SHE PLEDGED
HER HEART
IN HOLY
WEDLOCK
TO SAVE HIM
FROM THE
GALLOWS...
AND LOST
HER SOUL TO
UNHOLY DESIRE

eh

"YOU WANT ONLY ONE THING OF ME," SHE ACCUSED HIM, HER VOICE TREMBLING.

"And that is?" One of his brows arched in mocking question.

"My . . . my . . . you know! You want your way with me, you horrible beast!"

"My way with you?" He laughed, then he pressed up against her and she gasped as all her senses leapt. He nuzzled her hair, finding her ear with his mouth. "We both know I can have my way with you whenever I wish," he whispered hotly in her ear.

"Oh!" Rosalynde tried to free herself of him. "Let me go, you despicable cur!" she ordered as she sought to shove him away.

"From those perfect lips you vow your hatred. But, Rose, your body tells me otherwise." Despite her wish to deny his abhorrent words, Rosalynde knew with a sinking desperation that in this he had her dead to rights. A frisson coursed through her as his warm gaze held with hers. Then with a shudder she closed her eyes, unable to fight the truth anymore.

"Ah, my sweet Rose," he whispered in light kisses on her brow and then down her cheek to her temple. "Tell me once more how much you hate me. . . ."

Also by Rexanne Becnel

MY GALLANT ENEMY, winner of Waldenbooks' 1991 First Time Romance Author Award and winner of the *Romantic Times* Award for Best Medieval Romance by a New Author

THIEF OF MY HEART

THE ROSE OF
Blacksword

REXANNE
BECNEL

A DELL BOOK

Published by
Dell Publishing
a division of
Bantam Doubleday Dell Publishing Group, Inc.
666 Fifth Avenue
New York, New York 10103

The trademark Dell® is registered in the U.S. Patent and Trademark Office.

ISBN: 0-440-20910-2

Printed in the United States of America

Published simultaneously in Canada

June 1992

10 9 8 7 6 5 4 3 2 1

RAD

I fondly dedicate this book to all those who have contributed so much to my writing career.

SALLY LIVERETT, who read my first efforts with such wonder and enthusiasm;

PAMELA GRAY AHEARN, agent extraordinaire, who kept her faith in my writing even when I had lost it;

TERRY MCGEE, aka Emilie Richards, who coerced me into joining her writers' group;

RUTH GOODMAN, aka Meagan McKinney, who formed our first critique group;

BEVERLY WALSDORF, who gained me the job I needed to support my writing habit;

MARK GROTE, who was so wonderful to work for—supportive and understanding at all times;

DEBORAH GONZALES, aka Deborah Martin and Deborah Nicholas, who is much more than simply a critique partner;

and the SOUTHERN LOUISIANA CHAPTER OF RWA . . . especially the historical group.

If even one of you had not been there for me, I believe I would have given up writing long ago.

Prologue

1992

When the breeze is right and the flowers are in full bloom, the fragrance of roses permeates even the far reaches of the battlements at Stanwood Castle. The enduring stone, hard and unyielding, seems an unlikely setting for the romantic mood created by the gently wafting scents. Yet it is those very incongruities that contribute to the idyllic setting, for the forbidding protection of those ancient stone walls provides the environment that coaxes such exquisite blooms from the extensive rose gardens.

The castle is a popular stop for tourists and is well-known for its gardens, which are said to have been tended without break since the time of King Henry II. A formal herb garden laid out by an early chatelaine still provides milfoil and vervain, lungwort and sallow root. A small stand of beautifully espaliered pear trees are said to be descended from an original planting from the time of King Stephen.

But the castle's true claim to fame is its roses. No modern hybrids, these—grown for their long, spindly stems in regular rows for ease of cutting. Stanwood's roses bloom in riotous abandon, climbing up walls, clambering along eaves, sprawling over the outside stairways. They spring up in crevices and flourish in the most outlandish places. Even in the dead of winter there is bound to be some tenacious *Rosa* bravely putting forth blooms along a protected south-facing wall.

But one area above all others within Stanwood's mellow walls seems to beckon to the observant visitor. In a level spot at one end of the bailey, a thick hedge of *Rosa Gallica* surrounds an inviting green lawn. A solitary walnut tree shades a pair of carved stone benches at one end, while an ancient cast-bronze sundial stands at the other, supported on a simple fluted column and surrounded by a thick carpet of creeping thyme.

The years have given the bronze a deep patina, burned in by the sun and washed clean by centuries of English drizzle. But the letters on the sundial gleam as brightly as if they were newly cast. They are worn down, of course, and in some places barely distinguishable due to the many hands that have rubbed the message engraved there. A tale, so old that no one knows its source, promises long and happy life to those newlyweds who trace the sundial's aged words.

> A rose made sweeter by the thorn,
> A sword forged mighty by the fire.
> A love kept sacred by a vow.

It's a legend many have come to believe in.

1

England, A.D. 1156

The spindly rosebush was more thorns than foliage. Devoid of even a bud, it looked forlorn against the barren soil. It might have been only a dead stalk, not worthy of all the care being lavished upon it. But to Lady Rosalynde the meager bush was everything in the world she had left to give her little brother.

Her face was pale and sober as she knelt on the ground. She was unmindful of the dirt that stained the light blue of her celestine overtunic. She only concentrated on digging a suitable hole in the rich black earth, then added a generous portion of well-rotted stable sweepings to it. She wiped at her face with the back of one hand, leaving a black smudge upon her tear-streaked cheek, but she did not pause at her work. A sob escaped her, and then another as she centered the shrub. By the time she scraped the mound of soil back into the hole, she was weeping openly. But that did not deter her in her task. With hands now grimy and nails ruined quite beyond repair, she packed the soil firmly around the roots. It was only then that she sat back against her heels and stared pensively at the lonely little grave before her, marked now by the thorny rosebush and a new stone marker.

Beyond her, standing bareheaded and awkwardly gripping his Phrygian cap, the young page, Cleve, watched his
mistress. He was hesitant as he approached her with the
wooden bucket of water he had drawn from the garden
well.

"Shall I water it now, milady?" he asked in a hushed
tone.

Rosalynde looked up at him. Despite her own all-consuming grief, she recognized that he too was sorely distressed by young Giles's passing. But he blinked hard
against any threat of tears, and she gave him a sad and
rueful smile. "I'd like to do it myself."

He gave her the bucket without argument, but
Rosalynde could not mistake the concerned expression on
his normally matter-of-fact face. She knew everyone
thought she was behaving most strangely and that they
were all humoring her only because they did not know
what else to do. Death always seemed to make people
uncomfortable, as did dealing with the surviving family.
When she had told Lady Gwynne that she wanted to plant
a rosebush at Giles's grave, her poor aunt's eyes had filled
anew with tears. But she had only wiped her eyes, compressed her lips tightly, and nodded. When Rosalynde had
told Cleve that she would plant the rose herself—she
wanted no one to do it but herself—he too had accepted
her wishes and silently acquiesced. But now as she carefully poured water around the spindly plant's roots, she
felt as if this gesture of hers toward her only brother had
all been for naught. The rosebush changed nothing. The
fact that she had labored so hard at it would not undo what
had happened.

She drew the empty bucket against her chest and
gripped it tightly to her. Giles was still dead, still lost to
the fever that had racked his frail body for three torturous

days. Giles was dead despite all her frantic efforts to save him, and she had never felt more alone. First her mother. Then, for all practical purposes, her father. And now Giles. Despite her aunt and uncle who had been so good to her, she could not help but feel utterly abandoned.

Cleve shifted uneasily and once more his cap made the slow twisted circuit through his hands. Aware of his discomfort, Rosalynde took a slow, steadying breath.

" 'Twill bloom in his place," she said softly, as much for her own comfort as Cleve's. "I know it looks quite meager now, but by summer's end . . ." One last sob caught in her throat and she forced herself to look away from the lonely little grave.

"Please, milady, come along now. Let me see you back to Lady Gwynne and Lord Ogden. Your aunt was most concerned that you should rest. . . ." He took a hesitant step toward her small, bowed figure. "You're finished here now. Come away. . . ."

He trailed off as she turned a pale and haunted face up to him. Her eyes became even more brilliant than usual, their pale gold and green centers glistening with her tears.

"I *am* finished here," she agreed in a soft, wistful tone. She rubbed absently at the dirt clinging to her hands as the thought that had been lurking in her mind these past two days now became clearer. "I no longer need tend my little brother. There's truly no reason for me to stay here at Millwort Castle any longer, is there?" She sighed and looked down at her hands, unaccountably frightened by what she realized she must do. "Giles is beyond all help now. It's time that I went home."

"Home?" Cleve ventured nearer the mourning girl. "But, milady, this *is* your home. You needn't leave here. Why, my Lady Gwynne would be quite distraught to lose you. And anyway, until your father hears of Master Giles's death—" He hesitated and then made a quick sign of the cross. "Until he is told and decides what to do, then you mustn't think of leaving here atall. No, not atall," he stated quite firmly.

Rosalynde pushed a thick tendril of her dark mahogany hair back from her cheek. "And who's to tell the Lord of Stanwood about the loss of his son if not I? If not the very one he entrusted his only male heir to?" She turned her face back to the little mound of earth that was her brother's grave and to the scrawny rosebush that marked its presence. She remembered well her father's parting words to her despite her tender age so long ago. He'd said it that first time he had left her off at Millwort with her infant brother. And he'd said it each of the few times he had visited them these long eight years since. "Take good care of your brother," he had told her. "Take good care of your brother."

She had tried very hard to do just that despite Giles's weak constitution. But she had failed. For all that she had tried her best to save him, she had failed.

New tears started and fell unabashedly down her pale cheeks, and she was hard-pressed to know whether they were caused by sorrow or an inexplicable dread of seeing her father. Yet she knew she could not avoid him. Her eyes grew wide as she stared bleakly at her brother's grave. "I am the one who must do it. I must tell my father that his heir is dead."

Rosalynde took one last look about the cheerful chamber that had been her own for the past eight years. It was much more home to her now than was the castle where she had been born and lived her first eleven years. Lady Gwynne and Lord Ogden had been good to her since her mother died. They had opened their home and their hearts to a frightened girl and her newborn baby brother. When her mother had died in childbirth, it had seemed to Rosalynde that she had lost both of her parents, for her father had become an angry, unreasonable stranger after that. Then as soon as the tiny baby had been able to be moved, they had both been sent to live at Millwort Castle. Lady Gwynne had welcomed her only sister's children, and in the intervening years she had been as much a mother to them as was possible to be.

For Giles, Lady Gwynne and Lord Ogden had been the only parents he had ever known. The silent, scowling stranger who had visited them only three times through the years had hardly seemed a father to him. But Rosalynde had never forgotten her true parents. Her father's brief stopovers at Millwort had been joyfully anticipated but heartbreakingly cruel. All the old wounds had been opened each time by his aloofness, by the distance he kept between himself and his children. All the feelings of abandonment had become fresh once more, blinding her to everything but her private pain.

Giles had not understood. Lady Gwynne had only shushed Rosalynde's tears, telling her she expected too much, that a powerful knight like Sir Edward, Lord of Stanwood, could not be expected to display the sort of soft affection she wanted of him. Men simply weren't like that, she had explained.

But Rosalynde had known otherwise. She remembered a father who had swung her up on his shoulders despite her mother's laughing objections. She remembered a father who had carved two wooden horses for her—a mare and a stallion. He had promised her the foal as well. She recalled clearly when he had made that promise: Her mother had lain abovestairs, struggling to have a child while her husband and daughter had waited nervously below in the main hall.

But over the long hours of that day, into the evening and then the night, their hopefulness had turned to fear and then to awful dread. The babe had finally come, tiny and frail, hardly expected to last out the night. But her mother, the beautiful laughing Lady Anne, had simply faded away. No words to her husband or child. No complaints or even cries of anguish to the women attending her. She had just slipped away quietly, leaving in her wake a gloom that very likely still lingered at Stanwood.

Rosalynde sighed deeply and rubbed her burning eyes. Perhaps that was what had affected her father the most, she speculated unhappily. He had not had the chance to bid good-bye to the woman he had adored. As a consequence, he had turned a hardened heart to everyone, his children included.

But how was he to react to this latest loss? she wondered. How would he respond when she arrived unannounced with such awful news? Although he had never indicated the slightest feelings for the babe that had been the cause of his wife's death, Rosalynde was certain this new blow would hit him hard. Despite his emotional remoteness, she knew he cared deeply about his children's welfare and about his eventual heir. That was why he had sent them to Millwort. Rosalynde was to be well trained in the wifely arts, and Giles, when he was old enough, was to be trained in his letters and all the manly pursuits. She was to become a suitable man's wife. Giles was to inherit Stanwood Castle and the surrounding demesne.

As the years had gone by, however, her father had neglected Lady Gwynne's appeals that he decide on a husband for Rosalynde. He had delayed and delayed, although never with any real reason to do so. The good Lady

Gwynne had fussed that he simply did not want to believe that Rosalynde was old enough to be wed.

Rosalynde had been secretly relieved, for she had no desire to be removed to another home, far away from the only security she knew. She was happy at Millwort. Besides, although she knew her marriage to some lord of her father's choosing was inevitable, she did not look forward to it at all. She was content to live at Millwort Castle with her aunt and uncle. She learned her duties gladly and even participated in Giles's lessons. As a result she had learned to read and to letter quite proficiently. The somber monk who had taught her brother had been particularly outdone that a girl could cipher so well. Not at all proper knowledge for a lady, he had grumbled time and time again. But Lady Gwynne had always soothed him with extra sweets from the kitchens, and so the years had passed in relative peace.

Only now it had come to an end.

Rosalynde slid her hand lovingly one last time along the satin-stitched coverlet that adorned her high wooden bed. She and Lady Gwynne had labored long over it. Well, maybe one day she would return to its comfort, she told herself. Perhaps she might be back at Millwort before very long at all.

But deep inside Rosalynde did not believe it. She was going to Stanwood Castle because she felt she must. What was to come after that she could not begin to imagine.

"You need not go," Lady Gwynne beseeched Rosalynde one more time. "You still may change your mind and let Lord Ogden send the news to your father by messenger."

"It must be me who tells him. I owe him that much," Rosalynde replied earnestly to her aunt's concerned expression. "He left Giles with me—"

"He left Giles with Lord Ogden and myself," the good lady interrupted almost angrily. "You were but a child yourself, and only a little more than that now." Then her tone softened and she pressed her palms affectionately to Rosalynde's wan cheeks. "It was our heavenly Father's will to take Giles, Rosalynde. We may not question His purpose."

Rosalynde stared at her aunt's kindly face, wishing she could feel that same unshakable faith. But although she knew her aunt was right—indeed, prior to Giles's passing she would never have questioned God's will—now she was not so sure. She sighed and managed a weak smile.

"No matter the reason, 'tis time I went home. Even if my father does not want me there, that household no doubt needs a woman's hand."

Rosalynde knew that was one argument her aunt could not reason against, for she had many times voiced the same thought. Nevertheless, the older woman could only give her niece a watery smile and then pat her cheek one last time.

"Be a good girl," she instructed, though tears streamed down her lined face. She tucked Rosalynde's maidenly plait into the hood of her forest-green wool cloak. "Be a good girl and remember everything you've been taught."

"I will," Rosalynde reassured the dear woman as she gave her a tight hug. "Thank you. Thank you for everything—" Her voice caught on a sob as she realized she truly was leaving. "I won't let you down," she whispered through her tears.

"I doubt you could, even if you wanted to." Lady Gwynne gave a sad laugh as she squeezed her young charge's hand.

"And don't be fearing your father, young lady." Lord Ogden gave her a brief awkward hug, then stepped hastily back from her, uncomfortable with his own emotions. "He's a difficult man. Perhaps he doesn't meet the expectations of a young girl like yourself. But he's your father and you owe him your duty."

"I know that," Rosalynde murmured. "And I'll not disappoint you." She gave a sad smile to her aunt and uncle. Could she ever thank them enough for how good they had been to her and Giles? She stared at their downcast faces and bit her lower lip against the terrible sorrow that threatened to overwhelm her. How she would miss them.

Then her cream-colored palfrey was led around, and before she was quite prepared to go, she was mounted and everyone was ready to leave. Lord Ogden had a few last-minute instructions for the men-at-arms who would be her escort. She was to ride in their midst, never ahead or behind them. Because her regular maid was with child, another was to accompany her, but in addition to the reluctant maid, Rosalynde had asked for Cleve to come with her to Stanwood, and in a weak moment Lord Ogden had acquiesced. Now as the gangling youth guided his sturdy mount beside her mare, he gave her an encouraging look.

"It will be all right, milady. You'll see." Then he grinned, obviously excited at the prospect of the journey to his new home. He had never been off the Millwort holdings except for one brief trip to Abingdon Abbey. Now he was to go five days' journey east to Stanwood, and he could not contain his exuberance. If for no other reason than that, Rosalynde was pleased to have him along. A faint smile lifted her piquant features as she fell in line with two knights before her, another two following, and the pair of two-wheeled carts trailing behind with her maid, her belongings, and the necessary provisions for the journey.

"It appears that you are as anxious to leave as I am

anxious to stay." She gave Cleve a rueful glance. "Have you no regrets at all to be leaving your home?"

"None," he answered at once. "But you needn't go, Lady Rosalynde. You needn't. The messenger can carry the news to your father. It need not be you who tells him."

"Oh, but it must," she answered with a faraway look in her amber-green eyes. "I'm all that's left to my father, whether he cares or not. I was to look after Giles, and I'm the one to tell him of our loss."

She was silent after that and the boy decided it best not to press her. As time went by she would come out of this sadness that weighed so heavily upon her. Once she arrived at her father's home and gave him the sad news, she would begin to feel a little better. He maneuvered his pony as ordered by one of the knights but he kept his dark-brown eyes on his mistress's preoccupied face.

It was not like her to be so somber, so subdued. Her grief for her little brother affected Cleve sorely, for she of all people did not deserve such sorrow. He had always thought Lady Rosalynde the most beautiful, the most delightful maiden in the land. Or at least the fairest that he had ever seen. But it went far beyond the lustrous mahogany gleam of her long thick hair and the luminous glint in her unusual golden-green eyes. Any other maiden might have been quite vain to be possessed of such a slender yet curvaceous figure. Any other might have preened over such a translucently pale complexion, which still showed the bloom of roses in her cheeks.

But his mistress always thought of others before herself. She saw beauty all around her and goodness where it might otherwise go undetected and, in so doing, never saw what he and everyone else so clearly recognized. She was a jewel among common river rocks, a sparkling gem set amid pebbles of lesser worth. Where she walked the sun shone brighter, the grass grew greener, and the birds sang far sweeter.

He shook his head at his own poetic nonsense. He was halfway to being in love with her—so were most of the other serving lads at Millwort Castle, for she did not put herself too high to have a pleasant word for whomever crossed her path. But she surpassed his sixteen years by another three, and as for her social ranking, what hope had a mere page when it came to a lady of the realm? Still, that did not prevent him from enjoying her company whenever she required something of him. She might be far beyond him, but he only admired her the more for it. He would be willing to do anything for his Lady Rosalynde.

Now as he stared at her she straightened, inadvertently causing the dark-green hood to slip down from her head. In the crisp morning light her dark hair gleamed like a halo. Cleve blinked his eyes hard as he stared at her fragile beauty. Then she spoke and her voice, though soft and small, had the musical lilt of an angel's.

"We'd best not dawdle. The journey shall be long enough, and my father must be told."

2

Although she had made the journey years earlier, the trip from Millwort Castle to Stanwood was almost as new to Rosalynde as it was to Cleve. Whenever she would subside into morose silence, Cleve would still be alive with curiosity. He seemed never to tire of the changing scenery and had an endless stream of questions for her as well as for the better-traveled knights. Despite the grim purpose of her task, she found it exceedingly difficult to remain glum when Cleve's enthusiasm was so indefatigable.

" 'Tis an adulterine," one gravelly voiced knight replied to the lanky youth's question about a huge mound of gray stone ahead, hugging a hillside above the banks of the Stour River. "The new King Henry has ordered all the unlicensed castles built under his uncle, King Stephen, torn down, this one included."

Cleve shook his head and frowned. "It hardly makes sense to tear down castles when there are people living in mud hovels elsewhere." Then he brightened. "I suppose the stones could be used to build other houses. And perhaps to mend fences."

"Mayhap that's done with other adulterines, but not this one." The knight squinted at the hulking ruin. " 'Tis said to be haunted."

"Haunted?" Cleve's eyes grew larger, and even Rosalynde stared curiously at the remains of the castle.

"The peasants in these parts say Sir Medwyn killed his wife and then himself rather than accede to the new king's orders," the man answered with a chuckle, although he too sent a wary look toward the ill-fated castle.

Another of the knights joined in with a laugh. " 'Tis more likely that it's old King Stephen's ghost that still haunts the place. He still haunts the rest of the land," he added, disgust evident in his voice. "He was a poor king to England, and the castles built under his reign certainly proved poor protection for him."

With a puzzled shake of his head Cleve turned his chocolate-brown stare on Rosalynde. "Who's to understand a king who tears down castles?" He shook his shaggy dark head once more in confusion. "Is Millwort to be safe from the new King Henry then? Or Stanwood?"

Rosalynde could not help but smile at his youthful bewilderment. "Millwort and Stanwood Castles are safe. Never fear for that. But they are old fortresses, begun in the time of the Conqueror. Only the newer castles, like that one up there, are at risk."

"It still seems a waste," the boy answered as he eyed the towering rubble. "So much work ruined."

It did indeed, Rosalynde silently agreed as they approached the remnants of the fortress. But who was to understand the strange inclinations of royalty? On the one hand they protected their people. On the other they terrorized them with harsh assizes and incomprehensible edicts. Lord Ogden on numerous occasions had bemoaned King Stephen's contradictory practices. Her uncle remembered well the orderliness in the land under the first King Henry, and in the privacy of his own home he had not hesitated to bemoan King Stephen's many faults. But now

the old king's grandson was in power. Although Lord
Ogden had reserved judgment on the young Henry II, he
nevertheless hoped fervently for peace in England. As the
group of travelers drew up along the riverbank, just downstream of the adulterine, Rosalynde wondered if her father's views would coincide with Lord Ogden's.

At the edge of a low, grassy bank they halted. The day
was unseasonably warm and the sun shone brilliantly as
the group dismounted. As Rosalynde stretched her
cramped muscles, Cleve led the horses down to the river's
edge to drink, while the knights stretched out on the grass
in the shade of two gnarled yew trees.

"Come along, Nelda," Rosalynde called to the perpetu-
ally scowling serving woman. "The sooner we assemble
the meal, the sooner we may be on our way. And the
sooner you will be able to return to Millwort," she added
with a determined smile. Rosalynde knew the woman was
unhappy to have been uprooted from her comfortable routine at Millwort Castle. But even though Rosalynde had
not felt it necessary to have a maid on the trip—indeed,
Nelda had been more a hindrance than a help—Lady
Gwynne had been adamant. It would be quite scandalous
for a lady to travel alone among men, Lady Gwyne had
reminded her, particularly an unmarried maiden. A serving woman must always be at hand.

But as Rosalynde unpacked two loaves of bread, a half
wheel of cheese, and a pottery dish of raisins wrapped
securely in linen cloths, she couldn't help but wish a maid
hadn't been necessary. Nelda's presence had meant a cart
was needed, for very few serving women knew how to ride
horses. That, in turn, had meant they had to travel much
slower than if she and Cleve had simply ridden with the
knights by horseback. In fact, they would probably be ar-
riving at Stanwood today if they hadn't been held to such a

snail's pace by the slow-moving carts. As it was, they were little more than half the way there.

Still, for all that she wished to speed their arrival at Stanwood, Rosalynde was not really looking forward to the reunion with her father. Nor to relating the dire news she carried to him. With a heavy heart she cut herself a tiny square of cheese and tore off a small portion of the bread. Then she headed nearer the river and away from the company of the others as they ate.

"You mustn't fret so, milady."

Rosalynde looked up from her melancholy position atop a boulder that jutted partially into the river. "I'm not fretting, Cleve. And don't you worry about anything either," she said, forcing a smile as she looked over at the page's concerned expression. Then she tossed a piece of bread in the river and watched as two fish struck at the morsel. "Stanwood is a beautiful place. You'll love it there."

"What's it like?" he asked as he settled himself on a grassy hummock.

Rosalynde looked down at him, watching as he dug into his meal with a still-growing boy's gusto. It was clear he'd set himself to keeping her from worrying. Although a part of her would rather be alone with her thoughts, she nonetheless appreciated his sincere concern.

"Stanwood is . . . well . . ." She thought for a moment, trying to see her childhood home as it might appear to a stranger, trying to see past her emotional ties to her parents' castle. "It's big. And old." She smiled ruefully. "It's warmer than Millwort, as I recall. Because it's so near the sea. Sometimes, when the wind is strong out of the east, you can smell the salty sea air."

"Have you *seen* the sea?" Cleve stopped chewing as he listened to her. "Have you actually gone down to the edge of the sea and touched it?"

"Of course." Her smile was genuine as she took in his amazed expression. "I've walked in it. And so can you. We'll go down to the sea one day and then you can see for yourself."

"Now that would be grand indeed!" The boy grinned eagerly at her then and took a big bite of cheese.

"Stanwood is quite different from Millwort," she continued as she tossed another bit of bread to the circling fish. "It's half again as big, with a huge keep that has four floors and even its own chapel. And it has ever so many windows. It's actually quite light, even inside. And the bailey . . ." Here her face softened as she remembered. "The bailey stretches forever down a gentle hill. When I was little I couldn't run the entire length of it. My father—" She stopped and a frown marred her previously serene face. "Stanwood is not as elegant as Millwort. The walls aren't of big clean blocks but are built of mostly flint. Rubble walls, my father called them."

She stood up then and abruptly tossed the last chunk of the bread into the icy stream. "I'm sure I'm remembering it much finer than it actually is," she finished quietly.

"It sounds quite fine." The boy nodded encouragingly. "Are there many servants?"

Rosalynde paused before answering. "When I lived there it seemed like the entire castle was filled with people: cooks, serving women, squires, the steward, the seneschal, the chamberlain. It was a wonderful place to live, and I don't remember ever lacking for company."

But what would it be like now? That was the question Rosalynde had no answer for, and she was relieved when Cleve did not continue with his questions. What Stanwood was like now was anybody's guess. Still, Rosalynde was certain it was not the warm home of her childhood memories. It was her mother who had filled the castle with love.

It was she who had made her husband and her child so happy. When she had died, the love and the happiness had died along with her. Although Rosalynde dearly hoped to be happy again at Stanwood, she did not truly expect to be.

She jumped down from the rock to where her shoes sat abandoned in the grass, then stared pensively at the river, watching a short, rotted branch bump along several projecting stones, then scrape along the gravel shallows before spinning out crazily into deeper water. Cleve had stretched out in the lulling warmth of the spring sunshine. When the first shouts came from the knights who were a little downstream, Rosalynde did not even look up right away. She was so caught up in her own worried thoughts that she hardly heard the noise. But Cleve was not so soundly asleep as he appeared. At the first shout he opened his eyes and propped himself up on his elbows. At the second shout, however, he leapt up in sudden alarm.

"Get down, milady!" he hissed, crouching low and gesturing to her.

"What?" Rosalynde peered over at him, surprised by such perplexing behavior.

"Get down!" he persisted. "Something's wrong back there. I don't know what, but you must hide!"

Rosalynde turned sharply toward where Nelda and the four knights had relaxed with their noon meal. What she saw in that brief glance chilled her blood. A band of men, some mounted, others on foot, had attacked the small party with brutal precision. One of their knights already lay crumpled on the ground. The three others were fighting for their lives. She heard a shrill scream—Nelda's, she realized sickly. Then Cleve's hand closed over her arm and he unceremoniously yanked her down behind the protective cover of the boulder.

"My God! They're killing them!" she cried, frightened beyond measure by what she was witnessing. "We must help them!"

"How?" the boy asked curtly, although there was a tremble in his voice. "We've no real weapons and we're vastly outnumbered." He pushed her low, then tentatively peeked around the edge of the boulder. His short dagger was out, gripped tightly in his right hand, and Rosalynde stared at it with wide, terrified eyes. She had seen swords and long spears in the hands of the surprise attackers. In contrast, Cleve's weapon seemed woefully inadequate.

For what seemed like forever they crouched behind the boulder, their feet in the icy water as they were forced to listen to the gruesome sounds of the one-sided battle. Metal clanged cruelly against metal. There were shouts and curses and blood-curdling cries of pain. At each new outcry Rosalynde cringed in sickened horror. Her heart pounded painfully in her chest and yet she was frozen in a drowning fear. They were all dying. And it was just a matter of time before she and Cleve were found and killed as well!

"Watch the horses! The horses!" one guttural voice bellowed. Then there was a commotion of whinnies and frightened snorts from the horses before one of the animals thundered away from the melee. Unable to bear the suspense a moment longer, Rosalynde tried to look past the boulder as they heard the horse plunge into the water. But Cleve swiftly dragged her back.

"We've got to stay as still as this stone!" he admonished her in a fierce whisper. "Else they'll find us and then—" He stopped short at her horrified expression. He didn't have to say any more, however, for Rosalynde's imagination filled in the rest. But as they huddled there, exposed to the sun and the breeze and the river, it was impossible to feel hidden or very well protected despite the boulder's bulk between them and the cutthroat band beyond. The sounds of the gang's ultimate victory carried very clearly to Rosalynde and Cleve. Too clearly.

"Here's the wine, Tom boy," one of them said with a laugh. "Best have a tug afore 'tis all gone."

"Here, an' after I struck that one that cornered you, you would begrudge me my share? Hand it over, mate."

There was coarse laughter and much boasting amidst the distinctive sounds of the carts being emptied of all their contents. Then there was a long, low whistle and a brief silence that caused Rosalynde and Cleve to stare at each other in unreasoning fear.

"Lookee here, will you? Lookit this bit of finery. Silk, I vow. Some fine lady will be missin' her clothes this night." He snickered suggestively.

"Jewels too," another one chimed in.

"Lemmee see!"

There were sounds of a scuffle but Rosalynde and Cleve only pressed closer to the boulder, staring at each other as Rosalynde imagined the brutes pawing through her gowns and undergarments and the few pieces of jewelry she possessed.

"Huh. There's little enough of it. But e'en so, we'll do all right with this haul. He'll pay us a good price for these goods."

"But you know what 'e said," another voice cut in. " 'E said no more. 'E wouldn't take no more goods now that that unlucky bastard was caught and tried. 'E won't take no more stolen goods. At least for a while."

The other man, clearly the leader of the motley group, just laughed. "He'll take it, all right. And if he don't, there's plenty of others in Hadleigh what will."

The afternoon passed with an excruciating slowness.

Rosalynde and Cleve dared not move from the precarious
hiding place and therefore suffered alternating bouts of
paralyzing fear, unspeakable horror, and consuming rage
as the vandals amused themselves in drunken celebration,
arguments, and scuffles. It was only when the sun began
to cast long shadows across the riverbank and the sounds
from the gang of ruffians had begun to subside that Cleve
chanced a look around the exposed boulder.

"May God smite them down for this and see them rotted in hell!" he muttered as he stared toward the site of
the massacre. Then as Rosalynde rose to look as well, he
clapped a firm hand on her shoulder. "Oh, no, milady.
Don't look. It's too foul a sight."

But Rosalynde insisted. What she saw in the clearing
turned her stomach over. Three of the knights lay where
they had fallen, although their clothes had been stripped
away. Now their naked corpses lay white and exposed,
bloodied and mangled. It was enough to sicken a seasoned
warrior. It shook her to the core. She turned a pale face to
Cleve as she fought down the rising gorge in her throat.
Then she leaned heavily against the boulder. "What of
Nelda? And . . . and the other knight?"

"Perhaps it was they who rode away. Perhaps they escaped and will come back with help."

"But if Nelda didn't escape, those men will . . ." Her
words trailed off as she imagined just what those brutish
men would do to Nelda—to any woman they found. She
had heard the tales about William the Conqueror and the
Norman invasion. She had listened wide-eyed to whispered stories of the Viking marauders of times long past. A
violent shiver shook her as she realized that she was not
yet safe either. "Please God, let them have escaped. And
us too," she whispered in mortal fear.

Cleve's glum expression met hers and he clenched his

jaw nervously. "I hope God hears you, milady, for it's clear we must try to save ourselves."

Rosalynde's frightened eyes widened in renewed despair. What were they to do, a boy and one woman, against such a foul horde of murderers? She shook her head anxiously. "We cannot escape, Cleve. We can't defeat them either. What can we do?"

Cleve's gaze held with hers a long moment; his face was pale and grim. Then he peered over the boulder once more before taking a deep breath.

"We *can* escape. They don't know we're here. From the sounds of it, they've been drinking all the wine Lady Gwynne sent to your father. We can try to slip away when it gets a little darker. But not along the riverbank; it's too open. We'll have to head straight to those trees behind us and then skirt around the castle ruin. Then we can strike out for help."

Rosalynde was reassured somewhat by his clear thinking, and she nodded agreement with his plan. "But when?" she asked nervously. "If we wait until they leave it might be too dark and we'll never find our way in such strange territory in the night."

The answer to that dilemma was swiftly forthcoming. One of the gang rolled over with a groan and then rose. In a slow stagger he made his way toward the river. Beyond him the other men drowsed in drunken stupor or else continued to down the fine wines that had been stocked in the carts. As the man approached, Rosalynde cringed in fear. But the long hours of helplessness had given Cleve a new and reckless courage. Rosalynde watched in horror as he once again drew his pointed dagger.

She did not speak as they heard the brute pause just on the other side of the boulder. *Please let him stop there*, she prayed desperately. *Please don't let Cleve do anything rash.*

But Cleve shrugged off her restraining hand and ignored her pleading expression. Then they heard the man move again, coming around the boulder. Rosalynde froze in absolute horror, but Cleve was ready. With the stealth of a stalking cat, he inched around the cold granite stone. In the heart-shattering silence he crouched and tensed, and then, when the man came into view, he sprang forward.

Caught in the midst of loosening his braies so that he could relieve himself, the drunk had no time to protect himself. With a howl of pain he took the full length of Cleve's blade in his left shoulder. But perhaps due to the numbing effects of the wine, the wound did not at once bring him down. He only turned like a shaggy bear and, with a wild swing of his arm, struck out at his attacker.

Cleve was flung harshly against the rock. Rosalynde heard his sharp cry of pain and immediately sprang to his aid. The cutthroat turned as if to strike her as well, but suddenly he staggered and then went down on his knees. She heard a cry of alarm from one of his compatriots, but she did not waste time on any of them. With a strength born of terror and desperation, she looped Cleve's arm around her shoulder and then, without pausing a moment, lurched toward the trees, half carrying, half leading the still-stunned page.

"Milady . . ." Cleve mumbled as he fought to keep his senses.

"Run, Cleve. Run!" she cried as she urged him on.

She feared at any moment to be struck down by an avenging horde of assassins. Indeed, she feared to look back at their sure pursuit, not wanting to know how imminent was her death. But there was no blow, and as they gained the shelter of the shadowy forest, she finally chanced a fearful look behind them.

Rosalynde's breath came in huge gasps as she stared back at the riverbank. She saw the one man still lying where he had fallen after Cleve's heroic attack. His arm waved weakly for help, but his cohorts were clearly unable to assist him very well. One had tumbled over a root as he staggered drunkenly to assist. Another ran forward, looked around, then darted in another direction only to stop once more and stare stupidly about as if unsure just what it was he sought. He stared once in their direction and Rosalynde froze, certain they were discovered. But then the man lurched off in another direction, and with a shudder of relief she let loose her tightly held breath.

Without pausing to consider her actions, she plunged deeper into the thicket of shrubs and trees, still half supporting Cleve as she went. She was unmindful of the branches that plucked at her cloak and caught in her hair. She went on, heedless of the direction so long as it was far, far from the brutish men who had attacked, murdered, and plundered with no regard for the plight of their victims. Only when her bare foot caught on a curling vine and she nearly tripped was her headlong flight slowed. Cleve groaned in pain, tried to throw off her supporting arm and stand on his own, and then crumpled in a heap when his legs would not hold.

"Cleve. Cleve!" Rosalynde knelt at his side and lifted his head. Slowly the boy's eyes opened, but his stare was glazed with pain and confusion.

"Lady Rosalynde?" he muttered, closing his eyes again.

"Shh. It's all right, Cleve. It's all right. Just rest a moment while I see to your injuries," she murmured in a voice far more calm than she actually felt.

"Must get you away . . . safety. To Stanwood. . . ."

He jerked when her searching fingers found a tender spot on his head.

"Hold still. Let me see—" Rosalynde's words broke off when she saw the blood. It covered her fingers and matted the boy's thick brown hair. With a worried frown she tenderly parted his hair so that she could better assess the severity of the wound. Although the blood wasn't running freely anymore, only slowly oozing from the wound, the gash was a nasty one, and Rosalynde paused as she considered just what to do.

Their situation was precarious at best. Although they were safe for the moment, who was to say how long that would last? They were alone in strange territory, with no supplies, no one to help them, no weapons—

She glanced down at Cleve's hand and saw with huge relief that he had managed somehow to cling to his dagger despite everything that had happened. It was sticky with the blood of the man he had stabbed. Added to that, it wasn't much of a weapon to begin with. But they still had it and Rosalynde felt a little restored. They had a weapon and they were no longer being followed. That was a start.

She took a slow, steadying breath and then another, trying to calm her racing heart. Then with a firm set to her chin, she reached for the hem of her kirtle and tried to rip it. But the light linen was too well woven. She reached for Cleve's knife, but the still-stunned boy only gripped it tighter and struggled weakly against her.

"Give me the dagger, Cleve." she whispered urgently. "I only want to bind your head. Then we'll find a better resting place. Night will soon fall and we need shelter." She passed one of her slender hands over his head reassuringly. "I'll give the knife back to you just as soon as I'm finished with it."

Once more his eyes fluttered open, but this time he was more lucid. "Don't ruin your gown."

"Be quiet and cooperate," she replied, somewhat heartened that he might not be too seriously hurt. When his grip on the dagger slackened, she picked up the weapon with two fingers. Grimacing with disgust, she wiped it as clean as she could in a clump of new ferns. She quickly used it to tear two strips from her kirtle and then fashioned a bandage for his head. When she finished, he smiled weakly at her.

"Many thanks, milady." He struggled to sit up but would not have succeeded without her help. Although he tried to hide it, she could not miss his grimace of pain. "I must get you to safety," he muttered, staring a little vacantly about the dense forest stand.

"You're the one needs tending," Rosalynde countered as she also looked around, trying to take stock of their situation. "I need water to properly wash that gash in your head." She bit her lip in consternation as she pondered the problem.

"There's the river," he pointed out.

"No!" Rosalynde was quick to reply. "It's too easy for those awful men to find us if we venture down to the water's edge." A bird swooped through the trees and they both jumped. Rosalynde watched as it headed up toward the ruined castle that still guarded the hillside. A faint smile curved her lips as an idea formed in her head. "That castle must have had a well. We'll go up there—"

"You heard what the knights said," Cleve protested with rising strength. " 'Tis a haunted place. It would be foolish to enter such a place of death."

Unfazed by his dire warning, Rosalynde got to her feet. Her hose were in tatters. Her gown was ripped and still wet. Even her sturdy cape had a huge rent along one side.

But she was alive and so was Cleve. The threat of ghosts seemed far less a problem than the very real threat they had already encountered that day.

"Those ghosts will be our protection," she stated confidently as she bent to help him up. Cleve only stared at her with wide doubting eyes.

"They'll smother us in our sleep," he warned even as she put an arm about his waist and helped him start forward. "They'll sit on our chests and suck the life from us."

"They'll keep anyone else from following us," she retorted, although a small quiver of doubt snaked up her spine. "We mean them no harm. Surely they'll know that."

Cleve's expression was dubious. But as he had no better suggestion and was feeling exceedingly weak from the blow to his head, he leaned upon her. Crouching low, and with many backward glances, they slowly made their way toward the abandoned adulterine.

3

It was not the moans of unhappy ghosts nor the threat of menacing specters that tormented Rosalynde through the long hours of the night. She was not threatened by visions of the dead Sir Medwyn and his hapless wife as she huddled in the roofless remains of what must have been one of the kitchen's stores. She was instead gripped with fear for the feverish Cleve and haunted anew by the more recent deaths she had witnessed.

Nelda had not wanted to come on this trip. But because Rosalynde had insisted on traveling to her father herself, a maid had become necessary. If not for Rosalynde's adamant demand to go to her father herself, Nelda would still be alive, as would the four unlucky knights. Although she had seen only three bodies, Rosalynde could not banish the sight from her mind's eye, and she was certain everyone else in the party had also been murdered. And all because of her, she worried guiltily. Their poor souls had not even been dignified with a Christian burial.

Now Cleve was in a very bad way as well.

"Sweet Mary, mother of Jesus," she prayed with an urgency that clutched at her very soul. "Save this boy, I beseech thee. Have pity on him, for he does not deserve to die."

Through the moonless black of the night, as unseen

beasts rustled nearby and others howled from afar, she kept her lonely vigil. But try as she might to be thankful for their survival, for the protection of the ruined castle and the blessed remains of the old well in the rubble-littered bailey, Rosalynde was nonetheless besieged by both fear and fury.

It was not fair, she silently raged as she pressed a damp rag against Cleve's burning brow. Nothing was fair at all! Giles should not have died. Nelda and Lord Ogden's men should never have been so cruelly slaughtered. She should not be thrust into this terrible mess. And poor Cleve . . .

He groaned and tried to roll over. Then he flailed one arm wildly about before she was able to grab it and still his feverish thrashing.

"Look out!" He moaned as one tear escaped his tightly clenched eyes and trickled down his cheek. "Look out, milady."

Then his eyelids flew open and he stared up at her as if she were one of the very ghosts he had feared.

"Be still now," she crooned in a soft voice. She dipped the cloth she'd torn from her kirtle into a broken jug she had found and filled with water from a well. Then she wiped the sweat from his face. Despite the chill spring night, he was damp with the heat of his own body. She knew, however, that it was only a matter of time before the fever would give way to chills. Why hadn't she searched the woods for some vervain before the night had descended? She could have prepared a tea for his fever. Then she could have made a wash of common woundwort or a poultice of lady's mantle for his festering wound. Together the tea and the wash would have helped dispel the fever that tortured him now.

But she had not thought about it in her haste to find them a hiding place safe from the clutches of those murderous highwaymen. As soon as the sky grew light, however, she would venture forth. As soon as dawn broke the oppressive black of this night, she would do something—anything!—to help him.

It seemed forever before the faintest glow of gray-mauve light touched the eastern sky. She was cold and weary. Her muscles ached from the crouched position she had maintained at the injured boy's side all night. Her eyes stung and her vision was blurry, yet as soon as she was able to discern her surroundings, she knew she must move. Cleve had fallen into an exhausted slumber broken only occasionally by incoherent mutterings as he sought a more comfortable position. As she rose from his side she spread her cloak over his slight form and tucked it warmly about him. Then with teeth chattering from the cold, she picked her way warily from the lean-to shelter and out into the bailey.

The ruined castle had clearly not been very grand, yet Rosalynde could easily determine where the keep had stood as well as the main walls and the chapel. As she made her way to the collapsed gatetower, she wished, as she had all night, that the new King Henry II had not been so adamant in his orders to dismantle all unlicensed castles. If Lord Medwyn and his wife had not been summarily dismissed, those bandits would not have felt so free to roam the countryside, attacking at will.

She was brooding as she skirted a charred pile of timbers, thinking of the home it must have been, when a sudden idea struck her and she halted in her tracks. Any good chatelaine would have maintained an herb garden of both medicinal and cooking herbs. Surely some of those plants must still survive.

It did not take her long to locate the forgotten garden. Amid new green shoots of loosestrife and hedge mustard,

conkerwort and nettle, a sturdy group of the herbs necessary to any castle still thrived. There was no woundwort,
but shepherd's knot would do as well. And the inner bark
of the linden tree, once stripped and beaten, would make
an even better poultice than the dried everlasting leaves
she had carried in the cart.

Despite the cold and the hungry ache growing in her
stomach, as she hurried back to the sleeping youth,
Rosalynde felt infinitely better. Cleve would be all right
now. She would make sure of it. Then somehow they
would find their way to safety. Something good must come
of all this, she reasoned as she pushed a hopelessly tangled
strand of dark hair back from her forehead. Surely it was
not possible that anything else could go wrong.

"You cannot go!" Cleve muttered. He started to rise but
Rosalynde quickly pushed him back onto the pallet of
leaves she'd fashioned for him.

"Someone must," she argued back. Her angry tone
changed to a sympathetic one, however, when she saw his
grimace of pain. "One of us must go for help and you
clearly cannot," she explained more reasonably.

" 'Tis not safe," he persisted. But his eyes fell closed and
his shoulders slumped in resignation.

"No," she agreed softly. " 'Tis not safe. But think, Cleve,
what else is to be done? You cannot travel, and who knows
when those terrible men might return? Besides, the local
authorities must be told of this cruel and murderous
deed."

"But you cannot wander about," Cleve insisted, staring
up at her most earnestly. "What if those men should find
you? What if they try to ransom you to your father?"

"We cannot wait here forever," she answered quietly.
"Anyway, I've already decided. I'll take your cloak instead

of mine. As dirty as I am, with torn and ruined clothes and hair tangled beyond redemption, I shall look just another poor maiden of the village."

"And do you think just because they believe you're only a poor village maiden that they won't harm you?" he cried in exasperation. His face was pale but his eyes burned intently into hers. "They might not kill you, but they might do you even greater harm."

She started to reply, then stopped as his meaning of "greater harm" suddenly became clear to her. She had heard enough castle gossip to understand. "Oh. I-I see." She ducked her head in both fear and embarrassment.

"So, you see, you cannot go," the boy said with a sigh of finality.

"But I must," she said, although her voice trembled now with renewed fear. "Besides, those men are probably far away by now. I'll be careful, I promise you. It's very likely no one will take any notice of me at all."

Cleve frowned in agitation and shook his head weakly. "You wish it to be so, and therefore you believe it. But consider, milady, you have only to look upon a person once to be well remembered. No one will long believe your guise."

Although Rosalynde did not want to give any credence to his words, she knew in her heart he spoke the truth. Although she considered herself rather unremarkable looking, she had lately become more and more aware of men's eyes following her. But more than that, from her earliest memory her eyes had marked her apart from others. At times it had been a blessing. Today, however, it was a curse.

As a child she had been a curiosity. Her eyes with their clear green centers flecked with gold and rimmed with deep indigo had dominated her face. The story was told that upon her christening the priest had repeated his blessing, and not just once, but twice over again. To ward off any evil spirits that might dwell beyond her clear baby's gaze, he'd said. As she had grown, however, her eyes had become her best feature. More than one young man had sung their praise and sworn his faithfulness to her. But whether her startling eyes were considered an oddity or her claim to beauty, Rosalynde knew they nonetheless made her quite memorable. In frustration she chewed her lower lip and then looked back at Cleve.

"I'll keep your hood pulled low over my brow. And I'll duck my head and lower my eyes." She sighed, stood up, and reached for his coarse brown cloak. "It's the best I can do."

Cleve did not respond as she prepared to depart. Rosalynde glanced once at him, but the sight of his normally animated face so pale and stricken caused her to quickly look away. She felt as if she were abandoning him to the unknown even as she faced her own terrible fear that she was plunging into disaster. None of her options seemed promising. Yet to do nothing was foolish indeed.

"I've filled this bit of crockery with water. More linden bark is in it for you to change the dressing at midday. When the sun reaches its zenith, chew some of the shepherd's knot with a little of the water. Then again before the sun touches the horizon. And I've left some watercress here for you to eat."

"How long will you be gone?" the boy demanded with a doleful expression on his face. He managed to prop himself up on his elbows. "You should not stay away so long that it gets dark. You should not go at all," he added angrily.

"I'll come back before dark, no matter what." She turned to go, then paused in what was once the doorway to the partially demolished building. "I'll be very careful," she promised fervently. "And I'll find someone willing to help us."

She would, she repeated to herself as she walked swiftly along a partially overgrown path. She would return before dark no matter what. The very thought of being completely alone at night in unfamiliar territory left her petrified with fear. So long as the sun shone she would manage the grim task set before her. But once darkness fell . . .

She shivered and hugged Cleve's fustian cloak about her. It was fortunate they were near the same size, she thought absently, all the while keeping a wary eye about her. With any luck no one would pay her any mind at all.

This hope kept her going as she followed the footpath. Near a stream the path met up with a rough cart track. Rosalynde was certain a village could not be too far away. When the woodlands opened onto wastelands, the cart track widened. Then soon she saw stone fences, neat farm rows, and the distant squat tower of a small village church.

She was both encouraged and even more frightened as she neared the village, however, for something seemed most odd. No one worked the fields, although it was midmorning at least. At the first few stone cottages no wash lay over the bushes, nor children played about. Her pace slowed as she pondered this odd fact, but when she saw the flags fluttering and heard the sound of horns and drums and laughter, she understood. It must be fair day in this particular village. No one was afield because everyone had come to share in the festivities.

Rosalynde approached the village with great trepidation. But she soon realized that the crowd was a boon to her. What was one more girl in a square filled with merrymakers? What notice would anyone take of just another urchin come to partake of the day's revelry? Best of all, the

cobbled road that ran through the town appeared to be the
same old Roman road they had been traveling on before
the attack. They had only to continue on this way to reach
Stanwood Castle and safety.

The village was not large, but it did form the crossroads
of the old road and two other cart tracks. The river formed
one edge of the place, creating a wide, grassy bank that
clearly functioned as the town square. Rosalynde paused
and looked about, trying to get her bearings and to decide
where to begin her search for help while keeping her hood
low and her face somewhat hidden. *Don't be too hasty to
trust anyone,* she reminded herself sharply. For all she
knew, the same brigands who had attacked them might be
at this very fair themselves.

As Rosalynde progressed into the center of the festival,
she was amazed at the immense number and variety of
folk present. From meanest serf to prosperous craftsman,
from shabby villein to well-heeled merchant, they milled
about the square, partaking of the entertainments on every
side. Pedlars from far and wide displayed their wares. She
saw fine furs and hides, bolts of every imaginable sort of
cloth, goose quills, and linen napery Lady Gwynne would
have gushed over. Gamesters plied their trade, luring the
wide-eyed and unwary into the innocent-looking game of
colored stones and walnuts. Acrobats climbed upon one
another, twisting themselves with apparent ease into unbelievable contortions. Musicians fought for eminence
with rebec and lute, harp and gittern, all at odds with one
another, overwhelmed only by the shrill tones of the clarion. In one roped-off arena men wrestled a giant of a man.
Though quick and agile, one after another of the young
men were bested by the lumbering fellow who seemed
quite impervious to their repeated assaults.

There was a dizzying jumble of sound and motion, and

delectable smells of every food imaginable. Rosalynde's mouth watered as she sniffed first the fragrant aroma of roasted leeks, then the enticing scent of a pair of fat suckling pigs turning on an open spit. On another fire ducks and geese and chickens roasted. It was all so delicious that she could not resist approaching nearer the rare treats.

"I'll grant ye a smell for free. But to taste ye must ha' the coin," a stout fellow warned her, but not too unkindly.

"Oh, well. I'm not . . . I'm not hungry. Not just yet." She smiled apologetically and began to back away. Then she stopped, reminding herself of her purpose. "By your leave, sir." She drew nearer the man once more. "Can you tell me who might be the authority in this village?"

He grunted as he turned the heavily laden spit. Sweat poured down his neck and arms as he labored over the fire. "The mayor's about, s'pose." He jerked his head toward a boisterous crowd closer to the river. "Try over t' the bearbaiting."

The bearbaiting. Rosalynde grimaced in dismay as she stared at the knot of men and boys clustered around some entertainment she could not see. Her aunt had prevailed on Lord Ogden to disallow such gruesome sport at Millwort Castle, but Rosalynde had heard tales of it. Dogs disemboweled by ferocious bears. She shook her head in distaste, then swallowed hard and started forward. There was nothing she could do about it. She needed the mayor's help.

As she crossed the crowded square, however, intent on her mission, she was unexpectedly knocked over by the rough horseplay of two brawny toughs.

"Give way," one said with a grunt as his elbow caught her midsection. But when she landed hard on the ground and her hood flew back, the man halted in midstride.

"Well, well. What is it we have here, hidden in a lad's

short cloak?" Without a by-your-leave he bent down and
grabbed her arms, then roughly pulled the still-breathless
Rosalynde up. "Is she a pickpocket?" he asked his comrade with a snicker, his ale-laced breath assaulting her
senses. "Or perhaps a whore come to follow the fair and
ply her trade?"

"Surely not a whore," the other rowdy let out with a
drunken laugh and gave Rosalynde a disparaging look.
"She's hardly endowed with the usual whore's generous
equipment."

"Could be you're too hasty." The man pulled Rosalynde
against his chest, then nearly lifted her off her feet as he
rubbed her crudely against the length of him. "There's
more here than meets the eye." So saying, he flung her
cape over her shoulder and reached lecherously for her
rounded breast.

At the outset of the confrontation Rosalynde had been
too outdone and too frightened to respond. The memory of
the previous day's brutal attack had her nerves so on edge
that she wanted no more than to melt away into oblivion.
But when the man loosened his hold on her arms and
reached for her breast, she reacted instinctively. With a
loud crack she smacked his face. Then when he stepped
back in stunned surprise, she jerked her other arm free
and fled panic-stricken into the crowd. There was an uproar behind her, a furious cursing and then the heated
pursuit by the two. But Rosalynde was too scared to look
back, too alarmed to do anything but run for her life.

"The whore robbed me!" she heard him bellow like an
enraged bull as he tried to encourage others to grab her.
"Stop her! Catch the thief!"

But the crowd was too thick and the noise too loud for
him to be long heeded by the merrymakers. Ale and wine

had flowed freely since first light. Who would care if some fool was fleeced by a strumpet?

But Rosalynde feared pursuit on every side. Her blood roared in her ears as she dodged past a vagabond healer's cart, then insinuated herself into a bevy of women surrounding a colorful pedlar's tent. She could hardly catch her breath as she cast furtive eyes around her, terrified at any moment to be caught and handed back into that horrible man's clutches. While the other women crowded about, reaching out to finger the pedlar's goods and perhaps strike a bargain with the man, Rosalynde only huddled in their midst and pulled up her hood, praying all the while that she had escaped. She stared blindly at a length of fine red twill, and even reached forward perfunctorily to stroke a handsome blue samite, shot through with gold threads. But her mind was not on fabrics and gowns. She still needed to find the lord mayor. Yet how was she to venture about when that ogre could still be searching for her?

For the next hour Rosalynde debated just what to do, all the while keeping herself well surrounded by other village women. Twice she caught a glimpse of the pair of toughs who had chased her, but she hastily hid herself from their view.

She drifted from one pedlar to the next, hiding herself among the crowd that gathered to watch a pair of jugglers perform astounding feats of coordination. But although they tossed wooden bats, then daggers, and finally burning torches, Rosalynde could not enjoy their performance. When the rest of the crowd gasped in horror as one of the men donned a blindfold, she saw only the nightmarish danger of it all. The flaming batons were tossed faster and faster between the two men, and miraculously, the blindfolded fellow never missed a catch. But unlike the other spectators who cheered and tossed tokens of appreciation to the pair, Rosalynde only shuddered at the unnecessary risk the men had taken. Did everyone in this dissolute village thrive only on danger?

But as the crowd wandered off to seek amusements elsewhere, she knew she could hide amidst thém no longer. She must brace herself and seek out the mayor once more. She would explain her predicament to him— including her altercation with those two horrible men. Surely he would understand and come to her aid.

It took only a few inquiries for her to be directed to the mayor.

"He'll be near the gallows," one young lad told her. "Gettin' ready for the hangin's."

"There's to be a hanging?" Rosalynde asked, forgetting for a moment to duck her head as she stared dubiously at the scruffy boy.

"Three." He grinned and held up a like number of fingers. "Me da says they's a murderin' lot and we should all of us cheer when they goes up."

"Is that what this fair is for?" she asked with a shiver of revulsion at his eagerness for the killings.

The boy gave her a skeptical look. "Naw. 'Tis the Flitch of Bacon. The day of handfastin'," he said, disgust with her ignorance evident in his voice. "Only since no one has come forward to be handfasted, well, the mayor, he says we're to have the hangin's instead."

Rosalynde had heard of the custom of handfasting. It was a remnant of earlier times, a form of trial marriage. But it was not sanctioned by the Church, and although embraced by common folks, it was most certainly frowned upon by those of noble rank.

She murmured her thanks to the boy and then reluctantly turned toward the makeshift gallows where he'd said the mayor would be. A throng of curious bystanders had already begun to gather there for the gruesome entertainment, and she once again tried to hide herself within their midst.

". . . a bear of a man," one graybeard was saying. "With a sword as black as 'is heart!"

"Still and all, they was caught separatelike. Who's to say they're e'en part of the same gang?"

"Have ye heard of any attacks these several weeks since 'e's been in the gaol?" the old fellow retorted smugly. "No, you haven't. An' it's 'cause 'e's the ringleader. I saw 'im when I brought the lord mayor 'is ale. You'll see for yourself soon enough. 'E's the one, that Blacksword. The other two may be just as murderous, but mark my words, 'e's the ringleader. 'Tis unlikely 'e'd let any man give 'im orders."

Had those terrible men who had attacked them been caught? For a moment Rosalynde felt an enormous relief. But just as quickly she realized they could not possibly have been found and tried that fast. It was some other outlaws they had caught. She wanted to tell the men that bandits did indeed still roam the countryside. This Blacksword they discussed might be everything the old man said, but she and Cleve were living proof that he wasn't the only one. However, she decided that caution was in order and that she should go first with her story to the mayor.

"Excuse me," she interrupted the men, keeping her head meekly bowed. "Where might I find the lord mayor?"

The old man gave her a keen once-over, then gestured toward the gallows platform beyond them. "That's 'im up there. With the red cape and the big gut."

There was coarse laughter all around, but Rosalynde did not linger. She headed straight for the gallows, intending to speak to the mayor before she lost her nerve. She had left Cleve alone far too long already; it was time she conquer her fears and find the help they needed.

She had almost reached the steps that led up to the gallows platform when she finally saw a man who fit the description of the mayor. But before her relief could blossom, she was filled with a sudden dread. There, standing next to the mayor, gesticulating angrily, was the very same ruffian who had accosted her! Hurriedly she lowered her head and pulled her hood protectively about her face. But she nevertheless kept her eyes slanted sidelong at the man whose voice carried even over the hubbub of the crowd.

". . . full of thieves! One little whore picked my pocket while we were discussing—" He broke off then and lowered his voice. Although she could not hear his words, Rosalynde was certain he was accusing her further. Oh, how could she be so unlucky? she agonized as she melted back into the crowd. Why must the man whose help she so desperately needed be in the company of the very man she had been trying to avoid? And why, why, did the ruffian insist on accusing her of such thievery? She'd done nothing to him but try to escape his disgusting pawing.

But there were no answers for her questions, and Rosalynde's face creased in despair. She watched the two men from behind the sheltering bulk of a chestnut tree as she pondered this new problem. Eventually that man would leave. Eventually the mayor would be alone. But did she dare approach him? Would he listen to her, or would he simply believe that man and cast her in the gaol?

When the other man finally sauntered away, she crept nearer the scaffolding. But still she hesitated to approach the corpulent mayor. Then, to her dismay, a stout cart with the condemned men drew up before the gallows, surrounded by a jeering crowd. All other activities at the fair seemed to stop as everyone gathered around for the day's chief entertainment. Amidst considerable shoving and jostling for position, the crowd pressed close to the platform, thrusting Rosalynde almost to the forefront of the gathering. She could neither go forward nor slip away, for she was hemmed in by villagers all around. One rough-shod foot trod on her bare foot, but when she drew back, an elbow prodded sharply against her ribs. Like a mole caught in its tunnel she was trapped there, unable to escape and forced to witness the gruesome spectacle to come.

It was only the shouts of the mayor as he strode importantly back and forth upon the platform that brought any measure of quiet to the noisy, restless crowd.

"Hear me! Hear me, fine people of Dunmow!" He flapped his hands about for silence. "Quiet yourselves and hear me!"

When the uproar was down to a low murmur, the man puffed out his chest and stilled his nervous pacing. " 'Tis a fine day for a fair—"

"An' a foin day fer a hangin'!" someone shouted from the throng.

"So 'tis! So 'tis!" several voices added to the sentiment.

"Yes. Yes." The mayor waved once more for silence. "We shall have the hangings in short order. But I thought it only fittin'—given that this is the traditional day for the handfastings—that I offer one more time the chance for trial marriage to some willin' lad and lass. 'Tis only for a year and a day," he added in a wheedling tone.

"E'en a year and a day is too long for a man to be wed!" a crude, leering fellow hooted.

"E'en a *day's* too long for a woman to spend with the likes of you, John Finch!" a woman cackled back at him.

"That's just the point," the red-faced mayor continued.

" 'Tis always been the custom this day to let a man and woman try at marriage. If they don't suit, they may part ways in a year and a day, no harm done."

"Except to her maidenhead," a voice cried from the back, causing everyone to laugh.

"Might I take a new wife every year?" one drunken fellow called. "I might be tempted if I could have a new wench to warm me bed every year!"

"A girl would do better to wed one of those murderin' thieves than the likes of you," an answering taunt came from a woman.

But as the laughter roared once more, a crafty smile formed on the mayor's face. "There's never been a Flitch of Bacon Festival where Dunmow did not see at least one couple handfasted. Since it appears no maid is willin' to take her chances with one of our own fine lads, perhaps there's a lass among you who will take one of our prisoners to husband."

At that outrageous suggestion everyone broke into excited debate.

"Who'd wed a murderer?"

"They should all hang!"

"Yes, but a good woman can keep a man honest."

"Keep 'im satisfied, perhaps. But honest?"

"Huh! A woman's a worse sentence than a noose. Make them all three marry!"

Rosalynde stood just below the mayor, staring up at him in frustration. She cared nothing for this ancient custom of theirs and hardly more for the men who remained bound in the cart on the other side of the platform. She only wanted the mayor to dispense with this banter and finish this business. Then she could seek his help.

"Now hold on. Hold on!" the mayor shouted as he once

more attempted to quiet the restless people below him. "I only thought to provide you with more entertainment."

"I say, let us see the goods first," a young woman just behind Rosalynde cried.

Rosalynde turned to look askance at the girl. What manner of woman would even consider such a union? The girl, however, was already being sharply reprimanded by her mother.

"Shame! Shame, daughter!" the older woman hissed as she soundly cuffed her stocky daughter's head.

"What other choices are there?" the gap-toothed girl shrieked as she raised her arms defensively. But she was no match for her furious mother, who yanked her by one braid and dragged her ignominiously through the crowd. The mother gave no care to the uproarious laughter as she shouldered her way through the packed square, her daughter bawling every step of the way.

At their exit the people turned back to the mayor, who had been laughing so hard he'd gotten the hiccups. To cure that dilemma he guzzled ale from a leather skin he carried at his waist, but his speech was noticeably more slurred when he spoke again.

"D'ye wish to look 'em over, ladies?"

"Aye!" The roar came from men and women alike.

"Show 'em afore you condemn 'em—whether it's to be to the hangman or to the wife!"

To Rosalynde's utter dismay, the entire assemblage seemed now to want some hapless girl to wed one of the condemned men. This would take forever, she fretted. And to make things worse, it appeared the mayor would not last much longer. By the time she did get to speak to him, he would be quite lost to drink! She stared around her in despair, wondering if she could find someone else in authority who could help her. Surely there must be someone else.

But there was no one else, at least not still possessed of all his wits. To the last man, every villager was well steeped in ale or wine, celebrating the annual festivities despite their lack of understanding of the custom's source. It had always been done so, and it always would be. And as they probably did every year, they were all becoming completely and blindly drunk.

She tried to get through the crowd but it seemed hopeless. Then a chant started and she cringed with the cruelty of it all. "Bring 'em up! Bring 'em up!"

Between the awful noise, her helpless situation, and her worry for the ailing Cleve, Rosalynde almost burst into tears. Had the entire world gone mad? Were there nothing left but murderers and hangmen and bloodthirsty spectators? She clapped her hands over her ears and once more tried to escape. But she was perversely shoved even nearer the front, closer to the narrow stairs that led up to the gallows.

Then the tone of the crowd changed and she looked about in renewed panic. A group of village men had maneuvered the cart nearer the stairs and removed the back rails so that they could drag the three prisoners out. Rosalynde saw the group of men rear back, as if heaved all at once by a force too mighty for them to oppose. But then they quickly surged forward again to capture their quarry. She heard a cry of pain, and more than one vicious oath. Despite her determined disinterest, she could not help but raise up on her toes and crane her neck to see better. But everyone was now peering avidly toward the scuffling at the cart and she could not see past them.

Then the crowd suddenly drew back and Rosalynde was nearly toppled from her feet. By the time she regained her balance and glanced up, the condemned men were being herded up onto the gallows.

Rosalynde was overcome with unexpected compassion as she watched the repellent scene. Before she had been too consumed with her own miseries to worry about anyone else's troubles. But as she watched the first man ascend to the platform, she was overwhelmed with pity. He was a crude young fellow, dirty and mean-looking. But for all that, he was quite clearly terrified. The second man was older, with a mouth that fell open in fear, showing blackened stubs for teeth. Tears ran freely down his cheeks, leaving clean rivulets upon an otherwise filthy face.

She clutched at her cloak as she watched them shamble to stand beneath the waiting nooses, a burly guard on each side of them. Their feet were linked by heavy lengths of rope. Their arms were bound behind their backs. It was only by reminding herself that they were very likely murderers, of the same ilk as the deadly gang of cutthroats that had attacked her and her unsuspecting group yesterday, that she was able to fight back tears of sympathy.

Then there was another disruption at the stairs, and, with a loud outcry from the crowd, the third man was dragged up onto the gallows.

Rosalynde's eyes were as round and staring as everyone else's when the fellow found his footing and then shook his would-be captors off. Like the others he was bound hand and foot. But unlike those other hapless men, his bindings did not begin to lessen the threat he presented. Like a cornered wolf, beleaguered yet no less dangerous, he held the nervous men at bay, seeming almost to dare them to approach.

He was a big man—huge, Rosalynde noted—with massive shoulders and powerful arms. His tunic had been ripped and partially torn away, and as he strained against

the stout hemp ropes, his every muscle and sinew stood
out in sculpted detail. He was a full head taller than any
other man on the platform, and for the space of two heart-
beats Rosalynde wondered how such a fine specimen of a
man could ever have come to so poor an end.

The crowd was silent, in awe of the man who, even as
he approached his death, could be so fearsome, so intimidating. Then the man straightened a little, and with a contemptuous glance at the men who'd tried to hold him, he
moved of his own accord to stand beneath the third noose.

There was in that move an odd sort of nobility. Where
the other men were broken and afraid, he was proud and
brave. Clearly he did not wish to die, but he seemed to
have accepted his end with the dignity of a prince,
Rosalynde thought. He did not meet any eye after that,
but only stared grimly toward the horizon.

"Now there's a bloke worth having," Rosalynde heard a
woman somewhere near her murmur.

Yes, she silently agreed. There indeed was a man worth
having. If only he'd been at the river with them yesterday.
If only he'd been there to stop that pair of ruffians from
manhandling her and chasing her as a thief! She was so
desperately frightened, yet he seemed afraid of nothing.
Not even death. If only she could hire him to see her
home.

On that wishful thought she suddenly froze. He *could*
get her home if he was free. And *she* could set him free if
she would agree to be handfasted!

She shook her head in confusion, aghast at such a preposterous idea. Claim him for her husband in this heathen
ritual? She must be mad to even think such a thing. And
yet a part of her *was* mad, she admitted to herself, as she
stared wildly around her, still fearing to be caught by the

two bullies. She was mad with fear and mad with desperation. Could she afford to wait for another way home?

She stared up at the man once more. He might be a
criminal, but there was something oddly noble in his bearing. She was convinced he could get her home safely. But
would he? And could she take such a foolhardy chance?

She was still staring at him, dumbfounded and wondering what he looked like beneath the week-old beard and
long hair plastered damply to his head, when she realized
the mayor was again speaking.

". . . the three prisoners. Tom Hadley." He pointed to
the miserable young man at the end whose head hung
down pitifully. "Tom Hadley for thieving and murder, on
the King's Road to London. Roger Ganting for hunting
within the Bishop of Shortford's preserve and for attacking
the Bishop's guard and killing one man."

The mayor started to move nearer the big man but then
clearly thought better of it. "And then this fellow, known
only as Blacksword since he has not revealed his Christian
name very likely he's not even Christian! Blacksword,
also for thieving and murder. On the King's Road to London, on the highway to St. Edmonds, and in the village
of—" He stopped abruptly when the man slowly turned
his head and gave him a cold stare.

"The—the village of Lavenham," the mayor concluded
quickly. Then he took another step back from the menacing prisoner. "They've all been tried and found guilty.
Now we're to see 'em hanged."

"Wot about the han'fastin'?" a man beyond Rosalynde
called.

"Aye! Where's the maid willin' to rescue one of these
fine upstandin' lads from the noose?" an old man shouted.

Rosalynde did not pause to reason out what she did
next. She had heard the charges against him, yet she

harshly cast them from her mind. She had been horrified at the suggestion that some maiden be handfast wed to one of this murderous group. Yet now she clung to the idea as her only salvation. She had been disgusted by the crowd's perverse interest in seeing these men hanged or else wed to some unlucky woman, and yet . . . And yet the logic that prompted those earlier emotions fled when she once more spied the drunken visage of the man who'd chased her. If she did not act right now, she might not get another chance to save herself and Cleve.

As she raised her voice and fought her way forward, she knew he was the only man strong enough—and sober enough—to help her and Cleve. He was the only man with a reason to take her seriously. He had nothing to lose and everything to gain. Surely out of gratitude he would see her safely to Stanwood.

"*I* will be handfasted!" she cried, shoving her way past a stout village woman and her half-grown son. "*I* will have him to husband!"

At first the mayor did not hear her. There was too much noise from the restless spectators who surrounded the platform. But the people around her heard, and before she could reconsider her rash actions, she was pushed along, grabbed at roughly, and propelled forward until she stumbled to a halt at the foot of the crude stairway.

For a heart-stopping moment Rosalynde hesitated. All around her people stared and laughed. A new chant was springing up: "Handfast! Handfast!" She suddenly wanted no more than for the earth to swallow her up and deliver her from this hell she'd plunged herself so precipitously into. She looked wildly about for escape, but there was none. Before her a sea of avid faces swam, some malicious, some compassionate, others only eager for a new and novel entertainment. She had wanted to remain hidden and unnoticed, but now she was the center of everyone's attention.

She was shaking with fear as she tried to step back away from them all. But her heel struck against the rough wooden stairs and her hand bumped against the railing.

It was that rail that decided her, that gave her the strength to follow through on her mad and ill-advised scheme. Beneath her hand it was solid despite its rough texture and the splinters it promised. When she thought she would fall from the sheer fright of everything, the rail held her up. Although it made no sense—she knew it was only a desperate wish on her part—she kept thinking that this man might be like the rail: hard and strong, and prickly too. But beneath it he might be steady and reliable.

They need only be handfasted for a year and a day as the mayor said, she reminded herself. If she appealed to his better nature, he might help her. If she saved his life, he might feel obligated to her.

If she offered him a reward, he might do it.

She closed her eyes and tightened her grip on the wood. Then she took a slow, steadying breath, and with a fervent prayer for divine help, she turned and mounted the stairs.

"Well, well. What sport have we here?" the mayor leered as Rosalynde reached the top of the scaffold. "Come here. Come here," he gestured, clearly pleased that he'd been successful in enlarging on the day's entertainments.

Once she stood beside him he tugged down her hood, revealing her dark tangled hair and her dirty, frightened face. "What? No suitors of your own?" he scoffed, to the enormous pleasure of the raucous onlookers. When she didn't answer he prodded her forward, forcing her nearer

the three condemned men. "So, what's yer pleasure, m'
fresh young bride? Which of these earnest young grooms
pricks yer fancy?"

"They'll prick her fancy, all right," one drunken fellow
guffawed. "That, an' plenty more!"

"Pick the little one," an old woman shouted her advice.
"Ye can keep 'im in line easier."

"The big un'll tear such a little thing to pieces in the
bed," another one warned.

"Bet he'd fit *you* just fine," the malicious retort came
right back from another bystander.

With catcalls and whistles, hoots and shouted advice,
the crowd worked itself into a frenzy of anticipation. The
day of drunken merriment topped off by a handfasting and
public hanging! It was a day the people of Dunmow would
long recall with considerable relish. But for Rosalynde it
was a nightmare too awful to be believed.

She ignored the crude advice and taunts from the people in the crowd. With a shudder of revulsion she slipped
away from the vulgar pressure of the mayor's hand on her
shoulder. In doing so, however, she placed herself directly
before the last of the three prisoners, the one who had
prompted her to take such a mad course of action.

She was terrified as she slowly raised her eyes to him.
He was so big. So powerful and clearly dangerous. As her
gaze raised timorously from the tall boots that encased his
feet and calves, then farther, past his muscular thighs
wrapped in what once had been fine linen braies, she became even more unnerved than she already was. This was
like no man she'd ever seen before. There was a brutal
strength evident in both his magnificent physique and his
proud carriage. His tunic was half torn from him, as was
his shirt, and she saw a raw scrape where a portion of his

chest was exposed. His hands were still bound, yet the muscles of his arms bulged against the rough rope.

Finally, when she could bear the suspense no more, she lifted her gaze to his face.

Rosalynde wasn't sure what to expect. He was younger than she had first supposed, perhaps a half score years her elder. He was dirty, of course. Filthy. His unkempt hair was plastered to his skull, and she could not have guessed its true color. His jaw was stern and rigid, his nose straight save for a crook where it might have once been broken. All in all, however, he would probably be quite acceptable to the eye once cleaned and properly dressed.

But none of those things mattered to Rosalynde. He was a thief and a murderer. And yet he perversely seemed the only one who could help her. She had it within her power to save him, it appeared. Would he return the favor? It was that which she hoped to determine as she met his ferocious stare.

But the very fury in his eyes took her completely aback. He would as happily strangle her as look at her, she thought with a gasp of dismay. For an endless frozen moment she stared at him, her eyes wide with fear and desperation. Then he spoke, although it sounded more a low, menacing snarl.

"Begone from here, madame. I do not like your game!"

He had all his teeth, she noted obliquely. And better speech than she would have guessed. She shook her head sharply, trying to focus on the very real problem at hand.

" 'Tis no game," she whispered urgently.

But he only raised one of his straight eyebrows mistrustfully as his jaw tightened. "Then what? Why choose a husband from the gallows—"

"Is this the man you choose? Blacksword?" the mayor interrupted imperiously, although he did not venture too near. "You know, you might find one of the others a bit more biddable."

At this the crowd erupted in laughter, and he paused to take another gulp from the skin at his side.

"I want *him*," Rosalynde answered, raising her head to stare at the man known only as Blacksword. Her eyes searched his face for some sign that she was making the right decision, some reason to believe she wasn't delivering herself into the hands of the devil himself.

But his face was as hard as granite, set in the same rigid expression he'd assumed when he had first crossed to stand under the noose intended for him. Did he prefer hanging to marrying her? she wondered disbelievingly. Was he so lost to the world that he would seek his own death and perhaps doom her and Cleve as well?

In that moment anger flared within her, anger at everything that had happened to her, but mostly anger at him for being the horrible creature he was.

"I choose *you*!" she muttered through gritted teeth, her eyes blazing with fury. Without pausing to think, she grabbed hold of his grimy tunic and clenched a knot of the fabric in her small fist. "You have no other choice. Except to die. . . ." The rest faded away as his cold, colorless eyes met hers.

Fire leapt between them, angry and selfish and sizzling. Against her knuckles the heat of his skin seemed almost to burn her. She wanted to jump away, to protect herself from this menacing outlaw, this murderous villain. But her life might very well hang in the balance. Despite her every instinct to flee, she faced his icy rage.

When his agreement came, it was not in words. Indeed, it was hard for her to say just how she knew he had agreed at all. His posture was no less tense. His expression did not soften. But there was something in his eyes. A flicker, perhaps. A new light.

All Rosalynde knew was that she felt a sure and swift relief, as if he had somehow saved her life in that fraction of a moment. She released his shirt then and let loose the breath she had unconsciously been holding.

The mayor approached them and the crowd began to hoot and stomp with anticipation, but she didn't notice. Her gaze held with that of the man before her. It was then that she realized that his eyes, which she had thought only hard and colorless, were in truth a rare, clear shade of gray.

4

"They shall seek wedded bliss!" the mayor shouted to the mass of people crowded about the gallows. "Wedded bliss!"

With that announcement every throat seemed to raise a shout until Rosalynde clapped her hands over her ears at the din. It might have been the bloodthirsty howl of wolves, so unfeeling and pagan did it echo across the square. She floundered between renewed panic and enormous relief, between terror and hope as she stood trembling before the maddened crowd.

"Handfast! Handfast!" The chant reverberated around and around her. But the cry melded also with another call to "Hang them! Hang them!" until the two seemed one and she felt as if she were as much the subject of the one sentiment as the other.

"Handfast!"

"Hang them!"

In desperation she looked back up at the man she had just chosen to be handfasted to, but his grim expression provided her no solace. He only gave her a cold stare and then turned his eyes toward the horizon.

For a terror-filled moment she feared that instead of saving herself, she had indeed flung herself into a far worse snare. The riot of drunken villagers seemed as ready to cast her fate with this Blacksword and hang her as it was ready to see her wed to the menacing wretch. She turned to the mayor for help, but he was swilling back more ale and rousing the crowd to ever greater bedlam. She whirled to face the screaming horde, then stumbled back in fear as one leering fellow lunged partially onto the platform and tried to grab her ankle. He came up only with the tattered edge of her gown, but that was enough to unbalance her. Had she not been stopped by the solid bulk of the huge man behind her, she would have fallen hard on the wooden platform. As it was, she was barely able to right herself. But it was only when Blacksword took a threatening step toward the man still clinging to her hem that the drunken fool released his hold and fell back in very real fear.

Without thinking she ducked behind Blacksword, keeping his sturdy bulk between her and the crowd. Even though he was still bound, he seemed able to intimidate everyone near him. But his menacing posture toward the man who had grabbed at her had a surprising effect on the restless mob.

"Jealous, ain't 'e?"

" 'E courts her a'ready!"

And slowly the cry turned to "Handfast." From somewhere a chair was produced, and the mayor directed it be placed at the front of the gallows platform. Then he signaled Rosalynde to approach him.

"Wot's yer name, girl?" he demanded, fixing his hand on her shoulder again.

She glanced from him to the hulking Blacksword then at the crowd, which had subsided somewhat and strained now to hear what was being said. Then her eyes flitted back to Blacksword.

"Rosaly—" She halted, then swallowed hard. She had a

sudden and unaccountable fear of revealing too much about herself. "Rose. I—I am called Rose."

"A Rose!" the mayor jeered even as a loathsome belch escaped his lips. "We have here a thorny Rose to be wed to the outlaw Blacksword!"

" 'Twill be a union deadly to them both," someone cackled from the sea of faces below them. But it set the crowd to laughing again, and despite her fright Rosalynde sensed a more genial mood from the avid spectators. Still, she did not doubt their mood could just as easily turn black. If only she could be done with it all and make good her escape.

But that was not to be.

In short order the chair was dragged to a place before the two other condemned men. Then the intimidating Blacksword was freed of his bonds by a wary guard and thrust rudely toward the chair.

Rosalynde thought for a moment that her scheme would fall apart right there, for the fearsome rogue gave the guard such a quelling glare that the man raised his dagger protectively before him. But despite Blacksword's threatening posture, he seemed equally aware that this was not the time to seek revenge against those who had captured and imprisoned him. She saw him flex his shoulders as if to stretch them after their long cramped position. Then in a move she would never have expected, he turned toward the waiting crowd and gave them a victorious wave, with both his hands extended high over his head. Then equally surprising, he crossed the few steps to her and gave her a wide, mocking bow. "If you wish to live out this day, go along with whatever I say," he said quietly, for her ears only. Then he abruptly picked her up and tossed her most unceremoniously over his shoulder.

At once the crowd erupted into riotous waves of laughter and bold exhortations. From her upside-down position over his iron-muscled shoulder, Rosalynde heard the lewd advice and coarse suggestions. For a desperate, dizzying moment she feared she had delivered herself into the hands of Lucifer himself, a man who'd no sooner been set free by her intercession than he threatened her very life! What sort of madman had she bound herself to?

In a panic she kicked her legs and pounded her knotted fists against his back. But it was to no avail. He only strode back and forth along the platform, displaying her struggling, up-ended form for all to see and thereby goading the crowd to even more uproarious laughter. When he finally righted her, she nearly collapsed, she was so woozy from his topsy-turvy manhandling. But when he tried to steady her she furiously slapped his hands away.

"Cuff 'er one!"

"Teach 'er who's to be boss!" The laughter rang out.

For a moment Rosalynde cringed, fearing a blow from his mighty fist. But to her enormous chagrin he only scooped her up once more, then sat down on the chair with her firmly on his lap. Though she struggled, he clasped her tighter around the waist until she could hardly catch her breath at all.

"Be still," he said with a fierce growl in her ear.

But that only increased her terror and the tempo of her flailing arms. Then his other arm wrapped around her, holding her arms snug against her sides.

"I said be still and go along with whatever I say," he snarled once more, even as the spectators laughed anew at the antics before them.

"Oh, please, just let me go," she pleaded in a faint and breathless tone. She was unable to think or even move as her heart thundered painfully in her chest. What manner of man had she loosed by her ill-considered plan?

"It's too late to change your mind, wench." He pushed her hair aside so that his face was beside her own. "Just play your role and with any luck darkness shall see us free."

At this unpredictable remark Rosalynde turned a stupefied expression toward him. What did he mean, "luck"? Then in a flash she understood. It was not him she need most fear, but the crowd.

He glanced down at her frightened face while in the background the crowd became steadily drunker on both ale and pent-up anticipation. Once more she was struck by the vivid gray of his eyes, and she saw the sharp intelligence there. But before she could signal her new understanding of his meaning, his face descended over hers, and she was abruptly bent back over his arm in a harsh, impersonal kiss.

The wild cheering of the crowd echoed faintly in her ears. In some vague portion of her mind she even recognized that this too was just something he did to court the spectators' goodwill. But then logic fled and she was left conscious only of the hard forcefulness of his mouth, and how his lips gradually became softer and his tongue probed between her lips. As he'd ordered, she tried to play her role, but she was too undone by the sudden rush of blood to her head to clearly figure out her part. Should she protest? Should she succumb? No maiden would countenance such a public manhandling, would she? But that might not be true of a woman who would be handfasted to a condemned man.

Before she was able to make up her mind, he pulled back from her and gave her a quick and curious glance.

"Next time open your mouth," he mocked softly. Then he straightened her on his lap.

Rosalynde was breathless and weak, and completely be-

fuddled by this strange turn of events. She was unsure
now just what she was to do at all. It was the lord mayor,
however, who decided for her.

"We have here the man known as Blacksword. And here
the maiden called Rose." He strutted before them, stumbling from too much drink as he sought now to bring his
performance to a triumphant conclusion. "They shall be
handfast—wed in the old way—for a year and a day." He
belched and stumbled to a halt. "First the hangin's. Then
the handfastin'!"

What followed was grisly beyond Rosalynde's worst
nightmares. She still sat on Blacksword's lap, held immo-
bile as much by her revulsion of the goings on around
them as by his taut grasp. She refused to look behind them
as the other two prisoners were forced to stand on boxes
while the nooses were slipped over their heads and then
tightened about their necks. But she was horribly aware of
their helpless struggles and their pitiful pleading. She
bowed her head, squeezing her eyes tightly as she prayed
for this not to be happening. Around her the fierce Blacksword's grip tensed, and she was suddenly aware of his
heart thudding in his chest, pounding against her back as
he too tensed in awful anticipation. Then with a sinister
scrape the boxes were pulled out from under the two hapless men's feet and she heard the sickening cries as they
fell, the sound changing from wretched sobbing to abrupt
choking.

Rosalynde was never to be sure whether it was she or
Blacksword who jumped at the grotesque sound. Beyond
them the crowd let out a hoarse cheer, but it quickly
turned to an ominous quiet until nothing but the stran-
gling, jerking sounds of the doomed men behind them
could be heard. It was not until the silence was broken
only by the rhythmic creaking of the stout ropes as they

twisted and swayed with their heavy loads that the crowd began to shift and buzz with returning conversation. But it was not nearly as animated as before.

As for Rosalynde, she was trembling in violent agitation, tears brimming in her eyes. The man who held her seemed almost as affected as she. She heard his heartfelt "Thank you, Mistress Rose," whispered so quietly she was hardly sure he said it at all. But she had no chance to respond, for the mayor, who was clearly unmoved by the deaths he'd just witnessed, addressed the gathered throng once more.

"We've had the hangin's. Now fer the handfastin'."

In short order she and the man Blacksword were stood on either side of the chair. At the mayor's impatient gesture they joined hands across the chair, to the enormous approval of the waiting horde. Her hand felt small and cold when his larger one enveloped it. He held it firmly, although not painfully, and when they were declared wed she felt his short sigh of relief. But he did not look at her nor did he say a word.

The next two hours were a living hell for Rosalynde. Reseated in the chair, the two of them were lifted high and paraded around the square. Several times they were nearly dropped. More than once she thought she would slide out of his steely grasp and be trampled in the drunken mob. By the time they were lowered to the ground, she was trembling with fear and faint with exhaustion. Terror, hunger, and two days of brutality were taking their toll, and she was sure she would not last until nightfall. When someone tossed an apple in her lap she stared at it in dull surprise.

"If you don't eat it, I will," Blacksword said, reaching for the bruised fruit, which was clearly a leftover from the previous year's harvests. But Rosalynde was too quick. In a flash she snatched it up then proceeded to devour it like a starving woman. At such a desperate reaction, however, other festival-goers devised a new sport. Within moments they were being pelted with all sorts of foods. Raw carrots, onions, pears, beans, and even hard crusts of bread. Her arms, her legs, even her cheek caught the brunt of their new game, no matter how much she dodged. It was only when one man threw a particularly large turnip and nearly struck her in the head that Blacksword rose angrily from the chair they yet shared. Placing her abruptly aside, he glared furiously at the drunken lout who'd tossed the vegetable, sending him scurrying away. Rosalynde, meanwhile, lost no time in gathering up as much of the food as she could, stuffing it in her gown for Cleve.

"We must leave," she whispered to her new "husband" as he turned to watch her. "We must escape."

"Yes," he answered, looking around them as he did so. Then he spied a group of musicians surrounded by dancers, and he grabbed her arm and pulled her up. "Forget that cast off food."

The dancing was not the courtly movements she had been taught by her tutors. Men and women milled in wild abandon, stomping and swaying, drinking as they went and raising their voices in bawdy lyrics until the instruments were practically drowned out. Rosalynde was jostled and shoved, and nearly lost Blacksword in the confusion. Had she not grabbed determinedly onto the wide leather belt that circled his waist, he might have been gone, leaving her as stranded and alone as before.

But she refused to let go, and when he paused between two carts and looked back at her she was glad she had.

"I must leave you now," he said as he firmly disentangled her hand from his belt. He glanced once at her then turned his face away. "Many thanks for sparing my life."

"You can't just leave me!" she exclaimed, running after him as he turned to go. She grabbed once more at his belt, at his arm, at the torn edge of his tunic as he strode purposefully away. "You can't leave me!" she cried in renewed desperation.

He turned abruptly, grabbed her by the arms, and held her rigidly away from him. "I cannot help you! For whatever reason you chose to save me, I thank you. But I have my own affairs to tend. I cannot be any aid to you in yours," he finished bitterly.

"But you must help me!" Rosalynde pleaded, staring disbelievingly into his harshly set face. "I took a chance on you and you *must* repay me!"

"I told you, I *cannot* help you," he countered tersely. "Find someone else."

"But . . . but . . ." Tears welled in her eyes as her last hope for help began to disappear. She shuddered as she realized that everything she had endured this day had been for naught. Desperately she grasped his forearms. "You would be dead if not for me. Hanged like those other poor wretches." Her anger dissolved into frightened pleading. "I beg you, please don't abandon me here."

Through her tears his face was blurred; his expression was impossible to detect. She saw only his fierce gray stare, the stubbornly set jaw and brows lowered in a scowl. But she felt when his grasp changed. He thrust her away from him rudely, as if he were disgusted with his own forbearance.

"Who is it you fear?" he muttered, eyeing her suspiciously.

"No one . . . everyone." She shook her head then straightened up and wiped her tears away with the back of one hand. "I need to get somewhere and . . . and I thought . . . I want you to take me there."

"I cannot," he answered curtly. "There is an urgent matter I must pursue. A matter of vengeance—"

"You owe me this!" she interrupted him furiously, then ducked her head as a drunken couple looked over at them and began to giggle. "You owe me this much," she hissed.

"I owe—" He stopped and sighed. Then he gave her a disgruntled glance before he stared around at the lengthening shadows of approaching dusk. "If you want to follow me, so be it. That's as much as I can offer you. But you'll have to keep up. I'll not slow my pace for you." With that grudging offer he turned and headed past two stone cottages and toward an orchard beyond.

Rosalynde did not know whether to be infuriated with his callous indifference or relieved that he at least was not abandoning her entirely. But as she followed him, running to keep up with his ground-eating stride, she cast him more than one vituperative glance and silently cursed him for the black-hearted villainous reprobate he clearly was. His back was broad and inflexible as he strode through the shadowy orchard; his head was held high, like that of a fearless warrior as he proceeded on without so much as a glance behind him. In both his stride and his ease of movement he struck her as a man of incredible power and considerable pride. But he was a blackguard nonetheless, she fumed.

When they reached the edge of the orchard, he paused and Rosalynde collapsed onto a stone wall, gasping for breath. The vegetables she'd tucked into her tunic clustered in uncomfortable lumps at her waist, and she squirmed to find them a better resting place as she slowly caught her breath. When he turned to stare at her she met his gaze with an icy glare, but when his eyes did not waver, she began to feel uncomfortable. For all her frantic need to find help, for all her tears and demands that he not abandon her, as she faced that hard, assessing gaze, a tremor of fear slithered up her spine. She had thought he would be grateful enough to help her, but he clearly was not. Was he cold-hearted enough now to harm her?

When he took a step toward her, she let out a squeak of alarm and scrambled down from the rock wall.

"Have you any weapon?" His eyes ran down her dirty, lumpy form then up again to her face. "A dagger, perhaps?"

Rosalynde froze in indecision. Should she pretend to be weaponless—and thereby appear completely at his mercy? Or admit to having Cleve's small knife and perhaps have him take it from her? She hesitated and tried to break the hold of his perceptive gaze, but before she could formulate a reply, he gave her a cold smile.

"You have one," he stated knowingly. "Come, give it to me."

"No." Rosalynde backed away from him warily. "You may not have it."

"I can just as easily take it from you. Come now. Just hand it over."

As best she could, Rosalynde affected a measure of calm as she removed the meager weapon from the strap that held it to her leg. But she was shaking with fear and dread. Then, when he started toward her to retrieve it, she swiftly lifted it up and pointed it at him threateningly.

"Stay away from me!"

Her whispered warning slowed his pace, but a smirk curved his mouth into a half smile, and he looked at her in amusement.

"How now, wife?" The smirk grew broader as she stiffened at his use of that turn. "Is this any way to greet your new husband?"

"You're not my husband!" she hissed. "I only went along with that pagan ritual to get your help."

"You married a condemned murderer expecting his help?" He shook his head in mock disbelief even as he took another step closer. "It seems much wiser to ask the authorities for help than a 'convict' like myself. Why not go back and speak to the 'lord' mayor?"

"He's drunk. They all are," she answered, taking a wary step backwards. "Anyway, his friend grabbed me and then he accused me and—"

"Accused you? Of what? Thieving, perhaps? Are you a cutpurse, or maybe a whore?" One of his brows arched and he gave her a thoroughly insulting once-over. To her chagrin, she did not know whether to be relieved or angry at his obvious lack of interest in her womanly attributes.

"I've done nothing wrong!"

"Nor have I," he said sarcastically. "Do you believe me?" Then, at her look of disbelief, he let out a short, mirthless laugh. "I see you do not."

"I don't care about what you've done. If I had I would not have saved you from the hangman. But I *did* save you and now I want to be brought safely to my home."

"As I said before, I've needs enough of my own to occupy me, brat." His eyes narrowed until they appeared as dark as obsidian. "Where, pray tell, is your home?"

"Stanwood Castle. Have you heard of it?" she added hopefully.

But he only shrugged. "How did an urchin like you get so far from home?"

"I'm not an urchin!" she burst out. But at his clear look of skepticism she sighed in resignation.

"I-I was living at Millwort Castle and my brother . . . my brother died. I go to tell my father." She did not realize that her posture had slumped as she thought of her brother, nor that her hand had lowered somewhat with the dagger. "We were attacked. Everyone was killed but Cleve and me, and—"

"Cleve?"

Rosalynde stared at him doubtfully. How much of the truth should she tell this man? Should she reveal that she was a noblewoman and Cleve only her young servant? Should she let him know that Cleve was hurt? She needed to convince the brute that he would be well compensated for any help he gave her, but she did not want to appear so helpless that he might take advantage of her.

She was spared the necessity of reply by his sudden, lightning-fast lunge. In an instant he had her wrist in an unbreakable hold. She struggled frantically to grab the dagger with her other hand, but he swiftly jerked her against him, then spun her around so that her back was pressed against him and her other arm was pinned by his implacable grasp.

"Drop the knife," he muttered hoarsely in her ear. Then his hand tightened painfully around her wrist, cutting off her circulation until her fingers began to feel numb. "Drop it," he ordered once more.

When her nerveless fingers finally did release the short dagger, Rosalynde let out a small cry of despair. But whatever dreadful fears she had for her own safety fled as he immediately released her and grabbed the knife, almost seeming to forget she was even there. He ran his thumb assessingly over the hard steel blade and hefted the bone handle in his palm. "Small but effective in hand-to-hand combat." He gave her a piercing look. "I'll see you safe to the next village. That's the most I can do for you. Perhaps there you can get the help you need." He slid the dagger into the wide leather thong at his waist.

Rosalynde was too undone by his clear intention to

abandon her to weigh her words well. "You cannot just leave me off wherever you wish! I saved your miserable neck so that you could help me and Cleve! Have you no feelings whatsoever? Have you no honor?"

His expression turned black at her shrill tone and accusing words. Rosalynde knew it was reckless to berate a man such as he. She knew her words were foolish and rash. But too much had happened; she had been witness to too many horrors and had been too agitated in the last few days to care anymore.

"You have no honor! No . . . no soul! No heart at all in your chest!" Then she snatched one of the carrots out of her soiled tunic and flung it furiously at him.

He deflected it easily enough, but his scowl did not relent. "Think carefully, my thorny little Rose. If I have no honor, no soul nor heart either, then you are on precarious ground indeed. Count it a blessing that I have consented to take you to the next village. Do not think to get anything else of me. Now let's go." So saying, he scooped up the battered carrot, stepped easily over the ancient stone wall, and strode out into the open wastelands beyond.

Rosalynde watched him go with a mixture of hopelessness and fury. How could he be so cruel and heartless—so unfeeling? He had taken the knife, and he obviously had no compunction about abandoning her at the first opportunity he found. Even though that might be for the best, there was still Cleve to consider.

He was almost a third of the way toward the distant tree line, his tall form beginning to blend into the long shadows of dusk, when she finally made up her mind. No matter how awful he was, he was still her only hope. And he was heading in the wrong direction!

As fast as she ran across the open wasteland, she thought she would never catch him. He was almost to the

trees when he paused briefly at her breathless shout. But
then he turned and continued on his way, and she had to
force her bruised feet and aching lungs to continue on.

"Wait!" she cried as she finally caught up with him and
grabbed the hem of his tunic. "I said wait!"

He stopped so abruptly that she ran full force into him.
When she raised her dazed eyes to his face, he was once
again glaring at her.

"A woman who orders a man around—whether husband
or no—takes the risk of being severely cuffed for her im-
pudence."

"I'll pay you!" Rosalynde blurted out as she stared up
into his shadowed face. In the waning light he appeared
more beast than man, a shaggy creature of supernatural
strength, all her direst fears brought to unholy light. But
her worry for Cleve and her terror of being alone in a
strange, dark place overpowered her fear of his anger. "I'll
pay you. You'll be well rewarded," she vowed, half sobbing
in her desperation.

"With what?" Then he smiled coldly and gave her a
distasteful once-over. "I hope you don't think to bribe me
with your womanly favors. If I wanted that I would simply
take it. After all, we are handfast wed."

Rosalynde was aghast as much at his disgusting assump-
tion of her means of payment as by his humiliating rebuff.
But she was not about to let him leave. "My father will
pay," she insisted. "He will reward you well if you but
bring me safely to Stanwood Castle. And Cleve too."

This time he did not respond so quickly, and Rosalynde
felt the tiniest glimmer of hope. But then he laughed and
pushed his long matted hair back from his brow. "What
will he give me? A broken-down cow? Half of his wool
from the fall shearing? Or perhaps a share in his already
meager portion of the rocky ground he farms for some

noble lord? No." He shook his head bitterly. "I seek much more than that."

"My father is no mere cottar, no farmer to pay you in leeks and mutton!" she cried. "He is Lord of Stanwood. He will pay you in . . . in . . ."

"In gold? And jewels?" He laughed sarcastically and put his fists on his hips. "Yes, I can see now that you're quite the lady. How foolish of me not to have noticed. Here I thought I'd been wed to a mere village urchin, one who wanted a husband perhaps because she was already with child." One of his brows arched and his gaze moved down to the lump of vegetables inside her tunic. "No doubt your father will reward me with castles and land and riches far beyond my wildest dreams." He laughed again and started to move away. "What a poor liar you are."

"He'll give you weapons!" Rosalynde shouted in desperation. "A horse. And . . . and . . . and gold! Yes, he'll give you gold if you just bring us safely home." When that didn't convince him, when he gave her a last skeptical glance, she could not prevent the tears that spilled over her long thick lashes. "If you don't believe me then ask Cleve. By the holy rood! If you'll just talk to Cleve! He'll tell you. He'll tell you who I am and who my father is." She clasped her hands tightly before her mouth. "Please," she begged in little more than a whisper. "Please."

After a heartbreakingly long moment he turned to stare at her. His eyes were dark; his expression was unreadable. When he spoke his voice held a note she could not decipher. Had he been moved by her tears, or by her pleading? Or was it only his greed?

"What an odd little wench you are. What a thorny little Rose." Then he crossed to stand before her, and with one finger beneath her chin he tilted her face up to him. "Show me this Cleve of yours. But be cautious," he warned as the quick light of relief lit her face. "I'll not countenance any lies from you. Be truthful with me and we shall get along. Lie to me. . . ."

He left off without finishing, but Rosalynde was well aware of the threat inherent in his warning. Still, she was fairly certain her father would reward this Blacksword for any help he provided her. She did not pause to worry about that, however. As the violet light of nightfall began to shade the countryside, she quickly began the return trip to the castle where poor Cleve lay ailing. She did not let herself think about what would happen then, what Cleve would say, or about the days to come. She refused to dwell on the fact that she was entrusting herself and Cleve into the care of a condemned murderer who might, but for his previous capture, have been one of the bloodthirsty gang who had beset them yesterday.

Instead she concentrated on the knowledge that he wanted the reward. He was big and strong. And mean. He would get them to Stanwood safely in order to collect his prize. Then he would be on his way.

She drew her hood around her neck and shivered a little at the cool evening. No one need ever know about the handfasting, she decided. In a year and a day the vow would be broken, and she would be free to make a true marriage. Neither her father nor her future husband would ever have to know. She glanced curiously at the man who strode beside her in the dark moonlit night.

He would keep the secret, she assured herself. After all, he was not the sort who wished to be tied down to a wife. Besides, she recalled, pursing her lips in annoyance, he had already indicated his distaste for her. No, he would not tell anyone about the handfasting. With any luck she would be rid of him within a fortnight.

5

Rosalynde was cold, hungry, and long past exhaustion by the time they neared the ruined castle where Cleve was hidden. The moon had risen, a meager crescent in the eastern sky, and cast thin, ghostly shadows over the countryside. Trees, shrubs, stone outcroppings—in the pale metallic light each one appeared more sinister than the next. Her heart pounded with dread, for she expected at any moment that they would be beset by foul attackers.

The silent man who strode before her was small comfort, for she was sure he would be glad to be rid of her, even if it meant fighting his way free. He had agreed to see Cleve, and she wanted to believe that he would then be convinced she was not lying. But as they traipsed along the overgrown trail that led up to the ominous castle remains, she was hard-pressed to be optimistic. What if Cleve was out of his head with fever? What if he couldn't convince this Blacksword?

What if he wouldn't?

At that disconcerting thought she stumbled over a root and nearly fell headlong onto the path. Ahead of her, her taciturn companion only sent her a glance over his wide shoulder, then kept on at the same sure pace. Ungrateful wretch! she thought to herself. But she could not afford to dwell on such venomous thoughts. Instead, she needed to solve this new wrinkle. What would Cleve say when he found out she had bound herself to this menacing stranger, this condemned murderer? Although he was just a boy and only a servant, she was well aware of his protective nature toward her. Hadn't he proved that yesterday when he had attacked that horrible man at the river?

She bit her lip in dismay and debated her choices. If she told him that Blacksword was just someone she hired . . .

He would be skeptical and alarmed; however, he would have no reason not to believe her. But if he knew they were handfast wed . . . She shook her head and sighed. No, she could not tell him that, for even as small as he was, Cleve would very likely attack any man who dared claim his mistress's hand in such a vulgar fashion. And she could not imagine this Blacksword taking such an affront lightly. She did not like to lie, but if she and Cleve were to get home safely it seemed the only way. But she still felt uneasy as they approached the black shadow of the semidemolished adulterine.

"Where is this Cleve?" Blacksword finally spoke as they came upon a breach in the stone coursework wall.

"In an old lean-to," she answered as she tried to get her bearings. The night made everything look different, and for a moment she panicked, unsure now where she had left the page. But then she saw the overgrown herb garden and she was reassured. "This way," she said as she clambered over the rubble and started across the littered bailey. "We're nearly there."

But when she finally located the right shed and called out to Cleve, she received no answer.

"Cleve? Cleve?" she called more shrilly. Was she too late? Had he been hurt far worse than she had thought? An icy dread washed over her as she pushed her way into the roofless little building. "Cleve, are you here? Are you all right?"

"Milady?" The whisper came soft and shaky from the deepest recesses of the room. "Lady Rosalynde?"

In an instant she was at his side. She did not see the man behind her stiffen at the boy's mumbled words. In the impenetrable darkness she fumbled for Cleve, and even through his tunic and her cloak, which he clutched around him, the heat of his fever was unmistakable. She did not pause at all as she plotted what must be done.

"We need a fire. And water too." She found the broken bit of crockery and turned to where Blacksword stood, silent and faintly silhouetted in the gaping hole where a door must once have been. "The well is toward the far end of the bailey, opposite where we came in," she said. Then when he did not respond, her voice grew fierce. "Here. Take it."

"You go for the water and wood. I'll wait here with your friend." His answer was cold and unemotional, and for a moment Rosalynde's confidence wavered.

"He needs my help," she began. Then she paused as his concern suddenly became clear to her.

"This is no trick, *Sir* Blacksword, or whatever your name is. Cleve is hurt. Dear God, he's just a boy!" she cried. "Come and see for yourself."

There was an achingly long moment when he did not move. Then he advanced warily and when he squatted down near her, she reached for his hand to let him feel for himself the fever that consumed poor Cleve. But at the first touch of her hand on his arm he tensed. Had she not been so worried for Cleve, she would have pulled back from him, for she again felt that frisson of heat, like a warning jolt of danger when they touched. But her cause was too important. Cleve's very life might be at stake.

"Feel his head," she insisted as she tugged at his rigid forearm. "Feel for yourself." In the inky darkness she could see very little, but she felt when his arm relaxed, and she guided it to Cleve's overheated brow. "You see? I need water to cool him, and a fire for light to work by. I implore you, if you ever had a friend or a comrade you cared for, please, help me care for him."

Rosalynde could not hear the sincere plea in her own voice. She could not know that the meager moonlight shimmered in her dark hair much like a halo might. In the grueling afternoon she had appeared a dirty-faced raga-muffin, a desperate urchin scrabbling as best she could for survival. But shielded now by the night, and flattered by the silver glimmer of the moon, she was a different crea-ture entirely. The man, Blacksword, did not need to rea-son out the sudden confidence he had in her story. She had not lied so far, not about the boy nor about her noble rank. He'd heard the sick boy call her milady. And she had taken quick control of this new emergency as well, much as any accomplished chatelaine might. He stood up abruptly, taking the crockery with him.

"You'll have your fire, my thorny Rose. And your water. But we may not stay here overlong. I give them till their heads stop pounding—midday at the latest—before they come searching me out once more."

"Then you'll do it? You'll take us to Stanwood?"

"Aye," he slowly agreed. "For the promise of reward I'll take you to Stanwood."

So saying, he turned and left her there, wondering at his own perversity for lingering even this long near the cursed village of Dunmow.

It did not take him long to gather sufficient wood and build a small fire in the sheltered lee of the wall. He brought her water as well. Then as she began the difficult task of ministering to the injured boy, he settled back against a far wall, watching her as she worked. His stomach growled with hunger and the night air was cold where his arms and chest were exposed. But he suffered his discomforts willingly. Gladly. By every right he should be dead now, hanged by the neck, choking and writhing until his eyes bulged and his face grew mottled, like those other poor bastards today. But he was alive. Alive! And by the damnedest bit of good fortune imaginable.

He shifted against the cold stone wall, seeking a more comfortable position as he watched his curious savior. What had possessed her to claim him in such a way? he wondered as he took a bite of a bruised and overripe pear. Even with the ailing boy and the distance she yet had to travel, her gamble was still a foolish one. Were he even half the villain he was accused of being, he would not hesitate to slit her throat, and the boy's too. She was blessedly lucky to have selected him and not that vermin Tom Hadley who'd swung today. That slack-jawed coward had babbled incessantly last night, confessing to anyone who would listen every black-hearted, cold-blooded deed he had done in his brief but effective career as a highwayman. As if his confession at this late date could save his immortal soul.

He took a last bite of the pear and tossed the remains into the fire with a snort of disgust. If she had picked Tom to save her, she would be raped and left for dead by now.

At the sudden flare of the fire she glanced up at him, clearly startled. Although their eyes met only briefly before she returned her attention to bandaging the boy's head, there was no mistaking the fear in her eyes.

Smart girl, he thought cynically. It was best that she maintain a healthy fear of him and follow his orders without question if she expected him to get her to Stanwood

Castle. The promise of reward—a horse and weapons—was sufficient motivation for him to do as she asked. He owed her that much. But he would be damned if he'd risk losing the opportunity for revenge that he had so unexpectedly been handed.

Yet the fear in her eyes bothered him. If she knew he was not what he seemed . . .

He killed that thought before it could properly develop. No one in Dunmow had believed he was a knight—why should he think she would?

In London he'd been filled with his own success after winning that prized black sword at the King's tourney. Yet not three days later he'd been named a thief and thrown into that hole at Dunmow. It was bad enough to have fallen into such humiliating circumstances—to be brought so low as to be condemned as a common runagate! But now that he was freed, there was no reason for anyone else to know of it. Besides, until he knew for sure why he had been singled out and thrown in that gaol, it behooved him not to trust anyone in East Anglia.

He focused once again on the girl across the fire. Yes, he would take her to her father's castle and he would collect his reward. Although it rankled him to waste the time necessary to see her home, he knew his chances of finding his accusers were next to nothing without weapons to challenge them. It might take longer now—he would have to backtrack to the beginning and hunt them down—but he would not rest until he had found and killed the men who had used him as their pawn. He'd lost his well-trained destrier, his pack horse, his tournament weapons, and the black sword. That magnificent black sword.

His jaw tightened as he thought again how close he'd come to losing his life as well. Whether she was a thorny little Rose, or the Lady Rosalynde as the boy had called her, she had saved his neck to be sure. But gratitude was a poor second to the vengeance that consumed him now. Once these two were out of the way, he could get on with his need for revenge, he vowed. Once he had repaid his debt to her and collected his reward, he would then be better able to hunt down the men who had hoped to see him hanged.

And when he found them, he would kill them, and take complete pleasure in the doing of it.

6

Sir Gilbert Poole, newest Lord of Duxton, quaffed the remainder of his wine, then banged the heavy tankard down on the littered table with his one good arm. The cruel scowl on his face caused the man who stood before him to take a nervous step backward.

"Idiot! D'you think I gave the orders to cease the raids lightly? D'you think when I told you to lay low, it was not well considered?" In a fury he flung the metal tankard at the now-cringing man. "For your stupidity and greed you may have ruined everything! Everything!"

From his crouched and cowering position the man peered warily at his enraged lord. "But 'twas such easy gleanings. You see what we brought in. All that wine. The fine clothes you can—"

"That's a pittance compared to what I seek! For this meager gain—no gold!—we make richer travelers even more cautious! 'Twas no easy thing to lay a trap for that meddlesome knight, curse his hide. And then to bribe the mayor to forgo the trial and hasten the hangings. When word of this latest attack is heard—"

"N-no one will ever know. There was no one left among them to tell," the man stammered in self-defense. "We killed them all."

At that the furious Sir Gilbert's eyes narrowed. "All of them? You're certain?"

"Every one of them." The man did not hesitate to lie if it meant saving his own skin.

"What of the bodies?"

"We threw 'em in the river. They're half the way to the sea, like as not."

There was a tense silence. Finally the still-angry Gilbert rose from his seat and began to pace the chamber, rubbing his aching arm, which was bound tightly to his side. When he turned, he fixed his pale-blue gaze on the other man. "You'll receive only half of your portion of the profits this time. The rest is forfeit to me—to remind you not to make the same mistake again." Then, as if he anticipated the larger man's objection, he picked up a long sword that rested across the top of a wooden trunk and appeared to admire the fire-tempered blade.

"We've both benefited handsomely the past months. You need me to sell your 'goods,' and I need you to supply them. I see no need to quarrel over this matter." He paused and smiled coldly. "Do you?"

The other man opened his mouth as if to speak, but then his eyes fell to the sinister blade in Gilbert's hand. In the torch-lit room the rare black blade had a strange ebony sheen. The devil's own blade, it appeared. He clenched his jaw, then met Gilbert's cold, expectant stare.

"I'll not quarrel with you, milord," he reluctantly conceded. "But I cannot hold off much longer. My men grow restless. They cannot remain hidden in the hills forever."

"Did I say it would be forever! Dunmow has by now hanged its outlaws. We've nothing to fear there." Once again the young Lord Duxton twisted the sword so the magnificent black blade caught the light. " 'Tis time we moved our trade to fresher markets." Then he let out a dark malevolent laugh and struck out at the air with the razor-sharp sword. "Yes, 'tis time we seek riches farther afield."

After his minion left the room, Sir Gilbert laid the heavy sword across the table and rubbed his broken arm once more. Soon he would not need to soil his hands with the likes of such vermin, he thought as he stared at the wicked blade. That man and the others like him whom he employed had their uses, to be certain. He had kept his pockets well lined and himself well fixed in London while they'd ransacked the Essex and East Anglian countrysides at his direction. But now that his accursed father had finally died and he himself was ensconced at the castle in Duxton, he must be more cautious.

He'd thought it a stroke of genius when he'd decided to catch the "outlaws" who had been terrorizing the area. Not only would he ingratiate himself with the local populace, but he also had rid himself of those thieves operating outside his own hand-picked ring. How the people at Dunmow had fawned over him when he'd brought that pair of pitiful scum in!

But his greatest pleasure had been in bringing down that bastard knight.

An evil smile lit his face as he curled his hand around the intricately formed handle of the beautiful black sword. That would teach the fool not to humiliate Sir Gilbert Poole in the lists. No mere bastard could be allowed to unseat him in a tournament. No unknown, landless knight-errant could get away with breaking the newest Lord of Duxton's arm before London's finest nobility.

But he'd made him pay, Gilbert gloated. And most appropriately, at that. He'd killed two birds with one stone when he'd accused the man as an outlaw. A gold coin or two and that fat mayor had jumped at the chance to hang the man, no questions asked. By now the arrogant cur was tried and hanged and rotting in some ditch. Gilbert's only disappointment was that the presumptuous fool had not known who it was who had plotted his demise. That would have been too chancy.

He laughed aloud, the sound echoing darkly across the cold, empty chamber. Everything was falling into place. That fool—Sir Aric was his name—was taken care of. The authorities would now relax, thinking that the outlaws had been captured. Now that he was Lord of Duxton, it might be time for him to disassociate himself entirely from his band of outlaws, for he was able to avail himself of his demesne's riches as he wished now, without answering to anyone. It only remained for him to get himself a wife—a rich wife. Then he would be well fixed once and for all. She could bear him his requisite heirs while he enjoyed life at court.

Once more he picked up the fine weapon and admired it with a hard, assessing gaze. Too bad it was such a distinctive blade. He would like to have used it the next time he fought a tourney, but that might be too dangerous, at least in London. But elsewhere . . .

With a self-satisfied smile he picked up the sword and slid it into a leather-and-steel scabbard that hung from a wall peg. The blade was handsome, but it was only a symbol of his success. Then he filled his goblet with wine once more and toasted his own good fortune.

Demons plagued her. Faceless marauders hunted her down only to dissolve into horrible visions of grisly choking faces. She was hunted unmercifully, trapped in a hole with no way out, only to then be toasted and cheered by leering drunken faces. Far away she heard a child's voice calling. Giles, she thought in a moment of sudden joy. But when she turned, his pale face floated away from her to be replaced by Cleve's suffering features.

"Cleve . . ." she whimpered aloud, trying to reach him as he continued to cry out for her. "Cleve!"

But when she reached for him, it was not Cleve at all. The face that turned to her was harsher, and although he smiled, seeming almost to beckon to her, she knew she must go no nearer. She turned around to run away but he was there before her, blocking her path. Once more she turned, her heart racing now in terrible fear, but just as before, he was there. His smile was wider now, but his eyes were clear and watched her with uncanny perception. Lucifer, she thought as she flailed away from him. Lucifer.

Rosalynde sat up abruptly. Her heart thundered in her chest and every fiber in her being was tense and rigid with panic. Her eyes stared wildly about for the dreaded apparition, the pair of devil's eyes that seemed more dangerous than all of the other creatures who had crowded her nightmare. But there was no one there. She gulped two harsh breaths, fighting to control her skittering emotions. But as she looked about it seemed that her reality was almost as horrid as her terrifying dream. They were still hiding in the ruined castle. Cleve was sorely wounded although he seemed to be sleeping peacefully enough. And they were still far from home.

Her eyes widened at once as everything came back to her in a violent rush. Where was he? Where was the man she had claimed, the man who had agreed to see them safe? She scrambled to her feet as the sleep-induced cobwebs fled her brain. Where was he!

In the dense gray light of dawn, Rosalynde could see very little. The fire had burned down to a few glowing embers. Cleve was still huddled beneath her cloak, but his breathing came easy. When she touched his head, she was hugely relieved to feel only a normal, healthy warmth. But the place against the wall where that man had leaned— that Blacksword—was empty. Only a depression in the drift of leaves that had collected there gave any indication he had ever been there at all.

He had abandoned them! Disbelief and despair overwhelmed her as she stared panic-stricken about her. In spite of everything—the handfasting, the promise of reward—he had abandoned them. In utter hopelessness Rosalynde staggered the few steps to the storeroom opening, then leaned heavily against the rubble wall. What would she do? How would she and Cleve ever find their way safely to Stanwood? Tears started in her eyes, tears of helplessness and frustration and terrible, terrible fear. In anger she thrust them away, wiping fiercely at them with one small fist. She turned back to stare at Cleve, trying hard to contain the awful trembling that gripped her. Once more she had failed, she berated herself. If she'd picked one of those other men . . . If she'd not insisted on making this journey . . . If she had been able to save Giles . . .

If, if, if! She shook her head hard, then resolutely wiped the remnants of her tears away. It did no good to wish for what might have been, just as it did no good to cry, she told herself soberly. She looked again at the sleeping page. Maybe he would be better today, enough for them to venture out. Maybe if they kept to the forest and traveled by night they could make their way safely. Maybe . . .

She sighed deeply, daunted anew by their dire predicament. There was little she could do at the moment, yet to do nothing at all was to give all her fears free rein. Grimly she suppressed her fears. Cleve needed food and more of the healing herbs, she decided. At the moment fetching water and wood and preparing some sort of meal would have to be her first priority. She would worry about getting home after that.

Resolved, she stepped from the tumbled-down building, determined to be strong and brave for Cleve's sake. But with every bit of wood she picked up, she cast the vilest aspersions upon the ungrateful brute who had so callously abandoned them. He was a miserable wretch, she fumed as she found solace in her anger. An ungrateful cur with the morals of a serpent. As her ire increased, so did the pile of sticks and kindling grow until she had the beginnings for a veritable bonfire. Then she picked up the crockery and set off for the well, all the while vilifying the dishonorable ruffian, wishing vehemently that she had let him swing with those other two men. He was no doubt the ringleader, she decided bitterly, just as that old man had speculated. And she was a twice-cursed fool to have ever thought such a man might feel anything approaching gratitude.

She was in high dudgeon, searching her mind for any foul oath she had ever overheard to heap upon him. Although she'd never been one to curse—nor even to comprehend why some people did—she now understood completely. As she approached the well she was so caught up in her resentful thoughts that she was almost upon him before she realized it.

"Dear God!" The exclamation escaped her lips as she came to an abrupt stop. Her eyes grew as round as saucers as she stared dumbly at the scene before her. For his part, the man she knew only as Blacksword seemed completely unfazed by her unexpected appearance, as well as her undisguised staring. He only paused for a moment, sending her a hard look over his broad shoulder, then continued scraping his face with the sharp edge of the dagger.

Rosalynde's consuming fury over his cowardly abandonment of her was squelched at once. Clearly he was here; therefore all her suspicions were for naught. Yet now, as he calmly continued to wash himself, she felt a new kind of heat suffuse her. It was anger too, she told herself. Anger at him for scaring her so, and now anger at his utter lack of embarrassment to be caught in such an intimate act. And with his entire upper torso bared to her view! Yet despite the heat that crept up her neck to color her face, she continued to stand there, with her mouth opened in a little "O" and her eyes still wide and unblinking.

He had shed his torn tunic and his ripped chainse, and stood now in the chill early morning air, bare to the waist. He lowered the bucket into the well, then, when he pulled it up, dumped it over him. As the water coursed over his hair, down past his shoulders, chest, and back, then along his arms, she only stared dumbfounded, unable to say or even think one intelligent word. He picked up a piece of soaproot sitting on the rim of the well and began to lather himself vigorously with it. And still she only stared.

She had known he was a powerful man, broad shouldered and hard muscled. He was big and menacing-looking, and that was why she had claimed him in that pagan ritual. But she was nonetheless unprepared for the pure animal virility of him. He was like some magnificent wild creature, possessed of a primitive sort of power that sent a new type of fear skittering up her spine. Instinctively she stepped back, clutching the pottery container to her chest. But she was unable to look away. As the thin lather slowly slid down his body in dirty white rivulets, he flexed and stretched like some great beast of prey, confident of its own prowess. Then another time the bucket splashed into the well, and this time when he doused himself, a new man began to emerge.

She saw him shiver slightly. He shook his head, sending a spray of water flying around him. Only then did he turn to face her. He thrust his hands through his long hair, pushing it back from his face as he gave her a considering look. "Could it be you are waiting for someone to draw your bath, milady?"

The words were spoken in a most courtly manner, and for an instant Rosalynde was gratified that he at least acknowledged her rank. But she also recognized the sarcastic edge in his voice, and when his eyes flicked lightly over her, she understood his double meaning. She was filthy. Her clothes were torn and stained, her hair was grimy and tangled, and she hated to think how soiled her face must be. Self-consciously she tucked one long knotted tendril behind her ear, but she was irritated by his condescending attitude. He was a common criminal, she reminded herself, while she was a lady of the realm, despite her current shabby appearance.

"At the moment bathing seems a most frivolous occupation," she muttered in annoyance. "I've Cleve to attend. And you—" She gave him her most contemptuous glare. "You should be plotting our escape from this vile place."

But he ignored her ill-humored jibe and only bent down to remove his soft hide boots. "I know 'tis common for the nobility to anoint themselves with perfumed oils to cover the stink of their own bodies." He gave her a telling look. "I prefer to wash the dirt away."

So did she. But Rosalynde was in no mood to be conciliatory. "If you don't mind, I need water to cleanse Cleve's wounds." She took a deep breath then bravely came nearer him, determined not to appear afraid. He admitted she was a lady, despite her pitiful appearance, and he *had* stayed. Clearly he wanted the reward she'd promised. It followed, then, that he was working for her. It also behooved her to make sure he knew it. "Would you please draw a bucket of water up for me?" she asked in her coolest, most ladylike tone.

His answer was only a cynical look. But to her huge relief he did toss the bucket down into the deep well. As he pulled up the laden bucket she could not help but notice the smooth workings of the immense muscles of his arms and shoulders. She knew for herself how hard it was to draw the water up, for she had strained to do it the day before. With the well's cranking mechanism gone it was no mean feat. She had barely succeeded, yet he made it look easy.

Once the bucket was settled on the rim of the well, she handed him the pottery container so that he might fill it. But he only set it down beside the bucket and commenced to unlace the braies that hugged his hips so revealingly.

"You'll get your water when I finish my bath," he said shortly. Then without the least hesitation he began to draw the braies down.

Rosalynde was so horrified she could barely move. She stared aghast as the linen fabric slid low, revealing a few crisp curls of dark hair above his groin area. Then she abruptly whirled around, almost choking with shock and fear. He was truly a heathen! she thought in complete horror. A common criminal. An unconscionable murderer. And very likely capable of rape—

That thought caused her mouth to close with a snap and her stomach to lurch. Unwilling to run and thereby reveal how intimidated she was, she commanded her legs to walk stiffly away from him. If he meant to harm her, running would not help. Yet it took all her strength to maintain her dignified retreat. She kept thinking that any man who could murder—who could live by stealing from others, who could calmly undress before a stranger—was hardly likely to be above rape. At any moment she feared to hear his footsteps or feel his hands upon her.

Finally, near a section of crumbled wall, she paused long enough to glance fearfully behind her. To her enormous relief he had not pursued her, but what she saw at the well was no less unnerving. He had stripped off his hose and braies and stood now completely naked. His back was to her as he doused himself once more, and the early-morning light gleamed off his wet body. His legs and buttocks were paler than his upper body, she saw as her eyes widened in awe. But they were equally muscled, thick and strong, bunching and stretching as he bent forward to wash.

How long she stood thus, poised to flee yet staring boldly at him, she did not know. It was only when he straightened and looked over his shoulder to meet her gaze that she was shocked into motion. With a swift jerk, she turned and ducked behind the wall. But as she hurried back to Cleve's side, she could not banish Blacksword's image from her mind's eye.

When she reached the tumbled-down shed, she was still in a quandary. What had she gotten herself into now? she thought frantically. And what in the name of heaven was she to do?

As if he sensed her unease, Cleve's eyes slowly came open and he stared blankly about. Then they seemed to focus and, as if it were a huge effort, he slowly turned his head toward her.

"Mi . . . milady?" he croaked weakly.

At once Rosalynde's attention turned to him. "I'm here, Cleve." She knelt beside him and pressed her palm to his brow. To her enormous relief it was cool, and she sent a silent prayer of thanks aloft. "How do you feel?"

His answer was a frown. Then he raised a weak hand to

the crown of his head. "What happened?" he asked, wincing as his fingers found the bandaged wound.

"That man—the one you stabbed—he flung you against the boulder. Your head—" She stopped abruptly at the confused look he gave her. Her brow creased in concern as she stared at him. "Do you remember the attack? Two days ago when we had stopped for the midday meal?"

His brown eyes clouded over as he struggled to understand. Then suddenly his eyes cleared and his face grew fierce. "The unholy bastards!" he exclaimed, then immediately blushed. "Pardon, milady."

"It's all right," she said with a great sigh of relief. "But tell me, how do you feel? Are you well enough to travel?"

"Aye." He grunted as he tried to sit up. But his grimace of pain told her otherwise. "Ohhh . . ." He let out a painful moan, then lowered himself miserably to the pallet once more. "My head . . . ohhh . . ."

Rosalynde hovered over him with a worried frown. "You took a cruel blow, Cleve. That man flung you hard against the boulder. You've a nasty gash and perhaps even a crack in your head. You were feverish yesterday and all night too." She pressed her hand soothingly over the boy's creased brow.

"Then . . . then we've been here two nights and a day?" His face grew bewildered as he endeavored to remember everything. "You've tended me all this time?"

Rosalynde started to nod, but then she realized that wasn't precisely true. "Actually, you were alone most of yesterday. I went to find help."

"And did you?" he said, brightening a little.

Rosalynde hesitated and she felt the telltale heat of a blush begin to color her cheeks. "I-I did find someone—"

It was precisely at that second that their dubious savior chose to make his entrance. Rosalynde jumped abruptly, her fears of the previous minutes returning in a rush. Cleve started as well and immediately pushed up off the pallet to rise. For a tense, shattering moment the air crackled with menace: Rosalynde's concern that Cleve not know all the details of what she had done; Cleve's fear that outlaws had returned to attack them; and Blacksword's defensive reaction to the boy's sudden movement. With one swift motion he pinned Cleve to the floor, holding him helpless with a foot pressed harshly to his chest. At the sight of the dagger's quick flash Rosalynde immediately sprang forward and grabbed onto his arm.

"Don't!" she shrieked, holding onto the iron-hewn arm in alarm. "Don't hurt him!"

But the intimidating Blacksword seemed as unaffected by her desperate grasping as he was by Cleve's ineffectual flailing. Holding her off with one steely hand around her arm, he lowered himself to one knee and pressed the knife dangerously close to Cleve's white face. "Don't move."

At his fiercely growled command a sudden stillness at once gripped the room. Beneath Blacksword's overriding menace, Cleve shrank back, undone by his own terror. Rosalynde was equally frightened. It seemed certain the ogre meant to slay young Cleve! Her throat was dry; her mouth felt numb and it was an effort for her to get the words out.

"Don't hurt him," she pleaded in a quavering voice. "I'll do whatever you want. Just don't . . . don't hurt him."

The moment stretched out endlessly. She was conscious of his still-damp grip on her arm, wetting through her sleeve to her skin. Then she felt his fingers relax ever so slightly, and she let loose the breath she'd been holding.

"Stay still," he ordered the boy with a quelling stare.

Despite his fear, however, Cleve was not a coward. "I won't let you hurt her," he managed to say. But though his voice was not strong, his eyes flashed murderously. It was this, though, that seemed perversely to appease the man.

"What a fierce pup you guard yourself with." He gave Rosalynde a derisive glance, but she did not discount the seriousness of his next words. "Call him off."

"It's . . . it's all right, Cleve. Truly it is. This is the man—" She glanced fearfully at Blacksword, hoping against hope that he would not contradict her. "This is the man I-I hired to help us get home."

Once she had it out she shuddered, whether in relief or fear, she could not have said. Then she watched as Cleve's face turned from shock to disbelief and then to outrage.

"You hired *him?*" he said, casting her a look that clearly questioned her sanity.

"Yes," she replied weakly. Then "Yes," again more firmly when he seemed about to argue. In a frantic effort to silence him and thereby keep him safe from Blacksword's razor-edged temper, she adopted a stern and haughty tone that she hoped would sound sufficiently reproving. "You overstep your bounds in questioning me so."

To her relief Cleve closed his mouth. In the silence Blacksword stepped away from him, releasing Rosalynde as he did so. She was well aware that he was not inclined to humor either the disgruntled boy or herself.

"Can he walk?" he asked her, gesturing toward Cleve.

"Yes."

"No," Rosalynde countered, giving Cleve an annoyed look. Although she was more than anxious for them to be on their way, she knew Cleve was not well enough to walk. Head wounds especially required bed rest. But what Blacksword thought of their contradictory responses she could not tell. When he spoke his voice was equally noncommittal.

"See to his wound, then. And cook the remains of the vegetables." He gave her a stern look, then he tucked the knife securely into the leather girdle at his waist. Cleve's furious eyes narrowed when he saw that casual gesture.

"That's my knife," he bit out as he awkwardly propped himself up on his elbows.

" 'Tis mine now, pup." He gave Cleve a hard, flinty stare. "Behave yourself and I might eventually return it to you."

Rosalynde forestalled any further rash retorts from Cleve with a warning hand on his shoulder. "I'll explain," she whispered as she busied herself with the bandage around his head. "Just hold your tongue."

As angry and frightened as Rosalynde had been to discover the menacing Blacksword gone when she'd awakened, she was even more upset now when he lingered carefully within earshot of her and Cleve. He had dragged several long branches over near the shed, and now as she examined Cleve's head, washing it again with the woundwort and rebinding it with a softened linden-bark poultice, she was acutely aware of his presence. Cleve too was uncomfortably conscious of the big man's proximity and sent him a continuous stream of bitter glances and sullen stares. But despite their overwhelming preoccupation with Blacksword's nearness, he seemed, by contrast, completely unconcerned with theirs. While Rosalynde built up the fire to a healthy blaze, he only removed the twigs and leaves from the branches he had brought. While she brought a small amount of water to a boil and added the puny vegetables to it, he calmly lashed the two long branches together at one end, then lashed a short brace between them near the other. By the time the weak soup was ready, he had fashioned an odd contraption that had her and Cleve curious despite themselves. But he was decidedly uncommunicative.

Rosalynde fed Cleve a goodly portion of the plain broth and stewed vegetables. Then she ate also from the crude pottery that had to serve as pot, kettle, and trencher to all three of them. She was hungry, and yet her stomach was far too knotted for her to do more than pick sparingly at the food. When their doubtful protector finished his silent task and reentered the shed, she pulled the dish back from her mouth and stared warily at him.

"The remainder is for you," she said with as much grace as she could muster.

He immediately crossed the small space and squatted on his heels right next to her. "My thanks," he murmured as he took the dish from her hands. Then he steadily drank down the broth until the dish was empty.

She had pulled away from him when he first squatted down. Now, despite a conscious wish to appear unconcerned with anything he did, Rosalynde watched him with bewildered fascination. She saw how his wide, square palms with their strong, lean fingers enveloped the crockery dish. She watched with perverse absorption the rhythmic movement of his throat as he swallowed. He did not spill nor smack his lips, and when he finished he did not back hand his mouth to wipe off any excess. He only licked his lips once with his tongue, staring back at her as he did so.

Had she not been so rattled by his silent observation, she would have pondered more on this odd man. He was a murderer, yet he possessed the oddest social graces. He liked to be clean. He ate politely. And he had thanked her for the food. Of all the unexpected things, he had thanked her. His steady stare confused her, however, and her heart began to pound.

But if Rosalynde was mystified by his dangerous yet oddly civilized bearing, Cleve seemed only the more antagonized by it. It was his cracking, youthful voice that caused Blacksword to shift his eyes away from her.

"Who are you?" Cleve demanded. Then he turned toward Rosalynde, who was shaking her head in a futile effort to silence him. "Who is he and how can he help us? Has he horses? Has he weapons?"

"Cleve—"

"I'm someone who would as soon slit your throat as answer your questions." With that threatening statement Blacksword gave Rosalynde a sardonic stare. "Isn't that right, Rose?" he added with deliberate familiarity.

As much as she wished it were not true, at that moment Rosalynde was certain it was. But in her mind that made it even more important that Cleve not know the whole truth.

"He *can* get us home, Cleve. He's the only one who can," she insisted desperately.

But Cleve was in no mood to listen. "Is he the local sheriff, then? Or the lord of some nearby demesne?" The boy cast a disparaging eye over Blacksword's torn tunic and stained braies. "His only weapon is my knife. How can he save you if we are attacked again? And how can you be sure he will?"

Rosalynde did not have to look at Blacksword to be aware of his angry impatience. She was completely unnerved by the clear animosity between the two, and did not think out her response, so intent was she on diffusing the situation. "Everyone around here knows who he is! And they're all afraid of him!" she cried in a last attempt to frighten Cleve into holding his peace. "He has murdered many—"

She stopped abruptly, horrified by what she had revealed. Blacksword, however, finished her words for her. "I'm said to be an infamous outlaw who has murdered many *many* people," he said with deadly sarcasm. Then he pulled out the knife and both Rosalynde and Cleve jumped in alarm. He only put the tip of the blade to his thumbnail, however, and worked out a splinter. Then he looked over at them calmly. "Now it's time we leave this place. Unless, of course, you've changed your mind?" This last sarcastic sally he directed at Rosalynde.

Oh, how she wished she could do just that. How she wished she could be rid of this terrifying man. It seemed that they were endangered as much by his presence as by his absence. But she knew she must not risk losing his help now. Not after all she'd gone through to get him. He'd agreed to get them safely to Stanwood Castle, and despite her instinctive fear of him, there was still a part of her that believed he would do as he said. He wanted the reward she had promised. They would just have to suffer his temper and his moods until they reached her father. But she would have the devil of a time keeping Cleve calm.

"I haven't changed my mind," she said most seriously. She grabbed Cleve's hand and gave it a hard, warning squeeze. "But Cleve should not be up. Especially not doing anything so strenuous as walking."

The man Blacksword straightened to his full height then and gave them both what Rosalynde could only describe as an arrogant, superior smile. Once again she noticed how even and white his teeth were. And now, shaved as he was, the strong planes of his jaw and cheek bones were apparent, and she had to admit that he was attractive, albeit in a harsh and primitive way. For the first time she noticed that his hair was light, the color of autumn leaves

but streaked also with gold. Then, aghast that she should
be so distracted as to notice or care about his appearance,
she frowned. "Cleve cannot walk," she insisted once more.
His smile widened a fraction. "Then he shall ride."

7

The odd carryall bumped along the woodland floor, gliding over bracken and leaves, scraping along the rich soil and lurching occasionally over a small log. Despite her mistrust of the man, Rosalynde could not help but be impressed by the ingenious contraption he had fashioned with the three sticks. At the wide end he had slung her cloak between the two longest sticks to make a crude bed for Cleve. Then he stood inside the other pointed end, grasped the two branches in his hands, and strode forward. Like a beast of burden he pulled the crude cart, and despite its lack of wheels it carried the ailing boy remarkably well.

Cleve was not happy with the arrangement, but Rosalynde knew it was frustration more than anything else that had his face set in such a determined scowl. He had refused at first to ride, insisting he could walk. But dizziness had proven him wrong, and then, when his obstinance brought tears of desperation to Rosalynde's eyes, he had finally given in. But he had not been gracious about it. She knew he was sorely tried by their predicament, and more especially by his unaccustomed helplessness. It did not help things further that they must rely on such an immoral outlaw as this Blacksword to help them home. But while Cleve fumed in youthful outrage,

Rosalynde determined to maintain an air of calm. After all, it would do no good to aggravate the very man who was their sole means of safe passage. Moreover, she hoped by her example to cool Cleve's simmering anger over being indebted to such a vile person. They had several days more to spend in his company. She did not want the two coming to blows, for she knew well enough who would win. And she suspected as well that he was not the sort to go easy on a perceived adversary.

Yet all the logical reasoning and good sense in the world could not completely bury the resentment she felt toward the arrogant criminal, Blacksword. He might have agreed to get them to Stanwood, but only for the reward. He felt not the slightest bit of gratitude to her for saving him from the gallows. Why, he would have deserted her at the first chance if she hadn't been so persistent! She needed his help and so she must suffer his presence, she knew. It was even more galling to think that they were handfast wed. But that was only a temporary arrangement until they each went their own way. Until then, however, she had to keep the peace as best she could. But, oh, how she looked forward to seeing the last of him.

Even the way he pulled the crude contraption he had made annoyed her. He led the way with Cleve stretched out on the sling while she followed behind. As he forged through the forest's undergrowth, he seemed hardly strained at all, as if he were unaffected by the heavy load he dragged along. Indeed, as she took a deep breath and struggled to keep up with him, she began to wonder if he were completely tireless. He probably was, she fumed silently. He was Lucifer incarnate, devoid of any conscience or feelings whatsoever. Lucifer would not feel pain or weariness. He would just go on and on and on.

As they continued beneath the towering canopy of oaks

and beeches, under stands of giant chestnuts, elms, and yews, she became increasingly tired. Her feet hurt, for unprotected by the slippers she'd lost in the attack and subsequent escape, her toes seemed to catch every branch and find every stone. By the time he stopped beside a particularly dense stand of cedar trees, she had a pronounced limp.

"Why are we stopping?"

At Cleve's irritated tone Rosalynde gave him an exasperated look.

"Because we're tired," she answered crossly. She sat down where she stood and rubbed first her left foot and then her right. "And because my feet hurt," she added under her breath.

At once Cleve's petulant expression altered. "I'm sorry, milady. It should be you who rides in this infernal sling, not I."

"Don't be silly, Cleve," she replied. She was sorry now for her short temper with him, for she knew he was only feeling the effects of his unaccustomed confinement. "I'll be rested soon enough—"

"We'll stay here until nightfall."

At this, the first words Blacksword had spoken since they'd begun their trek, both Rosalynde and Cleve looked up. But he had gone deeper into the densely grown thicket. Taking advantage of this first opportunity to speak privately to Cleve, Rosalynde quickly moved nearer the boy.

"Please, Cleve, do not antagonize this man." She raised her hand, forestalling his quarrelsome reply. "Just trust me when I say that there was no one else who would come to our aid."

"But, milady," he whispered back most urgently. "He's an outlaw, you said, just like the men who attacked us. A murderer! He preys on those weaker than himself. And that's near everybody, from what I can tell," he added morosely.

"But he has agreed to help us."

"So he says. But why is he doing it?"

"I-I promised him a horse. And weapons too. I'm sure my father will honor my vow."

Cleve gave her a disbelieving stare. "A man like that agreed to help you merely for a promise? Where did you find him anyway?"

Rosalynde was so relieved that he had not waited for her to answer the first question that she rushed headlong into the second. "Dunmow. The village was called Dunmow and no one there would . . . could . . ." She faltered as she cast about for some believable explanation that had nothing to do with the handfasting. Then she remembered one of the fair's activities and she took a great breath.

"There was a festival, you see. And everyone was drinking. And . . . and placing bets," she added, trying hard to make her story sound true. "The mayor . . . well, he was too far gone in his cups to be much help." That at least was not a lie. "Then I saw this huge fellow betting on the bearbaiting."

"This Blacksword," Cleve cut in, saying the name as if it tasted bad in his mouth.

"He'd lost everything," she hurried on, consoling herself that this too was not precisely a lie. "But even then everyone was afraid of him. So, I thought . . . that is, I asked him if he would help me and he agreed to the terms."

Cleve stared at her, clearly hard-pressed to believe such a far-fetched tale. Yet Rosalynde knew the truth was far less believable even than her lie. Plus, the truth complicated things terribly. It was best for everyone involved if her handfast vow to one Blacksword was kept entirely secret.

"He agreed," Cleve repeated. Then he let out a great sigh and rested his head on the crook of his arm. " 'Tis still a puzzle why he agreed. If he's such a bold outlaw, why didn't he just rob someone and get what he needed?"

"Perhaps he wants to mend his ways," Rosalynde answered, biting her lower lip as she did so. "Perhaps he wearies of such a lawless life."

"Perhaps he plans to rob your father once he gets into his good graces," Cleve countered darkly.

"You are too suspicious by half," she replied in a huff. "We are hardly in a position to be particular."

"Hardly," a deep voice echoed from behind them.

With a guilty jump Rosalynde turned to look up at their dubious savior. He had come out of the thicket without a sound, and she wondered how much of their whispered conversation he had overheard. But if he was aware that she had deliberately lied—she preferred to think that she had just withheld the truth—he gave no indication of it. Still, she knew she must somehow speak to him privately about keeping the circumstances of how they met a secret.

To her vast relief, Blacksword did not pursue their line of conversation. Instead, he once more picked up the pointed end of the carryall and dragged it forward. But this time he pulled it directly into the dense green thicket with a curt order to her to "Come on."

She did not argue with his arrogant command, for she knew it would be pointless. But she wanted to. Cleve also kept his peace, but she knew by his tightly compressed lips that he too chafed under the imperious attitude of their murderous escort. Just suffer his arrogant superiority, she told herself in resignation. It's only for a short while. Once he got them to Stanwood she would ask her father to pay him and then send him far, far away. But that day could not come soon enough to suit her.

"Do you know where we are?" she asked in a subdued tone.

"East Anglia," he replied being deliberately vague. Then he seemed to relent. "The forest ends shortly. We'll have to cross a wide wasteland, and then fields beyond. We'll do it at night."

She could not argue with that sound bit of reasoning. Besides, Rosalynde doubted her sore feet could go any farther without a rest. With a weary sigh she sat down and then pulled out the supply of herbs she had taken from the ruined castle as well as the broken bit of crockery.

"Is there any water nearby?" She looked at the man who was standing now, staring at her. An odd little shiver snaked down her spine but she firmly thrust it aside. "A river perhaps? Or a brook?"

With a gesture of his head he indicated an area beyond them. "There's a spring. And a pool. Shall I show you?"

Rosalynde hesitated at this unexpectedly cordial response. A part of her wondered why he now asked instead of ordered. But she needed that water, both for Cleve's medicine as well as to refresh herself, and with only the briefest hesitation she agreed. "Is it far?"

"No." He watched her closely as she crossed the clearing to him. "The boy will be safe here."

Indeed, Cleve was already dozing off, quite clearly exhausted by his awkward ride. With one last glance at him Rosalynde turned back to the intimidating Blacksword and took a deep breath. Although Cleve was no protection against him, the thought of being completely alone with this man was nonetheless unnerving. Still, she did want to bathe her face and arms. And also to soak her sore feet.

With the bit of pottery clutched tightly in her hands, she proceeded down the meager trail he indicated.

In the early-afternoon sunshine, the woodlands were still shaded and cool. The heavy canopy of trees allowed only the occasional shaft of sunlight to pierce to the pleasant gloom of the forest floor. A soft light permeated everywhere, casting a peaceful green shade over all. Through this strangely tranquil scene they moved with a minimum of sound, slipping without speaking along a narrow path that wound between low rises and giant trees, steadily angling downhill.

When they finally came upon the spring it was almost a surprise, for there was no warning trickle of water spilling forth. Instead it gurgled up from a crevice of rocks, forming a small, still pond that then overspilled its banks to give birth to a thin sparkling brook. Sedges and ferns lined the banks, and white willows bent gracefully over the slow-moving water. All in all, it was a quiet, pristine scene, and they both automatically paused when they saw it. Then with a glad cry Rosalynde moved forward.

The man stood back, just watching as she knelt at the edge of the pond and filled the broken bowl with water. Then she placed that aside and pushed her sleeves up so that she could submerge her arms up to her elbows. Her thick, tangled hair fell alongside her face when she bent forward, hiding it from his view. But it was clear she was splashing her face and neck now, and that she was taking great pleasure from it. A sigh of pure contentment escaped her, and that simple sound commanded his attention.

She was a strange little flower, this Rose who had miraculously plucked him from the hangman's clutches. He'd thought her a bold and sassy urchin, and yet she was also as timid as a mouse, starting every time he moved too quickly. He knew she had every cause to react so to him.

He was, as far as she knew, a notorious outlaw and cold-blooded killer. And he'd not done anything to lessen her fear. He'd deliberately taken a menacing tone with the two of them if only to keep them quiet and completely responsive to his commands.

He'd not truly expected her story to be true. Had it not been for his guilty stab of conscience, he would have left her at the first safe village. Only she *had* turned out to be a lady, and then he'd felt honor-bound to return her to the safety of her own castle.

But had it truly been honor that compelled him? he wondered in a moment of honest self-examination. Had it been honor or the thought of reward? Christ's blood! he thought as a frown creased his face. What difference did it make why he was doing it? The fact was, it was none of his business how she'd come to be in such dire straits, just as it was no one's business why he was helping her. All he had to do was get her to her father's house safely and collect his reward. She would gladly be quit of him and he would be as happily rid of her. Then he could see to his other quest, his need for revenge against the unknown men who had conspired to have him hanged.

At the memory of his close brush with death, Aric's thoughts focused once again on just how he would satisfy himself on his unknown enemies. During his long hours in Dunmow's gaol, he'd had sufficient time to ponder his accusers' purpose. Innocent as he was of the crimes attributed to him, he had at first been sure that the local authorities had been looking for any stranger whom they might hang, in order to appease the terrorized populace. But as he had thought more on it, he realized that it might just as easily have been the bandits themselves who had wanted him hanged—to divert the search from themselves for a while. Now, however, the fact that the mayor had allowed him to be freed in the ritual celebration made it highly unlikely that it was the authorities who had wanted him framed for the crimes. No, it seemed obvious that it was the bandits themselves who'd sought a scapegoat. Whoever it was who led the villains in their reign of terror was clearly smart enough to know when to lay low and how to turn attention away from himself and his gang of cutthroats.

Still, even that did not explain everything. The night he had been taken he'd been riding from London, half asleep on the unfamiliar road to Lavenham and an upcoming tournament. He'd never even seen the blow coming. At one moment he'd been nodding in the saddle, exhausted from the long ride, and the next he'd been struck from behind with what had felt like a tree trunk. He'd hit the ground with a bone-jarring crash, but even in those first groggy minutes he'd heard what was said.

"Grab his sword!" The shout had come as innumerable men had swarmed over him. "Get his sword and bring it to me!"

Despite his valiant struggle, he'd been overpowered. His weapons had been confiscated and he had been bound with his arms behind his back and a cloth over his head. Then he'd been rudely pushed up onto a horse and brought into Dunmow. He'd never seen his captors, never put a face to the voices who congratulated themselves on the success of their plot. And even the voices would be hard to identify, for with a harshly barked "Keep quiet, fools!" one of the men—presumably their leader—had silenced them all.

Even now the ignominy of it caused his blood to heat in anger. They had trussed him up like a goose for the roasting and handed him over to the authorities as an outlaw known only as Blacksword.

Blacksword! he thought bitterly. It was that which bothered him most, for it indicated their vile deed had been well planned. And he'd ridden right into it. Yet if it was the outlaws, why not simply kill him and bring his body in to the authorities? Why have him killed by so roundabout a way as hanging?

Try as he might, he could not identify anyone with such a grudge against him as to plot so furtive an act. As a knight-errant he had ridden for any number of lords. In turn for an agreed-upon scutage fee, he performed their knight service due to their own leige lords. In between such service he rode in tournaments, earning his way through winner's tokens. Yet nothing in that would seem to warrant such animosity. Why did someone want him dead, and in such an unwieldy manner? There was a sinister quality to the entire affair that seemed to go beyond common outlawry.

Aric's fists clenched in frustrated fury. *Why* they wanted him dead did not matter so much as who the villains were, for he was determined to find the cowardly knaves and exact a terrible vengeance on them. Whoever it was, they had made a grave mistake when they selected Sir Aric of Wycliffe as their target, he vowed with a fierce scowl.

It was as he was scowling thus, still staring at the girl, albeit unseeingly, that she looked over at him. At the sudden fear on her face he came alert, mindful of how menacing he must appear. But when he took a step nearer, she jumped up in fright and splashed ankle deep into the water. He stopped at once, unwilling to frighten her further, but as he stared at her, a sudden unwonted thought leapt into his brain.

She was poised somewhere between flight and fury. Her body was tensed, ready to spring away and run for her life. But her face showed clearly her wrath as well as her disdain for him. Standing in the stream with her sleeves pushed up and her skirt dragged down by its now-soaked hem, she appeared young and slender, and yet he could see she possessed a woman's fullness. His eyes moved over her, noting the curve of hip beneath her sturdy wool gown and the press of youthful breasts against the unfitted bodice. Then he studied her face and his idea became more insistent.

She had washed away the days of grime. Her skin glowed with the soft health of youth, pale yet with a fair blush of pink in her cheeks. Sparkling drops of water clung to her, glistening like jewels against her skin and reflecting tiny sparks of sunlight where they clung to her thick lashes. Caught as she was in a single shaft of golden sunshine, she might have been a wood nymph, childlike yet womanly, frightened yet bold, unable to be caught and yet goading him relentlessly to pursue her. Then she blinked and he focused once more on her wide eyes.

They were unusual eyes. Startling, in fact. The centers were both yellow and green, a clear shade that seemed ever to change. But they were edged with a darker color, almost indigo it was so intense, and it was this that made them so mesmerizing. How had he not noticed them before? He took a step forward as the seeds of an idea began to take root in his mind. But she took two steps back, then glanced wildly about, searching for an escape.

"I do not mean to harm you, Mistress Rose."

She looked warily at him, distrust etched clearly in her face. "You've made a life of harming people," she countered, but the belligerence in her tone was belied by the fear in her expressive eyes.

"I would not harm one who saved my life."

He saw the disbelief in her face; he saw how she stared at him, then looked away, only to turn a half-curious, half-

skeptical gaze back on him. But despite her obvious
doubt, he was more and more sure that his idea could
work. She was heaven-sent! He turned and walked non-
chalantly toward the deeper end of the pool. There he
squatted beside the silently bubbling spring and carelessly
picked up several pebbles, which he idly tossed in one at a
time. It would do no good to frighten her away, not when
she might help him find the revenge he sought. Yet seeing
how she remained tensed, ready to flee at the least provocation, he knew he would have to work hard to undo the
poor image she had formed of him.

"Tell me of the robbers who attacked your party near
Dunmow."

Her expression changed then from suspicion of him to
angry remembrance of the deed that had turned her life
upside down.

"Were they your men?" she asked accusingly.

"No."

"But only because you were all in the gaol. Otherwise
you would not have hesitated to do the selfsame thing."

"Those other two men on the gallows were not known
to me." He gave her a calm and even stare. "And it's not
my way to attack innocent women and untried youths."

She digested that for a moment. Then her eyes narrowed. "Are you saying you're not a thief and murderer?"
Her dark brows lifted a fraction. "That you are innocent of
the charges that brought you to the gallows?"

Her skepticism brought a faint smile to his lips. "Would
you believe me if I said I was?"

She lifted her chin a notch and stared back at him with
ill-disguised contempt. "No, I would not believe that."

His smile faded. Of course she would not. No one could
possibly see a knight in his present guise as a condemned
criminal. But instead of dowsing his fledgling idea, her

scorn only strengthened his conviction. The time would come when she would not dismiss him so easily. "The subject doesn't bear discussing, then," he said, shrugging indifferently.

There was a brief, uncomfortable silence as they stared assessingly at each other. He knew she was trying to gauge how much danger he posed to her, how confident she should be about his taking them all the way to Stanwood Castle. For him, however, there was no longer any doubt in his mind. He would take her all the way to Stanwood, but it was more than just the promise of a horse and weapons that tempted him.

His eyes slid over her once more, noting her heart-shaped face and the masses of mahogany hair. She was no more a village urchin than he was a common outlaw. Through an accident of fate they'd been wed in a handfast ritual. But although they had both seen it only as a temporary solution to their own desperate situations, he now saw many more advantages. If her story of a dead brother was true, then she was her father's only heir. And now she was married to him.

His gaze moved down to take in her feminine shape and he felt an eager warmth suffuse him. They were wed, and whether she meant it to last or not, he now recognized the clear advantages of staying married to her. A year and a day be damned. She stood to inherit a castle and demesne, and he, though an unlanded bastard, was no less a knight of the realm and a suitable husband. It only remained for him to convince her—or more properly, to convince her father.

He stood up then, well pleased with his unexpected turn of luck. He'd never considered marriage before, but it now seemed a most welcome prospect. A comely little wench to warm his bed, and a sturdy castle to provide shelter and comfort. No more earning his way through tourneys and scutage fees. With property would come power, and with such power his revenge would be far easier to seek. He spared only a moment to thank the generous God who had answered his prayers with this curious angel.

"Go on back to the boy," he said, giving her a mocking grin. "I'll see what manner of game I can find." Then he turned and moved off into the woods.

Rosalynde watched him stride off with a mixture of alarm and bewilderment. What if he didn't come back? As much as she disliked the blackguard, she knew she needed him. If he abandoned them she didn't know what she would do.

Yet somehow she knew he would come back. In the long awkward moments when their eyes had met, something had changed. She didn't know what it was—perhaps he thought he might be able to get even a greater reward from her father, or else he might think he could ransom her to him—but whatever it was, she knew he bore watching.

She kept her eyes on his broad back until he disappeared into the greensward. Then she waded back to the bank of the small brook. He was not a man to trust, she decided once more. But he would be back—if only for the reward he sought. Her stomach growled and she rubbed the hollow spot with one hand. She hoped he would be successful in his hunt, for without a decent meal she was not certain she could keep up with the pace he set for them. But well fed, they would travel faster. And once they reached Stanwood, she reminded herself, she would be well rid of the man.

8

   Cleve was still asleep when dusk fell. By then
Rosalynde had foraged for mustard and arrowhead, sweet
rush and wild onions. When Blacksword returned with
two rabbits already gutted, she quickly built a fire while
he skinned the creatures and then constructed a simple
spit. She stewed the greens in a small amount of water,
but as their dinner cooked, there was little conversation.
Unfortunately, there was also little else to look at but one
another.

   He had clearly bathed before returning, for his clothes
were damp and his light hair was groomed back from his
face to fall neatly at his shoulders. She too had taken the
opportunity to wash her hair and the rest of her body in
the icy stream, although she had done so most hurriedly.
At each noise she had jumped, each creak of branch or
rustle of leaves. She'd been terrified that he might somehow return to spy upon her, and yet that fear had been
insufficient to prevent her from taking a bath. Stripped to
only her kirtle, she had submerged herself in the deepest
portion of the chilly pool, then quickly scrubbed her skin
with a clump of latherwort. Once satisfied and refreshed,
she'd wrung the linen kirtle out as best she could. Then
shivering in the wet and clinging garment, she had quickly
washed her tattered gown as well. While it had dried

draped over a glossy holly bush, she'd gathered whatever edible leaves and roots she could find. Now, although the gown was still damp in places, she nevertheless felt infinitely better.

Rosalynde ran her fingers through the length of her almost-dry hair, freeing a tangle and smoothing down the unruly mass. Once more her eyes veered to the man who sat so silently across the fire from her. In the shadows of the forest it was dark, although the dying sun still lit the western sky. But despite the dimness he was clearly revealed by the fire's golden glow, and Rosalynde could not pretend to be unaffected by his overwhelming masculinity.

There was about him a savageness, something akin to a huge beast of prey. His face was harshly etched in the flickering light of the fire: high cheekbones, strong jaw, and eyes that watched her with unnerving perceptiveness. Only his lips revealed any hint of softness, for they were finely formed, almost precise in their curving fullness. Unbidden the memory of the kiss he'd given her on the gallows pricked her, and she felt a faint heat creep up her cheeks. It had only been to please the crowd, she reminded herself. He had done it to keep the spectators entertained and thereby help the two of them to flee. Yet she also remembered his mocking jibe: "Next time open your mouth," he'd said. But when he'd tried to abandon her, he'd once more made it clear that her feminine charms were of no interest to him. All he wanted was a horse, weapons, and coins. An urchin, such as he considered her to be, interested him not whatsoever.

Logically she did not care. In fact, she was glad he was not the least bit attracted to her, for that would make things difficult indeed. But she nonetheless could not squelch the simmering anger she felt every time he was

near. He was too arrogant by half, she fumed as she poked
needlessly at the cooking vegetables with a pointed stick.
And he had neither honor nor morals to commend him
despite his physical prowess and unmistakable virility.

He leaned forward then too and turned the two hares
on the makeshift spit. But his eyes stayed on her and her
heart's pace unaccountably sped up.

"The meat is near done."

Rosalynde swallowed convulsively at his deep, rumbling
voice. "The vegetables as well," she murmured. She
frowned and ducked her head, letting her hair fall protectively before her to cut off his unsettling stare.

"We'll leave as soon as night is well fallen."

"I should awaken Cleve then."

"Let him sleep," he said before she could move to the
boy. "He appears to be resting well and besides, there are
some things we can discuss as we sup."

"Things?" Rosalynde's gaze returned abruptly to him.
There was something in his voice that alarmed her al
though she could not say why. "What kind of things?"

But he only gave her a shrug and an offhanded smile. "I
thought you might tell me of Stanwood."

"Stanwood?" she repeated, sure now that he planned
something.

"Yes, Stanwood. That is your home, is it not?"

"Yes. Yes," she replied as she bit at her lower lip. "But I
haven't been there in eight years."

He turned the spit again, then continued in a conversa-
tional tone. "Why were you away so long?"

Rosalynde paused before answering, trying to determine what he might be up to. But she could discern no
real harm in answering him with the truth. "My mother
died giving birth to my brother. We were sent to live with
my aunt and uncle at Millwort Castle. But now that Giles

is dead. . . ." She trailed off at that unhappy memory, and for a while the silence was broken only by the rush of the wind in the high canopy of the trees and the contented crackling of the fire.

"What will you do once you arrive there?"

Rosalynde raised her somber eyes back to him. "I'm not sure—oh, I see what you mean." She gave him a condescending glance. "I'll tell my father that you brought us home safely. That we would never have managed alone. If you're worried about the reward—"

"No," he interrupted her. "I meant, what will you do once you're back at Stanwood?"

"Oh." Rosalynde's brow creased a little at this unexpected question. Why should he care about such a thing? "I suppose I will take over the household duties, that is, until my father selects a husband for me—"

As soon as the words were out, she wished devoutly that she had not said them. They had not spoken outright about the unfortunate fact of their handfasting. However, now that the subject was raised, albeit in a roundabout manner, she was not so certain she really wished to discuss it.

There was an awkward silence. He removed the skewer and the two hares from the spit and placed them to cool on another pair of forked branches he'd stuck in the ground. Then he relaxed back and turned his clear gray eyes on her.

"You may not wed for a year and a day," he commented rather casually.

Rosalynde took heart at his forthright manner. "Yes, I know."

"Your father will no doubt understand," he remarked again in that same offhand manner. But this time Rosalynde started in alarm.

"I . . . It was . . ." She took a quick breath and then shut her mouth. Her father did not ever need to know about the handfasting. It was her fondest hope to keep it her secret. Sir Edward was a difficult man to predict. She feared enough telling him about Giles. To admit to such a pagan marriage would be too much for him to take. No, she'd decided before not to tell him, and she felt more strongly than ever that he should not know.

"You will get your reward," she said in her chilliest tone. "But only if my father does not hear of that accursed ceremony." Then she waited with bated breath for his response.

"But will I get the reward I *desire*?" he said. This time there was no mistaking the amusement in his voice.

A cold lump settled in Rosalynde's stomach. Here it was, she thought. Now that he'd had time to think out how best he could profit from her misfortune, he was about to bargain with her for her very life. And Cleve's as well. Her fear and resentment quickly mounted to fury. "You agreed to a horse and weapons. And perhaps some gold. I can promise you no more. My father is the one who will pay the reward. You'll have to bargain with him."

She stared at him belligerently, hoping her show of bravado would make him think twice about this greedy little plot of his. Her eyes narrowed as she watched him, and she tried to read his reaction in his face. But his expression had not changed, and for a moment she panicked. Surely he would not be so bold as to try to ransom her! He had no weapons, no means of escape, and no one to help him act out such a devious plan. He would be a fool even to attempt such a reckless move. But staring at him, seeing his confident face and unworried posture, Rosalynde wondered whether he might still try such a thing.

"As I recall, *you* suggested a horse and weapons and the

gold coins," he answered easily. "What I said was that I would accept a reward. But I reserve for myself the right to name it."

Rosalynde shifted anxiously on the log she was sitting upon. She could not deny his words, for she knew it was she who had suggested the form of reward. But if not a horse, weapons, and money, what did the ungrateful wretch want?

"I saved your life," she reminded him scathingly.

"Only because you believed I could save yours. I'd say we're even on that score."

"You haven't gotten us to Stanwood yet," she retorted with much heat.

"But I will," he answered smoothly. "And I'll want my reward when I do."

Rosalynde was too angry to think straight. She was infuriated by his overwhelming greed and his complete lack of normal human gratitude. Yet a tiny part of her was disappointed too. She'd thought that he was different from those other men when she'd seen him on the gallows. He'd had a certain dignity despite his filthy appearance, torn clothes, and desperate predicament. Yet now she knew he was as bad—no, probably worse—than them all. For he was cunning and manipulative in addition to being cruel and without any conscience whatsoever. How could she have been so wrong?

But Rosalynde knew the answer to that. She'd been desperate and she'd taken the only opportunity open to her. And now, just as then, she must make the best of her dreadful circumstances. She lifted her chin a notch and stared at him with ill-disguised contempt. "Go ahead then, name the unholy price you set as your reward."

He smiled then, with an expression completely at odds with the selfishness that she knew drove him. His eyes glowed warmly and his lips relaxed in what seemed the most natural and genuine smile. For a moment she almost let down her guard and a tiny little flutter stirred somewhere in her chest. But she resolutely quashed such foolish responses to him. This was only another example of how deceptive he could be. Especially now, when he was freshly cleaned and looking so handsome in the fire's gentle light, she must be ready for the worst.

"Well?" she prodded when he only stared at her with that same friendly if somewhat bemused expression on his face. "What is it you want?"

He tossed the twig he was holding into the fire, then took a slow breath. "Before this year is out, you and I shall be properly wed in the Church."

If he had demanded the moon from her, or the stars that littered the night skies like random jewels, Rosalynde could not have been more astounded. Marry her in the Church? She shook her head slightly, certain she had misheard him. Yet his face, so watchful and waiting, told her otherwise. She had heard him correctly, yet she could still not believe it. Then she realized her mouth was gaping open, and she hastily closed it.

"That . . . that's preposterous," she finally managed to say. "It's absurd. Why . . . why . . . it's impossible." Then she stood up nervously and moved nearer to where Cleve lay sleeping.

"We're already married," he continued in a reasonable tone, as if she had not responded to him at all.

"That heathen ritual hardly compares to a proper wedding with the blessings of a priest," she muttered fiercely.

"That's why I would be wed in the Church." Then he too stood up and began to approach her. "Perhaps if I told you a little of myself—"

"No!" Rosalynde gasped. She circled away from him,

trying desperately to keep the fire between them. As it became clear that he was not joking, that he was quite serious about this ludicrous demand for them to be properly wed, her heart began to race. Then when he tried to come closer, her shock turned to panic. "I already know enough about you! You're a common thief and . . . and a murderer!"

With the fire between them, he looked for all the world like a demon sent to torture her with a living hell on earth. He was so huge and powerful, his menace momentarily leashed but nonetheless indisputably there. And there was little she could do to protect herself from him. Then he smiled again, only this time it was less warm and more taunting.

"Tell me, Lady Rosalynde," he said, emphasizing her title. "Is it the fact that you believe I'm a criminal or that I'm common which upsets you more?" When she only glared at him suspiciously he continued. "If I was a criminal of noble title would you agree to my request? Or perhaps if I were a common man but honest, you would say yes."

Outraged by his mocking, Rosalynde lashed out at him. "Since you are neither honest nor noble, that hardly bears comment. You'd best content yourself with a horse and a sword, for that's the most reward you shall get!"

At that tension-filled moment Cleve let out a groan. Then he turned over a little and, with a sudden jerk, abruptly sat up. "Milady?"

The campsite was silent. In the flickering light of the dying fire, the three of them were each rimmed with gold and shadowed with black. The meal sat ready but untouched. The fire shifted as a log broke and there was a quick hiss and a small shower of sparks. Night birds had started to call and the evening breeze was cool and refreshing. But the animosity that crackled in the air completely belied the apparent peacefulness of the setting.

"Lady Rosalynde?" Cleve spoke once more as his eyes moved from her to the man who towered so threateningly across the fire from them. Then the boy's face lowered in a frown and he too struggled to his feet. "What is he up to?" he asked suspiciously.

Rosalynde was at his side at once, with an arm around him to provide the swaying page with support. "It's nothing, Cleve. Nothing. And you should not get up so abruptly," she added in as normal a tone as she could muster. But she shot a fierce glance at the still-staring Blacksword, half demanding, half pleading that he keep his peace before the boy.

When the wretch pursed his lips thoughtfully, however, then deliberately crossed the clearing to help her with Cleve, she was sure he meant to drag the ailing boy into their argument. But to her surprise he only lowered the protesting lad back to the ground with a curt "Stay there." Then he turned his steel-gray eyes on Rosalynde.

"Your mistress and I disagree on the best manner in which to proceed. However, since she asked me to guide her to safety, I reserve the right to make any and all decisions about exactly how that shall be accomplished." His glance fell briefly to Cleve. "I suggest we all eat now so that we can cover a goodly distance under cover of darkness."

To Rosalynde's great relief Cleve seemed mollified by the man's smooth words. She, however, read the double meaning in them and was hard-pressed to stifle the angry retort that rose on her lips. "The best manner to proceed," indeed, she fumed silently. But there was nothing she could do, not without revealing her shameful liaison with this man to Cleve. And that she would not do. It would be bad enough if Cleve knew of the handfast vow she'd taken. Even if she could restrain him from trying to defend her honor, she would then always have to worry that his hasty temper might give her away to someone else. More than anything she wished to keep this entire episode from anyone else's knowledge, particularly her father's. The best way to do that seemed to be through absolute secrecy. Yet if this dreadful man insisted that she honor her vow . . .

It was simply too horrible to even imagine, and she fought down the wave of panic that threatened to overwhelm her. Moving woodenly, performing the automatic task of serving the meat, she went over her options in her mind. Then when she found nothing there to cling to, she tried to recall anything he'd said or done that she might somehow turn against him or use to accuse him. She had no problem doing that, and she satisfied her thwarted fury by recounting to herself every time he'd slighted her or treated her poorly. For someone she'd known so briefly, there were an appallingly large number of such occurrences. By the time he put out the fire and erased all signs of their temporary campsite, she could barely contain her outrage nor her eagerness to accuse him. Unfortunately, Cleve remained awake as they resumed their journey. Although he reluctantly rode once more on the makeshift sling that Blacksword pulled, his eyes were open, watching Rosalynde as she trailed behind. But although Rosalynde kept her silence as they left the dark forest and struck out along a cart track that crossed the open wastelands, she knew the subject of her vow to the insufferable Blacksword had not been exhausted. He would bring it up again, and when he did, she would be ready. He would not catch her off-guard as he had this time with his outrageous demand.

They seemed to walk for hours. The moon showed its

silver crescent face in the east, then slowly wended its way across the vast sky while they moved relentlessly forward. Had it not been for that moon, Rosalynde would have been completely unsure of their course. As it was, she knew only that they must head generally east, toward the moon and toward the eventual dawn. The silent man who pulled Cleve so effortlessly might have been leading them anywhere, she knew. But the moon's constant presence reassured her that they proceeded generally as they should. Twice they passed stone-fenced fields and the dark shapes of slumbering villages. Once they saw a shepherd sleeping with his flock, probably due to the lambing season. But they carefully skirted anyplace with people. They were too vulnerable to attack to trust anyone.

Hours passed before the first streaks of dawn's light showed in the east. By the time they reached a willow-lined brook her feet were aching, her legs were numb with fatigue, and one of her toes throbbed painfully. It was difficult to avoid every stone in the dark, and more than once she had stubbed her toes. But she had been determined not to cry out or complain in any way. Even if she had, she thought spitefully, that crude brute would not have cared. He'd not looked around even once to ascertain that she was keeping up with him. Why, she could have collapsed in utter exhaustion and he would never have known. Then where would his demands have gotten him? she wondered sourly. Some husband he would make.

When he lowered the end of the carryall at the edge of the brook, she stalked past him in a huff and moved down to a grassy slope of bank. Then she lifted her skirts and waded straight out into the icy water.

"Ahh." A low moan of relief escaped her as the cold water soothed her burning feet. She flexed her toes against the slippery pebbles, then dug them into the loose bottom of the brook, reveling in the delicious relief it gave. She waded out a little farther, letting the refreshing water lap up almost to her knees, then bent over to scoop up a handful to drink.

"How are your feet?"

Rosalynde started at the quietly spoken words and jerked upright to find Blacksword standing directly behind her.

"They . . . they're fine." She stumbled back a step, clutching her skirt more tightly in her hand.

"I kept the two rabbit skins. If you like I can make some slippers for your feet."

He moved forward as he spoke and Rosalynde stepped back again. She was so unnerved by his nearness and so astounded by his surprising thoughtfulness that she was unmindful of the chilly stream, which caught now at her kirtle and heavier gown. But the current was stronger than she thought and the streambed more slippery. For an instant she tottered backward, unable to right herself in time to prevent a fall. But the imposing man before her quickly caught her arms, then unexpectedly pulled her nearer onto firmer footing.

"Be careful," he cautioned her with a hint of a smile on his harshly masculine face. For a long moment their eyes met. Rosalynde was obliquely aware that his hands slid a little way up her arms, then tightened ever so slightly. Like the pounding of a thousand drums, her heart's rhythm increased, and she was caught between terror and a sudden irrational thrill. Something sparked between them, sharp and strong and unmistakable. She'd felt it on the gallows when she had grabbed his tunic in anger, and she felt it now even more vividly.

It was fear, she told herself, as his gaze held her mesmerized before him. The snake entranced the mouse just so, as the owl also froze the helpless hare. He was a predator and she was his unfortunate prey. Yet a part of her knew he meant her no harm, at least not in the way she would have expected. Warmth seeped up from somewhere in her belly, spreading an unaccustomed heat throughout her body, and still she stood ensnared by his powerful yet gentle grasp on her. Then he moved a half pace nearer and logic miraculously leapt to her rescue. With a violent jerk she wrenched herself away from him.

"Unhand me. I am quite able to take care of myself."

"Oh?" One of his brows raised skeptically. "That must be why you took a husband from Dunmow's gallows, because you are so able to take care of yourself."

Rosalynde wished she could call back her angry words. She should not stoop to argue with such a man as he was. Drawing herself up as best she could, she gave him her coolest stare. "I *did* find a way out of my predicament, didn't I? And a way for you out of yours."

Then, slipping and stumbling, she stalked upstream, until the broad security of a cedar tree stood clearly between them.

She did not see the faint smile that played across his face, nor quite hear his softly murmured words. "From the fat into the fire you have leapt, my sweet little wife. And it appears I have assumed one life sentence for another."

She peered nervously at him, wondering at his odd mood as she tried in vain to slow her breathing and ease the pounding in her chest. What deviousness did he plot now? Did he think to woo her over to his ridiculous plan with his offer of rabbit-skin shoes? Did he think she was fool enough to be influenced by his potent stare or his masculine embrace?

Had he meant to kiss her?

She stared back at his shadowy form still standing

alongside the stream and nervously licked her lips. She frowned when they tingled with unexpected sensitivity, and unwillingly she recalled once more the kiss he'd given her on the gallows. That kiss had pleased the spectators enormously. They'd cheered and clapped and raucously called for more. She, however, had been shocked and horrified.

But that wasn't precisely true, and as Rosalynde watched Blacksword stoop down to cup water in his hands for a drink, she could not hide the truth from herself. She had been horrified by the terrible predicament she was in, and shocked by the boldness of the kiss. But something in her had responded to the unique feel of his hard mouth pressing down on hers.

"Sweet Mother of Jesus," she whispered in prayer, then made a quick sign of the cross as that same unsettling warmth twisted in her stomach once more. What in the name of heaven was wrong with her? she worried as she bent down to splash her overheated face with water. Yet she could not help but wonder what that kiss would have been like if she had opened her mouth, as it appeared was the proper method for kissing. She slid her tongue experimentally along her lips, marveling at the strange sensuality of it. Then in quick mortification she ceased such foolishness and frowned at her own perversity. Such feelings should be reserved for her husband—her true husband, she amended hastily as she glanced back at the intolerable cad who irked her so incessantly. But he was gone and, to her complete chagrin, she felt a faint wave of disappointment. Despite her every reason for caution where he was concerned—he was black-hearted in every sense of the word—she was nonetheless consumed with a new curiosity. She justified it as only the normal reactions of a young woman of marriageable age. Yet as Rosalynde slowly picked her way through the dawn's dim shadows, she could not deny that a new emotion had joined her other feelings of fear and dislike and mistrust. Before he'd only been someone whose presence she must endure in order to find the safety of her home.

Now he was a mystery, enigmatic and intriguing. A challenge she found hard to ignore. Anything further she refused to consider.

9

They ate the remnants of the cooked rabbit and a salad of dandelion greens, yarrow, and plantain leaves that Rosalynde was able to find. For the first time Cleve displayed a good appetite, and she was much heartened by his improvement. But with his returning health there came an almost tangible increase in his hostility toward their mysterious protector.

"We've no need for him any longer," Cleve hissed when Blacksword volunteered to fetch water from the brook. "And I can full well go down to the water myself!"

"I know you think you're well, but head wounds are very serious," she whispered back. "Besides, I'll not renege on my promise to the man," she added. It occurred to her that she was breaking one promise to him already, one vow. Yet she was not exactly breaking it, she told herself. She would stay his wife for a year and a day, albeit secretly. But she had not entered into the vow with any intentions of keeping it. Despite all her rationalization and reasoning, that one fact bothered her sorely. Marriage was a holy sacrament. Even though their vow had not been made before a priest or within the hallowed confines of the Church, it had nonetheless been made before God. Until he had brought up the possibility of a proper marriage in the Church, she had eased her conscience about the moral repercussions of her handfast marriage. After all, if he didn't want to remain wed she could hardly force him to. But now he wanted to honor the vow and *she* was the one who balked.

Cleve was oblivious to her inner turmoil, and when the object of his ire suddenly reappeared with the water he glowered at him openly.

"How far is it to Stanwood?" he demanded angrily.

The taller man squatted down on his heels next to Rosalynde and handed her the water. Then he turned an expressionless face toward Cleve. "Two more nights' travel."

Cleve grumbled something under his breath, then looked at Rosalynde stubbornly. "I can walk from now on."

She started to object but it was Blacksword who answered the boy. "Then it will take at least three nights."

It was just the provocation Cleve needed to release his pent-up hostility. He lurched to his feet and faced the larger man fiercely. "I'll walk and it may take three days, but we'll be well rid of you!"

"Cleve!" Rosalynde leapt between the two, for she fully expected Blacksword to react violently to the youth's reckless taunt. To her surprise, however, it was Cleve she had to restrain. He was tensed and poised to attack, while the other man only eased himself back to a sitting position and then pulled something from his open tunic.

"Come here so I may measure your feet." He gave her a steady look, pointedly disregarding the lad's angry outburst.

Rosalynde was so relieved that he was not going to hurt Cleve that she did not hesitate. With only a meaningful glare at Cleve, she crossed quickly to Blacksword's side and sat down meekly beside him. When it was obvious the man was not going to rise to his bait and that Rosalynde would not back him up, Cleve's anger began to dissipate into bewilderment.

" 'Tis *my* duty to protect you," he said plaintively. "Not his."

"If you wish to do your duty, Cleve, then please, *please* just abide by what I say," she replied most earnestly.

For a long tense moment he stood there in the slowly building light. She could see the struggle in his face, his need to protect his mistress from a man he perceived to be dangerous, when it was clear he could not possibly win. Cleve was nothing if not loyal, and his stubbornness about protecting her from harm warmed her heart.

Yet Rosalynde knew that it was not overt physical harm she faced from the man who now sat so placidly beside her. He would not gain anything by hurting her. The harm this man could do was of a different nature entirely, especially if he chose to pursue his claim to her hand through that pagan handfasting ritual. As her father's only remaining heir, she was the conduit through which Stanwood Castle would pass to her husband. But only to her rightful husband—not an immoral ruffian such as this Blacksword. Now that he realized all he might gain, she would no doubt have the devil of a time convincing him that such a union between them was impossible. Still, if she soothed him with enough gold he would eventually come around.

Much reassured, she gave Cleve a smile, all the while profoundly aware of Blacksword's overwhelming nearness. "Please rest, Cleve. We have so far to go."

When the boy finally sat down it was with great reluctance, but she nonetheless felt tremendously relieved. Unfortunately, she was immediately faced with a new and far more unsettling dilemma. To her enormous confusion, Blacksword bent forward, then grasped her ankles and unceremoniously pivoted her around so that her lower legs rested on his lap, and one of his hands cupped her left foot.

"What are you doing?" she exclaimed, too flustered by his possessive touch to be angry.

"You need shoes," he replied matter-of-factly. Then he pressed the fur of one of the skins against her much-abused sole and her objections disappeared at once. Shoes. Something soft against her feet.

At that tacit approval, Blacksword wrapped the ends of the rabbit skin over the top of her foot and held them with one hand wrapped around her ankle, so that her entire foot was encased in the smooth fur. It was a most impersonal action, or at least it should have been. Certainly if it had been the tanner at Millwort Castle who'd measured her foot so she would not have given it a second thought. But this man was not the grizzled old tanner, and they were not at Millwort. Every instinct for self-preservation told her to snatch her foot from his grasp and get as far away from him as possible. It was far better to suffer the sharp stones and branches of the cart track than to endure his unnerving touch.

But Cleve was scowling at them from across the small clearing, and more than anything she did not want to give him further cause for animosity. So she suffered Blacksword's sure touch as best she could, sitting stiff with tension as he moved the skin back and forth until he found the best position for it.

"How does that feel?" He looked up at her then and their gazes collided with breathless impact. All thoughts of Cleve and Millwort and the graybeard tanner fled as she stared into his granite gray eyes. She vaguely heard him say something about cutting away the excess and she was aware that he pulled out Cleve's dagger and was cutting

several slits into the skin. When he put that skin aside and
then picked up the other she continued to stare at him,
suddenly confused by her conflicting feelings. She
watched as he took her other foot then fit the rabbit skin to
it. His hand was so warm. His fingers were strong and
callused, and yet also gentle. He cut the fur with quick,
deft strokes, then he met her gaze once more.

"I scraped the skins well, and I'll coat them with a paste
of water and ash while we camp. But they will not be as
supple as properly prepared leather."

Rosalynde nodded her head although little of what he
said registered. She was too caught up in her own mud-
dled thoughts to care about a pair of shoes. Just as she'd
been struck by his noble bearing even when he was bound
and forced to mount the gallows, so was she now aware of
an odd dignity, a rare quality under normal circumstances,
but in a convicted murderer . . .

". . . bindings from your hem," he was saying when
she finally came alert.

"Bindings?" She stared at him in momentary confusion
before she understood what he was saying. "Oh, you want
a strip of the fabric."

"It would help," he answered with a warm yet still
searching glance.

She took the knife he offered then quickly removed an
adequate strip from her ruined gown. But as she automatically started to hand the short dagger back to him, Cleve
interrupted.

"That's my knife."

Once more Rosalynde found herself caught between the
two of them, but this time she was not so alarmed. Despite
all logic she felt certain Blacksword meant to protect
them, especially since he wished to wed her once they
reached Stanwood. Even though that demand of his was

completely outrageous, it still made sense that he retain possession of the sole weapon at their disposal. Cleve might not be able to understand that, but she did. She still had no idea whatsoever about how she was going to deal with the man's ridiculous demand for his "reward," but she did know that Cleve could not be allowed to disrupt things, no matter how aggravated he might be. With a warning look at the page she handed the knife back to Blacksword.

There was a muffled expletive from the boy, and he shot her a most aggrieved stare. Then he drew his cloak tight around him and stormed off into the bushes. Rosalynde heard the snapping of twigs and the rustle of leaves. Then he obviously found himself a resting spot, and after a few moments it was quiet once more.

Yet if Cleve's departure quelled one sort of tension, finding herself alone with her strange protector created another tension entirely. To make matters worse, her right foot still lay in his lap; her calf rested quite intimately upon his muscular thigh. In sudden mortification she started to pull away. However, he was too fast. Before she could get away, he caught her ankle in his grasp.

"We're not through yet," he said quietly as his eyes locked with hers.

At that all her aplomb fled. "I-I don't need the shoes. Truly," she added as a hint of amusement lifted a corner of his mouth.

But his hand only slid a little up her calf and his other hand cupped the sole of her foot. "You've bruises here." He caressed the heel of her foot. "And scrapes and cuts." He stroked along the side of her little toe.

A shiver coursed up her spine, followed by a ripple of warmth. To her chagrin he seemed quite aware of her reaction to him, and he gave her a disarming grin.

"Why don't we agree to work together on this one task? It won't take long. Then once your shoes are finished, you can go back to disliking me if you want."

It was said as if she were a petulant child and he the tolerant adult. As a result, she found it most difficult to take umbrage with his statement, for she would only look more the fool. Although her jaw was clenched in clear annoyance, she managed a curt nod. He rewarded her with a touch of his knuckle to her chin. Then he set to work.

As he fitted the rabbit skin to her foot, she tried to appear as dignified as she could. But with his warm hands on her foot and his unexpected touch to her chin, she found her nerves completely unsettled. As dawn spread its sparkling light over the little clearing, she could hardly control her skittering emotions.

Whatever had possessed her to side with him against Cleve? she wondered hopelessly. Even if it was a logical choice in this case, this Blacksword still was not someone to trust. And now she had put herself practically in his lap! To make matters worse, her emotions were running completely awry. Every time he touched her, no matter how impersonal it might seem, something turned over deep inside her. She must get hold of herself!

"I can do that one," she blurted out when he reached for the other fur. "I saw where you put the holes and how you strung the cord through." She bit her lower lip as he stared deeply into her eyes. "Thanks . . . thank you for doing this one."

"You're welcome," he said simply. Then he handed her the skin and the knife, and leaned back on his elbows to watch her.

Rosalynde was so relieved that he'd not argued that she set to the task with pleasure. She made a series of holes along the two long top edges, then three more along each of the short sides that would circle her ankle. She worked swiftly and with sure hands, for she was no stranger to the sewing room. As she was beginning to feed the narrow strip of cord through the holes, however, she suddenly sat up very straight.

To her complete shock and total bewilderment, Blacksword was running one hand slowly down the length of her hair, from the bend of her neck, down her back to where her hair pooled on the ground behind her. Then he gathered a handful and gently twirled it around his wrist and hand.

"You have beautiful hair," he murmured as she turned in astonishment to face him. His gaze moved up to her stunned expression. "And captivating eyes." He moved his hand up to her face and lightly caressed her chin once more. "If I didn't already know that you were flesh and blood—warm," he added softly, "I'd think you were some wood nymph sent to bewitch me."

"Don't," she warned, albeit breathlessly. "You have no right." She grabbed his wrist to push it away, but he would not budge.

"I have every right," he countered, staring deeply into her eyes. "Every right."

Rosalynde was so undone by his startling words and the compelling force of his gentle touch that any retort died unsaid. When he sat up, the hand at her chin came around to circle her neck. Her heart raced ferociously and every fiber of her being seemed intensely alert.

"You are mine. My wife," she heard him murmur. Then his lips met hers and she became oblivious to everything else.

His kiss was neither harsh nor demanding. Indeed, his lips were astoundingly soft as they moved over hers. Yet she did not mistake the possessiveness with which they claimed hers. Perhaps it was the way they teased her own lips apart with soft nibbles and subtle pressure. Perhaps it was only the heated stroke of his tongue on her lips. She was far too dizzy to be sure. She only knew that she went from numb to light-headed to wildly intoxicated in the space of a few seconds. Bending to the seductive pressure of his hand, she was drawn down onto his chest, and then somehow rolled over until he lay above her, kissing her more and more insistently. His tongue slid silkily along the seam of her lips and, without being aware of it, she opened to him.

At once he deepened the kiss, using both lips and tongue in the most erotic manner imaginable. Heat flared in her belly and raced like wildfire through her. He moved and she was suddenly conscious of his weight against her breasts and stomach and legs. One of his knees slipped between her thighs, and the fire flamed even higher as every part of her responded to him. Then his tongue found hers and her reaction was acute. Like a stroke of lightning, it stunned her and she stiffened at the intimate caress.

But even as her body was flooded with the most sultry of sensations, the very power of it helped her shake off the lethargy that had overwhelmed her.

"No," she pleaded as she twisted her face away from his searching mouth. "No!" she repeated as she finally began to push him away.

"You are my wife," he murmured low against her ear. "Don't deny me. Don't deny yourself this pleasure."

In her ear his voice was warm and seductive, and she felt a forbidden thrill run through her. But he spoke of a wife, and that was a point she would not relent on.

"Let me up!" she insisted as panic overcame this unfamiliar passion. "Get off!"

This time her words got his attention, but he did not move from his dominant position over her. Instead he only lifted his head and stared down into her huge, darkened eyes.

"You opened your mouth this time," he said with a slight mocking grin. "I told you you would like it better."

"I didn't!" she muttered, shoving ineffectively at his wide chest.

"What a little liar you are," he said with a low chuckle. He caught her mouth once more in a lusty, demanding kiss, clearly proving his point. Then, while she lay there, dazed anew by how easily he commanded her emotions, he rolled off her to lay on his back in the grass.

For a moment Rosalynde could not move. She had no power over her ragged breathing nor her limp muscles. But when he reached one hand out to slide a stray tendril from her neck, she reacted as if she had been burned. Up she leapt, scurrying away from him as if her life depended on it. Only when she saw that he still lay where he was did she slow her flight at all.

"You . . . you . . ." she sputtered. But she was too flustered to think straight, and too undone to compose her thoughts. "You are a wicked man!" she finally hissed as unseemly tears started in her eyes. He was wicked and without morals or even a shred of human decency. Yet in spite of that, it was not the reassuring heat of anger that filled her. Instead, she was bewildered by a myriad of confusing emotions and strange, lingering sensations.

"Why did you do that?" The words came unbidden to her lips even as she dashed her tears away with the back of one hand.

He rolled to his side and propped himself up on one elbow. "It's only normal for a man to kiss his wife," he answered, but his eyes grew watchful and his expression turned serious.

"I'm not your wife," Rosalynde insisted, thoroughly unsettled by his too-perceptive stare.

"You made the vow willingly," he countered. "You sought me out."

"You know why I did that!" she cried. Then she glanced fearfully to where Cleve had gone to sleep, and lowered her voice. "You benefited as much as I."

"And now I will benefit even more." So saying, he sat up, propping his forearms on his bent knees. "You may deny me now, but eventually you'll admit to the truth."

"If you tell my father I'll say you lie," she warned, although the very thought of her father knowing any of this terrified her. "He'll never believe you."

One of his brows arched in arrogant amusement. "It's an easy enough fact to verify. Dunmow is little more than a good day's ride from Stanwood."

Rosalynde could not stay to hear any more. His words were too true, too horribly true. With a cry of anguish she turned and stumbled blindly into the copsewood. Branches caught at her gown and tugged at her wildly streaming hair, but she didn't care. She had to get away from him. It didn't matter where as long as it was far, far away.

When Rosalynde finally stopped her headlong flight, she was gasping for breath and holding her throbbing side. She sagged against an ancient oak tree, then slowly, hopelessly slid down along its trunk to sit in a desolate heap amidst its spreading roots.

Why had he kissed her like that? Why? she agonized as tears quickened once more in her haunted eyes. And why, *why* had she let him?

But Rosalynde knew she had done far more than just let

him kiss her. She closed her eyes with a groan and sagged back against the uncompromising bulk of the old tree. No matter how she wished to blame him for everything, she knew she had gone along with the kiss of her own free will. He might have lulled her into complacency with his deceptively mild behavior. He most certainly had manipulated her into siding with him against Cleve. And he had used that episode with the rabbit-skin shoes to get near enough to stroke her and practice his powers of seduction on her. But from the first moment his lips met hers she could have rejected him. Instead of accepting his indecent attentions, she should have reacted with revulsion and disgust.

Only that had not been what she'd felt.

A shudder of complete humiliation shook her and fresh tears streaked down her cheeks. She'd accepted his kiss, opening freely to the vivid sensations he'd raised in her. And, oh, how incredibly vivid they had been! How shamefully wicked! But no amount of self-abasement could erase the truth. She had been stupid, reckless, and sinful in the extreme, yet her entire being buzzed still with the remembered pleasure of his tongue moving sensuously along hers. She swallowed a sob and shook her head hard against the undeniable fact. He was a practiced seducer, but she had been his more-than-willing accomplice. If he was insistent before about this farce of a marriage he aspired to, how much more relentless would he now be?

Rosalynde rubbed her damp eyes with the edge of her sleeves, then tried to dry her cheeks as well. What would she do? she agonized, curling into a tight ball in a hollow between the roots. How could she face him again? Now it would truly be impossible to keep him silent about their handfast vow. She buried her head in her arms as another sob shook her exhausted body. Why had she given him this new power over her?

But she was so physically drained and so thoroughly traumatized by the long night's events that she could not properly fashion any answers to her desperate questions. As she huddled in the hard security of the oak tree, trying to block out the harsh light of another day, she was beyond all rational thought. Her mind closed against the terrible reality of her situation and sleep brought the only promise of relief.

But even in her dreams she was tormented by clear gray eyes and the seductive power of a beckoning smile.

When Aric found her he was taken aback by the scene that met his eyes. She had fled in tears, angry and frightened and horrified as well. She had kissed a murdering outlaw, a common criminal, and he was certain that her sheltered upbringing had not prepared her for such a thing. The fact that she had enjoyed it no doubt troubled her sorely.

He had enjoyed it as well, he recalled with vivid clarity as he looked down on the sleeping woman before him. He'd not wanted to let her go at the time, but he'd thought it best not to scare her off completely. So he had let her escape and just waited. There was nowhere for her to go, and perhaps a little time alone would help her to think things out a bit. It had given him time as well, and as he had lain there in the little clearing, staring up through the branches of the beech trees, he'd decided to force her to listen to the truth. Maybe if she could see him in a better light, if she knew he was of noble upbringing, the idea of marriage to him might not seem so abhorrent. He was already certain she would not long object to the duties of the marriage bed.

Now as he took in her slender figure curved within the dark embrace of the ancient oak root, he vowed to convince her, no matter what it took. Once more the image of a wood nymph came to mind. A fairy rose. There was an air of sweetness about her, of fragility. Yet he knew she was far tougher than she appeared. She had survived that attack, then fearlessly gone for help. In a moment of desperation she'd been brazen enough to claim a man who, by all appearances, was capable of the direst crimes, and she'd done so solely with the hope that he might be coerced into helping her for sufficient reward.

He shook his head in bemusement and his eyes followed the gleaming curve of her mahogany colored hair as it fell along her neck and draped over her arms. One of her hands showed beyond the heavy, dark tangle. Small and pale, the palm was slightly open; the fingers were curled loosely in repose. Her hand was small and pale, her feet were soft and pale. No doubt beneath that shapeless gown she wore she was small and pale all over. Yet he recalled the press of her breasts against his chest, and he knew her woman's curves were soft and ample. She was no young girl, but a woman, old enough—and ready enough—for marriage.

At that thought he felt a returning rush of warmth to his loins. By rights she was already wedded—to him. And he was more than ready to consummate their vow. With a muttered oath at his own burning impatience, he bent down on one knee to gather her up. He'd allowed her this temper tantrum, but he could not let her stay so far from the safety of his protection any longer.

When Rosalynde came slowly awake she had the oddest sensation of floating, of lifting from her cold, uncomfortable bed to float in warm security somewhere above the ground. Her bed at Millwort had been warm and secure.

Yet she knew somehow that she was not in her old familiar bed. Then she was shifted slightly against something hot and solid, and she reluctantly opened her eyes.

At first she thought she was still asleep. She'd dreamed of those eyes. And of that smile. But then she felt his arms tighten beneath her and she knew that this was real. He had her in his arms and was boldly walking off with her as if she were some prize he had just stolen.

"Let me down," she gasped as she came fully, abruptly awake.

"Soon," he answered, giving her a faint smile.

"No, now!" she insisted, struggling aginst the firm hold he had on her. She kicked her legs and shoved hard at his chest and shoulder. But his only response was to hold her tighter, although his face did grow more stern.

"You have no right to do this! Get your hands off me, you vile cad! You disgusting . . . disgusting—"

When he suddenly released her she let out a shriek and automatically grabbed at his neck to prevent herself from tumbling to the ground. But he caught at her too and then, with a deft shifting of his arms, turned her upright.

In the space of a second Rosalynde found herself face to face with him. Her arms were still twined around his neck, holding on tightly, and her entire body was pressed close to him. His arms circled her waist, keeping her near and holding her up just enough so that her feet did not touch the ground. It was a far worse position than before, she realized at once, and she found it far more unnerving. For a long moment their eyes met in conflict, hers darkened to green in anger and outrage, his hard as granite, determined not to give an inch. But then his eyes changed, glowing from within as if a fire smoldered there. Slowly he let her slide down his hard-muscled length as he still held her eyes captive.

"I have every right." The words came low and husky, and she knew what was to come. She knew he was going to kiss her, but in the space of that one shattering moment she lost the will to protest. Logic deserted her as did any remnants of rational thought. His face seemed to descend in slow motion. His mouth lowered to hers with torturous delay. Yet when their lips finally met and clung, everything else sped up to a dizzying speed. The world was spinning too fast; her heart pounded furiously; and her blood seemed to roar in her veins. In desperation she clung to him as the only sturdy thing in an out-of-kilter world. But that just made it worse, for the pressure of his body against hers only added fuel to the fire. In a rush all the confusing emotions she'd tried to stifle earlier came back, but with far more urgency.

His lips moved on hers with a sureness that stole her breath away. When his tongue came out to trace a possessive path along her lower lip, her mouth opened of its own volition to give him entrance. As if the torrid kiss they'd shared before was only a harbinger of things to come, he teased her with the power of his seductive mouth. Promising, demanding, and then rewarding her with new and higher thrills of pleasure, he erased every objection from her mind.

One of his hands cupped her derriere and she let out a low moan. But that only fired his ardor higher. More and more demandingly he laid his claim, stroking deep within her mouth, tantalizing her until her tongue joined with his. It was new and frightening to her, and yet there was a part of her that responded instinctively to his virile dominance. It was an ancient dance they performed. The moves came innately to her, from some wellspring of her feminine being.

When he tilted her back and moved his kiss down to

her throat, she clung to him helplessly. When his lips
moved urgently across the rough wool of her gown to
press heatedly against the valley between her breasts, she
shuddered with longing. Only when he pressed her hard
against his thickening loins did her eyes come open and
any semblance of reason return to her.

"You mustn't," she whispered, although every fiber in
her demanded that he continue.

"I must," he murmured hoarsely, stirring her anew with
his breath in her ear. "There's no other way it can be
between us."

There's no other way . . . The words echoed in her
mind as he lowered her to the grass-lined earth, pressing
new and more feverish kisses on her. There was no way to
stop him. And no way to stop herself. For a moment she
fought the all-consuming lethargy that overwhelmed her.
This was sinful. Despite the pagan ritual binding them,
they were not truly married.

Yet her body betrayed her logical mind. This exquisite
pleasure, this heaven on earth could not be wrong. It
could not be a sin. Then his hand found her breast and
even that weak debate was quashed. As his mouth de-
lighted hers with sweet desire and fiercely flaming passion, so did his hands begin to work an incredible magic
on her body. They strayed to where no one had ever
touched her, to where she hardly dared to touch herself.
But it was no accidental straying and he was not hesitant.
One of his hands cupped her breast; the thumb stroked
rhythmically back and forth against the already stiffened
nipple. With his other arm he rolled her over to lay upon
him and he boldly stroked her derriere once more, sliding
his palm back and forth across her bottom in the most
provocative manner.

A feeling unlike anything she'd ever experienced

washed over Rosalynde. It was hot and yet she shivered. It felt natural and, oh, so right, and yet there was something in her that said it was wicked and forbidden. She knew she should fight the all-encompassing lure of it, and yet she could not. She could not.

When his hand found the bare skin of her thigh, she shuddered with ever-increasing delight. Then, when he rolled her over and pressed his full weight against her, she gasped at the dizzying rapture. His hands pulled at her gown, tearing her girdle away and loosening the ties at her waist. But all the while he kissed her, deeper and deeper, striking a chord somewhere inside her, awakening feelings in her that she'd never dreamed could exist. She was lost in the physical splendor of their mutual passion. It was only when he tugged her gown free and slid her kirtle from her shoulders that he pulled a little away from her.

As she gazed up at him, her eyes dazed by the maelstrom of emotions he roused, he removed his tunic and chainse in one swift motion. His boots and hose were hastily followed by his braies, and only when her eyes swept over his magnificently naked body did the enormity of what they were doing strike her.

"No—"

Her cry was stifled before it properly escaped. As if he anticipated her sudden reversal, Blacksword covered her near-naked body with his own. His skin was firm and warm and heavy with possession. His lips were adamant, almost fierce as he plundered her mouth.

With only the feeblest of protests her words died unsaid. Her hands fluttered a moment at his hard chest, then slid up to circle his neck. Her kirtle was only a crushed bit of linen between them, pulled down to her waist, lifted up beyond her hips. Beneath his heavy form she melted against his hardness. Everything that was feminine in her responded to that which was masculine in him. Even the heated press of his rigid male flesh was met by the soft concave of her belly.

Then he nudged her legs apart and she complied.

"Be my wife," she heard him whisper hoarsely against her lips. "Be mine," he murmured as one of his hands slid down to her secret triangle of curls, then slipped even further to stroke the very center of her being.

At once she felt a quickening, like lightning striking a dry tree, sending it immediately into flames. Hot and slick, his fingers played against her with devastating results. She could hardly catch her breath, and though she squirmed away from the fiery delight, she wanted it so badly. Then his hand was replaced by another probing heat and she arched up to him in a mindless plea.

"Blacksword . . ." she entreated, tossing her head back and forth, then reaching up once more for his mind-drugging kiss. "Blacksword."

"Aric," he whispered against her lips. "My name is Aric."

"Aric." She panted as he pressed a little farther into her, beginning to fill her with fire and fury and a primitive sort of power.

"You are wife to Aric of Wycliffe." His teeth pulled at her lower lip, refusing her the deep kiss she was pleading for. "Say it," he insisted breathlessly, as he rocked his hips back and forth against her, torturing her with a deliberateness that was driving her mad. "You are wife to Aric . . ."

"I am your wife," she whispered in a voice that shook with passion. "I am . . ."

With a groan he finally let his weight come down upon her. His mouth met hers with an explosion of passion; his chest and hard-ridged belly crushed her into the soft green earth; and the full length and strength of his male flesh slid with unerring accuracy into her.

She wanted to cry out, to pull away in fear and pain at the sudden tearing she felt. As he found her virgin's barrier, then pushed beyond it, passion fled and an abrupt and horrible reality startled her.

But he would not let her go and he would not end their kiss. Though she struggled, he held her firmly beneath him. When she sobbed he seemed to absorb all her fear and pain into himself, and only deepened the kiss. Though no less fiery and demanding, his lips nonetheless moved to please her. His tongue stroked her inner lips; they forced her to respond. And when her own tongue moved out to meet his, she was rewarded by a renewed leap of the same passionate fire. He still filled her with a heat and pressure completely foreign to her, but the pain was gone. And when he shifted his hips slightly, she let out a gasp of unexpected pleasure.

It seemed the signal he waited for. As he raised his face from hers, he began a slow and rhythmic motion, pressing his hips to hers then rocking back, pushing deeper then lifting away, sliding his full length into her, then pulling almost completely out. Exquisite waves of undiluted pleasure rippled through her as he steadily increased his tempo, filling her then pulling back. Rosalynde's eyes widened with wonder as she stared up into his passion-filled eyes. She arched up in unthinking response, accepting him fully into the feminine warmth of her body, urging him on as she innocently responded to his expert caress. Their movements increased and the fire flamed higher. A rush that was wet and hot and filled with light swept over her, and in a moment of near panic she clung desperately to him. Then she was overwhelmed by a tidal wave of

passion and she cried out at the very ferocity of their lovemaking. Wave after wave shook her. Like a storm she was
battered by its very violence. She heard his cry buried
deep against her neck. It seemed to have been wrenched
from deep inside him, and it filled her with awe. Yet the
one emotion she did not feel was fear. She was not
afraid.

He shuddered over her as if he too shared in the same
cataclysm of emotions. Then his weight came fully, heavily
against her and she released a huge sigh.

Her breath was short, matched by his own ragged
breathing. With hearts pounding in unison, their bodies
melded together, still intimately joined, their breathing
almost a shared effort, Rosalynde felt absurdly as if they
were no longer separate beings but part of the same
whole. He lay above her, absorbing her into himself, it
seemed, and though she felt nearly crushed by his massive
weight, she did not care.

Then he moved a little to the side, sliding from her
sweat-slicked body. She let out a faint groan of dismay, but
he quickly stilled it with a stirring kiss as he gathered her
close to him. Legs tangled, arms still wrapped about one
another, they lay in the dappled shade. Rosalynde's exhaustion was complete: Her mind, body, and emotions
had been taxed beyond previous comprehension. She
could not think about the wondrous things that had just
happened to her. She could not be logical or dwell on
what was to come. She only relaxed in his heated embrace
and listened to the rhythmic beating of his heart beneath
her ear. Steady and reliable, the sound gave her a sense of
security she could not quite understand. In the past days
she'd had enough of death and sorrow and fear to last her
a lifetime. But this—this was the sound of life and of hope.

With a faint smile she sighed again and moved a little nearer to his comforting bulk. She was safe. She knew that without a doubt. Then she gave herself over to sleep and the watchful observance of the man who still held her.

10

This time Rosalynde awoke in one sudden jolt. Blacksword had shifted slightly and his hand had, even in his sleep, moved unerringly to her breast. It was this that brought her slumber to an end, and for a few seconds she simply lay there, reliving in growing horror the full extent of her degradation.

There was no denying what had passed between her and the man whose body curved now so intimately around hers. She could not believe it, and yet every portion of her body gave vivid proof. Her lips were sensitive and swollen from his fierce kisses. Her breasts were full and even now her nipples peaked and tightened at the remembered passion they had shared. But it was the lingering warmth down there . . .

A flush of heat and color crept up her chest and face as she recalled the way he had touched her and entered her down there.

"Sweet Mary, what have I done?" she whispered, truly appalled at her unpardonable behavior. She had lain with him—a man she hardly knew and whom she hoped soon to be rid of—and to add to her shame, she had then quite obviously fallen asleep still clasped in the rogue's embrace! If she spent the remainder of her life on her knees in fervent prayer, she could not hope to be forgiven for such a reprehensible act!

In desperation she glanced around, searching for a way out of her predicament. They lay in a bed of thick grasses, sheltered by a half circle of willows. Somewhere behind them must be their camp. And Cleve, she realized with a start. She must get away from this man—this Blacksword —before Cleve found out, she thought wildly. They must slip away while he slept and somehow—somehow!—make their way to Stanwood before he caught up with them.

Even as she made her plans, she knew it was madness. There was no chance they could escape him, and even less chance that he would not follow. But she could not pause to consider that. If she had to confront him—*when* she had to—she would decide then how to handle him. She would lie if he told anything to her father. She would! But first she must make good her escape.

She edged slightly away from him, as if only in her sleep, and managed to free her leg of the weight of his thigh. For a few seconds she rested, listening to his steady breathing to ascertain whether she'd awakened him at all. Then with ultimate care, she lifted his arm and moved it from where it draped over her, and laid it on his own hip. His wrist was wide and sturdy, she noted during the endless seconds it took to accomplish this move. Her hand could not even span its brawny width. He was possessed of such strength, she despaired. If he caught her he could easily crush her in his hands.

Yet it was these same hands that had caressed her so provocatively, she unwillingly recalled. He had used his hands in tenderness and passion. Was it possible he could use them in violence against her? She paused as she carefully let go of his wrist, confused by the many facets of his personality. Yes, he could use violence against her, she

told herself vehemently. If he had to he would. She was
sure of it. Only she was not going to give him the chance.

With that thought uppermost in her mind, she inched
with infinite slowness away from the warm curve of his
body. A shiver raced through her when she was finally free
of his touch. She told herself it was fear, but there was a
tiny doubting voice in her head that denied it. She had
enjoyed the towering passion they'd shared, the voice said,
despite her every wish to pretend she had not. She had
enjoyed it and now it was over.

But Rosalynde refused to listen to the voice. She refused to look back at the man sleeping so quietly, so unconcerned by his own nakedness. And she adamantly
refused to think about the repercussions of what she was
doing. She only rose to her feet, clutched her kirtle up to
her breasts, and scurried behind the slender trunk of one
of the willows.

Once she had her kirtle back on, she glanced around
wildly for her gown. To her chagrin she saw it lying just
behind Blacksword, a pitiful heap of dark-green wool
abandoned during their wanton episode. Terrifed at any
moment that he might awaken, she circled warily behind
the protection of the trees. Once he stirred, and she froze,
holding her breath as her heart slammed furiously against
her chest. But then he stilled, and after only a moment's
hesitation she crept forward again.

It seemed to take forever. Every sound from the cry of a
hunting kerlew to the scolding of a pair of squirrels magni-
fied in her ears, rolling like thunder across the silent
glade. Surely he would awaken! But he slept on as if he
were drugged, and when she finally reached her gown she
could have cried with relief.

His back was to her, marked with lingering bruises and
scrapes—probably from his imprisonment, she thought. It

rose and fell lightly, signaling his continuing slumber, and despite her fear, she scrutinized him one last time. His shoulders were wide and tan, as if he often went without either tunic or chainse. But for all its muscled width, his back tapered gracefully to a trim waist and then further to lean, hard-muscled buttocks. She stared wide-eyed at him, hardly able to believe what she and this man had done together. Yet as her eyes moved down to his iron-hewn thighs, the feel of his lightly furred leg slipping between hers came vividly back to mind.

"Oh!" She gasped softly into the scratchy wool of the gown she held clutched in her hands. Then, humiliated by the perversity of her own thoughts, she turned away. Her hands trembled as she struggled with the gown. It was twisted and knotted, and she thought she would smother before she pulled it down past her head and shoulders, and then shoved her arms hurriedly into the sleeves. She fought the difficult fabric down to her waist then turned to flee, but three unexpected words stopped her.

"Don't leave yet."

In horror Rosalynde turned her head to see Blacksword staring at her. He was propped up on one elbow, smiling at her, and completely unfazed by his lack of clothing.

"You don't have to run away in such a panic," he continued in the same husky tone. "It's hours till dark. There's no rush."

"I-I . . ." Words failed Rosalynde as she stared at him. He appeared so relaxed. His tone was so beguiling. And that smile . . .

She compressed her lips tightly together and forced herself to look away from him. That smile of his was far too confident, far too gloating, she fretted. But she knew that was to be expected. In his eyes he'd won. He had gotten what he wanted, and that was the right to claim her as his

wife. To make things worse, she quite obviously had cooperated with him every step of the way. Like a complete
wanton, she had let him do what he would, and cried out
with the pleasure of it!

For a moment she stood still, consumed with guilt and
horror and too many other emotions to understand. Then
from the corner of her eye she saw him move, and she
swiftly turned to face him, prepared now for the worst.
But he only stood up, stretched his arms wide, and let out
a huge yawn.

Rosalynde's eyes widened in shock as she stared at him,
revealed as he was now in his full masculine glory. This
unrestrained view she had of him showed a man of pure
muscle, without an ounce of excess flesh. She had determined that before, but now the fact was driven home. In
the filtered light of midday every part of him was clearly
displayed to her, and despite her unwillingness to appear
in the least affected, she stared at him with mouth slightly
agape and eyes wide with surprise, quite transfixed by
what she saw.

A pale scar contrasted against the darker skin of his
side, a neat slice near his belly. Another puckered crescent
marred the smooth flesh of one side of his chest. A mottled
purple bruise still showed angrily against his ribs, and a
raw scrape was just beginning to heal on one of his forearms. But those lingering marks of the harsh life he'd lived
did nothing to mar the masculine beauty of his virile body.
If anything they enhanced it, giving him a disturbing aura
of power, of confidence, and especially of danger. It was
this last that should have terrified her the most, but somehow it also attracted her most unwisely to him. Only with
the sternest exercise of willpower was she able to force her
gaze away.

"Must you be so . . . so . . . so shameless?" she muttered as hot color suffused her cheeks.

"Must you be so prudish?" he countered with a rakish grin. But to her enormous relief, he reached for his braies and pulled them up to cover his loins.

Rosalynde was poised between stupefaction and an overwhelming urge to run away. As she watched him knot his braies securely at the waist then roll the fabric over twice, she searched her mind desperately for some remedy to her newly worsened predicament. But her mind was an uncooperative blank; no solution presented itself at all. If she ran he would catch her. If he took her all the way to Stanwood he would reveal the handfast vow to her father. And if she tried to deny it he could now reveal what had passed between them this day. She was caught in an intolerable situation, trapped no matter which direction she turned. Oh, if only he would just go away!

"Come now, sweet wife. Come greet your husband with something other than this timid expression and shy reserve." His eyes slid possessively over her, and his faint smile seemed nonetheless filled with an enormous amount of satisfaction. "Come here, Rose, and give me a kiss."

It was this last—both gloating and insulting to her ears —which finally goaded her into action.

"Don't you touch me," she warned, jerking her skirt all the way down, then eyeing him as if he were the lowest form of life. "Don't you ever presume to touch me again!"

His expression altered slightly at that, as if he had not quite expected such a rebuff from her. Not anymore, at least. What an arrogant oaf he was! she fumed. But he seemed to reconsider his approach, and this time when he smiled it seemed almost genuine. But she knew better than to trust him. She knew.

"If you'll just hear me out, Rose." He spread his arms

placatingly and took a step toward her. "You'll find things not so black as they appear."

"Not so black!" A sudden tremble crept into her voice and she swallowed hard to hide it. More than anything she did not want to cry before him. That would be the final humiliating admission of defeat. She swallowed again. "You have ruined me."

"It is not ruinous for a wife to lie with her husband—"

"I'm not your wife!" she shrieked as she finally lost all control. "I'm not your wife!" Then she whirled away from him and ran as fast as she could from the still-undeniable pull of his masculine presence.

"Rose!"

She heard his call but only ran the faster. She wasn't sure where she was going, only that she must get away. Even though she knew he could catch her if he wanted to, she could not stay a moment longer in his presence. The knowledge of how he had so easily seduced her, so effortlessly convinced her to throw away everything she'd been taught, everything she believed, fueled her flight with improbable speed.

"Christ's blood! Would you just listen to me!" Then he let out an irreverent oath, and she heard the sound of his determined pursuit.

She didn't get far in her headlong flight. Before she could reach the security of the deep woods or find the comfort at least of Cleve's presence, he had her. Like a squalling kitten she was caught and lifted off her feet. Then he spun her around, yanking her up against him as he circled her waist with his implacable grip.

"No. Stop!" she cried, striking out blindly at him. "Let me go!"

"Be damned, woman! Would you just listen for once without interrupting me or running away?"

"No. No!" She fought him even harder, kicking his hard shins with her bare toes.

But it was another furious cry that silenced her and brought a momentary pause to their struggle.

"Unhand her, you unholy bastard!" Then with a bellow of pure rage Cleve charged them. Like a dog attacking a bear, the boy flew at the man.

Blacksword stood staring at the enraged boy for a moment, as if he could not quite believe his eyes. Then with another muttered curse he thrust Rosalynde aside and turned to face his puny but scrappy adversary.

Rosalynde fell to her knees at the abrupt change of events, and when she looked up she viewed their confrontation with equal portions of relief and horror. Cleve, pale with fury, was almost upon the larger man, with a stout branch his only weapon against Blacksword's considerable size advantage. Yet branch and boy together were still no match for the more experienced outlaw. With a quick feint and a sudden turn, Blacksword threw off Cleve's timing and then jerked the branch easily from his hands. As he swung it high Rosalynde was certain he meant to bash in the boy's head, and she screamed a warning at Cleve. Instead of pressing his advantage, however, Blacksword only heaved the stout branch into the trees and then turned angrily to deal with Cleve. Yet despite Blacksword's clear advantage, the boy would not back down.

"I'll kill you, you son of Satan!" he growled as he circled the imposing man.

"Dear God, Cleve. Get away. Get away!" Rosalynde cried.

But Cleve's sense of loyalty was too ingrained, and his need for revenge against this man who tried to dishonor his mistress was far too strong. "I'll kill you," he hissed as once more he charged.

This time he caught Blacksword around the waist. Or perhaps Blacksword caught him, Rosalynde was later to wonder. But the battle went no further than that for with a sudden blast of a horn, a group of horsemen burst from the woods. In an instant the trio was surrounded.

In the confusion of those first few seconds Rosalynde's emotions seemed to work in slow motion. First came shock at the complete unexpectedness of it all. Then came horror as she relived the initial attack that had started this entire disaster. But then she recognized the deep green and gold pennants that the lead rider flew and her horror turned to surprise and then overwhelming relief. "Stanwood!" she cried, hardly daring to believe they were saved. "Stanwood!"

At once the tenor of the battle between Cleve and the huge Blacksword changed. Sensing the shift in his favor, Cleve abandoned his aggression and instead stumbled away from the grasp of the now-wary man.

"He's a murderer! A thief who set upon us!" he cried to the uncertain riders who milled around them, stirring up a blinding cloud of dust. "He attacked the Lady Rosalynde!"

He had, Rosalynde silently concurred. He had indeed attacked her and used her most cruelly. But as the riders drew swords and daggers and closed in on the single man on foot, she was suddenly terrified for him. "Don't hurt him!" she screamed as the horses and dust blocked her view of the suddenly dangerous situation.

"Don't kill him!"

Yet her words were only one more cry of alarm lost in the pandemonium of the moment. Without warning she was whisked up before one of the knights who then abruptly wheeled his horse. As they rode out of view of the fight, she was left agonizing over her last sight of Blacksword. He was shouldered to the ground by one of the horses, and she screamed to think he would be trampled even as she knew he deserved whatever harsh hand fate dealt him. But something in her just could not rejoice in his suffering.

Cleve was plucked to safety by another stout knight, and they were quickly flanked by two others. But Blacksword was left far behind, surrounded by angry warrior knights with weapons drawn. Despite his physical prowess, Rosalynde knew that on foot and unarmed he did not stand a chance.

Once beyond a stand of trees, they stopped and dismounted. The leader of the knights who found them was an older man called Sir Roger, whom she vaguely remembered from her childhood days. He was clearly overjoyed to have found her, but not nearly so much so as Rosalynde, who deemed it a veritable miracle to have been saved, and by her father's own knights! Even more astounding was the fact that among them was one of her uncle's knights, the only survivor of the four men who'd originally accompanied her. The man told her that he and Nelda had escaped, and the two of them had managed to reach Stanwood on one of the horses and summon help. More than anything else, Rosalynde thanked God for sparing at least those two lives.

But when she tried to intercede on Blacksword's behalf, Sir Roger would not hear a word of it.

"Don't bother yourself on his part," he told her as he resettled her on the pommel before a silent young knight. "My men will take care of him, have no doubt." But as vague as his words were, the significant arch of his bushy brows sent an unwarranted shiver of fear through Rosalynde.

"What does that mean?" she demanded from her perch

over the war-horse's withers. "What are you going to do with him?"

"Only what's due a man who attacks innocent women and children," he answered curtly. "Don't even turn your mind toward the likes of him, milady."

"He should be strung up!" Cleve interjected, shooting her an angry look. "He's a thief and a murderer and a—" He halted abruptly and after a moment his eyes fell away from her mortified face. "And he should be hanged," he ended lamely.

For the space of one moment the older knight stared from the outraged boy to the suddenly pale girl. Then he shifted uncomfortably from one foot to the other and noisily cleared his throat. "Did he . . . that is, has he . . ." He faltered, then cursed softly under his breath. "Did you suffer any harm at his hands, milady?"

Rosalynde felt the rush of blood to her face, and though she feared it gave her away, she did not even pause to consider her answer. "No," she muttered quietly. Then no again, louder. "He helped us get this far," she stated, giving Cleve a quelling glance.

"He hardly looked to be helping you," Sir Roger quipped sarcastically.

"I tell you, he should not be treated so!"

But for all her insistence, Rosalynde was not to know Blacksword's fate. He was still in the half circle of willows while she and Cleve were surrounded by the other knights deeper in the woods. When Sir Roger led the small band away, she tried frantically to catch a glimpse of Blacksword. But her efforts were in vain. The knights deliberately skirted the spot where he had been captured. As the horses thundered away from the abandoned campsite, she bowed her head in abject contrition and prayed that another man had not been killed because of her.

The burly fellow whose horse she shared said not a word to her as they rode. They were surrounded by several other knights, and Cleve trailed somewhere behind on a laden packhorse. As for Blacksword, she simply did not know—and that was the worst of all. It did no good to console herself that he would have died on the gallows if not for her. He had met his part of their agreement; he'd been taking her home as he'd promised. The fact that he had taken advantage of her now seemed a much smaller matter when compared to the loss of his life. Although she'd not thought so before, she now knew that nothing he had done deserved so cruel a fate as that. The deed had not been so terrible. If anything, it had brought her unexpected and undeniable pleasure. She hardly dared admit it, even to herself. But the truth was indisputable. For all his brutality he had been possessed of the most tender of touches. With hands and mouth . . .

A sudden trembling came over her and she felt a telling heat rush through her body. In dismay she closed her eyes against the bittersweet memory of it. She was a woman now, no longer a maiden. She'd lain with a man—her husband, no matter what the circumstances of their marriage. But he might already have paid for that with his life. Added to that, there was the possibility now that she could end up with child. And how was she to explain any of this to her father?

Rosalynde was so exhausted by everything that had happened, so defeated by the emotional turmoil that gripped her, that she could hardly sit upright in the saddle. She sagged against the rigid knight's grasp and a fat tear escaped her eye. Then another came, and another. As the riders made their way at a bone-jarring pace, she wept hot salty tears for all that had happened, and all that could never be again. She cried for her brother, for the knights

who had died, and even for the loss of her mother, so
many years before. But mostly she cried for the man
Blacksword—Aric of Wycliffe, he'd said was his name.

   She cried for Aric of Wycliffe, and she cried for herself.

11

They rode as if the devil himself chased them. Even when night fell over the land. Even after the moon's cold thin light abandoned them. Even though darkness shrouded the countryside with an impenetrable blackness. Still they pressed on, though both riders and beasts suffered with their weariness.

They arrived at Stanwood at the bleakest hour of night. Yet torches burned in the gatehouse, and even to Rosalynde's beleagured senses the castle appeared to be in a strange state of unrest. The gate was down, men and horses milled in seeming aimlessness, and in the flickering orange light it looked almost as she imagined hell might, all dark disjointed shapes and jerky movements.

Rosalynde could not quite collect her senses as they clattered to a halt in the stone-paved bailey. Her wits were still befuddled from her uncomfortable catnap, and her emotions were far too battered. To further confuse the situation, a low murmur rippled through the people there, then quickly escalated to shouts and calls. Sir Roger dismounted first. Then she was swiftly handed down into his waiting hands and set onto her own wobbly legs. Cleve quickly found his way to her side, and in spite of her lingering anger at his unswerving obstinance, she was nonetheless grateful for at least his one familiar face. Then a tall austere figure hurried through the gathering throng, and before she realized what was happening to her, she was unexpectedly swept into her father's fierce embrace.

At the urgent feel of his arms crushing her to him, all of Rosalynde's disparate emotions combined to dissolve the last of her stamina. Hot tears clouded her vision and a sob caught in her throat as she clung unashamedly to the man she both loved and feared. "Papa," she whispered against the coarse wool tunic at his chest. "Papa," she cried as she gave way to a flood of tears.

"You are safe. You are safe," he muttered over and over into her dark, tangled hair. His hands clasped her even closer as if he feared she might disappear. "You are safe."

The rest of her confusing homecoming was lost in the curious chatter of the onlookers and the barked orders of Sir Roger. Somehow she and her father made their way to the great hall. The inquisitive spectators were shut out when the huge pair of doors was closed. Only Sir Roger, her father, and another nervous-looking fellow accompanied her, and it was there that her father finally released his tight hold on her.

"I thought I'd lost you too," he whispered hoarsely as he held her at arm's length. He blinked hard, cleared his throat, and then let his hands fall away from her. "Are you hurt at all?"

Rosalynde shook her head in reply, for she could not speak, she was so overcome with emotions. He loved her —the thought circled round and round in her disbelieving mind. He still loved her and had grieved to think he'd lost her. It was a wonder, almost beyond comprehension, after the long years he'd all but ignored them. Then his words registered more clearly and her breath caught in her throat. He thought he'd lost her *too*. He knew about Giles.

"Papa." She approached him and hesitantly reached out

to touch his dark-clad chest. "I came because of Giles. I . . . I'm sorry."

At this softly worded expression of her own grief, he stiffened and she could almost feel him pulling back from her. In the brief passage of only one second he changed from the loving father she recalled from her early years, back to the cold unyielding man he had been ever since her mother's death. Panicked that she was losing him all over again, Rosalynde gripped the loose fabric of his tunic. "I tried to save him, Papa. I did! I used everything I knew—cleansed his blood with elder shoots, dandelion, and nettle; purified his lungs with lungwort and shave grass; cooled his fever with vervain and sallow bark. I even burned mugwort and St. John's root in his chamber." She babbled on faster and faster. "But nothing would do. I tried . . . I really tried—" She broke off as tears flooded her eyes once more and a sob choked in her throat.

Rosalynde felt her father tremble as he sternly put her from him. His face was pale, even to her blurred eyes, and his jaw was clenched as if he fought for control. Then he spoke and no trace of softness lingered in his voice. "Giles was ever a sickly child. It was God's will."

But he turned away from her then, and even though he placed none of the blame on her, Rosalynde felt the weight of his rejection keenly. He did not blame her with words, but his reaction. . . .

A paroxysm of trembling rushed over her and she was suddenly light-headed. Only Sir Roger's timely grip on her arm prevented her from collapsing on the floor. He seated her on a high-backed chair, then quickly called for something for her to drink. By the time Rosalynde swallowed the potent red wine, sputtering and coughing as it seared down her throat, her father was bending over her once more, his brow creased in concern.

"Are you hurt? Were you harmed in any way?" he demanded almost angrily.

But though she shook her head no, it was Sir Roger who answered her father.

"We found her about ten leagues to the west, half the way to the Stour River. She and her serving lad were being attacked by a giant of a runagate—Blacksword, the lad called him."

"And did you kill the bastard?" Sir Edward growled furiously.

"Ahh . . . well, you see, sir, I would have. Only—" He shot Rosalynde an uncertain look. "Your daughter demanded we not kill him. So I had him brought back here for your pleasure, milord." He let out a slow sigh of relief when his liege lord's eyes narrowed and he nodded in angry approval. "I might add, sir, that the serving lad gave a good accounting of himself. Puny bit that he is, he faced the man as bravely as you could ever hope to see."

"He shall be well rewarded," Sir Edward replied curtly. Then he stared once more at his pale-faced daughter. "And what of you, Rosalynde? Did the man—did he—" He faltered as if the words were too ugly to say, too awful even to contemplate. But Rosalynde knew whereof he spoke, and her mind twisted away from a truthful answer. There was nothing good to come of the truth, she rationalized. Not for her. Not for her father. Certainly not for the man Blacksword. She'd felt an intense rush of relief when Sir Roger revealed that Blacksword still lived. But she knew he would not live long if her father knew what had passed between them. When she finally spoke the lie came most convincingly to her lips, although it burned like gall on her tongue.

"I am tired, Father. And dirty. My clothes are ruined. My feet—" She broke off as she recalled the rabbit-skin shoes that had led to her ultimate downfall. But she took a hard, shaky breath and continued. "I was frightened beyond the measuring, but I am not hurt."

Their eyes met in silent assessment. Did he believe her? she wondered nervously. Could he read the lie in her eyes? Then he gave her a slow nod and she let loose the breath she'd unconsciously been holding. As he gave orders for a bath to be prepared for her and a chamber readied, she sat there, numb from all that had happened. Her mind cried out for sleep, her body was almost beyond her own control, so exhausted was she by her ordeal. But there was still one thing she had to do. With the last reserves of her strength she stood upright and crossed to where her father gave instructions to the sandy-haired man.

". . . her chamber in the east tower," he was saying as she timidly plucked at his sleeve. Then he waved the fellow away and he turned to face her.

"Father, about that man."

"Cedric?" Sir Edward questioned, gesturing to the quietly departing seneschal.

"No. No, not him." Rosalynde clasped her hands tightly together. "You know, the man, Blacksword."

At once her father's expression hardened. "Do not let that knave disturb your thoughts even one moment longer, daughter. His punishment falls to me, and mark my words, he shall pay the ultimate price for daring to harm me or mine."

"But he didn't!" she cried in renewed fear for the man who had been both villain and savior to her, both knave and lover.

"If he did not harm you, it was not for want of trying. It was only the lad who prevented him from doing his worst."

"That's not true!" She shook her head wildly, casting about desperately for the words to convince him. "I hired him to see us home. Cleve was hurt. We were alone. He was the only one willing to do it. Oh, don't you see? To punish him is wrong. I promised him a reward!"

Rosalynde knew she dared much by challenging her father on this, a matter more proper for men to attend to, and far beyond the affairs of a mere woman. But her conscience nagged at her too sorely for her to let Blacksword be tortured or killed for his deeds. Despite his unforgivable behavior toward her, he nonetheless had the right of marriage on his side. Her father did not know that—if he did he would very likely be even more inclined to kill the man. But she knew it was true, and she could not allow him to die for it.

There was no time for her to plan what to do, how even to stop Blacksword from revealing all to her father should his life be spared. She would face that problem later when she had to. Right now she knew only that any pain he suffered would be on her head, and she simply could not bear any more guilt.

"I promised him a reward," she stated more softly. "You cannot just murder him."

" 'Twill hardly be murder." Sir Edward gave her a hard, scrutinizing look. She had to fight down the color that threatened to rise in her cheeks, but she met his gaze squarely. She knew instinctively that he preferred very much to believe what she said if only because any other story was much too unpleasant for him to stomach. He wanted his daughter whole and unsullied. Unless he were faced with undeniable proof to the contrary, he would accept her story.

The uncomfortable silence was broken by the entrance of a serving girl who halted, then waited in the corner to show Rosalynde to her chamber. But Rosalynde stood there silently pleading with her father to relent.

"I will look into the matter," he finally conceded. "I promise you I'll not make my decision in haste." Then as if any further discussion of the matter was closed, he turned to leave. "Sleep now, daughter. We'll speak later of what will be done."

One prison was very much like another, Aric thought with disgust as he cast a bleary eye about the black hole he'd been thrust into. Cold. Dark. Smelling of urine and mold. With a grunt of pain he pushed himself up to a sitting position then gingerly raised one hand to his brow. An enormous egg had raised up on his forehead; his knuckles were raw from the one blow he'd managed to get in against the group of knights who had overpowered him; and his left arm felt as if it had been yanked from his shoulder. But he was still alive, and he tried hard to take some comfort in that.

Damn the bitch! he thought bitterly. Damn her to hell for throwing him to the wolves the first chance she got.

With the cold assessiveness of a man long accustomed to fending for himself in difficult circumstances, he examined this latest prison into which he had been cast. The chamber was small, less than twice his length square. The walls were rubble and stone, too rough to lean against with any degree of comfort. The floor was stone as well, covered with a stale layer of straw. The only light admitted was from the steel bar grate in the heavy oak door, and it was barely enough to see by. A small bucket chained to the wall held water; a hole in the floor allowed human waste to be washed away. All in all, it was not a place he wished to spend much time in. But then, it was unlikely he would have to, he reasoned cynically. Once she ran to

her father with her sad tale of woe, it was unlikely he'd
live out more than a day or two. He well knew that the one
thing prized above all in a noblewoman was her virginity.
Handfast ceremony or no, her father would no doubt
rather kill him than risk the chance that his daughter's
imperfect state might be revealed to anyone.

Once more he cursed the moment of insanity when he'd
thought he might win both maid and demesne for himself
merely by the bedding of her. He must have been mad!
But then, as he recalled how she had looked standing in
that quiet pool with the sunlight glinting sparks off her
wet lashes, and her slender arms and shapely ankles exposed to his view, he knew just what sort of madness it
had been. He'd been completely and unexpectedly overcome with desire for the strange nymph-like creature she
was, and it had totally clouded his thinking. Now it appeared he would pay dearly for his mistake.

In the hollow darkness of the little cell, he tried hard to
attain that same state of calm he'd finally reached in the
prison at Dunmow. It had not come easily. He had fought
the unfairness then of being falsely convicted, the frustration of not knowing who had singled him out in such a
way, and the incompleteness of a life not lived out as expected. Yet in the long days and nights as he'd awaited the
inevitable hanging, he'd come to a grudging acceptance of
his fate. He'd vowed to meet his maker with as much
dignity as he could muster.

But then when the sudden intervention had come, he'd
been almost angry. The peace and resignation had been
ripped away, and all the raw fear and pain were exposed
once more, much like a wound torn wide apart after it had
barely begun to heal. The ragged urchin who had so fearfully mounted the grisly gallows had appeared at once
both an imp of the devil and an angel of God. He'd been

unable to believe she was more than a figment of his imagination, a manifestation of his suppressed prayers for salvation. Yet she had stood there, timid . . . terrified . . . made bold by her own desperation. In her fear she'd grabbed hold of his tunic and her startling eyes had blazed with heated emotions. But it was not the heat in her eyes that had swayed him. Perhaps in different circumstances he would have been moved by those huge, piercing eyes. But that day . . . that day it had been the unexpected warmth of her knuckles grazing the skin of his chest.

In a strange way he had already started to die by the time she had made her way up before the jeering crowd. When he'd finally resigned himself to his fate, he had begun to let go of life. But her warm touch . . . It had been like the touch of life itself, enticing him—goading him—to take one last chance, to not give up.

Aric leaned back against the rough wall, ignoring the sharp jut of stone against his sore shoulder. He'd taken the chance and he'd escaped the hangman, but now he could see that it had only been a stay of execution. A temporary reprieve. Now it was over.

With a vicious oath and a grunt of pain, he got to his feet and then flexed his left shoulder gingerly. God's blood, but he did not want to die! Restlessly he paced the small dank chamber. Three strides across the foul-smelling space then back to where he'd started. Just as impatiently his mind turned round and round, seeking some escape, some way out of this hellish pit he'd landed in. But here too he met only with stone walls. No matter how he struggled to find a solution to his dilemma, it all came back to the same thing. Unless she chose to defend him, he would die. Unless she denied that he had spoiled her virginity, his chances were grim indeed. What he said would matter less than nothing to her father. It was all up to her.

On that thought he placed both of his hands against the stout door and leaned his weight against it in resignation. If his fate was in her hands he was doomed.

Rosalynde descended the ancient stone stairs one groggy step at a time. She was home, she kept telling herself over and over. That was what she had wanted and she should be happy at last. Yet that did nothing to dispel the awful feelings of dread that hung over her like a heavy shadow. She was still exhausted and completely disoriented. Although she'd just awakened, something told her it was long past dawn. And even though she'd been bathed by some maid last night and now wore a new gown that, though not fancy, was nonetheless reasonably clean, she still could not quite enjoy her newfound safety. Too much was still unresolved from last night. As her senses sharpened she had a nagging feeling of guilt for her lengthy slumber. The situation with Blacksword was still uncertain, and she needed to know whether her father had set him free. Then she spied Cleve sitting alone at a table with a huge platter of cheeses, broken meats, and dried fruits before him, and looking far too pleased with himself. If Blacksword had been freed, Cleve would hardly appear so content.

"Cleve!" Her cry stopped him in the process of stuffing one more chunk of cheese into his already overfilled mouth. "Cleve!" she repeated, this time in an accusing tone.

At once he jumped up, a look of complete guilt on his face. A fresh bandage was wrapped about his head and she noticed that he too looked newly bathed. But she had something far more important than his appearance on her mind as she approached him. Something was going on, and she was certain he knew exactly what.

"Why did no one awaken me earlier? What hour is it?" she demanded. Then her stomach let out an embarrassing growl, and she could not help reaching out for a handful of raisins and devouring them ravenously. "Why is there no one about?" she added suspiciously.

"It's near midday, milady. And as for the whereabouts of the castlefolk, well, as far as I can see, there aren't too many inside servants to begin with." He cast a disdainful glance around the admittedly shabby surroundings. "And those that there are have all gone out to view that villain. That Blacksword." This last he said almost boastfully. Even her sudden frown could not quite diffuse his obvious satisfaction.

At once Rosalynde was alarmed. She had slept more than half of the day away. With Cleve's hostility toward Blacksword—Aric—he might have told her father anything. But more than his lies Rosalynde feared that Cleve might have told her father the truth, and throughout it all she had been left to sleep, blissfully unaware. As frightened as she was angry, she rounded on him with her fists planted imperiously on her hips.

"What is going on around here, Cleve? Tell me now what you've done."

But Cleve was not easily cowed, even by her, for he keenly felt the righteousness of his own anger. With a stubborn jut to his chin he stood up and scowled right back at her. "Your father questioned me this morning and I told him nothing but the truth of it—how that man bullied the both of us. How he is a thief and a murderer—and boastful of it too!" The boy pushed his shaggy hair from his brow. His dark eyes glittered with emotion. "And then there's what he did to you!"

Rosalynde gasped at the painful truth of his words. "You

. . . you didn't say anything . . . not to my father," she finished weakly.

Under her horrified gaze Cleve's angry glare slowly faded until he finally looked down at the floor. "That swine should hang," he muttered furiously.

"What did you tell my father?" Rosalynde whispered urgently. She crossed the remaining space, grasped his arms, and stared fearfully into his eyes. "What, Cleve? What?"

Anger warred with loyalty on the young page's face. Rosalynde knew instinctively that he would never deliberately do anything to hurt her. He'd proven beyond any doubt that he would risk his very life to protect her. But she also realized that he saw Blacksword as a threat to her. It was as pure and simple as that. Even though she knew her own shameful part in the deed, Cleve saw only Blacksword's guilt. He would no doubt say anything to see Blacksword punished for his crime. But in doing so, had he sentenced the man to death?

"I told him—" Cleve's face took on a mutinous expression and he shook off her desperate grasp. "I told him what I saw. That he was accosting you, trying to . . . trying to . . ." He stopped abruptly. "It's true, isn't it? I told your father that I stopped him before he could—" He looked away then and took a harsh breath before he peered resentfully back at her. "I told him nothing happened. But it did, didn't it?"

Rosalynde could not answer him. No matter how true it was, no matter how undeniable, she simply could not bring herself to say the words aloud. Yet her very silence seemed to condemn her.

In the awful stillness of the great hall Cleve's eyes seemed to go almost black. The petulance in his face jelled into a harder emotion. Had she not been so consumed by her own self-reproachful thoughts, she might have even imagined that he shed the cloak of boyhood at that moment. His youthful ideals had been crushed by reality. He could never be a boy again.

"You don't understand," Rosalynde finally choked out. Her mouth was as dry as dust even though tears clouded her eyes. She felt hot with shame and yet her face was pale and colorless. "You don't understand." Then she whirled away from him and fled recklessly from the hall.

She did not plan her pell-mell flight from Cleve's accusing eyes. She could not think or reason what she must do. But when she charged into the glaring sunlight of the inner bailey, into the unexpected clusters of castlefolk gathered there in the midday sunshine, she came to an abrupt halt.

To Rosalynde's still-disoriented senses, the scene in the bailey was not quite real. It was a bad dream, a familiar reassuring place, yet possessed now of a strange and ominous tension. It was her home and yet everything was somehow wrong. Several faces turned at her sudden appearance. Then a wave of murmurs and whispers swept through the crowd until every neck craned to see her, every eye peered her way. Rosalynde was taken aback by her sudden preeminence, and in her beleagured state of mind it seemed that Cleve's accusing stare echoed now a hundredfold in these new and unknown faces.

As she stood there, frozen, she realized that this was very much a recurrence of her dreadful ordeal in Dunmow: all those expectant faces waiting to be entertained, no matter that it was at the dire expense of another. Panicked anew, she nearly turned and fled, so unnerved was she by it all. But then she heard Cleve's step behind her and at once her resolve strengthened.

It took only a quick glance across the sea of faces to

ascertain what was going on. At the far end of the bailey beyond the alehouse, a man was tied to the gate that led into the stableyard.

Blacksword.

Aric.

His arms were spread wide; his back was bared to the waist. Before him a knot of men clustered, and a little beyond them stood her father. Then the brawniest of the group of men separated himself from the others and approached the bound Blacksword, shaking out a long leather whip as he advanced.

"No!" The scream tore from her lips as she dashed down the few steps then pushed her way through the staring crowd. She heard the sharp crack of the whip even from across the bailey, followed by the gasp of the crowd, and she winced as if the wicked leather had cut her own skin.

"No! No!" she cried out once more, unaware that it came out only as a frantic sob. But the spectators' attentions were no longer focused on her. Everyone had heard the gossip: Some fiend had been foolish enough to attack Sir Edward's daughter. Now he was to pay with a painful stripping away of his flesh until he begged for the final relief from his pain at the hangman's noose. With every snap of the vicious whip, the entire assemblage jerked in response. Yet they waited still for the next and the next, both repelled and uncontrollably drawn to watch the grisly flogging.

But Rosalynde felt only a sickening anguish for what was happening. Sobbing and gasping for breath, stumbling blindly as she ran, she broke into the little clearing as the whip drew back then snaked cruelly out once more. She watched in frozen horror as the stiffened tip of leather cut through the air then flicked with deadly precision across Blacksword's broad, sweating back.

"Stop! Oh, please God, stop!" she prayed aloud as her stomach twisted with revulsion at such a cruel deed. Standing unbowed, his hands tied in place against the sturdy wooden gate, Blacksword could not see her. But she could see him, and what she saw filled her with terror and shame. His back already showed the fierce red welts of too many strikes of the whip. The last one had finally drawn blood. Before her unbelieving eyes the whip struck once more, and she saw with agonizing clarity the thin red tear against the firm brown flesh and then the several bright lines of oozing blood that slid down that strong unyielding back.

Unable to bear it even a moment longer, Rosalynde tore her eyes away. Then she saw her father and she knew what she must do.

"Stop this, Papa! Stop it!" she pleaded as she rushed to his side. She grabbed both his hands to force his attention to her. "You can't let this go on! You can't!"

Her father's face was grim as he finally met her eyes. "He gets no more than he deserves."

"He deserves none of this. None of it!" she begged, heedless of the tears that flooded her face. "I promised him a reward."

"So you said before, but 'tis clear he was too impatient to wait for it. In his greed and lust he wanted something more—" He broke off then and signaled to the man with the whip to resume his gruesome task. Once more the unforgiving leather cracked, and this time Rosalynde felt as if it struck her to the very heart, tearing her—ripping her—asunder. She could not let this go on! In a fury she rounded on the man, seeing in her fear and pain how he drew back once more to flog the unbending man who refused to sag or whimper beneath the whip's savage bite. In an outburst of energy she flung herself at the thick-muscled arm that held the whip.

Her strength was not enough to stop the man. Had she been able to think clearly, she would have recognized that fact at once. But the scowling fellow knew better than to strike the very woman whose honor it was he now avenged. One swat of his other hand would have rid him of her pesky interference. But he dared not. It was her father who finally dragged her away. It was Sir Edward who grabbed her and shook her until her teeth fairly rattled in her head.

Then he took an angry breath and glared down into her frightened, stubborn face. "Mind what you do, daughter! Do not shame me by this unseemly display!"

"If you flog him—" She gasped for breath as she locked her haunted eyes with his furious ones. "If you flog a man whom you should reward, then you shame yourself."

There was an unearthly silence in the castle bailey. Not a soul moved. No one dared speak. Every ear strained to hear what passed between father and daughter, and a hundred possibilities circled in as many minds. But their words were low and muttered, and no one heard a word save the two of them.

Finally the glowering Sir Edward turned and, with only a terse shake of his head, signaled the man with the whip to halt. Then, ignoring both the waiting crowd and the still-bound prisoner, he dragged his unruly daughter away.

12

"Impossible!" Sir Edward shot his daughter a furious look. "I'll not reward a ruffian for his misdeeds."

"Papa, please. I beg you!" Rosalynde clutched her hands tightly at her stomach as she watched her father's angry pacing. "You've listened to Cleve. You've listened to Sir Roger. Why can you not listen to me?"

"This is not your concern. Women should not interfere—"

"It is solely my concern!" she shouted in self-righteous indignation.

At such a blatant contradiction of his words, her father turned and gave her a baleful glare. "Is this the same biddable child I sent to Millwort? Is this foul temper a sample of the lessons you learned at your lady aunt's knee?" He studied her with ill-concealed impatience. "I am Lord of Stanwood, miss. Everyone—everything—here falls under my protection. Those who dare to threaten anything of mine do thereby threaten me. And I take no threat lightly. There is no way but for him to pay, and harshly."

"But not with his life," she pleaded in a voice gone softer with her rising fear for Blacksword.

Her father did not respond for a long moment, and in the nerve-racking silence Rosalynde considered the wisdom of confessing all to him. If he knew the man was her husband then perhaps . . . She pressed her fingers to her mouth as she struggled to decide. Perhaps he would free him, she hoped. But the stubborn frown on her father's face held more promise of dire consequences to the man who dared compromise his one daughter than it did reward. No matter that pagan ritual of marriage—if her father was angry now, he would be uncontrollable if she was to tell him everything that had happened. No, she decided reluctantly, she must never reveal her secret, for that would be the final death sentence for Blacksword. Yet even so it seemed he faced much the same fate unless she could somehow convince her father to spare him.

With a vow to remain calm and unemotional no matter what, Rosalynde lifted a reasonable expression to her father. "Cleve has told you grim tales of Blacksword. I know he has. But you must understand—"

"What sort of name is that anyway? Blacksword, indeed. 'Tis the name of a ruffian, a knave, and only confirms what the boy has said."

"His name is Aric," Rosalynde put in. "He is from a place called Wycliffe."

Her father stared at her with narrowed eyes. "He told you this?"

Rosalynde nodded and stepped nearer to him. "He did not deny that he had an unsavory past, but he agreed to help us. And he was most solicitous. He even built a sling to carry Cleve in."

"A sling?"

At her father's curious tone, Rosalynde felt a faint spark of hope. "Didn't Cleve tell you? He was hurt and unable to walk. Blacksword—I mean, Aric—built a clever frame so that he could pull Cleve to safety." She watched as her father digested that bit of news and thoughtfully pulled at his chin. Then before he could dismiss that information she continued. "He hunted for us and kept us fed. He even made me a pair of slippers from the two rabbit skins."

Her father pursed his lips and looked away from her. When he finally returned his gaze to her, his face was still suspicous.

"The boy said that the man was struggling with you. That he had to protect you from—" He halted abruptly, clearly loathe to bring up the one possibility he wished not to think about.

"Cleve misunderstood." The lie slipped softly from her lips and she cringed inside at the unfair light she cast Cleve in. She would make it up to him, she promised herself. But she just could not let Blacksword die. "Cleve was still groggy from the wound to his head. He was suspicious of the man. He—he was perhaps a little ashamed that he was unable to provide for me."

Rosalynde held her breath, fearful to hope, yet unable to discount the considering expression on her father's face. Please, God, she earnestly prayed, please let him spare Blacksword.

There was a short silence before Sir Edward cleared his throat. In his solemn eyes Rosalynde fancied she could see his need for vengeance warring with a desire to be fair. Then he spoke and her hopes plummetted. "He is still a self-proclaimed murderer. A thief. A blackguard." He spat the word out in disgust. "The name Blacksword no doubt was earned through less than noble endeavors."

"But . . . but . . ." Rosalynde fumbled for words. "He wants to change. I know he does. If you could just give him a chance . . ." She trailed off despairingly.

"Mother of God, but you ask much of me!" he muttered with a scowl. Then he sat down in a sturdy chair and glowered over at her. "He's been flogged." He stopped. Then he took a slow breath and Rosalynde knew he had made up his mind. One way or the other, he had decided Blacksword's fate. "He's been flogged but he stood it well. I'll spare his life, Rosalynde. I'll spare his life. But that's all I'll do. There'll be no reward for him, only a hard job under a watchful eye. He'll be fed but he'll work strenuously for his due. Then when he proves himself—*if* he proves himself . . . Well, we'll see what happens then."

At this unexpected compromise, Rosalynde was completely taken aback. He would spare Blacksword's life! Blacksword would live! In a rush of heartfelt emotions, relief foremost among them, Rosalynde flew to where he sat. "Thank you, Papa. Oh, thank you," she cried as she hugged him fiercely. Then, when he stiffened in surprise, she stumbled back, embarrassed by her demonstrative outburst. But it was her turn to be surprised, for her father was staring up at her with a face suddenly stripped of any protective expression. For the span of less than a second he was not the strong father, the invincible man she'd always known. She saw a softness there, something touched by her spontaneous display of affection. In that instant she was reminded of the father he had been in her early years. Before everything had happened. But then he blinked and the father of the past eight years returned.

They stared at each other without speaking until he rose and dismissed her with a nod. For another moment Rosalynde lingered, still staring at him, but hesitantly now. Then she gave him a wavering smile and murmured another quick "Thank you," before she turned and walked away on legs that trembled. She did not see the bittersweet expression of both longing and sadness that swept over his face, nor the way his eyes followed her out of sight.

But her heart was lighter than it had been in a very long time.

Aric was dizzy from the pain, yet he refused to yield to it. In red-hot waves it washed over him. Every beat of his heart drove fresh daggers of fire into his back; every least trickle of sweat stung him with new and cruel agony. Flies buzzed around his head and settled on his tortured flesh, and he was torn between the excruciating torment of shrugging them off and the unbearable misery of letting them stay.

Christ's blood! When would this accursed waiting end? He'd stood the ungodly flogging, refusing to break no matter what torture her father meted out. He would die on his feet without a whimper or moan if it was his last act on this earth! But then the flogging had abruptly halted and he'd been left now, these long, agonizing minutes, to stand in the glaring sunlight, surrounded by the restless castlefolk, waiting for God only knew what would come next.

He closed his eyes against the bead of sweat that traversed his brow, then he shook his head sharply to clear his vision. Only by the most stringent exercise of willpower was he able to suppress the groan of pain that immediately rose to his lips, and he trembled from the very exertion of it. Once more he considered revealing the truth to her father. Maybe if he knew they were wed. Maybe if he knew she could already be carrying the fruit of his seed . . . Maybe there was still a way to save himself. Yet Aric was not so blinded by the painful blows to his back to realize the absolute futility of that line of reasoning. He gave a frustrated tug at each of the ropes tied so snugly at his wrists, then clenched his jaw in anger. She had probably run straightaway to her father with her tale of woe, painting him as foul a blackguard as she could. No doubt this flogging—and now this interminable wait— could be traced directly to her lily-white hands.

He swung his head slowly from one side to the other, searching among the faces that waited for the culminating of this public punishment. There were tradesmen and serfs there, men-at-arms and servants. Children crowded in among the women, clinging to their skirts as they peered in round-eyed awe at him. One little girl off to his left did not look afraid, however, only curious, and for some reason Aric stared at her. But then her mother grabbed the child and hustled her behind her skirts. "The devil dwells in those eyes," she hissed at her daughter and for everyone else's benefit. "Don't stare at him over long."

It was this which irritated Aric the most. He was beneath the contempt of every soul present. Even the little children were frightened of him, for their parents made certain of it. God, what hope was there for anything but a quick and merciful end to his suffering? Then a commotion rippled through the crowd and he braced himself against the expected resumption of the vicious flogging.

But to his surprise four burly men-at-arms approached him, and he was unexpectedly released from his helpless position. Quickly, before he could react to his sudden freedom, they tied his arms behind him. Then he was led across the bailey, through the crowd, which murmured now in bewilderment equal to his own, and hustled back down into the gloomy, foul-smelling donjon. His arms were untied and he was shoved painfully into the same fetid cell. Only then did one of the four guards say anything that shed a small light on these new goings-on.

"Use the water to make yourself presentable. Sir Edward will speak to you directly."

The door screeched shut, the bar was lowered with a

hollow thud, and Aric heard the tramp of the men's foot-steps as they ascended from the dank donjon. He stood there in the chill air, his damp skin shivering and lifting in goose bumps, and his mind filled with a myriad of questions. He did not know what was going on, nor why he was to be brought before her father, Sir Edward. Perhaps it was a miraculous reprieve.

More likely the man wished to cast the killing blow himself, he thought sourly. But then, why have him wash? It made no sense at all. Still, whatever the reason, Aric took some solace that he was at least to have a chance to face the man who would decide his fate. How he would proceed, what he would say, how he could defend himself against the accusations cast at his door, he could not yet predict. That would depend on the nature of the accusations and the temperament of the accuser. But *she* would not escape the truth with an accusation of rape, he vowed as he reached for the bucket of water. He grimaced in pain as his tortured flesh pulled against the muscles of his back. If she cried rape he would reveal the marriage. Though either of those was sufficient to condemn him, he would not let her escape unscathed.

The treachery was hers. She must suffer the consequences as well.

Sir Edward did not look up when the group of men approached. He sat at his huge table with papers and quills, ink and blotting sand strewn in seeming confusion before him. He remained purposefully absorbed in the boring list of fields and tenants and crop assignments as the men came to a clattering halt before him. Let the knave squirm, he thought as he moved his finger quite deliberately down the parchment. It would do him good. Yet honesty demanded that Sir Edward admit, at least to

himself, that he was nearly as uncomfortable with this in-
terview as this cursed fellow no doubt was.

His finger paused and a frown emphasized the creases
of his deeply lined face. Christ's blood, but it would be
easier to just stretch the man's neck. But in a moment of
weakness he'd promised otherwise to his daughter, and
now he found himself in an untenable position. In unfamiliar frustration his mind veered from fury to bewilderment, from absolute conviction to total bafflement. It was
not his way to be indecisive. By God, when a man made a
decision he must be true to his gut feelings and stick
closely to his words! To punish the man who mistreated
his only daughter had taken no great struggle of conscience. Yet Rosalynde's pleadings on the man's behalf had
created an unwelcome debate between his need for revenge and his need for justice. Between his common sense
and his emotions.

For a moment he saw how she'd looked up at him, with
her eyes so huge and her face so pale. How like her
mother she was, he thought. It was what he'd feared when
he'd sent her away those many years ago—to be reminded
every time he gazed upon her of the wife he'd lost. Yet
now he found an unexpected comfort in it. Like her
mother she was fair and sweet, like any rose, yet not so
fragile as she appeared. The same lips that had trembled
with emotion were as likely to thin with anger and purse
with displeasure, he realized. His frown eased as his own
wife's face came back to him. She had possessed those
very same lips that had been just as prone to smile with
tenderness and laugh with joyous abandon. He'd never
been able to deny the Lady Anne a thing. Was it any
wonder he could not deny their daughter?

One of the men shifted restlessly and Sir Edward came
back to the present with a blink of his suddenly mist-filled

eyes. His hand trembled slightly as he put the ledger page from him. But he firmly buried the image of his wife as he attended the unpleasant business before him. She'd been gone from him these eight long years. The fact that Rosalynde had her mother's same lustrous mahogany hair and that her mouth was cast from the identical mold changed nothing. He was still without his wife, though it pained him every day of his existence. But now he had his daughter back and he would be a good father to her. He was still Lord of Stanwood, however. No matter his promise to his beloved daughter, he still must ensure the safety of his people, her included. The hard-eyed brute before him would not be hanged; he'd already said as much. But as Sir Edward slid his narrowed gaze over the arrogant-looking knave, his resolve hardened. He would not be hanged. But he would damn well be brought to heel.

Sir Edward leaned his elbows on the table and made a steeple of his fingers as he watched the man closely. "You survived the flogging well enough, I see."

The man met his gaze evenly. "Aye."

Sir Edward's chin raised a notch. Too arrogant by half, he decided with grim amusement. But that would not last. He picked up the quill and dipped it into a pottery dish of ink. "Your name?"

There was a brief hesitation, just enough for Sir Edward to wonder if the answer given was a truthful one. "I am Aric."

"Aric." Sir Edward stared steadily at him. "From whence?"

Again the hesitation. "Wycliffe."

This one would be trouble, Sir Edward decided on the instant. On the pretext of writing down that information, he turned his eyes away from the even stare of the man before him. He was trouble and he would bear watching.

But he was big and looked strong as an ox. It was a rare thing to find a man of such physique. Even among his own knights few appeared his match. There was only one thing for it, Sir Edward decided. The man would be worked dawn to dusk, at the hardest, most taxing and menial of jobs. If he were bone-tired and dog-weary he could cause no mischief. Work and sleep would become the whole of yon Aric's life. He would either rise to it or bolt. At that moment Sir Edward was hard-pressed to decide which eventuality he would prefer.

"So, Aric of Wycliffe." He threw the quill down and leaned back in the heavy hide-covered chair. "You've taken your flogging well. Another less-just lord would have seen you hanged as well. However, since there is some doubt as to the precise extent of your crimes, I have decided to offer you a choice." He smiled slightly, pleased by this brilliant ploy he'd just thought of. "You may choose to work in my employ—to prove yourself, as it were. Or you may be treated as are all outlaws, and hanged."

His brows lifted in wry amusement when the man's jaw tightened at his words. "So, what say you to this? You bear the brunt of your own decision."

For a long moment the man did not reply. The silence stretched out so unnervingly that a blood vessel began angrily to throb in Sir Edward's temple. But just as he was about to leap from his chair in a fury over the man's outrageous effrontery, the huge brute gave a barely perceptible nod of his head.

"I thank you for making the choice my own," he said stiffly. He raised his chin and stared boldly at Sir Edward. "I accept your offer to work in your service. You may count me among your loyal subjects."

Sir Edward had to stifle an amazed chuckle as the man was escorted off by the four frowning guards. By God, but the knave made it seem *he'd* been the one to confer the favor instead of the other way around! And now he would be a most loyal subject? There was scant chance of that. A week of working with his back still afire from the flogging would test that loyalty well. Added to that, the grim dislike of the castle guard and the fear and contempt of the castle-folk would very likely see him straining in the harness.

Sir Edward felt well pleased with himself as he pushed away from the table and the remainder of his unfinished work. That fellow was too cocksure of himself to long endure such ignominy. Eventually he would break, and when he did the penalty would be great. No leniency would be forthcoming for even his least infraction of any castle rule. The man had been given his one and only chance. If he stretched the boundaries even the smallest bit, Rosalynde would not be able to object or intercede on his behalf.

13

Despite her all-consuming worry about Black-sword's condition, Rosalynde knew she must prepare for the evening meal—and her next meeting with her father—with great care. At midday, given all the commotion caused by the flogging, and then her own public display of temper, there had been no meal other than the hasty distribution of broken meats, bread, and cheese. Even the ale had been consumed on the run as men-at-arms, servants, and tradesmen alike had hurried from Sir Edward's furious path. But now the castle was calmer and a proper meal was called for. Accordingly she buried her concerns for her outlaw protector as best she could. She donned one of the several gowns her father had given her—gowns that had once been her mother's—and combed her long hair until it gleamed. To calm the rebellious waves she pulled two long tendrils back from either side of her brow and wove them together down the back of her head until she could not reach any farther. Then she took a short bit of cord and tied the strand securely, adding a sprig of lavender into the knot for good measure.

She had none of her ornaments, no jewels or ribbons, nor gowns of silk bedecked with braided trim. Yet she did not mourn their loss, for such items seemed quite insignificant to her now. Life was what mattered, she told herself as her thoughts once more veered to the man who had saved her at Dunmow. Being alive, being safe—those were the important things. The most sumptuous gown made from cloth of gold, worked entirely with silver threads and sparkling pearls and caught up in a girdle of the finest golden links, would mean far less to her than simply being able to breathe deeply and without fear, secure in the bosom of her own home.

Rosalynde spun slowly around on her heels, taking in the oddly shaped chamber to which she had returned. The room was quite the same as she recalled: rough stone walls built at flat angles to make almost a circle; six tall narrow windows so that a view of nearly the entire countryside could be had. Each window was set back into a recess, just the right size for a child to curl up in—or for a woman to sit back in, holding a fretting babe or comforting an ailing child.

For a long moment she stared around her, seeing the dusty plank floor, the plain high bed, and the slightly worn tapestry that hung above the bed. Yet what she saw in her mind's eye was a far different scene entirely. Oh, the chamber was much the same, but in her imagination it held a certain glow, a satisfying warmth. How happy she'd been then, she recalled as bittersweet memories tugged at her. How completely and utterly happy. She wiped away a stray tear, then stared around her as reality intruded once more. There was no warm glow now, though a small blaze fought the evening chill away. There was no happiness either. The room was the same except for the accumulated dust and its decidedly shabby appearance. But nothing else was the same.

With a deep breath she tried to shake off such depressing thoughts. It did no good to dwell on the past, she told herself as she rubbed her hand aimlessly across a sturdy wooden trunk. She frowned at the thick gray dust on her palm, then brushed her hand clean. When her mother had lived, the castle had shone like a rare gold coin. Now it was dark and dirty and sad.

Rosalynde squared her shoulders as she crossed to the door. If nothing else she could at least set the place to rights. She could see Stanwood dusted and scrubbed and clean once more. She might not be able to restore it to happiness—who could possibly know how to accomplish such a thing? But the rest of it she could handle. After all, managing a large household was precisely what her aunt had trained her to do.

Feeling somewhat better for having at least some course of action open to her, Rosalynde banked the fire, pulled the wood shutters tight across the windows, then finally left her chamber and headed for this next meeting with her father. They had seemed to have a confrontation every time they'd met so far. But this time she was determined it not be so. After all, she reasoned, there was no longer any cause for it. He already knew about Giles, and although she still felt the dire weight of responsibility for her younger brother's loss, she also knew there was nothing to be done for it. Time was the best healer for such pain, although in her father's case it seemed he'd not yet even recovered from his wife's death. Still, she thought as she moved silently down the steps, there was nothing she could do about that either.

The other matter of discord between them, that of the treatment of Blacksword, would also resolve itself, she hoped. She'd watched from a window in her chamber as the guards had untied him and led him away from the clearly disappointed crowd. Her relief had been immediate and overwhelming. He would not be killed! Yet fast on the heels of relief came a new fear. What might he reveal now that his life was spared? She had promised him a reward—a horse, weapons, even gold. But her father had made it clear he would not reward a man he considered a base scoundrel. However, despite her father, it would be in her best interests to find Blacksword some sort of reward, if only to buy his silence. Now that he had narrowly escaped with his life, he must realize how foolish it would be for him to claim her as his wife. Her father wouldn't hesitate to kill him if he knew all that had passed between them in the woods. No, she reassured herself, Blacksword would take whatever she could find for him as a reward and flee.

Rosalynde stopped at the base of the dim stairwell, absently noting how many torch bases were broken or simply not replenished with tallow-dipped rushes. But her concentration remained on Blacksword and how she should deal with him. Foremost among her worries was the condition of his cruelly flogged back. If it was not to fester it must be properly tended, and she was the best person to do it. But once again she was certain her father would object.

By rights she should not care if he suffered from his punishment. He'd behaved abominably toward her. But every time she thought of him suffering because of her, she cringed inside. It did not matter that their handfast vow and her promise to reward him were the only choices open to her at the time, nor that he had benefited far more than she had. She nevertheless could not completely absolve herself of the guilty feelings that consumed her.

He ruined me, she reminded herself harshly. He did it knowing that she would be ruined and knowing that their handfasting was not a marriage at all. He did it only to satisfy his own lust and greed. Yet when she thought of that despicable moment, when she remembered the de-

grading way he had used her for his own selfish pleasure . . .

A tremor rippled through her, dredging up unwanted
feelings and stirring a shameful heat deep in her belly.
Her entire body reacted most traitorously, tensing and
warming in her most private places, tingling with remembrance all over. She steadied herself against a solid stone
column as a faintness stole over her.

Oh, but she was too, too wicked, she berated herself, a
shameful hussy to have this disgusting response to such a
man as Blacksword. Yet no amount of self-reproach could
alter the undeniable facts. She had heard of the sin of lust.
It had been a common theme among the priests who visited Millwort. But she'd never truly understood precisely
what lust was. It had been easy to nod and agree with the
priests as they'd condemned those who sinned so wick-
edly. Only now was she beginning to understand the
power of such feelings, the overwhelming pull of one body
to another.

She took a shaky breath, willing calmness back to her
still-trembling limbs. After the evening meal ended she
would retire to the chapel, she decided. With fervent
prayer and the help of the Blessed Virgin she would surely
be able to conquer these sinful feelings. She would pray
for forgiveness, and pray for strength. And she would pray
especially that Blacksword would keep his silence.

"Eat, daughter. Eat," her father encouraged her as he
piled his own trencher high.

"I will," she replied, but with little enthusiasm. Even if
the food had been appetizing, she was too worried about
Blacksword's condition—and how she would see to his
wounds without her father's knowledge—to eat.

In her honor the meal was intended to be a feast, and

she had smiled warmly and spoken graciously to the several servants and numerous men-at-arms to whom she'd been introduced. But now that they were at the high table, all appearances of a celebratory feast ended, at least to her mind. As her father immersed himself in food and conversation with Sir Roger, who sat to his left, so also did the outside steward and Cedric, the seneschal, turn their attention to food and hearty conversation. Soon the entire hall reverberated with loud and raucous discourse and the constant clunk of wooden cups against wooden tables. As she stared around, completely ignored by the men who by far made up the bulk of the diners, she was consumed with a crushing loneliness. Even Cleve, whom she spotted at the far end of the hall seated with the other pages once the serving was done, clearly found no fault with the casual method of dining. At that moment she would have given anything to be with her dear lady aunt Gwynne, comfortably seated at the high table at Millwort.

She stared down at the unappealing meat and let herself succumb to homesickness for Millwort. There they did not rush to eat like swine to the trough. There each meal was a gracious occasion, complete with orderly servings and soothing music. At Millwort conversation was polite and subdued. But here! She cringed as a particularly foul oath floated up from the masses below. Here no one cared the least for proper deportment. She cast an irritated glance at her father. No one cared the least because the lord of the castle did not care either.

But she cared.

Her aunt had drummed the lessons into her head. But it was the example of good housewifery she'd set that had impressed Rosalynde the most. With a sudden gleam in her green and gold eyes, she stared in renewed interest about the hall.

As in the stairwell, fully a quarter of the wall-mounted torches were unlit due to unrefreshed rushes in tallow. The walls were grimy with soot and dirt and cobwebs. The floor was strewn with rushes that had twice outlived their usefulness. Old rushes meant table leavings, dog droppings, and a host of crawling and hopping vermin. And then there were the tables themselves. No cloths to cover them and none too clean. A sticky wine stain marred the oak trestle table she sat at. Crumbs marked the joints in the wood and nicks of various sizes gave evidence that many a knife had been crudely stuck upright on the surface. By every right they should have been immaculate and draped with pristine white cloths.

Her jaw jutted forward in righteous anger as she viewed the scene before her. Stanwood had not been so while her mother had lived. In the intervening years it had clearly become a man's abode, with no consideration for those comforts dear to a woman's heart. But now that she was here, Rosalynde intended to set things to right. And perhaps in the process she might be able to attend Blacksword.

Renewed by that prospect, she turned her determined gaze on her father. He was chewing vigorously, gesturing with his knife, which boasted the leg of a chicken on its greasy point.

"Father," she said as she mentally plotted out her course of action. "Father," she called a little louder, plucking at his sleeve. "Father!"

At that Sir Edward turned to face her. "You needn't shout at me, child—"

"Oh, but 'tis clear I must. How else might I be heard in this din?" Then at his disapproving look she hastily changed her sharp tone. "It's just that I'm not accustomed to such a rowdy meal. And . . . and . . . the table was not even washed."

Her father glanced down at the table, then out over the boisterous group who peopled the hall. He opened his mouth as if to speak, then slowly closed it and stared about him even more intently.

" 'Tis a trifle untidy. I'll warrant you that," he finally conceded. "And as for their rowdy manner, well, 'tis only right considering the days of searching for you. They celebrate now in your very honor."

Rosalynde was wise enough to look suitably humbled, and to her relief he appeared somewhat mollified. He laid his knife down and took up his goblet instead, drinking deeply before he spoke again.

"I'll see that Cedric has the tables cleaned." He gave her a long look. "And the rushes refreshed." He met her steady gaze once more, then let out a loud sigh. "It shall all be cleaned. I'll see to it."

"Perhaps you would let me see to it." She held her breath, hoping he would agree.

"Cedric is the seneschal. 'Tis his place."

"A good housewife runs her own household. This is what Lady Gwynne has prepared me for."

He seemed to take that in well enough and even nodded his head twice as he considered her words. "But you are not a wife yet, are you?"

Rosalynde's eyes widened at his casually stated words, and for a moment her heart leapt in fear. Only by the most stringent exercise of self-control was she able to calm her rapid pulse. He did not know, she told herself firmly. He did not know the truth, that she was by rights wife to Blacksword.

"No," she said, slowly and carefully. "I am not precisely a housewife, but I have the skills nonetheless. I would gladly take over the keys to Stanwood, Father, if you would but let me."

When his grin of approval came, followed promptly by a fatherly pat on her hand, Rosalynde felt a heady burst of power. She was to run a household of her own at last! And though he'd balked at her initial outburst, her father had willingly succumbed to her meekly worded request. So that was the lay of the land, the realization dawned on her. That was the way to best achieve her ends. Was that how her mother had handled her intimidating husband, through mildness and sweetness? As she finished her meal in companionable silence with him, she vowed to curb her too-quick tongue and stifle her often-hasty temper. If it meant killing her father with kindness to see Stanwood Castle set to rights, she would do it. Though he agreed now, she did not doubt that he would balk later, for it was more than cleaning she intended. Uniforms, fresh linens, new tapestries—these and more would be required to see Stanwood attain its deserved glory. He would mislike the inconvenience and complain of the cost, no doubt, but in the end he would be pleased. And he would be proud of her as well.

Rosalynde did not give her father the opportunity to forget or to renege on his promise. No sooner was the meal done and the men's gaming and gambling begun than she cornered him.

"There's much to plan and much for me to see before I can begin my work. How would you have me proceed, Father?"

Sir Edward looked down at her sincere face then glanced distractedly about the teeming hall. "The rushes, I suppose. Cedric will see that fresh ones are cut. And the tables, of course—"

"No, no. I do not mean what must be done. I've faith

enough that I can find those necessary tasks. No, what I mean is, will you tell Cedric and the cook that they must consult now with me? And will you give their keys over into my keeping?"

At first he appeared very prone to balk, and words of argument rose in her throat. But she determinedly smiled up at him, a hopeful, enthusiastic expression on her face. Finally he expelled a great gust of air and rubbed his chin absently. "Can it not wait till the morn?"

"I would like to plan this evening so that I may begin the work at dawn's light."

Once again he sighed and this time he nodded. "As you wish, Rosalynde. Come along then, let's be done with it so I may all the sooner retire to my games." He had a disconcerted expression on his face as they left the hall, but Rosalynde was smiling broadly.

The cook was resistant although he did not say a word as Sir Edward took his keys and handed them to Rosalynde. However, she could see the displeasure at being usurped written clearly in the stout fellow's eyes. Cedric, by contrast, seemed almost relieved. He untied the metal ring of keys from his girdle and handed them over to her with a shy grin and several bobs of his head. Reassured by his acceptance, she laid a hand on his arm before he could follow her father back to the great hall.

"Could you perhaps show me to the stillroom? Healing is a particular interest of mine, and I thought I might begin by inspecting the supplies kept there." She started forward, allowing him no time to protest. "And along the way you could tell me which key opens which door."

The bailey was cloaked in darkness by the time Rosalynde finally exited the stillroom. She had long before sent Cedric off, and as she'd examined the pouches of dried leaves and ground roots and mentally catalogued the

valuable vials of essences and tinctures, the time had sped
by unnoticed. But that was to the good, she decided as she
hurried across the grassy yard with the concoction she had
prepared held tight in her hands. Since most of the
castlefolk had already sought their beds and pallets, perhaps she would not encounter any opposition to her desperately conceived plan.

Ever since she'd seen Blacksword led away, the condition of his sorely abused back had tortured her. Throughout the tiresome afternoon and the dismal evening meal
she had been consumed with both guilt for her part in his
flogging and concern for the cruel injury he still suffered
from the whip's vicious bite. She'd been determined to see
to his wounds, but she'd been equally certain that her
father would not approve. It was only when her father had
agreed to let her run the household—and had given her all
the keys—that she had come up with this idea. Now, with
a wash of goldenrod and a decoction of milfoil mixed with
boiled and cooled tallow to form an ointment, she meant
to seek Blacksword out, see to his wounds, and somehow
convince him to keep their secret to himself.

She was not precisely sure where to look. She had managed to get some information from Cedric under the guise
of general inquiries about the organization of the castle.
She learned that unmarried male servants slept in the
great hall during cold weather, or else in several of the
stairwell niches. But in the warmer months many of them
slept in the stables. The pages slept in a group adjacent to
the knights' quarters. What few women servants there
were slept either adjacent to the kitchens or near the areas
of their particular duties. She had not seen Blacksword
anywhere near the great hall. In addition, logic told her
that her father would not allow a man he considered dangerous to roam the castle freely. For despite her father's

grudging assent to spare Blacksword's life, Rosalynde knew he would be watching and waiting for him to make a mistake. Under the circumstances, it was most likely that Blacksword was consigned to some corner of the stables.

Her heart began to pound as she neared the black shadow that was the main stable building. A single light glowed weakly from an opened shutter, but all else lay still and dark as she felt her way along the wood-timbered building. When her fingers felt the rough frame of the opening, she paused and took a shaky breath.

You have nothing to fear from him, she tried to reassure herself. In her home castle her safety was assured. He would not dare to harm her.

But it was not the threat of harm that had her trembling so, a small voice taunted her. His hands had not hurt her at all, but instead had caressed her with exquisite tenderness. *God save me from just such caresses,* she prayed with quickening breath. It was only the fearful knowledge that he must be in terrible pain that forced her to step cautiously into the stable opening. Neither revenge nor passion would be on his mind this night, she told herself bravely. Relief was what he would want most, and she carried the promise of relief in her own hands.

The stable was feebly lit by a lone flickering candle in a scraped-hide lantern. Unsure where exactly to look, Rosalynde was drawn to the weak golden light. Past the stalls of the great destriers she crept on silent feet. The lantern was hung at the entrance of the last stall, and when she reached it she stopped. A few low murmurs had already alerted her that someone was about. Despite her tiny tremor of fear, she crept farther until her eyes were able to fully take in who was occupying the stall. Even in the full gleam of the flickering light she could hardly believe her eyes. Blacksword sat on an overturned hay bier, bare to the waist, and some hussy had her hand on his bare shoulder. Even worse, the tart was bending forward, providing him a clear view down her loose blouse of the cleavage between her overdeveloped breasts!

Rosalynde noted with some satisfaction that at least his eyes were closed, but that was small comfort. It was clear the girl was there to offer him solace for his pain, but what sort of solace was highly questionable to Rosalynde's mind. The two were so engrossed—her making soft cluck- ing noises as she slid her hand back and forth on his shoul- der, and him wincing as he tried to find an easier position —that Rosalynde had no idea how long she might have stood there before they would have noticed her. But when she saw the girl reach out for an old horse rag to wipe the sweat from Blacksword's cruelly cut back, Rosalynde could not keep her silence any longer.

"Don't touch him with that!"

At once two heads swiveled around to stare at her in wary surprise. The girl's face quickly assumed an expres- sion of guilt and subservience as she hitched her blouse higher on her shoulder. Blacksword's face, however, al- tered from caution to curiosity and then, it seemed, to satisfaction. But it was suspicion that ultimately lingered as his gaze narrowed and his lips thinned in sarcasm.

" 'Tis a hard-hearted pair you and your father make. He sees the wounds formed with an unjust flogging, and you make sure no healing may take place. Do you begrudge me the ease of this kind maiden's ministrations?" he fin- ished with an ill-disguised taunt.

Rosalynde was too aggravated to think straight. "Her ministrations . . . Her ministrations!" she sputtered. "If you wish the wounds to fester, by all means, let her minis- ter to you with that filthy rag!"

Had it not been for the mortified girl's hasty exit,

Rosalynde might have stormed away from the little stall herself. As it was, however, when the girl sneaked silently past her, she was left alone to face the scowling Blacksword. Under the circumstances she was hard-pressed to recall exactly why it was she had sought him out.

For a long, uneasy moment he continued to glare at her. Then with a movement that seemed effortless but that she was certain pained him greatly, he rose to his feet and faced her. "What in the name of hell do you want?"

In the narrow confines of the low-ceilinged stable, Rosalynde was suddenly intimidated by the powerful man who stood before her. He was the one who was hurt. He was the one who needed help. Yet she felt unaccountably like fleeing his awesome presence.

"Well?" he prompted with a sneer. "You came here for a reason, so let's have it. Or do I dare suspect that it was only jealousy that drew you here?" He smiled sarcastically. " 'Tis not likely a newlywed like yourself would long abide her husband's dalliance with the dairymaid."

It was that repugnant comment with its attendant innuendo which drove her at last to a furious response. "I'm no newly-wed bride and you are most emphatically not my husband! And I don't care if you . . . if you—"

"Be careful, my sweet wife." He goaded her still further. " 'Tis said that walls may have ears. Would you flaunt our marital discord so openly?" To this vile remark he added more insult by arching one of his brows in mocking superiority.

"This is not marital discord," Rosalynde hissed, but with a cautious glance over her shoulder toward the rest of the darkened stable. "This is not marital discord," she repeated in a quieter yet no less adamant tone. "This is . . . this is . . . it's pure dislike!"

She stared at him belligerently, daring him to deny that

she heartily disliked him. A part of her was firm in her
position, ready to argue that she found him completely
detestable and thoroughly unlikable. But that same small
voice crept through her defenses to whisper that there
were some things about him that didn't repulse her. There
were some things she didn't dislike about him at all. But
though she tried to ignore that irritating voice, as she
glared at Blacksword it became more and more difficult.
He was so overpoweringly masculine; he had such a com-
manding presence. In the closeness of the room as he
stood bare-chested before her, she began suddenly to
grow warmer as unwelcome remembrances of his heated
embrace overwhelmed her. To make matters even worse,
his thoughts seemed to follow the same path, for his implacable gray gaze slowly slipped down to take in every
aspect of her appearance. Even though she was completely covered by the high-necked aqua wool gown, she
felt the full force of that gaze, and its effect on her was
immediate.

Of a sudden she felt surrounded by his virile presence,
suffocated by unwanted memories and wicked desires.
She took a harsh breath as his eyes rose back up to meet
hers, and in his gaze she saw a promise—a threat—of
things to come. In a panic she stepped back, determined
only that she must escape while she could. But Blacksword was too swift. As if he read her mind, he reached a
quick hand forward to grab her arm. At once the two vials
of medications she'd prepared fell onto the layer of straw
between them. He glanced down at them, then back up at
her again.

"For me?" he asked with mocking courtesy. "Has my
wood nymph come back to heal me? Can this be the same
girl who had me flogged? God's blood, but I believe she
must be feeling guilty if she's come bearing healing oint-

ments." He tugged on her arm, drawing her forward against her will. "Is that it, my wild Rose? Are you feeling sorry for the deep slice of those cruel thorns of yours?"

" 'Twas not of my doing," she cried as she tried unsuccessfully to free herself from his firm clasp. "I've no cause to be feeling any guilt on your account!"

But the truth was she did feel guilt, and to her chagrin he seemed somehow to know.

"You feel the guilt," he averred. "But it is no more or less than any noblewoman feels. A man risks life and limb while the fair maiden applauds and cheers. 'Tis only when the fanfare is done and the excitement over that she feels remorse for the injuries he suffers." He released her hand abruptly and let go a cynical laugh. "Come, my fair Rose, assuage your guilt." He turned his back to her and squared his shoulders. "Smooth your balm over my wounds. I daresay it will sting more bitterly than ever the whip did."

Freed of his confining grasp, Rosalynde's first instinct was to turn and flee. But the sight of the angry red welts that crisscrossed his back and the brown crusted blood that had dried in place held her rooted to her spot. She had caused those terrible marks. She had caused him to suffer untold pain—to suffer it even yet. Despite her fear of his anger and her mistrust of his motives, the cruelly marked flesh before her would not let her leave. Her fury dissolved into hot choking shame, and tears blurred her eyes as she finally stooped, shaking, to retrieve the two vials.

"I-I need water," she whispered to that broad, unmoving back. "I'll return directly." Then she grabbed a nearby bucket and fled into the dark. But if Rosalynde thought to find some solace in the empty night, she was sorely disappointed. When she returned with the water, her throat was still thick with emotion and her heart pounded an unsteady rhythm. But her tears were gone and her hands trembled no more.

Blacksword still stood as he had, although to her eyes he seemed not so erect as before. But he stiffened at her entrance and his voice was as taunting as ever. "Ready to begin, *milady*?" he asked with biting emphasis on that last word.

But Rosalynde did not rise to his baiting words. She was too undone by the gruesome task before her and too distressed by her part in his pain. "Could you sit?" she asked in a small voice. After only a moment's hesitation he once again sat down on the overturned hay bier.

Viewed up close, Blacksword's back was a dreadful sight indeed. Although she had a talent for healing, Rosalynde had never acquired the ability to stifle her stomach's adverse reaction to the ravages of the flesh. Yet on this occasion, more than any other, she knew she must suppress the horror and force herself to hold steady. Her deepest dread was that in order to soothe and heal his fiery wounds, she must first cause him even further pain. But it could not be helped, and with a deep calming breath she set to her task.

"This will be painful," she murmured after she ripped a generous length of linen from the hem of her kirtle and soaked it in the cool water. Then, clenching her teeth against what she knew she must do, she pressed the cloth to the welts across his upper back. She felt the tremor through the fabric, the silent quiver as his tortured skin reacted to the pressure of her hands. Something in her quivered too, something deep inside, and she had to muffle her own moan of dismay. But he gave no voice to the agony he surely felt, and she could do no less. With hands as gentle as was possible, she swiftly soaked the crusted-on blood and washed it away. She braced her left hand against one of his arms as she worked, and oddly enough, it was the warmth and solidity of that unharmed skin which gave her the strength to continue. Down the valley of his spine and across the hard muscles she cleansed away the dirt and blood and tatters of hanging skin. The cleansing wash was next, and finally she gingerly applied the ointment, sliding it across welts and tears alike, smoothing it across his ravaged flesh, feeling it soften and melt against the heat of his skin. Only when Rosalynde was finished with her work did her rigid stance give way, and her slight sag must have transmitted itself to him.

"Well done, milady," he mocked in a voice low and filled with tension. "But know you not that the gentlest touch of a beautiful maiden's fingers causes far more torture to a man than does the severest flogging?"

She jerked upright and glared at the back of his tawny head. "Is it as painful as the hangman's noose?"

At that his head twisted slightly and he peered at her with eyes of the deepest slate gray.

"That's something I cannot answer with any degree of knowledge."

"Well, I can answer it!" she snapped, furious that even in the midst of his pain he could still mock her. "Those men hung there, choking and . . . and twisting. They tried to breathe . . . You heard them! That could have been you! Why cannot you be content to at least be alive!"

In her outburst of anger and frustration and awful memory she was not immediately aware of the tears that filled her eyes. When they spilled over her dark lashes to splash down her cheeks, she brushed them away with the back of one hand, humiliated to cry before him. But as she turned to flee his presence, he stood up and caught her wrist once more. For one galvanizing moment her shimmering eyes locked with his glittering stare. Then his grip tightened and his eyes narrowed with emotion.

"I am very glad to be alive, *milady*. But content? I'll only be content when what is rightfully mine becomes mine."

"But . . . but I tried to get your reward for you," Rosalynde stammered. "I really did—"

"And what of yourself?" he interrupted her. "You are mine by right of your handfast vow." His eyes bored into hers with an intensity that was frightening. "You are mine by right of possession."

"No," she whispered, wishing to deny the terrible truth of his words. "No, I am no possession, most especially not yours." But saying the words did not make it so, and she quaked at the awful truth of what he said. There was a long, tense silence before he dropped her hand.

"Will you tell your father, or shall I?" he asked in a voice low and quiet, yet filled nonetheless with menace.

"You can't be serious," she gasped. She stared up at him in horror. "Surely you know that would be a death sentence."

"Shall you tell him we are man and wife—truly and in every way—or shall I?" he persisted, as if he'd not heard her words at all.

"I shall deny it. . . ." Rosalynde shook her head slowly, her eyes never leaving his face. "You are mad," she whispered when she recognized the dark determination in his face. "He will have you slain," she insisted. "You will not live to spread your tale."

" 'Tis no doubt he would not see the truth come out any more than you," he replied caustically. "But as for me—" He stopped and his expression grew grim. "There are things I must do. Things I will not delay." He reached for his shirt then turned a mocking smile on her. "Take heart,

Lady Rosalynde. If he is so bloodthirsty as you believe and has me struck down for saying the truth, then you will at least be free of me. After all, that *is* what you desire most, is it not?" Again he fixed her with a piercing look.

Rosalynde was flustered and confused by his paradoxical words. She was not sure at all what she wanted of this man, but one thing was certain: She did not want to see him struck down, especially at her father's hands.

"I would not wish you dead," she answered, so quietly that the words went all but unheard.

He cocked his head slightly, and one brow lifted skeptically. "You refuse me to husband but you would not see me dead," he mused aloud as if he pondered a weighty matter. Then his gaze sharpened and his voice grew harsh. "Unfortunately, there appears to be no other choices. If the truth comes out you say I shall be slain, and yet I cannot live with less than the truth. So you see. . . ." He trailed off with a mocking smile that seemed to make light of the words which struck her so deeply. "There is no middle road. You may have one or the other, but nothing else."

"But why?" she cried, more unsettled than ever. "Why must it be only one or the other? Why can you not be content—"

"Because the vow was made," he cut her off as he dropped the shirt and grabbed her by the arms. "Because we are handfast wed." His head lowered and his searing gaze met her stunned eyes. "Because you are my wife. Mine."

Then his lips descended on hers with a fierce ardor that rocked her back on her heels. Anger, pain, and desire flared between them in that kiss. He was harsh and demanding, forcing her mouth open, slipping his tongue between her startled lips. Yet any rational thoughts of repugnance and horror melted away in the heat of his emotion. The very savageness of his kiss, the hard possessiveness of it, seemed perversely to make her softer and more pliable until she was fitted intimately against him, tilted backward in his implacable embrace.

When he at last pulled back from her she was off balance and gasping for breath. Their eyes met and in that instant Rosalynde felt as if he'd discovered some secret about her, as if she'd somehow given herself away. Then he smiled and she was suddenly sure of it. She struggled out of his arms, confused and frightened by the unsettled feelings inside her.

"There's no reason to put if off, Rose. I would have the truth of our union made known. Already I have delayed too long, dallying at your skirts when there are urgent matters that require my attention." He halted and his features darkened. For a moment he seemed lost in thought.

In the brief silence Rosalynde found her voice. "Dallying at my skirts!" She sputtered in outrage. "You cannot blame your foolishness on me! Oh, but you are truly quite mad!"

"Perhaps I am, Rose. Only time will tell. So run to your father and tell him. Tell him I kissed you in the stable. Tell him I made love with you in the forest." He laughed at her wide-eyed look of shock. "Tell him we are man and wife, or else I will. And then my blood will be on your hands."

It was this last that lent wings to her feet. She fled through the stable, uncaring of where she ran so long as she escaped his mocking words and taunting laugh. Out into the castle yard she dashed, across the dusty bailey until she reached the great hall and the narrow stone stairs that led up the east tower. But even when she attained her own chambers and slammed the door closed, she was not able to dismiss his tormenting words from her mind.

She was gasping for breath as she hastily disrobed, still panting as she nervously twisted her long hair into one thick plait. She could not tell her father the truth. Yet would it not go even worse for Blacksword if he was the one to reveal it all? Torn by her conflicting emotions—he was horrid and deserved whatever hand fate dealt him, but she could not bear to see him hurt again—she climbed into her bed and flung a heavy sheepskin over her. The dark warmth of her bed, however, was of no comfort whatsoever, for no matter what she did—tell or keep her silence—it would all come to the same end. If her father knew, he would most certainly have Blacksword punished, undoubtedly to the point of death. She knew that with a surety she could not shake. And then, just as Blacksword had said, his blood would be on her hands.

She buried her head in her arms, wishing to blot out the entire world as she huddled in her misery. Why must he be so stubborn? Why must he be so inflexible?

But as her utter exhaustion gave way to the numbing relief of sleep, she was not entirely certain whether it was Blacksword's inflexibility that disturbed her so, or her father's.

14

Rosalynde was awake before dawn. As she made her way down to the great hall, the fire was just being lit and the tables were being assembled by four menservants. Two harried women came in carting fresh pitchers of ale and baskets filled with the previous day's bread for breaking the night's fast.

The rushes were more than disgusting, Rosalynde noted in passing. They appeared even worse by day than by night. Yet the many tasks that faced her in order to put the castle to rights were not uppermost in her mind. Not at the moment.

She had slept fitfully, waking over and over again to worry about the ultimatum Blacksword had given her. Either she would reveal all, or he would; that summed up his unyielding position. Yet she was equally determined to keep their secret from her father. Now, as she slipped past the tall oak door, she intended to confront him once more. If she could just get him to delay. If she could just convince him to hold his tongue, even if it was only for a little while.

On the ramparts the guards were changing, while in the castle yard servants and men-at-arms both were beginning their day's tasks. A gang of young boys made their way to the well, carrying empty buckets on either side of their shoulder yokes. They ceased their boisterous chatter when they spied her and speedily doffed their assortment of misshapen caps. But they gaped at her with mouths half opened and stared without the least thought for their manners.

Another area lacking, she thought as she gave them a wan smile and hurried past. Stanwood was sorely lacking in any of the amenities of life. Last night's meal had been mediocre at best. The housekeeping was deplorable. The castle children had no manners. And where, she wondered with a frown, were the women servants? She'd seen only the two in the great hall this morning, and a few more last night. There was the dairymaid as well, she recalled sourly. But she quickly dismissed that hussy from her mind. The women of the castle were few and far between, and those she'd seen were ragged, poorly trained, and clearly overworked. Stanwood had obviously become a man's domain in the years since her mother's death. But all that was about to change.

Rosalynde lifted the end of her girdle and felt the reassuring weight of the keys that hung there. She was mistress now and she would see things put to right, one way or another. And the first thing she would do was buy Blacksword's silence.

The storerooms yielded a suitable beginning to her plan —one well-mended but clean chainse of soft linen and a supple tunic of deep-green kendal. With that in hand plus clean wash rags, and more of the balm she'd prepared, she was ready to face him. But when she reached the stable, she was taken with a terrible case of nerves.

What if he kissed her again? Her logical self knew that a kiss was the very least she should be worried about. What really mattered was what he might say—or even worse, what he might do. But as in every other instance, she was not at all logical where Blacksword was concerned.

She halted at the stable door and pressed one hand to her fluttering stomach. Do not think of him in that way, she ordered herself sternly. He was only another of her father's many servants, and in need of her healing skills. No more, no less. But despite such sensible reasoning, her heart thundered furiously and her mouth was as dry as carded wool. As she forced one foot forward and then the other, she consoled herself with the thought that he might not be there at all.

But he was there. She heard his low voice and then his grunt of pain, followed by a heavy thud. Fearing the worst, she flew around a low wall only to stop short at the scene that greeted her. Blacksword squatted next to a heavy granite block. The thick-bellied stable marshal was staring at him with undisguised awe, a foolish grin of pleasure on his brown-seamed face.

"I'd ne'er ha' thought it possible if I ha'n't seen it with me own eyes!" The man patted the block proudly, then lifted a short steel mallet and brought it down once sharply on the solid stone. "Now I can work easier without them fool boys gettin' in me way." He glanced at Blacksword again and screwed up one side of his mouth. "Ye've got the brawn, boy. Now it remains to see if ye got the brains." Once more he patted the stone before he turned and then spotted Rosalynde.

"Milady!" He looked at her with wide, disbelieving eyes, as if the thought of the lady of the castle setting foot in the stables was quite beyond him. He bobbed his head respectfully. "Is there . . . is there somethin' I can be helpin' you with, milady?" He bobbed his head again.

Rosalynde's eyes strayed from him to Blacksword and then quickly back to the tongue-tied marshal. It was far easier to look at him than at the hard-eyed man whose gaze even now was causing her skin to heat.

"You . . . you may go now. I only came to tend this . . . this man's wounds." She thrust out the vial with the ointment in it as if to verify that she spoke the truth. "He will not work so well if . . . if his wounds should fester."

But the stableman seemed unlikely to argue with her no matter what reason she gave. He was clearly uncomfortable around a noblewoman and was only too happy to leave her to her task.

"I've harness to mend. And two shields." He shuffled around, giving her a cautious sidelong glance. "Just send him back to me when ye've finished with him, if ye please, milady."

With no further excuse to avoid it, Rosalynde finally looked back at Blacksword. He had remained as he was, squatting beside the great stone he'd obviously moved for the older stable marshal. But when her eyes met his he slowly stood up. Once again she was struck by the sheer animal beauty of the man. He exuded a raw power, tempered by the shrewd light of intelligence in his clear gray eyes. There was a pride evident in him. It was there in the way he squared his shoulders, the way he held his head. The way his gaze never faltered. In that moment she was sure that he was more than what he seemed. He was no common servant, no serf born to an existence of toil and labor. He'd known more than that in his life. And yet she could not get around the fact that he was still a common criminal.

Rosalynde bit her lower lip as she stared at him, all but forgetting her original purpose in seeking him out. It was only when he glanced briefly at the stable marshal who was busy ferrying the tools of his trade nearer the relocated stone, then returned his gaze to her that she forced herself back to the task at hand.

"If . . . if you'll remove your clothes. Your shirt," she hastened to clarify in a strained voice.

"Yes, milady," he murmured politely. But he let his eyes travel over her in a leisurely fashion before he gave her a faint mocking grin, then pulled the torn, soiled shirt over his head. He tossed it unceremoniously aside and stared boldly at her.

"Turn around," she croaked out as she blushed scarlet from his impudent gaze. He was a wretched beast, purely a devil, she seethed, until the sight of his mutilated back chased every other thought aside. She stared at it sickly. Scabs had formed in the night, but his efforts in moving the stone had clearly broken the wounds open. Fresh blood trickled across the crusted remnants of the ointment. That, combined with the many raised welts gave his wide back a horribly scarred appearance. Even though she was confident of her ointment's ability to heal the wounds without serious scarring, if he continued to break the wounds open, no amount of her skill could help.

"Why was this man put to such heavy work? Look at his back!" she demanded of the silent stableman. Once given vent, her anger would not abate. "Can't you see what your thoughtlessness had caused?"

" 'Tweren't me, milady. 'Tweren't me," the man vowed earnestly as he faced her furious scowl. " 'Twas Sir Roger as said he was to be worked dawn to dusk, and hard too. I'm only doin' as I was told. Truly, I am!"

"Sir Roger?" She glared at the older man. "And who does Sir Roger get his orders from?"

The man did not answer. He did not have to. Rosalynde guessed at once from his suddenly pale face that Sir Roger must answer only to her father. And that brought things right back around to the original problem that had driven her here to the stables: Blacksword and her father. A vein throbbed in her temple and quickly grew to an aching rhythm. Her father and Blacksword. Between the two of them and their unreasonable stubbornness she was stretched like a taut rope. It was awful enough when they both tugged with equal pressure, but the two of them were pulling at her in erratic bursts and always from unpredictable directions. How long could she balance between them?

Seeing the stable marshal's nervous shifting from one foot to the other, she let out a weary sigh. "I'll speak to my father. You need not worry on that score."

The man needed no more than that to consider himself dismissed. With a final bob of his head he backed to the door, then eased himself through and disappeared. But though he was relieved to escape an awkward confrontation, Rosalynde was granted no such favor. Alone in the stable once more with Blacksword, she felt her righteous anger at his mistreatment give way to near resignation. He was going to be difficult, that was clear. She'd been a fool to hope otherwise.

"So," he said as his clear gray eyes locked with hers. "You shall speak to your father. And on my behalf. But just how much shall you say?" His brow arched skeptically. "I await your answer, sweet wife."

"Don't call me that!" she hissed, casting an alarmed glance about them.

"Do you deny it yet?"

Of course she did. She must. Yet Rosalynde knew that she had to take a different tack with him. She bit down on her lower lip and took the stopper from the vial. "I came here to see to your wounds. Can I not attend that without quarreling with you?"

There was a brief silence. Then she made the mistake of raising her eyes back up to his. He was staring at her with an unfathomable expression on his face. Not angry, for a change. She could detect little discernible emotion at all. But her stomach nonetheless tightened in complete awareness of him.

"It's hardly quarreling I have in mind," he said in a slow, husky tone.

It was enough to send all thought of ointments and wounds flying right out of her head, to be immediately replaced by other thoughts far too wicked to be proper. But she refused to respond to his innuendo and instead addressed the real topic that rested so uneasily between them.

"I have thought long on what you said last night," she began, lowering her eyes from his unsettling gaze.

"And have you come to a conclusion?" he asked lightly, although she detected an edge of tension in his voice.

Rosalynde took a slow breath and deliberately moved to his side. Her hands trembled slightly as she poured a palmful of the ointment, then began intently to apply it to his back. She was relieved that he did not stop her but only twisted his head slightly to keep his eyes on her face. Still, she knew she could not avoid answering his question.

"I need time," she finally whispered. "Just a little time," she hastened to add before he could reply. "If you knew how dangerous your position is—"

"You apply your medicine to my back even now. Do you think I do not know how dangerous it is for me here?" he snapped back.

Her hands fell away from him and he turned to face her. Only inches separated them. "I am your father's newest slave." He said the word as if it tasted foul upon his tongue. "You promised me a reward. You took the handfast vow with me. But once here you deny it all." His angry eyes bored into hers. "You are my wife. I'll take only that as my reward."

"But he will never have you as husband to his only daughter! Don't you see?" she pleaded. "You have no title . . . no lands."

"And if I did? Would he have me then? Would you?"

The words that had risen in her throat died suddenly at such a strange comment from him. It was beyond comprehension for a noblewoman and a commoner to wed. It was simply unheard of. Yet in the long moment that they stared at one another she thought once more how unlike any common man he was, even from the first time she had laid eyes on him. His bearing was too noble. His pride too apparent. Then her brow creased suspiciously even as unreasonable hope welled in her breast.

"Who are you?" she murmured. She stared at him as if he were someone she'd never seen before. "Who are you and how did you come to be on the gallows of Dunmow?"

He stared back at her too, and for a moment she thought he might reveal some startling story to her. Perhaps he was a prince bewitched, as in the tale of the two sisters and the bear. Or else a nobleman tormented by a jealous and vengeful sprite. Yet just as her rational self knew that there were no sprites and no bewitchings except in stories and legends, she also knew that for all her hopes to the contrary, he was unlikely to be any more than he appeared: a blackguard and a rogue. Charming at times. With a rare streak of compassion, even. But he was a rogue nonetheless, and her father would never see him as suitable.

He shrugged and his eyes seemed to become harder, as if he deliberately wished to shut out the past.

"I am Aric. From Wycliffe. I told you that before."

"Who was your father?" she pressed. She was suddenly angry at his apparent evasiveness and his threat that still hung over her.

"My father was a man of no great note," he replied after only a moment's pause. "I was the last of my mother's children. Wycliffe held naught for me, so . . ." He shrugged as if that should explain the rest. But it explained nothing, and Rosalynde became even more angry.

"Wycliffe held naught for you? Probably because you'd already stolen everything of value that there was. Then you moved on until finally they caught you in Dunmow." She grabbed the stopper and slapped it back into the mouth of the vial. "Yes, I promised you reward! Yes, I wedded you, knowing you were already condemned to die! But I never thought you would . . . you were . . ." She stumbled over the words, for even to her they sounded exceedingly foolish. She'd not expected him really to be a thief or a murderer? It was only the secret wishes of a child, she realized.

But not only of a child, the unwelcome thought came to her. She had played the woman to his man. The wife to his husband. And the very intensity of that joining—the never-suspected pleasure of it—had blinded her anew. She wanted him to be more than he was because . . . because it somehow made what they'd done together seem a little less wrong.

"You never thought I would be around to demand that I be paid?" He finished her sentence with his own conclusion. "Can this be true?" He grabbed both of her arms and gave her a hard shake. "What a truly heartless wench you are, *Lady Rosalynde*. So tell me, why do you hesitate to tell all to your father? If you are so certain he will punish me with death, why not tell him all and be finished with it?"

"I do not want you dead!" Rosalynde cried in answer to the last of his questions. "But if you hold fast to this mad course of yours—"

His grip changed at her stammered-out words. His hand tightened, but now he only pulled her a little nearer. "If not dead, then alive? But I have to question why. Why, Rose? What will you gain by my presence at Stanwood?" His eyes swept her pale, frightened face. One of his hands moved to pluck a bit of straw from her hair. Then he ran his knuckle lightly along the curve of her cheek. "Could it be that my thorny little Rose wants both the sun and the storm?" He smiled at her look of bewilderment, but there was no warmth in his eyes.

"I am not acceptable to you as a husband," he explained mockingly. "But as a lover . . ." He pulled her up against him then, and the heat of his body and hers together sent a fiery shiver through her. As much as Rosalynde wished to deny his insulting pronouncement, the flare of desire that curled up from her belly would not allow it. The sin of lust. Once more it was upon her, surprising her when she least expected it, catching her fast in its unrelenting grasp. Dear God, she prayed frantically. She had not known it could be so strong. Never could she have known. . . .

With a jerk she pulled herself away from him, shaking from the terrible turmoil of emotions he had stirred in her. "You are a conceited oaf!" she cried in self-defense. "A disgusting . . . a disgusting bastard—"

"Yes, a bastard, but also your rightful husband," he ended her frustrated litany before it had properly begun. "When shall you admit as much to your father?" He tormented her with a mocking half smile.

For an instant Rosalynde was tempted to do just that: tell her father the whole truth and let him do what he would with Blacksword. The heartless brute deserved

whatever sentence he received. But just as quickly the
image of him bound beneath the cruel bite of the whip
chased away her vengeful thoughts. He was arrogant and
presumptuous and a knave of the first rank, but something
in her simply could not bear to see him suffer further.
With a supreme effort she choked back her angry words
and instead tried to recall why she had originally come out
to speak to him.

"I've a proposition for you," she stated as calmly as she
could. When he only gave her a skeptical glance, however,
her tone became more shrill. "If you will just hold your
tongue. For a little longer," she added quickly before he
could interrupt. "I promise you, I will manage to find you
a suitable reward."

There was a breathless silence. A horse shifted in its
stall a little beyond them, but all else was still.

"You know the reward I want."

"I'll get you a horse. And gold too. I promise. I can't be
sure about any weapons, however." She stared up at him,
hoping against hope that for once he might be reasonable.
But her hopes were dashed by his next few words.

"That's not enough."

"Then what, by all that is holy, will be enough?" she
exploded, forgetting to keep her words quiet.

The answer he gave was clear, though he did not speak
a word. But his eyes spoke volumes as they slipped over
her slender figure, lingering at her breasts before raising
to her lips. To her dismay, however, the emotion that sent
her pulse racing at such an unwarranted perusal was neither insult nor shock. Instead a shameful wave of desire
radiated up from her nether regions and she felt an insane
stab of longing for him. She was mad to feel so, and he was
a devil to inspire such lust in her. Yet she could not will
such powerful feelings away.

"You are mad," she whispered. "Truly mad."

"Perhaps I am," he said, advancing on her slowly. "But I don't think so. There's very little that a man needs, my wild Rose. As a woman it behooves you to understand this. A full belly." He rubbed his own flat stomach languorously. "Shelter from the cold." He cast a wry expression around him at the snug stable. "A woman to ease himself upon." His grin lost its sardonic edge as his eyes bored into hers. "And the chance to choose his own path."

She backed away from his predatory approach. Her voice was barely above a whisper. "I notice you make no mention of honor."

He shrugged, then stopped. "Honor is not something a man needs. Rather it is something he either has or does not have."

"And you have none!" she accused, though her lips trembled as she spoke.

"I have enough," he countered. "Certainly far more than you."

At that she grew angry once more. "I came to you today to honor my promise. To assure you that you shall get your reward—your *rightful* reward."

He gave her a keen look and started to speak, but then stopped. For a moment longer he studied her. Then in some vague, hardly discernible manner he seemed to relax. "How long is a 'little longer'?" he asked noncommittally.

Rosalynde was suddenly wary. What was this change in him? Why was he offering her compromise? For an endless moment she did not answer him for she sensed a trap. He was up to something. Yet with no other options available, she had no choice but to agree. After all, it was the very agreement she'd come here to get.

"You'll wait a few days? Or even a week or more?" She

stared at him suspiciously. "You'll keep your silence and go about your duties as any good servant might?"

"Slave, Rose. Not servant. I am slave here now, but only because I choose to be." He picked up his shirt, all the while watching her. "There are all sorts of enslavement, however. Some better than others." He grinned then. "Some *much* better than others."

Her heart was pounding as he turned to leave, and she was sorely perplexed by his odd choice of words. There was something prophetic in them, she was certain of that. But as much as she wished to believe that it only meant he had changed his mind about his new role at Stanwood, she was nonetheless filled with a foreboding that he meant something else entirely. Something that had to do with her.

It was only the sight of him donning his shirt that pressed her to shake off her strange feelings.

"Wait. I've a fresh chainse for you. And a tunic. Yours are not clean," she finished lamely when he gave her a searching look.

He took the clean shirt without comment, relinquishing his other to her. Once it and the dark-green tunic were settled over his wide shoulders, he favored her with a faint smile. "Thank you, Lady Rosalynde," he said in a most courtly manner. Yet there was a taunt in his words nevertheless. His gray eyes held with hers for a breathtaking moment before he turned and sought out the stable marshal.

Once her breathing had slowed to a more normal pace, Rosalynde tried to find something positive in this the most recent of their confrontations. He had agreed to keep silent and that was good, she thought as she stood there in the empty work space. He also appeared to be settling into his role as a stableman. Certainly he had pleased the old stable marshal with his first task. Things might work out well after all, she speculated. Yet as her hands gripped his ragged shirt and she felt the remnants of his lingering warmth, as his scent of skin and sweat and her own ointment drifted up to her, she trembled. He was cooperating for the moment, she realized, but he was still the same man as ever. Strong-willed. Single-minded. Possessed of an appeal that was surely the mark of the devil. He outraged her with every word he uttered and every glance from his flinty gray eyes. Yet he made her blood sing.

She wanted to fling the grimy tunic away. But instead she balled it up and tucked it under her arm. Then with her pale face set in a frown, she hurried away to the many other tasks that awaited her.

It was almost midday before Aric saw Rosalynde again, crossing the dusty castle yard. He held tightly to the rope in his hand and murmured a soothing word to the tall destrier that tried to prance away from him.

"Easy, my fine fellow. Easy." He patted the steed's velvety muzzle even as he determinedly held the great creature's head down. But his eyes never strayed from Rosalynde until she disappeared into the kitchen sheds.

"Hand me that mallet," the marshal said with a grunt as he muscled the high-spirited animal's hind leg up. The horse started forward and would have dumped the man on his back but Aric anticipated the move, and with a swift downward pull on the rope, he stilled the beast. It took only another few minutes for the marshal to complete his farrier's duties. As he backed away from the heavy horse, he mopped his brow with the sleeve of his stained tunic. "That 'un's the worst of the lot. T'others will be easier." Then he squinted at Aric. "I'm thinking you've been around horses."

Aric ran one hand down the tall bay's neck. "Some," he replied noncommittally, his mind still on Rosalynde.

As the day progressed and he worked beside the stable marshal, first with the horses and later handling the heavy metal bars that would be worked into hinges, spear points, and wheel rims, his mind veered constantly to the woman who had brought him to this new low point in his life.

No, he admitted honestly. This was not the lowest point in his life. That had come when he'd stood on the gallows at Dunmow waiting to die. He might be a slave now—her slave, even—but at least he was alive. And he intended to stay that way. The skin on his back burned like fire every time he stretched too far or bent over. But that only served to strengthen his resolve. He would stay alive and he would ultimately wreak vengeance on his enemies. And all through the innocent aid of one slender, dark-haired maiden. She'd saved his life; now through their marriage he would gain the power needed to find those who had sought to murder him.

He lifted another iron bar and grimaced at the shooting pain across his back. He would continue to work as a slave, but only for so long. Sir Edward's pretty little daughter had bought his silence for a while, or so she thought. But time would work to his advantage, he realized, not hers. She was too squeamish to see him hurt or killed. Her instincts for healing were too strong for that. She would much prefer to buy him off and have him simply disappear from Stanwood. But he had decided to stay. She was his wife both in the eyes of the law as well as through their joining. If her inheritance hadn't been enough to entice him to claim his husbandly rights, her warmth and passion surely were.

He had a year to convince her that he was the only man for her. Considering her fiery response to his lovemaking, he was certain it would not take nearly that long. As for her father's objections, once it was clear he had bedded her and possibly gotten her with child, her father would come around. He would be so relieved to find that Aric was a knight that he would agree to their marriage in the Church at once.

In the meantime it would be his pleasure to bring the sweet Lady Rosalynde to heel. She turned her pretty little nose up at him because she thought him beneath her. But he knew well enough—and so did she now—that the pleasure they'd found in one another had been mutual. It would not be long before she came to him again. It would not be long before she admitted her feelings of desire and longing for him.

He wanted her to wife; he had revealed as much to her already. But he would not have her until she admitted as much to him.

15

Rosalynde left the kitchen sheds in a foul mood. She had taken inventory of the food stores, inspected the buttery, and visited the alehouse. She had seen the linen storage rooms earlier and the stillroom. Now she meant to take stock of the herb gardens, but she was quite certain already what she would find. Anything to do with the male pleasures, such as hawking, hunting, and drinking, was more than adequately maintained—although the cleanliness of the alehouse and the buttery left much to be desired. But the food storerooms were abysmally stocked and in horrendous disorder, as had been the stillroom and linen closets. She did not doubt that the herb garden was completely overrun with weeds.

She rubbed her throbbing temple but her stride was no less determined as she made her way down the bailey to the flat sunny spot where her mother had cultivated her herbs. Stanwood Castle was in hopeless disarray and she had a huge project on her hands, Rosalynde realized, even larger than she had expected. For a moment it seemed far too complex for her to handle at all—who was she to think she could set to rights what her father clearly considered of no importance? But at the same time, something in her rose to the challenge. This was her true home. It always had been, and now, since she was her father's sole heir, it appeared it would be even after she was wed.

At the thought of being someday wed, Rosalynde could not repress a shiver of dismay. Even though it was her duty eventually to wed and produce heirs, the very thought frightened her. She already had a husband—albeit temporarily. But how would she ever explain that she was not a virgin? She frowned as she hurried across the yard. Maybe her future husband would not be able to tell, she thought hopefully. Yet she knew that hope was not enough to ease her fears, for the fact remained that she could not imagine lying with another man as she had lain with Blacksword. Except that she could no longer pretend he was only Blacksword the outlaw. Now he was Aric of Wycliffe, a man she hardly knew but who had laid a claim to her which she was hard pressed to deny.

With a forlorn sigh Rosalynde shooed a rambunctious pair of overgrown puppies from her path as she neared the garden. The question of a husband was beyond her control, she told herself firmly. For the time being she might as well just tackle each and every one of the castle's shortcomings. She was going to be here a very long time.

Yet when she passed a group of unpruned pear trees and the herb garden came into view, she almost changed her mind. She remembered a well laid out garden with stone paths, green lawns, and deep borders of herbs interspersed with flowers. What presented itself before her now was a wild jungle of untended shrubs. Paths snaked through in completely unintended locations, and even as she stared at it hopelessly, three more dogs came racing from within the tangle of weeds, nearly bowling her over in their canine delight.

"Out. Out!" she cried, stamping her feet and flapping the ends of her overtunic at them. What had they done to the peaceful little garden she remembered from her childhood? But the dogs only romped past her, yelping foolishly and following the path of the two mongrels she'd spied previously.

Rosalynde was nearly undone. Everything that was wrong with Stanwood—the crudeness of the fare, the absence of court manners, the lack of a woman's touch at all —was summed up by the condition of her mother's herb garden. Even the abandoned garden at the adulterine castle had not been as bad as this one! Her shoulders slumped in defeat as she stared at the remnants of the herbarium. This garden alone would take all of her efforts. But there was everything else to attend as well. She would never manage it all. Never.

" 'Tis a sorry sight, isn't it?"

Rosalynde turned at the unexpected voice to find her father standing several paces behind her. Had his expression not been so forlorn and his eyes so sad she would have vented her frustration on him at once. After all, it was he who had allowed her home to sink so low. But she could not heap further guilt on him, not when he so clearly felt the effects of it already.

"It can be repaired," she said, although the enthusiasm in her voice was sadly lacking.

"Can it?" he asked as he slowly advanced toward her. "Sometimes I think not."

As she heard the loneliness in his voice and recognized the true meaning of his words, Rosalynde's natural inclination to nurture came to the fore. "It can be put to rights. I'm sure of it." She hesitated. "But I shall need your help."

He looked up at her and she saw how he fought to bury any trace of his sorrow. "I'm no gardener," he stated gruffly.

"Yes, I know. But I am. You need but give me a man to use as I see fit. Perhaps two."

Her father stared at her a long time before answering. "Two days you are here. I give you the keys. Now you would take two of my servants to make a garden."

"I brought two with me. Plus myself," she countered. His ill-humored words did not worry her at all. Then she smiled and crossed the rest of the way to stand before him. "You will be pleased with the results, I daresay."

His eyes held with hers for another long moment before he nodded his head. "I daresay I will," he admitted. Then he took his leave of her.

Rosalynde watched him go, and her heart filled with a mixture of love and sorrow. She had been referring to far more than his just being pleased with the garden, of course. But then, she was fairly certain he had known that.

She made her plans that night after a dissatisfying meal of stringy boar haunch, oversalted fish, and porridge. In the privacy of her own chamber, by the light of one flickering candle, she brushed her hair and decided how best to proceed. Cleve would start in the garden along with someone else whom she would find in the morning. As it was spring, they must make haste to prepare the garden now. Cedric would be given strict orders to have the kitchen, the alehouse, and the storerooms cleaned first and then reorganized. She would handle the linen stores and the stillroom herself.

As for the great hall, she would enlist that group of ill-mannered boys to clean out all the old rushes, scrub down the stone floors with lye leached through the ash pots, then cut and spread new rushes. The great fireplace would have to be scrubbed as well. And when they finished that

she would have them scrape all the torch bases and can-
dleholders too.

Of course she would have to supervise each group herself. She trusted none of them to see the tasks completed
to her satisfaction. But if she had to labor from before
dawn until after dusk, she would see it done. The sewing
and spinning, the cleaning of the lesser chambers and the
making of soaps and candles, she would address at a later
date. For now she would satisfy herself with the neces-
saries.

At first light she rousted Cedric from his pallet near her
father's chamber. She was already dressed in a plain gray
smock with her hair bound up in linen. The keys to the
castle jangled gaily from the end of her girdle.

"Good morrow, Cedric. I trust you slept well, for we're
to begin a considerable task today."

"Mi-milady?" he stammered out, still bleary from sleep.

"Please assemble a goodly group of servants in the great
hall. Four or five of those shiftless lads and the two serving
women. Instruct the cook to relinquish at least two of his
assistants. He won't need them as we shall feast on dried
fish, bread, and cheese until this task is done. Oh, and I'll
need Cleve and . . . and . . . and anyone else you can
find." She gave him a satisfied smile. "And do make haste,
Cedric. The day is wasting even as we speak."

He stared at her a moment longer, as if he did not quite
understand what she had said. Then he bobbed his sandy
head and gave her a faint smile. "Aye, milady. I'll see to it
at once." He grabbed up his shoes and sat down to put
them on as his smile broadened. "I 'spect there's to be
some changes around here."

"I expect there will," she concurred.

The others proved to be far less accommodating than
Cedric, yet Rosalynde was not dismayed. Old habits were

hard to break, but she was determined that the dreadful habits and routines that the servants of Stanwood had fallen into would be broken once and for all. The serving women were sent to clean the kitchens, top to bottom, floor to ceiling and everything in between. The two kitchen helpers she sent to purge the storerooms. The five clumsy boys she turned to with especial vengeance.

"Every crumb," she told them sternly. "Every sliver of bone and glob of fat is to be swept and scrubbed away." As she left the great hall she turned a deaf ear to their groans of dismay. They would soon learn their places, she vowed, and soon know that the orders of a lady were as inviolate as that of a lord.

But it was from Cleve that she received the loudest complaints.

"This, a garden?" he said in disbelief when faced with the disaster that was the herb garden. He watched as one of the dogs began to bark at them, then turned to her with a pained expression. "'Twould be best to leave it to the dogs and start elsewhere anew, Lady Rosalynde."

"I think not," she replied, giving him a firm look. "First locate the old stone paths beneath all those weeds, and clear them. Then we'll mark the shrubs that must go and those that must stay."

"'Twill take a year and more!" he exclaimed when he saw she would not be swayed from her purpose.

"You have two weeks." But at his stunned expression she relented a little. "Cedric will send someone to help you."

"Best he send someone with the strength of an ox," he grumbled, eyeing several sturdy willows that had sprung up unwelcome amid the ruined garden.

At his disgruntled words, a picture of Blacksword sprang to her mind, for he was indeed as strong as an ox.

But she determinedly beat back that image and concentrated on the many tasks at hand. When she left Cleve he was scratching his head and muttering to himself.

It took all of Rosalynde's willpower to stay away from her small crew of laborers during the morning. But she knew they must learn to be responsible without her constant overview. It was time for the midday meal before she completed her cleaning and inventory of the stillroom. The faces that greeted her as they partook of the meal in unusual silence were somber indeed. And dirty as well. Her father cast her a curious glance when he was presented with the meager fare. But he did not raise a comment and only set to the spare offerings with a great display of gusto. Rosalynde was enormously gratified for his show of support, for if he accepted her unpopular methods, no one else could dare complain. As she left the great hall to attend her other tasks, she gave the much-subdued cadre of young men further and more explicit instructions for the continuation of their work.

In the kitchen the cook gave her a disgruntled stare that spoke volumes. But Rosalynde refused to be baited and addressed the two serving women who were already scraping years of greasy dirt from the rafters above the cutting and preparation tables.

"Save your scrapings in a tub, Edith," she directed the older of the pair. "I'll be forming a garden pile, and any waste from the kitchen should be brought there."

"Aye, milady." The maid nodded. " 'Tis shameful to say how much of it there'll be." She slid a huge brown blob of mingled dirt and grease off the knife blade for effect. "To think we've been eatin' such." She raised her eyebrows dramatically.

Rosalynde looked at her for a long moment, then also at

the younger, stouter Maud. "Can either of you cook?" she asked on impulse.

Maud was the first to reply. "I'm a fair hand, particular to soups and stews." She glanced at Edith as if weighing the wisdom of her next words. Then she plunged on. "Edith here makes a pear tart to weep over."

"Pear tart?" Rosalynde stared at Edith in astonishment. But as her mind whirled with new possibilities, the two women mistook her expression.

Edith's face paled with fear. "Please don't hold it again' mo, milady. It was only that the pears were fallin' to rot. And the flour, well, 'twould have gone rancid before too long. I'm not a thief, milady. Truly, I'm not!"

"Oh, never fear as much." Rosalynde hastened to reassure the trembling woman. "I was just thinking . . . Well, you see—" She glanced around but the cook had disappeared in a huff. "I'm thinking of making some changes around here."

Cedric had the storerooms and the alehouse fairly well in hand when Rosalynde checked. The servants he'd enlisted were busy under his watchful eye, and to Rosalynde's mind he appeared more animated than she'd ever seen him. But when he spied her he at once became his more subdued self.

" 'Tis a considerable task, milady. But we'll not pause till you are well satisfied."

Rosalynde smiled at his words, for despite his seriousness she detected a true enthusiasm on his part for this undertaking. In him, at least, she was sure she had an ally.

"Although I too long to see our work completed, I hardly expect to accomplish it all in one day, Cedric. However, I must say you've made a commendable start of it."

At that casual compliment his fair face turned a noticeable pink. "I-I've also sent a stout fellow to assist in your garden."

"Oh, yes, the garden."

Rosalynde had purposefully put off returning to the garden. For one thing, once she turned her energies there she did not want to be drawn away to another task. She wished to spend the entire afternoon in the overgrown garden. But in another way she dreaded going back there, for she was still not entirely comfortable in Cleve's company. Although on the surface they had returned to the proper relationship of servant and lady, there was a strain there that had not previously existed. She had not, by her actions, given him leave to bring up anything of what had happened between them and Blacksword—Aric. However, she knew that she and Cleve had been too familiar in the past for him to hold his opinions to himself overlong. It was only a matter of time.

She sighed and then gave Cedric an absent smile. "I suppose I must see to the garden now. I shall be there until dusk, should anyone seek me out."

As Rosalynde approached the herb garden, her mind spun with plans for the spot. It would take time but she would make it far more than merely an herb garden. She would follow in her mother's path and make it the loveliest spot in Stanwood, a pleasaunce, her aunt had said they were called in the great castles. In addition to the lawns and paths and borders, she imagined a quiet pond in the center, perhaps with one of those wonderful sundials nearby. And all around there would be a thick hedge of roses. It would be fragrant and beautiful. And it would keep those unruly dogs out, she thought with satisfaction.

But then she reached the sunny spot, and all thoughts of lawns and flowers and a restful garden flew quite out of her mind. She saw the start that had been made in clearing the weed-choked area. She saw the huge pile of discarded plants and the beginnings of a path into the center of the garden. A nondescript tree had even been dug up and cut into lengths for the woodpiles. But none of those things were what caused her eyes to stare and her mouth to gape open. That instantaneous reaction was caused by the man who squatted at the beginnings of the path, scratching one overgrown pup behind the ears as two of the mongrel's kin bounded about, yelping and whining for a chance at his affections.

"You!" Rosalynde exclaimed without even realizing she had spoken aloud.

Aric looked at her. "A slave goes where he is told and does the task given him," he said in smug response. He slowly stood up, watching her all the while with that familiar mocking expression. "Are you pleased with the progress, Rose?"

"Lady Rosalynde to you," she snapped. "If you value your stubborn hide, you will not be so impudent with me."

"If your husband may not be intimate with you, then who? Besides, no one is near enough to overhear us," he countered.

"What of Cleve?" she replied nervously, trying to peer past him. "And you are not my husband!" she finished with a hiss.

He ignored her last words. "Cleve went off in search of you, I believe. He was rather disgruntled when Cedric sent me here to labor with him."

"Well, you can just go right back to Cedric. I don't want you in my garden," she stated furiously. "I'll not have you here!"

"I intend to stay." The words were quietly said, and yet the steely quality of them was unmistakable.

"It is not necessary," she insisted. "You can be better used elsewhere."

"I will not be *used* anywhere, *milady*," he said with an icy calm. "Not by you or any others."

"Then . . . then why are you here? Why not flee?" Rosalynde shivered under his suddenly cold stare. Even the pup at his feet whined uneasily. "If it's your reward that holds you here, I promise to pay you soon—"

"I stay because it serves me best. That's all you need understand. Cedric told me to work in this little garden, and that is what I shall do. And I suggest you abandon any thoughts of having him send me elsewhere."

Rosalynde was too undone to reply. She was mistress here and he only a slave, less even than a serf. Yet he stood before her in all his villainous glory dictating to her and she had no choice but to surrender to his will. No matter how much she abhorred her predicament, she could not forget that he had only to reveal their handfast vow—and his subsequent seduction of her—to ruin her reputation forever. At the moment the fact that he would very likely pay for such a revelation with his own life seemed almost appealing! Still, she knew that she must be careful and not make a misstep with this man.

Stifling an impatient oath, she glared at him. "You wish to work here only to irritate me. Well, you shall work then, but you'll be very sorry that you ever crossed me!" So saying she picked up a branch and swished it angrily through the air. "Remove that willow there. And all these saplings. Clear the remainder of the stone paths. And . . . and . . ." She glared at his complacent face and her temper rose even higher. "And get rid of those infernal dogs!"

Rosalynde stormed away before he could laugh and thereby goad her into doing something she might later regret, such as striking him with the switch she still clutched in her hand. At once she flung the branch away, horrified that he could propel her into such a towering rage that she could lose all control of her temper. It was not her way to shout at servants, nor to heap them with unreasonable amounts of work. And especially not to strike them!

Only he was not your everyday sort of servant, she fretted as she fled as quickly as was seemly across the bailey. He was a common criminal. No, she amended. He was quite an uncommon criminal.

He's also your husband, her conscience reminded her. And the man who had claimed her maidenhead.

What an awful, awful coil she had entangled herself in, she agonized as she hurried toward the great hall. What a dreadful mess. Then she spied her father in conversation with young Cleve, and her heart fell to her feet. No doubt Cleve was in enough of a temper to reveal everything he knew to her father. If that were the case . . .

She refused to speculate on that horrible eventuality and instead took a fortifying breath and changed her direction to head toward the two men.

"Ahh, Rosalynde," her father exclaimed as he saw her approach. "I've good news to share with you." His smiling face eased her fears quite a bit, but Cleve's wide grin confused her completely.

"I've decided to reward this brave young lad. I've no doubt you will agree with my decision, daughter."

"Reward him?" Rosalynde repeated. Then she smiled, for she could not help but be pleased. Cleve had always been a good and loyal page. He'd proven his mettle when he'd defended her at the river and again when he'd challenged Blacksword, even though he'd been somewhat misguided at the time. He of all people deserved reward. "I hope it is something very good, for he has saved my very life. During the attack at the river," she hastened to clarify.

"Yes. He is by all accounts an exceedingly brave lad. It is therefore my decision that he shall join the ranks of my squires, with the opportunity to train for knighthood."

It was hard to say who was more stunned. Cleve's face froze in a look of disbelief. His eyes shifted from Sir Edward to Rosalynde then back again to Sir Edward as his face reflected alternate feelings of wonder, terror, and then disbelief once more. Rosalynde knew that, considering his birthright was only that of bastard to a minor knight, he never had thought to aspire to more than an inside servant's position. To his mind it was far better than laboring in the fields. But now! Rosalynde was the first of the two to recover her wits, and with a clap of her hands and a laugh of pure delight, she caught Cleve's hands in her own.

"A squire! And mayhap a knight? I had never thought to call you Sir Cleve," she exclaimed with a happy smile. "But I look forward now to the day with great anticipation."

"He is not Sir Cleve yet," her father interjected sternly. But there was still a twinkle in his deep-set eyes. "There is much hard work ahead of you, lad. All sorts of lessons in comportment and language and history, as well as tilting and swordplay and a hundred other things."

"Oh, thank you, my lord! Thank you," Cleve answered in a hushed, awe-struck voice. "Thank you so much. You will always have my undying gratitude, my complete loyalty, my endless faithfulness—"

"Yes, yes. I understand," Sir Edward chuckled. Then he laid one of his hands on the boy's narrow shoulder. "I suggest you finish this day's tasks. But afterward you may remove yourself to the squires' quarters above the storerooms. And tomorrow you will report to the captain of the guard along with the others to begin your new responsibilities."

At this reference to the day's tasks, Cleve came down a little from his euphoria and sent Rosalynde a questioning look. But she gave him a determined smile and waved him away.

"Never mind the garden. Be off with you," she said.

"Yes, milady. Thank you, milady. Thank you, milord." He backed away, bowing as he did. "Thank you, milord," he repeated yet again. Then he turned and, with an exuberant leap, dashed off.

"He seems a good lad," Sir Edward remarked as they both watched Cleve's joyous departure.

"He will make you proud of your choice." Rosalynde turned to face him. "He won't let you down."

"I never thought he would. I consider myself a fair judge of a man. And this one possesses the integrity a true knight needs. The honor."

The honor. Those words haunted Rosalynde as she made her way back to the garden. Yes, Cleve possessed an innate sense of honor. But Aric had spoken of honor too. She'd accused him of having none, for he certainly could be the most horrible and contentious man alive. Yet even at his most dreadful he still maintained that odd air of nobility. Even when he'd faced the hangman, and then again when he'd been flogged before them all, he'd managed by his very bearing to hold onto his dignity. Once more she wondered where he'd come from and how he'd been brought to such a pass as the gallows.

By the time she reached the garden plot, her anger had all but disappeared, suppressed beneath her undeniable curiosity about him. Already the second tree was uprooted and dragged out of the garden space. The pack of hounds lay in various poses of relaxation near the beginning of the path, and beyond them Rosalynde could see Aric's broad back as he bent and pulled, bent and pulled, yanking weeds and small shrubs from their stubborn hold on the fertile soil, then tossing them over his shoulder, roots and all, to leave an ever-mounting trail behind him. As she watched, he paused and straightened up. Then he pulled his tunic over his head, tossed it aside, and bent back to his work, clad only in his shirt.

Gardening was hardly considered proper work for a man. Serfs farmed of course, and a few women servants would always work in the castle garden. But mostly it was a chore reserved for boys. Yet even in this most menial of tasks Aric did not appear in the least demeaned. He tackled the work as he did everything, with force and determination. Rosalynde had to admit a grudging respect for the progress he'd made in such a short time. Already one of the stone-paved paths was cleaned almost to the center of the garden. At this rate her pleasaunce would take shape more quickly than she'd dared hoped.

Much calmed from her earlier angry mood, she made her way down the roughly cleared path toward Aric. Although she was behind him and he could not see her approach, he nonetheless seemed to sense her proximity. Like a wary beast he turned before she was within striking distance. At the sight of her, however, his wary stance relaxed and his watchful gaze turned assessing.

"Come to check on my diligence, *Lady Rosalynde*?" he asked in that ever-mocking tone. "Or perhaps to threaten me with still further labors?" He grinned as if neither of those possibilities worried him at all.

Rosalynde found herself hard-pressed to come up with an honest answer for her return. Why had she come back to the garden so soon? She could just as well have seen once more to the great hall, or perhaps to the kitchens. But she'd been drawn back here instead.

It was the garden itself, she told herself. Gardening was her particular hobby, and this garden especially meant very much to her. Certainly her return had nothing whatsoever to do with the man who faced her now. If anything, she was more likely to avoid the garden due to his presence in it. But that wouldn't do either, she reprimanded herself. If she was to impress upon him that he could be no more and no less than any other servant at Stanwood, then she could neither seek him out nor avoid him any more than she did the others.

But that terribly logical thought held no sway in the least upon her splintered emotions. As she stared up at the hard planes of his face, her heart's pace trebled and she was suddenly quite short of breath.

"I am here . . ." she began feebly. "I am here because this garden means very much to me."

"Then it must mean as much to me."

Such a courtly reply took her completely by surprise, and for a moment she could only stare at him, confusion clearly evident on her face. Then she frowned and looked away. "I am no fool. Do not patronize me."

"Yes, milady," he said, again with that smooth, well-mannered speech.

"Do not mock me!" she snapped, glaring at him furiously.

"And how would you have me treat you, Rose?" he answered, although his eyes glittered now with harder emotions.

"I-I am your mistress, whom you should treat with respect. And I will treat you equally well. Just do your work willingly, and you will be dealt with fairly at Stanwood."

He considered her words a moment, all the while keeping his eyes fastened on her. "Have I not done my work well today?"

"Yes. Yes, truthfully you have."

"So it follows then that you should treat me well."

"But you are being treated well. You have a place to sleep. Food to eat—"

"That meets two of the four needs of a man," he said, reminding her of their earlier conversation. "There's still the matter of my freedom. And my woman," he added more quietly. Then before she could recover from the shock of those bold words he continued. "Come to my bed, sweet wife. Even though I have granted you a little more time, that need not prevent us from lying together again."

This time Rosalynde jumped as if she'd been burned. Indeed, his smoothly said words seemed to scorch her and she was at once heated through and through.

"You . . . you . . ." She sputtered ineffectually. "You are mad!"

"Mad with desire."

"A-a villainous blackguard!"

"You are my wife."

"A disgusting . . . a disgusting—"

"You were not disgusted, Rose. No matter how you try to convince yourself of it now, it was hardly disgust you felt at our joining."

"Oh!" Rosalynde was unable to face one more dreadful word. She took one step backward, then turned to flee those too-perceptive eyes of his. But he caught her hand before she could escape and held her there before him. If his words had unnerved her, his possessive grasp drove all logical thought from her. Like a moonstruck fool she gaped at him, unable even to disguise her emotions from him.

"Your hair should be free," he murmured, staring deeply into her eyes. "Free to spill over your shoulders; free to slide between my fingers." He pulled her nearer and for that moment Rosalynde forgot everything: the castle, her father, all the reasons he was the wrong man for her. "Come to me tonight," he urged her as one of his hands circled her neck.

Then she felt the linen slip loose from around her head and in a moment her hair tumbled free in glorious abandon. She heard his quickly indrawn breath. His hands moved to slide through the thick dark masses. But she was too disconcerted to remain even a moment longer within his disturbing embrace.

"You . . . you should not," she whispered as she backed away from the mesmerizing warmth of his hands. "Someone could see us—" She stopped abruptly, horrified that that was the only pitiful excuse she could come up with. That was not what she'd meant to say at all. But as he continued to stare at her with his compelling gray eyes, every logical thought flew right out of her head. She'd meant to tell him not to touch her so. She'd meant to say that he was impertinent in the extreme even to suggest such a thing. But the words would not come. With her heart racing furiously, Rosalynde could only back away from him, then, on legs that shook from the effort, walk carefully away.

She was soon safely locked in her own room, flung upon her own bed with the shutters locked tight against the light. But the pull was still there, and nothing changed that. Like a strong invisible tether, it tied her to him and she could not free herself from its power.

Heart to heart, she thought for one weak and fanciful moment.

No, she amended harshly. That was only wishful thinking. Loin to loin was a far more honest appraisal.

Tears filled her eyes at such a sinful admission, and with a sob she flung herself down onto the hard floor and huddled on her knees.

"I confess the sin of lust," she whispered as she clasped her hands in desperate prayer. "I confess the sin of lust for a man I should abhor. Dear God, help me. Sweet Jesus, have mercy. Blessed Mother, I beseech thee . . ."

But though she prayed long and hard, to every saint that might heed her plea, she feared her prayers would receive no answer. And she would receive no relief.

16

Time flew by too quickly. But in other ways it crawled by at a snail's pace.

The stillroom and storerooms progressed very well. The shelves were purged and cleaned, then only the worth-while contents stocked, and in logical order according to regular usage. In the buttery the various wines in their butts were tasted and either sealed or drained, as Rosalynde's delicate palate dictated. The alehouse, like the kitchen, took a little longer. Too many years of baked-on dirt and grease had resulted in thick leavings that were most difficult to remove. By each day's end the scraped-off goo had transferred itself to the aprons and headcloths of poor Maud and Edith until they both looked veritable frights. But bit by bit progress was made.

Rosalynde's greatest satisfaction came from the improvements in the great hall. Clean walls and floors plus fresh rushes sprinkled liberally with lavender and mint made a marked difference in both the appearance and odor of the place. The first evening her father had even commented favorably upon her efforts and given her a fond pat on her hand. Since then she had prodded the unwilling group of serving lads into dragging the tables outside and scrubbing them with strong soap, then leaving the boards to dry in the ever-strengthening afternoon sun.

Benches received the same treatment. Eventually she planned to purchase adequate linen for tablecloths. Only then would the tables be completely presentable to her sensibilities.

By far the most difficult task the boys undertook in the great hall was cleaning the torch bases and candlesticks. Endless layers of wax and burned-on tallow raised all sorts of muttered oaths from the reluctant fellows, but she ignored them completely. They could mutter to their hearts' content so long as their curses were not too loud and their work proceeded apace. And proceed it did, day by day, until even the grumpy boys began to exhibit a certain pride in their accomplishments.

The garden, however, was another matter entirely. Cleve had abandoned her completely, embracing his new duties as squire with enthusiasm and vigor. To her carefully worded requests of her father for an additional laborer from the fields, she received a huffy no. He could spare not a single man, he told her quite adamantly. For not only must the serfs plant their own strips of land, they must also put in their prescribed days of labor on Sir Edward's lands. While the weather was fair he absolutely refused to relinquish even one man.

That left her with only Aric.

It aggravated her to no end that neither her father nor Cleve seemed worried that such a rogue outlaw was working for her without further supervision. But Cleve had seemed to sum it up the last time she'd tried to coerce him into helping her.

"It does me good to see such a haughty one as him brought so low as to labor at what is rightfully women's work," he had said, giving her a self-important look. "And should he object, there's not a man in the guard who would not slice him down at once. Besides, 'twas you who wished him spared, was it not?"

To that she had no argument. And she dared not go to her father with any further concerns about Blacksword's constant presence, for she feared that might lead to questions and revelations of things she wished kept secret. At times she thought her father actually wanted Aric to revolt against his menial duty, for on more than one occasion she had caught him observing the man at his labor in the garden. But he did his work well and the garden improved daily, so neither she nor her father had an honest cause for complaint. Only to herself would she admit that it was not the threat of physical harm that she feared from Blacksword. The watchmen on the ramparts and the numerous castlefolk protected her from any such danger.

No, the menace Aric presented was far more subtle, and far more pervasive. Something in him drew her. She might curse it as a madness on her part, and pray endlessly for relief, but it was nevertheless always with her. Whether they spoke or not, whether she labored nearby him or sought respite as far from him as she could, the pull was ever present and seemed perversely to be growing greater still.

Even in her sleep he haunted her, for more than once or twice she was awakened by dreams of him. And even if they were not distinct dreams, the early-morning hours invariably found her filled with a great lassitude and a sultry awareness of her own body that she'd never known before.

It was only that she was no longer a maiden, she would tell herself sternly. But her body said it was more. Her nipples would tighten, a warmth would creep up from her belly, and a restlessness that was completely foreign would steal over her. It was then, as she lay in her plain bed, waiting for dawn to bring light to the world, that she admitted the depths of her depravity.

She wanted him just as he clearly wanted her. Lust was a beast with its own mind and heart, and it tortured her unmercifully.

One warm morning Rosalynde awoke with that now-familiar coil of heat deep inside her. For a few disturbing moments she simply lay there, resigned to her disquieting feelings, resentful that Aric could affect her even in her own chamber but, above all, dismayed by the intense curiosity and unresolved questions building in her. Every morning it was worse. She felt as if she were waiting for something, and not just for Blacksword's reaction when he learned she had not yet obtained his reward for him. It was a physical thing, something her body wanted, but she did not know what.

Or more precisely, she did not know why. Why did she want his touch? His caress? Why did she relive the exquisite feel of his lips pressed to hers, of his tongue stroking into her mouth and igniting a wondrous panic in her?

She twisted restlessly on the mattress, then flung the covers from her in frustration. Why must she ever be tormented by the wicked remembrance of his final possession of her? Over and over in her mind it played, and every time it left her more wrought up than before. With a muttered oath not at all becoming to a lady, she rose from the bed and padded on bare feet to the pan of water that she'd brought inside the night before. With trembling hands she splashed her face, then soaked a cloth in the water and pressed it to her warm cheeks. Yet that did no more to cool her overheated body than did the cold floor beneath her feet. She doubted that even a bath in an icy spring could put out the fire that burned inside her.

She tossed down the cloth, unmindful of the water that

sprang in drops from the shallow pan. A pox on that man, she fumed as she found a clean kirtle and tugged it over her head. He was a devil, she decided as she thrust first one arm and then the other into the sleeves. Lucifer himself, she vowed as she yanked the fabric down. The only way to rid herself of such sinful feelings would be to rid herself of him. And the sooner the better. But how was she ever to do that?

It was this worry that beset her through the early breaking of the night's fast. By now Aric was taking his meals in the great hall with the rest of the castlefolk, sitting at the last table, nearest to the entry doors. But Rosalynde knew he was there, and despite her best intentions her eyes crept repeatedly to watch him.

He ate neatly, not like so many others of the servants. He had no knife so he ate only with a spoon and his fingers, yet still he was cleaner and more fastidious than the others at his table. Bread and cheese was the fare, along with a small bowl of gruel and a mug of ale. Rosalynde watched surreptitiously until he finished and rose to leave. Only then did she hurriedly finish her own meal.

It did not take long to dispense with the day's instructions to the castle servants. They were finally becoming resigned to the fact that life at Stanwood was never again to be as it was. Cleanliness, orderliness. These were what the new chatelaine required, and she—and they, as a result—would not have their rest until it was so.

By the time Rosalynde left them to their work and made her way to the garden, Aric had already begun to dig up the last of the unwanted willows. With a heavy garden fork he loosened the earth. Then with a curved length of hammered metal attached to a stout length of oak, he began to scoop the earth away. Bend, dig, scoop, and straighten. Again and again he moved as he slowly circled the sturdy sapling; and she, like one stupefied, stood and watched. One of the mongrel pups circled her, stepping on her toes and whacking her legs with his tail as he sought her attention. But although Rosalynde stooped to scratch the mutt amiably behind his ears, her gaze remained on Aric.

Once he had circled the tree, he put his spade aside and leaned his weight hard against the trunk. It was then that he spied her and straightened up.

"Good morrow, Rose," he said in a tone far too familiar for a servant to use with a lady. But Rosalynde knew it was useless to protest. It wouldn't change his manner at all, and she was certain he took perverse pleasure in baiting her thus. Instead she gave him a perfunctory smile and moved toward the bed of perennial herbs she had been weeding and transplanting.

"Did you sleep well?" he persisted as he watched her approach. "Perchance did you have any dreams of me?"

"Hardly," she snapped, but color rose in her face to think how close to the truth he was.

"I dreamed of you," he murmured as she sidled past him on the cleared path. "I dreamed you were there beside me . . . beneath me . . ."

"Oh! You are truly vile!" she hissed in horror, even as a spark somewhere inside her leapt into sudden flame. "You court disaster by such unseemly speech!"

" 'Tis not unseemly for a husband to desire his wife in his bed," he countered. "And, Rose, make no doubt, I do desire you in my bed."

"Your bed! Your bed! Why, 'tis less than a pallet is your bed! A pile of hay! You dare much—"

"Yes, I know," he bit out, pinning her with his dark gaze. "My bed is a mean one indeed. No bed at all, in fact. And yes, I dare much to want what is mine. I court disaster to speak the truth. That's where we differ, *sweet wife.*

I'll dare much for the truth, while you run from it. Cringe from it!" At that he drew her beneath the branches of the doomed willow, hiding them from view. Then he pulled her closer until the entire lengths of their bodies were but inches apart.

Rosalynde was sure he meant to kiss her. His grasp was tight, his eyes burned into hers with a fierce light, and his lips poised just above her own. She did not consciously halt her struggle, yet as his face drew nearer her own, something inside her seemed to melt. Her heart pounded in her ears as she waited for his kiss.

But the kiss she received was not at all what she expected. His lips touched her brow once, then again, before moving to caress her temple.

"Sweet Rose," he murmured against her cheek. "My thorny little Rose," he whispered heatedly against her sensitive ear.

In sudden discontent, she leaned her weight slightly against him, even as she turned her face up to him. Something in her burned for him. Like hunger. Like her very need for air. Logic deemed this food a poison. To breathe deeply would surely be her undoing. Yet still she wanted it, no matter the risk. Nothing in her young and sheltered existence had prepared her for this onslaught of new and forbidden emotions. Nothing could have.

She breathed in the scent of sweat and earth that clung to him and without even being aware edged a little nearer, wanting the taste of his mouth on hers. Their eyes met in fiery collision and she knew she was completely transparent to him. But once more he surprised her. He bent down as if to kiss her, then halted before their lips met.

"You are mine, and soon the whole world shall know."

"No!" The word was out before she could stop it.

"Yes," he countered, holding her head still when, in her

panic, she would have pulled back. "I've allowed you enough delay. It's time to confront your father."

At this broaching of the subject she had hoped to avoid, Rosalynde's emotional elation came to a crashing halt. She tried to twist out of his rigid grasp, but his hold on her was adamant. In his steady gaze she recognized determination and a reckless daring that frightened her. "He will kill you! It's too soon!"

"It will always be too soon," he retorted darkly. "You'll put me off and put me off until a year and a day is done."

"No. No, that's not it. It's just that . . . that . . ." Rosalynde could not formulate a reply, at least not an honest one. It was true she sought desperately to escape the year-and-a-day constraints set on her by the handfasting ritual. But her primary fear was for her father's furious reaction. She had only to recall the horrors of the flogging to know her father would deal most harshly with the man who had ruined his daughter. Even though Blacksword seemed ready to risk her father's fury, she was not.

"He will kill you," she whispered quietly, staring into his slate-gray eyes. "I know you don't believe that, but it's true."

His hands tightened but something in his eyes flickered. "Your concern is flattering, sweet. But I'm willing to take my chances with him. This yoke of slavery weighs too heavily on me."

"But it's not so bad," she argued, seeking some way to convince him. "Truly. The work is hard, but you have enough to eat and a safe place to sleep. You are well treated here."

"You still do not understand. A man needs more than a full belly and a warm place to sleep. It is the freedom to go —or stay—that I want. And my woman." He pulled her up against him so that she was pressed close against the entire length of his male form. It was a shock of heat and hardness, and although her body would have rested willingly against him, her mind pushed her away.

"You are a madman! You want too much!"

"I want only what every man wants. I'll not rest until I have it. Come, wife." He stared deeply into her wide eyes. " 'Tis time we spoke to your father."

"No!" Rosalynde squeaked as he made to leave the willow's protective embrace. "Wait!"

"There's no use in waiting any longer."

"Another week. Just one more week!" she pleaded in desperation.

He halted and stared at her keenly. "Why wait? Why?"

"Because . . ." She faltered. "Just because."

In the filtered light he stood before her, his hair a dark gold, his face burned brown by his outdoor labors. He was so completely male, so unbelievably virile. A part of her responded innately to him, and it was a wonder to her that he seemed to desire her as well. It was that thought which prompted her next rash words.

"If you will just wait, just not do anything or say anything . . ."

His eyes glinted with silvery light. "If I will wait, what?" he pressed her.

"I will kiss you," she pronounced very gravely.

For a moment their eyes held. "You would have kissed me anyway," he mocked. "Kissed me and more."

Her serious stare dissolved into a glare. "You think overmuch of yourself," she snapped, even though she knew he had the truth of it. But her need to buy his silence overrode her need to prick his pride.

His smile faded. "You dare much to place yourself above he who is your legal husband. Lady you may be. Wedded to a mere slave. But that changes nothing of the facts." Then his curt tone relented. "But there are forms of slavery not so objectionable." His hands slid up her arms. "Make me a slave to your kisses, my Rose. Make me your slave and I will make you mine."

For an endless trembling moment he held her within his gaze, within his grasp. Forgotten was her anger; forgotten the bribe she'd offered him. As she stared like one mesmerized into the smoky depths of his potent stare, Rosalynde felt every defense against him ebb away. Like the taut string of a longbow her emotions stretched to the point of breaking, until she was forced to admit to herself that she wanted his kiss. She *needed* his kiss with a desperation that made her want to weep.

"Kiss me," he murmured softly. "Buy my silence with your lips. With your tongue," he coaxed in a voice grown low and husky.

In unquestioning response Rosalynde leaned into him, lifting up on her toes to reach his lips. When he bent down to meet her kiss, when he shifted to fit her against him, she pressed herself freely to him, never thinking of payment or bribes or the silence she bought. In that moment her thoughts reeled and logic disappeared. She knew only the warmth of his nearness, the magic of his touch, and the exquisite sweetness of his kiss.

He did not demand anything of her in that kiss. Indeed, there was almost a caution, a reserve in the intimate pressure of his firm mouth against hers. But his very reticence seemed to goad her on, and without thinking she parted her lips and ran the tip of her tongue along the seam of his lips.

At once everything changed.

His hold on her tightened even as he opened to her hesitant approach. He took her tongue into his mouth and met it with his own, and before she could protest she was overcome with unnameable delight. She had initiated the kiss, yet even in her passionate haze she knew it had been at his command. And now as desire exploded inside her, she knew that in every way he held her in his thrall. She was a slave to her desire for him. He had made her thus, and willingly did she now succumb.

One of his hands moved down to cup her derriere, and she groaned against his mouth. His hand moved possessively, stroking against the place where the heat that consumed her began, and she gasped in both fear and yearning. At that, his mouth moved to her neck, kissing, nipping, stroking the sensitive skin with his tongue. In small wet circles his tongue traced patterns of pure delight even as his palm circled her bottom, pressing and exciting her with daring promise.

"Blacksword," she murmured on a short intake of breath. "Aric." She felt the full strength of his arousal press demandingly against her belly.

He lifted his head and stared into the melting amber of her eyes. "Whether you be Rosalynde to my Aric," he whispered, "or Rose to my Blacksword, I will have you yet. I will have you yet." Then to her complete bewilderment, he put her from him.

For a full minute they stared at one another across the span of his stiff arms. Rosalynde fought for breath and for control of her spinning senses, only partly aware of his equally breathless state. But she could not hide the bewilderment on her face, nor the impossible desire.

"For such a kiss," he began, still fighting for breath. "For such a kiss you have my silence, sweet Rose."

"You . . . you will not confront my father?" she asked, hardly able to gather her wits again.

"It cannot be avoided forever," he warned her. Then his eyes moved to her reddened lips and he let out a self-deprecating chuckle. "But should I pursue the matter too hard, I suspect you now know how to silence me once more."

So saying he released his hold on her arms and then pushed his hair back from his brow. "And now, as much as I would like to tarry with you, I fear our absence might soon be noted." He gave her a low, sweeping bow before straightening up. Then he gave her a bawdy wink and turned back to his tasks.

Rosalynde stood in the little enclosure of the willow long moments after Aric had left. She heard him in the garden as he worked and knew she too should begin the many tasks that awaited her. But rue and basil and sage were forgotten as she remained where she was.

For the first time she recognized the true depths of the problem she had created. The handfasting had been a necessity, a vow made but never intended to be honored. Then they had lain together and everything had changed. Her virginity was lost and could never be reclaimed. But even in that, as wrong as it was, there had still been the hope for some resolution, some possibility of resuming her life with a degree of hope for the future. And for marriage to some respectable fellow one day.

But this kiss . . .

In the few seconds they had clung together, in the brief embrace they had shared, Rosalynde had come to a new and shattering realization. Blacksword or Aric—he touched something deep within her, something primitive and vital that she'd never known even existed. She thought of him constantly. Waking or sleeping, it made no difference. Her mind was consumed with him, and her body . . .

She closed her eyes and leaned against the little willow. He made her body sing.

If ever there were a man to whom she would cleave herself, he was most certainly it. Rogue that he was, commoner, outlaw, murderer—he drew her in a way no man ever would again. She was as sure of this as of anything she'd ever known. She was a lady. He was a slave. And yet no other man could be husband to her before him.

No man.

Sir Gilbert of Duxton scratched futilely at his bound arm, then picked up the parchment before him. "Have I met this Sir Edward?"

"Sir Peter of Kiln was godfather to both your father and Sir Edward of Stanwood. They squired together and were old friends."

"I've not heard his name mentioned lately. He certainly has not been in London. Is he in disfavor with the crown?"

The seneschal shifted from one leg to another, clearly not at ease under his master's pointed gaze. "Word carries that he has kept to himself these past years since his wife died. He concerns himself with his crops and his fields. And his serfs," he added more quietly.

Gilbert did not notice the man's implication. He was too engrossed in his own thoughts, and his face relaxed in a small smile. "Stanwood must be a profitable demesne under such close supervision. Has he any other heirs besides this daughter?"

"Only a son who died recently."

"So there is no other claim. The land would go with her hand. As would the income." Gilbert leaned back, scratching absently at the itch that continued to plague his healing arm. He gestured for more wine and read the neatly lettered paper once more.

His father's old friend invited him to the spring festivities. Feasting, games, a melee. And the chance to meet his only child, a girl called Rosalynde.

He tapped the corner of the stiff paper against his freshly shaven chin and pursed his lips.

Perhaps this was an omen. He'd been considering abandoning his less savory activities. There was too much outcry against highwaymen and runagates to think he could much longer avoid being found out. Perhaps the rich demesne of a pretty little wife would be a better source of income. Or even the rich demesne of an ugly wife.

He laughed out loud and threw the paper down on the table. "Send word to this Sir Edward that we are pleased to attend his festivities. And Feron," he added before the man could leave the chamber. "Have my captain of the guard come to me. If this Sir Edward is at all like my father, he is more impressed by a man's ability with the sword than by his cleverness. Duxton must make a fine showing in the melee, and I would plan my strategy well."

After the seneschal had departed, Gilbert took up his tankard and drank deeply of the stong red wine. How opportune was this invitation. A wife and another demesne. Yes, this was a very good sign.

He flexed the shoulder of his injured arm, then began abruptly to loosen the bindings around it. Enough time had gone by. Surely the bone was knit. It would not be good to meet his future father-in-law in less than his finest fighting mettle. No, he must strengthen his arm and prepare his men for the melee.

He glanced over at a long sword that hung in a simple leather-and-steel scabbard from a peg on the wall. Perhaps he'd even have a chance to use the newest and finest of his weapons. It had not yet seen battle. However, the upcoming merriments might be the perfect time to christen it.

17

Rosalynde's return to Stanwood Castle brought a myriad of changes. Many were obvious, for even the most slovenly of castle residents could not help but enjoy the new regime of cleanliness that the lord's daughter enforced with a sweet voice and an iron hand. No one complained at the change in authority when Maud and Edith took over the now-spotless kitchen. Even the grumblings about the new work required of everyone were slowly dying down, for everyone was equally affected, and the truth was, the servants took a certain comfort in knowing precisely what their duties were.

Each morning, noon, and evening Sir Edward presided over the meals in the newly pleasant great hall. The castlefolk had begun to respond to the higher expectations made of them. Even his personal garments were clean and mended; indeed, his entire life had brightened in the two weeks since his daughter had returned to him. He was well fed, well housed, and well clothed, as content as a man might hope to be.

"Come walk with me," he requested of her one particular day when the noon meal was complete. "I would have a moment of your time before you hurry away to your next task."

Rosalynde gave her father a surprised look. Although

she knew he approved of all she'd done, he had rarely singled her out to speak with. She welcomed his attention now.

"Will you accompany me to the bailey? I've several vats set to boil and I must check their progress."

"What new labor have you begun?" he asked as they made their way out of the hall and into the midday sunlight.

"We melt tallow and beeswax and wax bark to skim the dirt away. There are candles to make and rushlights to replenish."

They strolled on in silence before he spoke again. "Stanwood shines under your deft hand, daughter. I'd not noted the loss of comforts until you began to restore them."

His eyes were straight ahead as he spoke, never touching her own, and his voice was somewhat gruff. But Rosalynde nonetheless felt the approval there, and a warm rush of feeling went through her.

" 'Tis not so much," she demurred.

" 'Tis enough to make me know that you are a woman now, not a child as I had persisted in thinking. You are a woman fully grown and a chatelaine to be proud of." He halted when they reached the huge vats, and he turned to stare at her expectantly. " 'Tis time to see you wed."

Rosalynde gasped in shock at his unexpected words, and in the first moments after his pronouncement she only stared at him in horror, looking for all the world as if she had just learned she was to be executed at dawn. Her heart thundered furiously and her throat grew dry as she stared mutely at him, her eyes wide and her mouth gaping open.

It was clear he anticipated a pleased reaction from her, even though it might understandably be tempered with a natural hesitance. Every noblewoman expected to marry, and there was no reason for him to think she would feel any differently about it. When his brow creased in a puzzled frown, however, she abruptly closed her mouth and assumed a less revealing expression. But her father was not to be fooled.

"What is this, Rosalynde? You gape at me as one amazed. Yet was it not you who said you were well trained in the housewifely arts? You have proven that well enough. It only remains for you to take a husband. And yet methinks the idea does not set well with you."

For a moment Rosalynde could not think of a reply. At least not one that did not threaten the well-being of Aric. "I . . . it's only that, well. . . ." She faltered. "I have only just returned to Stanwood and already you would send me away."

"You cannot think I would send you from Stanwood, daughter. As my only heir, you and your husband should be here." His lined face smiled reassuringly and he patted her shoulder. "Never fear. I'll not send you away again."

Had it not been for her terrible predicament of already being bound to Aric, Rosalynde would have been very much comforted by her father's words, for there was a wealth of revealing emotion in them. In his own awkward way he was expressing his regret for the long years he had kept her away. In his own way he was showing his love to her. Rosalynde recognized that at once. But the urgency of her own situation prevented her from savoring the knowledge. Instead she clasped her hands together and turned nervously toward the nearest vat.

"There is no rush, is there, Father? I mean, certainly I expect to wed, but . . . but I had thought we could spend some time together first. And also," she added, grasping truly at straws now. "Also, it would be unseemly to host a wedding so soon after poor Giles's death. . . ."

She trailed off as sorrow for her young brother combined with her own panic to choke her voice.

"There, there, Rosalynde. Do not fret for this." Sir Edward hovered near her, clearly discomfitted by this unanticipated turn of events. " 'Tis not my wish to send you tomorrow into marriage. I but thought to begin the process. Make the inquiries."

"Oh." Rosalynde turned a hopeful face to her father. "Oh, I see," she said with relief.

"And since you have worked such wonders with the castle," he hurried on when he saw her change of mood, "I thought to begin by entertaining a few guests."

Rosalynde's relief skidded to a halt. "When?" she asked fearfully.

"Oh, soon," he said evasively. "But don't worry on that, daughter. A guest or two now and again will hardly trouble you." He shifted his gaze to the ramparts and frowned somewhat. "I . . . ah . . . I must see to something. If you will pardon me? I must speak to Cedric . . . to Sir Roger, I mean. Well . . ." With those parting words he strode quickly away. Rosalynde was left to stare after him, her emotions in a quandary as she pondered the new complication that had just been thrust upon her.

She refused to work with Aric that afternoon. The thought of dealing with his ever-strengthening demands was too much for her to face, especially after her troubling conversation with her father. But it was not only his demands that she feared. More than that, it was her own weakening resolve.

A week had passed since she'd bribed him with that kiss, and in that time he'd only become more and more familiar with her. He hadn't kissed her again. It would almost have been better if he had. Instead he talked to her most easily, did not hesitate to touch her in passing—at least he did that only when no one was in sight—and all too often smiled at her. It was that smile—sometimes friendly, sometimes mocking—that proved her biggest trial. His eyes would sweep her lazily. Possessively. And he would smile, showing strong white teeth beneath curving lips.

Those lips fascinated her, and more and more she found herself dwelling on them. Whenever she was alone, whether working or resting, the memory of those lips pressed to her own haunted her. She imagined him kissing her neck, her shoulders. Her breasts. Something deep inside her would tighten into a hot churning knot and she would even imagine him sweeping a trail of kisses down to her belly, as if he might be able to release the pent-up tension that coiled in her down there. Then, appalled at the wicked wanderings of her own thoughts, she would retreat to the sanctuary of prayer. Many long hours she spent on her knees. In the small chapel. In her own chamber. Sometimes even in the garden. She would kneel on the small fustian pallet, pulling up nettles and felonwort and friar's cap, and she would pray for divine intervention. Nothing but God's own intercession seemed likely to contradict the overwhelming emotions that so perversely drew her to Blacksword. Only God could help her.

She was staring at the huge vat of tallow, seeing but not really noting how industriously the young lad stirred the bubbling mess and how carefully he skimmed away the scum. Her mind was preoccupied with Aric and with her father's words regarding her marriage. When the first shout came she did not at first look up. But when she heard a frightened cry followed by a babble of alarmed calls, her head jerked up. Across the bailey, just beyond the great hall, she could see a knot of people. But above them, dangling from a rope, a man twisted crazily. He'd been repairing crumbling portions of the wall earlier, sitting in a sling that had been lowered from the ramparts above. But one of the ropes had broken, and unable to crawl up or get down, the man could only cling to the single remaining length of jute.

She did not stop to think as she dashed toward the man. From all across the bailey people stopped to look, then hurried toward the excitement. But one person reacted more quickly than the rest. Instead of heading toward the screaming man, Aric rushed to a narrow stone stairs that led up to the ramparts. Then before anyone else could even formulate a plan to aid the hapless fellow, Aric was standing above him, gripping the rope in his mighty fists. With one hand he lifted the man a foot, just enough to unloop the other end of the rope, which was anchored to a huge timber. Then in slow, steady movements he lowered the terrified man hand over hand to the ground.

When the poor fellow finally reached the ground, a huge shout went up from the gathered crowd. Cheers and clapping greeted the trembling mason, and for a moment he was unable to speak. Then he looked up at the brawny man who now pulled up the rope and coiled it neatly in his hand.

"Ye have me thanks, friend," he called up to Aric. He gave him an abbreviated bow, then smiled up at him again. "Ye have me thanks and me undying friendship."

As cheers followed that pronouncement, Rosalynde also stared up at Aric. In the late afternoon, with the sunlight glancing golden off his hair and backlighting his powerful silhouette, he looked almost an angel of deliverance. Most certainly he had rescued the mason from sure injury. With his quick reaction, shrewd thinking, and physical strength he had saved the fellow before his arms gave out. He had not waited for instructions or orders. Instead he had taken control of the situation and averted disaster.

Her brow creased as she studied him. He was not a follower, but a leader. He was too smart and too capable to be a mere runagate, yet how had he come by such qualities?

Rosalynde knew this one act would go far in establishing the outlaw Blacksword among the rest of the castlefolk. He would be Aric the hero now, and accepted, instead of remaining an outsider.

Yet in his dark tunic and braies, with nothing to commend him but his native intelligence and uncanny strength, he appeared to be as much devil as angel. Lucifer, the fallen angel, her fanciful thoughts named him. He had a considerable capacity for good. Why had he ever been drawn into a life of crime?

She watched as his eyes skimmed the crowd. She trembled when they stopped on her. For a tense moment their eyes clung and she sensed the taunt he sent her. She'd avoided him today. He knew it and he would not let her get away with it. On shaking legs she sought to turn away from that mocking stare, to flee to the safety of her candles and wax. But her father appeared in the bailey then, and with a wave of his hand called her to his side.

"Are you hurt, Tom?" he asked the old mason with the concern of a good lord.

"I'm shaken, milord, and none too steady in my knees. But I'm sound, and I've that young fellow to thank for it. If he hadn't been there . . ."

"So it seems," Sir Edward agreed as his eyes turned up to where Aric stood. As he and Rosalynde watched, Blacksword gathered the ends of the rope, whipped them tightly around the loops, and tucked them securely in place. Then he slung the heavy coil over one shoulder and made his way toward the stairs.

"This Aric," Sir Edward mused, watching the man's sure descent. "He's one not easy to fathom." Then he turned his eyes on her. "If you've finished with him in your garden, I've another more likely place in mind for him."

His words created unexpected confusion in Rosalynde. Logic deemed it best that she and Aric not spend any time in company together. That only created all sorts of temptations for her. But she quite perversely did not want him out of her sight. She justified it as only self-preservation. Away from her he might accidentally—or intentionally—give their secret away. But she could not completely pass it off as such, at least not to herself.

"What would you have of him?" she asked her father quietly.

"If he is so inclined, he would make a good man-at-arms. He has the strength and the quickness. He's not a stupid fellow. I'm just not certain of his loyalty," he added thoughtfully.

"I had thought—" Rosalynde started to speak, and then had second thoughts.

But her father pinned her with his astute gaze. "You had thought what?" he prompted as the crowd began to disperse.

"Well, I mean . . ." She hesitated, knowing she must tread carefully. "It has been only a fortnight since you had him flogged, and then you spared him only because I interceded. Yet now you would make him a man-at-arms with weapons at his disposal?" She looked away, unnerved by her father's steady gaze. "It's just that I am surprised, that is all."

"Is there something about this man that I should know,

Rosalynde? Something you are aware of that would better help me to judge his character?" When she did not answer, but only shook her head mutely, he sighed. "The man is an odd one. I mark that well. There is that side of him that is a savage. I have seen it in men of war and I recognize it in him. But he has a self-control that sets him apart. I know he but bides his time, daughter. He was not meant to till earth. But I have only to channel his savagery and shrewdness to my own use. Eventually I will find the proper niche for him here at Stanwood. That's the only sure way to ever inspire loyalty in a man. Make him fit in."

Rosalynde was much taken aback by her father's well-considered words. She'd not noticed that her father was even aware of Aric's whereabouts, let alone the vagaries of the man's personality. Yet she could not but agree with his assessment. Aric was most assuredly possessed of a savage side. And he was a man accustomed to danger, to war, as it were. She'd not thought about his self-control, yet now that her father had put voice to it, she recognized it well. He'd kept silent during that brutal flogging. And since then he had most definitely been biding his time, waiting for his reward even though what he demanded and what she offered seemed far beyond compromise. Oh yes, he was a man possessed of both savagery and self-control.

For a weak moment she wondered which of those traits fascinated her more. But her father was watching her, and she sternly willed such thoughts away.

"He is a man hard to understand," she admitted slowly.

"Do you fear him?"

This time Rosalynde could not hide her startled expression. "I . . . well, no. No," she said in a firmer voice. "I have never feared harm at his hands," she declared. At least not the sort of harm her father meant, she thought to herself. What she feared from the man was the singular power he seemed to have over her body and her emotions. That was what made him so particularly dangerous to her.

"Never?" Sir Edward's gray brows raised doubtfully. "How come you by such faith in a man of his questionable past?"

"What I mean is, once I got to know him I was not afraid. At first . . . well, at first I was too desperate for help to worry. But once he agreed to help us . . ."

"You trusted him to keep to his word."

"Yes, I trusted him to keep his word." And he had, she knew. The only problem now was that he also trusted her to keep hers.

She pressed her lips together, unable to suppress the guilt that besieged her at that thought. More than anything she wanted to escape her father's keen gaze, but for once he seemed determined to keep her in his company. "Aric will make you a good man-at-arms, Father. He is strong and smart, and can be very determined. My garden nears completion. Take him with good heart. I wish you well of him. As for me, however, I've much left to do this day. If you will excuse me?"

Sir Edward watched her depart with a small frown on his face. Twice in one day he'd left her side bewildered by her reactions. Was it only that she was a woman and he a man? Was that why nothing he expected from her came to pass?

He'd thought to find a girl too young and too spoiled to take over the workings of a household as vast as Stanwood. Instead, he'd found her to be capable and willing, a young woman of admirable talents and grace. He'd anticipated her excitement at the thought of her own marriage, yet she'd clearly been dismayed. Resistant even. And now, when he'd only offhandedly remarked on the uses of one of his many servants, he'd gotten a strong sense that she was vitally concerned with whatever befell the man.

For a moment he wondered at such concern, and a vague voice of doubt tugged at him. Had something passed between the two of them before they'd been found and brought to Stanwood? Had the boy's accusations been true?

But if they had been true, if the man had attacked her and done his worst with her, she would hardly have defended him at the flogging. Although she might be tempted to lie to preserve her own reputation, if he had misused her she would surely not have balked at seeing the man punished. No, he decided with a slow shake of his graying head. Rosalynde felt gratitude toward the man, but nothing else. He had saved her and the boy, and as a result, she would very likely always have a particular interest in this man's well-being. Under the circumstances she should be well pleased, for as a man-at-arms his life would improve considerably. Assuming, of course, that the taciturn fellow was bright enough to appreciate what was being offered to him.

Aric was wary when he was called into Sir Edward's presence. He had seen the man staring at him after the mason had been rescued, but his own eyes had been drawn to Rosalynde who had stood at her father's side. Now he wondered whether she had finally confessed, finally revealed the truth of her marriage to her parent. Since she had pointedly avoided him all day, there was no telling what he might expect.

If Rosalynde had told her father of the handfast vow, the man would undoubtedly be furious. Just as Rosalynde had foreseen, her father's first reaction would most certainly be violent. Aric's only defense would be the revelation of

his own noble upbringing, and he counted on that to ensure the marriage stood.

He frowned as he strode across the bailey, and once
again he wondered at his own perversity for not simply
revealing the truth of his identity. Day by day his chance
for revenge against his unknown foes was slipping away
from him, confounded by his feelings for this one slender
maiden. Even worse, being so near Rosalynde and yet not
having leave to bed her taxed him almost beyond the lim-
its of his control. It did not help at all that the dairymaid
constantly dogged his path. That one's willing and ample
form interested him not the least, and only served to increase the desire he felt for the dark-haired mistress of the
castle.

Rosalynde desired him as well—there was no mistaking
that fact. But her noble birth held her apart from him, and
although he suspected she would accept him better should
his true identity be revealed, for some reason he wanted
more than that. He wanted her to admit to her desire. He
wanted her to come to him willingly, disregarding all the
reasons she should not. Only then would he be sure that
she wanted *him,* the man she knew him to be. Only then
would he tell her the truth of who he was.

When he entered the great hall and stopped before her
father, he was immediately certain that Rosalynde had not
revealed a thing to him, for Sir Edward's smile, though
reserved, was nonetheless sincere. This time there was no
waiting in silence, wondering what was to come. This time
Sir Edward laid down his quill and leaned back in his
chair, eyeing him with friendly interest.

"That was a commendable feat I saw this morning.
Quick thinking, even more quickly carried out. I thank
you both for myself and for Tom."

Aric considered Sir Edward a short moment before

bowing his head slightly in acknowledgment. "It was little enough to do for a man in need."

"Yes," Sir Edward mused. "Perhaps so. But I am as inclined to reward good deeds as I am likely to punish bad. We did not meet under the best of circumstances. But I am ready to let the past be, and move on to the future. If you can agree to that, I offer you a position among my men-at-arms."

This Aric had not anticipated, and he was momentarily taken by surprise. To have weapons in his hands once more! To test himself daily in exercise and combat. If he must maintain this disguise, far better to be a soldier than a farmer. But as a soldier, how likely was he to see Rosalynde? It was for this that he hesitated until Sir Edward's smile began to fade.

"Well?" the older man demanded more brusquely. "Is my faith in your quick wits so soon proved foolish?"

"Nay, sire. Not foolish at all. I had but wondered . . ." Aric halted, then his resolve jelled. He would see Rosalynde, one way or another, and in a better light. She would be his yet, as would the whole of Stanwood some day. But it was the woman he wanted above all else, and with a sudden grin he faced Sir Edward. "I had but marveled at your generosity, sire. Most assuredly I do accept your kind offer. I only hope, Sir Edward, that I may prove worthy of your trust."

So do I, Sir Edward thought once he had sent the intimidating fellow off to Sir Roger. *So do I.*

18

Rosalynde stood beneath the one tree in her garden. The ancient walnut provided the only shady spot in the otherwise hot and dusty castle yard. Two of the lads from the great hall were laying an edging of river stones around one portion of the garden while two others were off collecting more of the smoothly rounded rocks, and still another pair struggled to shift an oversize block of stone to the far end of the neat little lawn.

Aric would make short shrift of that task, she decided as she watched the boys' sweaty efforts. Then she immediately berated herself for such a perverse thought. So what if he could move the huge stone single-handed? That meant nothing. He was still a condemned criminal. Yet her eyes could not help but stray once more to the broad-shouldered figure on the far side of the bailey. Even among the many like-clothed men-at-arms he stood out. It was as much his arrogant carriage as his considerable size; the man was simply not the sort one could ignore. Even among the other men-at-arms that proved true. Although she observed him from afar, it was nonetheless obvious that the other men were in awe of him and his incredible prowess with whatever weapon they practiced with. Some responded by seeking his friendship. Others reacted with scowls and quiet mutterings. But there was not a man among them who did not react in some way. Blacksword was not a man easily overlooked.

Even Sir Roger had made a point of observing him. It was the day they had practiced with the stout oak staffs. Back and forth in the dusty yard the men had fought. Feint and parry, then strike. High and low the staffs had swung with the thud of wood on wood a constant echo across the yard. Aric had been paired with the most proficient of the other men. When that poor fellow had been deftly un-armed with a particularly swift upward stroke, Sir Roger's second-in-command had stepped in to take his place. All other activity had slowed to watch the two men's eager exercise. Even Rosalynde had moved reluctantly nearer.

This time the fight had been long and tiring. Before a clear victor could emerge, Sir Roger had called it to a halt. Rosalynde thought it was to save the other man's dignity, but another odd sensation had struck her as well. Aric had seemed to be holding back, she had noticed during the fight. His movements were slower and not nearly so aggressive. It was almost as if he too had not wished to belittle the man by his victory. But that had made no sense at all.

Now as she watched them scale the inner walls of the castle, throwing their pike-ended ropes to catch on the parapet walls, then hauling themselves up until they gained the walkway, the mystery of the man plagued her anew. Sir Roger wondered about his remarkable physical skills. Her father was intrigued by his considerable talents. And she . . . she was plainly besotted with him.

With a frustrated oath she pushed herself away from the walnut tree, then snapped the small dried branch she held in two. If it had been a torture to work with him every day in the garden, it seemed doubly so now that she only saw him from afar.

"Does this please you, milady?" one of the lads inquired respectfully.

"Yes, yes," she answered with a vague wave of one hand. She gave the fellow a cursory glance, then sighed, annoyed by her constant preoccupation with Aric. "It looks very well," she said, this time actually looking at the finished work. "Until the next cartload of stones arrives, go ahead and fetch water for the new row of rosebushes." Then she saw her father across the yard and her attention was once more turned away from her labors.

Her father stood next to Sir Roger. From this distance Rosalynde could not determine what passed between them. But she watched, as did they, while Blacksword speedily scaled the wall, catching up to the man before him, and allowing that lagging fellow to use one of his shoulders as a boost up to the top. Her father turned at once to Sir Roger, and their heads bent close for several seconds. Then Sir Edward turned to stare at her and all at once her heart began to race. She'd not spoken at length to her father in the five days since he'd pulled Aric from the garden and made him one of his men-at-arms. Yet she knew that something was afoot.

It was not until the evening meal, however, that she received the least inkling of what it could be. She was freshly cleaned. Her hair was loosely pulled back from her face, then caught halfway down her back by a pierced leather strip that was woven with the hair into a braid falling past her waist. She wore an apple-green gown, the first of several gowns she'd begun for herself, and her face glowed with color from the many hours that she spent outdoors. When she spied Aric entering with the other men-at-arms to eat at a table in the middle of the hall, an astute observer would have noticed that the golden-rose hue of her cheeks deepened even further. But Rosalynde quickly averted her gaze, and in the flickering light of the hall, her emotions were easily hidden.

When her father joined her, he too appeared in fine spirits. But his old eyes were sharp as he watched his daughter signal the chamberlain to begin the serving. With an occasional nod of her head and gesture of her hand, she orchestrated the meal from her place above the salt.

"The fowl is good," he commended her as he did justice to the whole duckling before him. "The bread and the sauce also." He licked gravy from one finger, then grinned at her. "Your husband shall be blessed indeed."

"Husband!" Rosalynde's eyes widened in sudden alarm. What did he mean? What did he know?

Her father's amiable expression dissolved into a frown. "God's blood, daughter! Can I not speak of your marriage without you staring at me as if I were sending you to your execution? 'Tis your duty to marry. Especially now. And do not think to enter the abbey no matter what the priests may say. Stanwood is held only through you. It is just this choosing of the right man that awaits."

"I-I do not mean to imply that I would shirk my duties," Rosalynde answered, recovering from her shock. "I know I must marry, and truly, I do seek it. It is only the choice that concerns me. Nothing else."

"That is good, then. That is good. And I plan to be generous with you on that account. You shall see any fellow I consider and I will not deny you comment on their merits. The decision, of course, will be mine. However, I would see you happy with the choice."

"Thank you, Father," she said with a small sigh of relief.

"To that end," he continued, after drinking deeply of his wine. "I propose a spring festival. The planting nears completion. The weather has cooperated. I would reward one and all with a day of feasting and games." He cleared his throat and gave her a watchful smile. "Several men of my acquaintance have expressed interest in the games."

"Several men?"

Sir Edward met her dismayed gaze, then looked away. "There will be a small tourney. It will give you a chance to meet several unmarried men and perhaps find one to your liking. Since I'll not invite any whom I would not also accept, you will have much freedom in the choosing. More than most fathers would allow," he added somewhat belligerently. Then his tone softened. "Stanwood has not hosted such a gathering in many a year. Until you returned the place was hardly presentable. But you have taken things well in hand, daughter. I have given you leave to manage the household as you will. You must now trust me to do my duty to you with regard to a husband."

"I-I cannot but agree," she replied, aware that he asked nothing unreasonable of her.

"Good," he said, then signaled a page to refill his cup. "You prepare chambers and meals. I'll see to the entertainments. Oh, but there *is* one matter you could help me with. Pertaining to the new man. Aric."

"Aric?" Rosalynde echoed. Once more her equanimity was destroyed. "How can I . . . What do you mean?"

Sir Edward bent toward her, his voice lowered. "That fellow you brought here has me mightily perplexed. Beyond his brute strength, he possesses a shrewd intelligence."

With that assessment Rosalynde could not but agree. Still, her father's interest made her wary. "But what has that to do with me?"

"He reveals nothing of himself. Not how he came by his talent for combat, nor how he has spent these past years. Yet I am not one easily fooled. The man fights like one trained to it. His skill was learned and then tested on the field of battle. He is not a mere brawler. But he keeps his secrets to himself."

"Perhaps it is for the best, Father."

"Aye, sometimes that is best. But one of the entertainments at our festival shall be the melee. If he can be trusted he could very well turn the tide in our favor. Sir Virgil of Rising will be here, and I have not bested his men in the melee's battle games in many a year."

Rosalynde's relief at her father's concerns was so great that she let out a great sigh. Then she smiled brightly at him. "He can be trusted to fight with you. Of that I am absolutely certain."

"So I thought you might say. But I would nonetheless like to know more of him. You spent time with him before. You saved him from my punishment and probably even tended his back." His one brow arched perceptively. "You trust him and I wouldn't doubt he trusts you, at least more than he might trust anyone else around here. Talk to him, Rosalynde. See what you can learn of him. The man has much to offer but I must know more."

"I must know more." Those words of her father's bothered Rosalynde through the remainder of the meal. "I must know more." And yet there was much that he must never know.

Still, her curiosity about Aric was even stronger than her father's. The man was a complete enigma. His arrogant attitude was sorely at odds with his lowly station in life. It was no wonder that her father had noticed him. The fact that he was so adept in battle only piqued her father's interest, for Sir Edward was primarily a man of war. He had not hesitated to back Matilda and her son Henry II in his bid to claim the crown from Stephen. In the two years since that conflict had been resolved, he had clearly been

chafing at the bit. Now that he proposed the tourney and
the melee, it was no surprise that he would seek out the
best warriors to fight with him. And just like him, she had
no doubt that Aric was among the best.

But how had he gotten to be the best? That was the
question that puzzled her father and that plagued her as
well.

She left the meal early, leaving her father to his own
devices and the now well-trained boys to the clearing of
the tables. As she made her way past the edge of the
crowded tables she saw Edith. Remembering a matter
they needed to discuss, she made her way over to her.

"Good ev'nin', milady," Edith said, starting to rise from
her half-completed meal.

"Please, I do not mean to disturb your meal," Rosalynde
said with a smile, pressing her back into her seat. "I only
wished to tell you that tomorrow after the first meal I will
explain to you which spices go best together. We'll measure and tie into bundles the prescribed amounts so that
you may more easily use them in your cooking."

"Thank you, milady. I promise you, your faith in me
shall not be wasted."

"Of that I have no doubt." She patted Edith's shoulder
then turned to depart. It was then that she met Aric's gaze.
He was still sitting at the table, but his meal was done and
he was just finishing his cup of ale. Their eyes met only
briefly; she quickly averted her face and continued on her
way. But in that single moment of contact there was a
wealth of communication. Her skin was warm and her
heart raced as she made her way out of the great hall. A
knot twisted deep in her belly, and once outside she
paused to take a calming breath. But she hardly had time
to get over that one potent look they'd shared before the
very object of her disquiet appeared through the twilight.

As if he knew she were there—as if he expected her to be waiting for him—he crossed to the deep shadows where she stood on trembling legs.

"Come walk with me," he said in a low and husky tone. His hand reached up and with the backs of his knuckles he stroked down the curve of hair that lay against her cheek.

The ready retort she had for his unseemly invitation died unsaid when his hand met her hair. Instead she only pressed herself harder against the rough stone wall, wishing he would go away, wishing that he would not force her to confront the terrible feelings he roused in her.

"I have missed you," he murmured when she did not respond. His fingers found the line of her jaw and he traced a path down to her chin. "Have you missed me as well?"

"No," Rosalynde replied, although she knew it was not the truth. "No," she repeated the lie in a breathless voice.

She heard his soft chuckle and felt his warmth as he moved a little closer. One of his hands moved to rest against the wall, effectively blocking her escape. With his other he tilted her face up to him. "Such a sweet little liar you are, my Rose. Lips like honey, waiting to be feasted upon. Yet from those very lips spill the most blatant of lies." He rubbed the callused pad of his thumb across her full lower lip. "You tell me lies; you break vows that were made before God and man. How is it that I still would have you to wife?"

"You want only one thing of me," she accused him, her voice trembling.

"And that is?" One of his brows arched in mocking question.

"My . . . my . . . you know! Your way with me, you horrible beast!"

"My way with you?" He laughed again, then he pressed

up against her and she gasped as all her senses leapt. His chest was hard against her full breasts. His belly was firm and his thighs like iron where they pressed against her soft form. He nuzzled her hair, finding her ear with his mouth. "We both know I can have my way with you whenever I wish," he whispered hotly in her ear. To make his point he rubbed his loins aggressively against her until she felt she would melt from the heat he inspired in her. "It only remains for me to gain the castle through a proper renewal of our vows."

"Oh!" Rosalynde tried to free herself of him at that cold and self-serving revelation. "Let me go, you despicable cur!" she ordered as she sought to shove him away.

"From those perfect lips you vow your hatred. But, Rose, your body tells me otherwise. Here." His hand moved up to stroke the side of her breast. Then his thumb slid to the hardened crest. "And here," he added as his eyes stared deeply into hers. Despite her wish to deny his abhorrent words, Rosalynde knew with a sinking desperation that in this he had her dead to rights. A frisson coursed through her as his warm gaze held with hers. Then with a shudder of defeat she closed her eyes, unable to fight the truth anymore.

"Ah, my sweet Rose," he whispered in light kisses on her brow and then down her cheek to her temple. "Tell me once more how much you hate me."

Rosalynde swallowed hard, then swallowed again when his lips found the vulnerable exposed hollow at her throat. Her arms lifted to circle his neck; in the quiet dark of this corner of the bailey she pressed her entire length to him, succumbing to the desire that simmered so near the surface and that now threatened to erupt and overwhelm them.

"I hate you," her words came, faint and trembling. "I do," she insisted on a sigh.

He pulled her away from the wall and gathered her into his arms. "If this is your hatred, then I must work harder to gain your love—"

But before he could complete his statement, before his lips could meet hers, the door to the great hall opened, spilling a slash of light down the three stone steps and into the starlit yard. Instinctively Blacksword turned, hiding her identity with his broad form. His lips touched hers lightly, whispering a mute warning to be quiet. Then on silent feet he turned, moving deeper into the shadows, still holding on to her as two men paused on the step.

Rosalynde was too unnerved by her reaction to Aric to be mindful of the men who stood so near yet were oblivious to their presence. She buried her face against Blacksword's neck, breathing in the unique scent of his hard-muscled body, intoxicated by the wild feelings he roused in her. Yet when one of the men spoke, her nerves came painfully alert and she was overcome with fear.

" 'Tis a chance you need not take," Sir Roger said in his familiar gravelly voice.

It was her father who responded. "He has the talent. You saw him today, Roger. You know he could have made short shrift of Harold if he had but wished to."

"But there's the rub! Why *did* he **hold** back? And who's to know when he might hold back again?"

Rosalynde sensed Aric's sudden tension when he realized they spoke of him. In the dark corner formed by the outer wall and the great hall they stood, pressed together, both straining to hear her father's response.

"He had a reason for holding back, I'll grant you that. Though I cannot be sure of his reason, however, I am nonetheless fairly sure that he will not do so in the heat of battle."

Sir Roger let out a grunt of disapproval. "He is an outlaw. Mark my words, 'tis more than likely he'll go too far and let serious blood during our sport. Either way, I'd as well not learn you misjudged him on the field of honor."

With a low chuckle Sir Edward moved down the steps and out into the yard. " 'Tis only a melee," he reminded his captain of the guard. "Best to find out now instead of in a true battle."

"Aye, it is only a melee," Sir Roger agreed as the men began to walk away. "But Sir Virgil of Rising will be there and I would rather be completely sure of our troops. And 'tis not only Rising's forces who will be eager to best us. Every man who aspires to your daughter's hand will want to prove his mettle before you."

They were soon out of earshot, but Aric did not immediately move away from her. He seemed preoccupied until she shifted in his arms. Then he leaned back and looked down at her.

"Those fools who aspire to your hand will have me to contend with," he said sternly. Then his expression relaxed. "It appears the father is coming around toward me. So, it seems, is the daughter." His hands moved down her back as he stared into her eyes. "How soon until we tell your father he already has a son-in-law? How soon until you will be mine, my night Rose?"

More than anything Rosalynde wanted to say "now." More than anything she wished to complete the passionate exploration they'd begun, to allow the fire they'd started, to build to an inferno until it consumed them both. But the conversation they had overheard had forced reality on her. As she lingered in his stirring embrace all her questions came back to mind, the very same questions her father had about the uncommon servant she had brought him.

"Who are you?" she whispered, trying to make out the expression in his shadowed face. "Please tell me who you really are."

There was a moment's pause before he answered, a moment when she sensed a strange yearning in him, as if he fought a part of himself before replying. "I'm the same man you saved from the gallows. The man you wed. The man who claims you as wife. What more do you wish to know?"

In frustration she pushed against him. "That's not what I mean and you know it. My father offers you an honorable life. He asks only for the truth of your past so that he may know whether you will truly protect his back. Is that so hard for you to understand?"

"I'll protect his back, Rosalynde. I pledged him my loyalty and I always stand by my vow. 'Tis time you stand by yours."

"Must you always come back to that!" she cried, truly frustrated now. She tried to slip from his encircling arms but he easily thwarted her.

"Your vow is where it all started between us. It will always come back to that. But if you would know more of your husband, 'tis easily enough done. Just bribe me with your kisses. If you doubt my willingness to serve your father honorably, promise me your tender caress. Tempt me with the memory of our joining." His husky words sent a warm shiver through her. "Come to my bed, my sweet, sweet wife."

If only she could, the wild thought careened through her head. If only it was that easy she would follow him right now, whether to a bed of straw, a pallet of hides, or a mattress of feathers and down. He would lay her back and remove her clothes. Then he would remove his as well, and cover her trembling body with the heat and power of his own.

Rosalynde turned her face away from his seeking kiss, but her hands twisted in the sturdy fabric of his tunic. "You don't understand," she whispered miserably. "What you want . . . it can never be."

"You're wrong in that, my honey Rose. We may have whatever we want *if* we are willing to take the risk."

"But the risk is your *life!*" she blurted out angrily. "Can't you see that?"

His hand caught her chin and he turned her face up to him. She felt the rough warmth of his palm against the sensitive skin of her neck. But his eyes were hard and as dark as obsidian.

"I think, perhaps, that it is the risk to *your* life—to your way of life—that worries you most." So saying, he bent forward to take her mouth in an angry and forceful kiss.

There was no teasing this time, no beguiling and seducing with lips and tongue. This time he did not ask nor did he coax. Instead he took what he wanted with no regard for her feelings at all.

Rosalynde felt the heat of anger and frustration in his demanding possession of her. As he twisted her hair in his hands then plundered her mouth voraciously, she recognized the desire that drove him to such a violent outburst. Within her there was an answering desire. She was thunder to his lightning, as much a cause of this storm of emotions as she was a reaction to it. She felt the rigid strength of him pressing against her; she felt the melting heat as she became pliant against him. But everything else was lost as she succumbed to the intoxicating power of his kiss.

There was no right or wrong as Rosalynde yielded to his steely embrace. Logic and the proper order of society played no part in her reaction to him. In truth, it never had. Whether he were a black-hearted criminal as had been proclaimed, or something else as she often suspected, there was no denying him. In reckless abandon she rose to his forceful possession of her. In a dizzy rush she accepted his rough caress and in so doing found an even greater pleasure. She was crushed in his arms, drowning in the powerful emotions that erupted between them. And when his hand slid down to cup her derriere, to press her most intimately against his fierce arousal, she whimpered helplessly against his lips.

"Will you have me, my thorny Rose?" he murmured in a voice thick with passion. He moved deliberately against her, starting an erotic ripple that coursed up from her belly to encompass her entire being. "Will you have me at last?"

Rosalynde was beyond denying him anything. One of her hands circled his neck, sliding along the pronounced muscles of his shoulder and back. *There's a man worth having,* she recalled the awestruck comment made by some woman of Dunmow. She'd agreed at the time and she still did, but for reasons that could not be more different. He was a man worth having no matter what the chasm between them was, and that very realization erased even her last few doubts. It was as if joy suddenly filled her, as if an odd sort of serenity washed over her with all its attendant happiness. There was no wrong when two people shared such intensity of feeling. Such desire was a gift to be treasured, a blessing bestowed upon them by a benign and understanding God. It was not lust, she understood with almost painful clarity. It was not lust but love.

Tears started in her eyes as that thunderous truth struck her. Emotions caught in her throat and in a sob she turned her face away from him.

"Blacksword . . ." she whispered as his mouth pressed feverish kisses to her ear and neck and throat. "Black-sword . . ."

"Aric," he murmured as his tongue traced an exquisite pattern in her ear. One of his hands cupped her breasts, and she stiffened at the perfect thrill it sent through her. "I am Aric, Rosalynde. Your husband."

"Yes," she replied as her nipples tightened in response. "You are Aric, my husband."

My love, she added silently when his lips caught hers in a fiery kiss. As she succumbed to this new wonder, this new understanding of his place in her life, Rosalynde's thoughts tumbled in disjointed happiness. They'd kissed at the handfasting ceremony, but this, she now knew, was the true kiss that pledged her vow. As he slowly turned round and round, holding her with desperate fervor, kissing her as if he must consume her, she did not hold back a thing. She came to him with complete awareness and total acceptance. His breath was her breath. His heartbeat was her own. Their passion was a mutual thing.

Their love was inevitable.

But their lovemaking sadly was not. Once more the door to the great hall opened. Once more light spilled out across the darkened yard. But this time a lantern swung from the hands of a solitary figure, and this time the light found their corner.

Rosalynde was much too overwhelmed with emotion to react at first. Too besotted by the name she'd put to her feelings to think or even to move. But Aric's response to the interruption was immediate.

"Begone from here, fool!" he said with a snarl as he used his wide shoulders to protect her identity from pry-ing eyes. "Begone from here or suffer the consequences."

Yes, begone, Rosalynde echoed silently as she pressed a kiss against the rough wool at Aric's chest.

"If that is the Lady Rosalynde, then 'tis you who shall suffer the consequences!" young Cleve's voice hissed furiously.

At once Rosalynde's head came up. Aric's hands tightened on her arms, but he did not stop her when she wrenched free of his embrace. As she faced the boy who shook now with the depths of his anger—or was it disappointment? she wondered as she took in his pale face—she tried to marshal her thoughts.

"Please, Cleve. You must understand—"

" 'Tis clear enough for even a fool to understand!"

"No, no. If you would just listen!"

"This is not your concern, pup," Aric said warningly. His arm came around Rosalynde's shoulders and he pulled her possessively against him. "I suggest you take yourself off."

The boy sent the towering man a scathing look, then his eyes turned urgently to Rosalynde. "Come with me, milady. Just leave him now and this can all be forgotten," he pleaded.

Behind her Rosalynde felt the warmth of Aric's chest, and also the tension he barely restrained. With a slow shake of her head she stared at Cleve.

"It's not that simple."

"Bedamned if it is not! D'you think you're the first maiden to swoon at the feet of a man she can never have!" His eyes narrowed and he took a step forward. The light swung wildly in his hands, casting grim dancing shadows across them all. "D'you think you're the first maiden to go to her marriage bed no longer a virgin!"

"Hold your accursed tongue, boy. Or else I'll tear it

from your head! If you care for her as you profess to, you'll not be so loose with her honor!"

Cleve drew himself up to his fullest height and glared at the man who held Rosalynde so easily. "Her honor is defiled only by you. She's too besotted to see that, but I am not." His eyes came back to her. "I beg you, milady. Put him from you before you come to grief. Even now your father seeks an honorable man to be your husband. Do not ruin your life with a one such as him!" Then with a stiff bow that was more an insult, given the circumstances, he turned and stalked away.

But Cleve's departure did not ease the tension that gnawed at Rosalynde. As darkness enveloped them once more she was forced to face reality. No matter the feelings that swelled within her for Aric, no matter his noble bearing and the thread of decency she knew ran deep within him, she could not change facts. She was from noble lineage; for her, marriage to another of her class was inevitable. Aric—Blacksword—was a criminal, a slave, a servant. No father in his right mind would sanction such a match. Most especially not hers.

Aric's arm moved down to circle her waist, and with an easy tug he turned her to face him. But his expression too was serious as he met her somber stare.

"This changes nothing. He knows. Your father must soon know. But it changes nothing."

"It changes everything," she whispered as an infinite sadness engulfed her. She bowed her head and leaned heavily against him. "It changes everything." Then she straightened up and pulled back from him. "I must return to my chamber. You'd best go to your own . . . wherever it is you sleep."

"If Cleve chooses to tell your father, the fact that you sleep alone tonight will change naught." His hand reached out to finger a loose tendril of her wild dark hair. "Stay with me, Rose. We'll face your father together. I promise you, it will be easier than you think."

Tears started in her eyes at the sultry pull of his slow, husky words, tears of frustration and helplessness and overwhelming sorrow. It could not be, no matter how much she might want it. He and she could never be together. To meet secretly, even this one time, would only make it worse later on. Unable to speak, she lifted her misty eyes to him and shook her head. Then she backed away, turned, and fled across the yard.

Rosalynde did not seek her chamber, for she knew too well the tortures that awaited her in her bed: Visions of Aric. Dreams of his caress. No, her chamber was the last place she could go. But there was no other place of solace either. When she paused at the edge of the garden, winded from her rapid flight, she knew it too was the wrong place. The garden was filled with memories of Aric. But then, everything was.

In final desperation she made her weary way to the dark and empty chapel. In the quiet of the night it seemed almost to protect her in its close, tomb-like atmosphere. But though she slumped down onto her knees, though she clasped her hands together and tried desperately to pray, this time she found no comfort. Whether the oft-repeated phrases of the well-known prayers, or her own fumbling attempts, this time the words would not come.

As she huddled there in the dark, miserable and silently weeping, the truth was inescapable. She could not pray to be rid of this problem, of this man who tormented her night and day. She could not pray to be rid of him because in her heart she knew that she could not bear to let him go.

19

The rising sun was but a faded spot of light in a heavy gray sky. It was most appropriate, given Rosalynde's dismal mood. After a miserable, sleepless night she had risen with no clearer idea of what to do than before. She stood in the still-empty yard, staring across the way toward her little garden—her pleasaunce—and wondering if it might rain. It had not rained once since she'd come home. Not once. That was good for the planting, of course. The villagers had labored long and hard to prepare the fields. But now they needed rain for their crops and she needed relief from the forced cheerfulness of endless sunshine.

As if to punctuate her feelings, a distant rumble sounded the threat of a storm to come. With a disconsolate sigh Rosalynde raised her face to the oppressive sky. Rain would be good, she thought. She would welcome it gladly, if only because it might wash everything clean, take the dust from the air, and freshen the stale earth.

But it would still not bring relief to her dire predicament. It seemed that nothing would. Cleve would inform her father of all he'd seen; Aric would either be punished or banished; and she would be forced into marriage with the first acceptable suitor her father could find. But Aric was unlikely to accept that situation easily. He would reveal their handfast vow, and then only heaven knew what would transpire.

She wrapped her arms around her waist, trembling from the emotional exhaustion. In the long hours of the night she had wrestled with her feelings. From one extreme to the other she had swayed, sometimes hating Blacksword for coming between her and her father, and at other times admitting to the love that she bore for him. Yet no matter how her moods swung, there seemed no way to avoid the inevitable. He would tell her father the truth and he would very likely die for it. That, above all, was the one thing she could not resign herself to.

A gust of wind stirred the dusty bailey, building a quick whirlwind before it subsided. Across the yard several squires stumbled from their quarters, shoving and jostling one another good-naturedly. As she watched, Cleve came into view, walking alone, not participating in the others' horseplay. When she started toward him she was not sure what she would say. She only knew she must convince him to hold his peace.

"Cleve." Her call brought him up short and he gave her a wary look.

"Lady Rosalynde," he replied stiffly. But he said no more, and as Rosalynde nervously twisted her fingers together, she knew he was deeply hurt by what he saw as her defection to Blacksword.

With a fortifying breath she faced him. "I would speak privately with you, if you please. About last night," she added when he only stared at her from heavy-lidded eyes. In guilt and humiliation her eyes slid away from his. "There is nothing to be gained by involving my father in this matter."

"It is not for gain that I would speak to him! Not for myself! But for you—" He stopped short, clenching his jaw as he fought for control. "If you have not the sense to end this matter, then your father must."

"But he will be so angry! You don't know him!"

"You should have considered that before you fell in with that man. You should have considered just what your punishment would be when you dallied with one so far beneath you!"

" 'Tis not *my* punishment I fear, but *his*," Rosalynde pleaded in response to his angry charge. "You were there at the flogging. This can only be worse."

"Then we will all be well rid of the villain," Cleve answered in a voice that wavered between its new adult timbre and its old youthful pitch.

"But I love him," she whispered in desperation. Against her pale face her extraordinary eyes were wide and haunted. "I love him."

For an endless moment they stared at one another. On the one face was horror and disbelief, on the other, desperation. It was Cleve who looked away.

" 'Tis not love you feel, but something else entirely. You will feel it again for your husband."

She came perilously close to revealing everything to Cleve at that moment—that Aric *was* her husband by right of the handfasting ritual. Only her fear that the young squire could never keep his silence on the matter prevented her from confessing the entire truth to him.

"You're so wrong. I shall never feel this way for any man but him."

"Christ's blood!" The boy exploded in anger. "Are you fool enough not to know that love or not, it does not matter!" But when tears started in her eyes, his tone softened. "Milady, I cannot in good conscience keep this from your father. He has been good to me beyond all expectation. I am his man now. Surely you can see that."

She nodded weakly, but two teardrops spilled past her lashes and trickled down her pale cheeks.

"Don't cry, milady. Please, I cannot bear it," he whispered urgently, drawing nearer as he did so. His dark eyes stared mournfully at her.

"What am I do to, Cleve? Whatever am I to do?"

He did not answer at once but only took her arm and steered her toward the garden. Once there, however, he faced her with renewed conviction. "If you would not have your father be rid of the man, then you must do it yourself."

She shook her head and wiped at her damp eyes. "He will not go."

"Then make him."

"But how?" She sniffed, even as she fought the idea.

"I don't know," he replied, angry once more. "But 'tis clear he is encouraged to stay by your acceptance of his impudent attentions. Reject him out of hand. Offer him gold or whatever else you think he might want. But *send him away!*"

The problem was, he didn't want gold, he only wanted her, Rosalynde thought later as she sat in the quiet of her own chamber. Aric wanted only her—and everything that entailed.

Yet if he was to live, he must not stay any longer at Stanwood. As she weighed Cleve's words, the truth of what she must do became painfully clear. As he had said, she must get rid of Aric or else her father would. More than anything else, her yielding to him as she had last night would encourage him in his mad pursuit of her. It remained for her to squelch the burning passion between them. No matter how she felt, no matter how desperately she yearned for him, she must reject him.

It would not be easy. He would react with anger and

perhaps even violence. He might even force himself on her. But she must reject him, even make him despise her if that's what it took.

She must do it though it killed her, for if she did not, it would surely kill him.

For once luck seemed to be with Rosalynde. The threat of rain came to reality, and during the slow steady drizzle the daily routine of castle life was altered. The men-at-arms were put to repairing harness and weapons, and so long as Rosalynde avoided the stables she was saved the possibility of running into Aric. Although she knew she could not put off confronting him for long—Cleve's threat to tell her father still hung over her head—she did not want to meet him before she was ready. Then just after midday a small group of riders presented themselves at the castle gate. In the confusion of rain and mud and unexpected visitors, Rosalynde was so busy that she was able temporarily at least to ignore the pressing urgency of Cleve's demand.

With efficiency that her father noted with silent approval, she had the several knights settled in the guest chambers, ordered a light repast prepared for the tired travelers, and sent orders to the kitchen for a change in the evening meal. Instead of the normal light supper, a substantial meal had to be planned in honor of their guests. It was only when she'd seen to all those details that she was able to take a momentary break.

"Rosalynde. Daughter." Her father's voice carried to her. At his side she saw the refreshed knight who was leader of the group. With a welcoming smile pasted on her face she took a breath, then made her way toward them.

"Sir Gilbert Poole, Lord of Duxton, may I present to you my daughter, the Lady Rosalynde."

With a polite curtsy she greeted the man and took the hand he extended. When she straightened it was his turn to bow and press a light kiss against her knuckles. It was a perfectly appropriate gesture, and yet when he raised his gaze to hers she felt a sudden and unwarranted prickle of apprehension. His eyes were uncommonly pale, the blue of snow in moonlight. He was a comely enough man, well formed and of goodly height. His nose was straight, his teeth well, and his skin unmarked by pox scars. But there was an odd quality about him that she could not pinpoint. His lips curved in a pleased smile and she lowered her eyes in confusion. Straight teeth, yes, but his mouth held a cruel slant. Still, on the surface he was no more than a well-favored knight, the very sort of man her father no doubt would see her paired with.

At once her eyes jerked back up to his as she understood. Her father must have summoned this Sir Gilbert here. His visit was not completely unexpected.

" 'Tis my great pleasure to meet you, Lady Rosalynde. You are too kind to offer such gracious hospitality to me and my men."

" 'Tis our pleasure," Rosalynde countered as good manners demanded. "I'm afraid our remote location precludes many visitors. We welcome you and whatever news you may bring. From whence have you traveled?" she added politely.

"We come most recently from Elsing, but we have been these several weeks afield."

"Gilbert hounds the outlaws who are a plague upon the land," her father explained. "Do you meet with success?"

"Enough to know that there are many still left to be caught."

" 'Tis an outrage." Her father swore. "I would see them all hanged and damned unto hell." Then he glanced hastily at her. "My pardon, Rosalynde. But my temper festers to know that even one such vermin remains to prey upon the land."

"Have you suffered at the hands of such renegades?" Sir Gilbert asked with narrowed gaze.

"Nay," Sir Edward blurted out, sending Rosalynde a telling glance. She knew at once that he preferred her several unchaperoned days be kept from common knowledge. It left too dark a stain upon her purity and his power to protect her. "No, we've seen no outlaws nearby. However, there was rumor of an attack near the Stour River."

"Near Dunmow?" Sir Gilbert raised his brows slightly, and Rosalynde thought him momentarily alarmed. But he recovered quickly and his expression swiftly changed to one of smug self-satisfaction. "You will be glad to know that we sent three ruffians to the gallows at Dunmow. One we believe to be the ringleader of the entire area." His eyes fastened on Rosalynde's suddenly pale face with frank admiration. "Never fear, fair lady. It is my intention to rid all of East Anglia of such vermin. Only then will such lovely flowers as yourself be at ease to bloom."

Rosalynde escaped Sir Gilbert's presence as soon as was seemly, her heart still pounding and her stomach knotted from his unexpected revelation. Sir Gilbert had been the one who had captured Blacksword! It didn't matter that Gilbert was ridding the countryside of the dire scourge of outlaws. It didn't matter that he was well favored and unmarried, or that he was everything an unwed maiden should hope to gain, as her father had made quite plain to her. His presence at Stanwood would be absolutely disastrous should he recognize the outlaw Blacksword.

Or should Aric—Blacksword—recognize him.

Rosalynde felt for all the world like a poor ruff caught between warring hawks of the air. Her father, Aric, Cleve, and now this Sir Gilbert. They all made demands of her while offering threat to one another. She was prey to them all and yet she must nonetheless keep them well apart.

A headache hammered in her head as she saw to the feeding of the group of visitors. She felt no compunction at all about leaving them in her father's company on the pretext of tending to supper preparations. As much as she wished to avoid it, she knew she must find Aric and alert him about Sir Gilbert. With any luck this might be the impetus she needed to send him well away from here. If he would just flee Sir Gilbert's threat, all might yet be set to rights.

Only she knew, as she hurried through the misty rain down the slippery stone path, that when Aric left, nothing would ever be right again. Not for her, anyway.

She found him under the shed that projected from the tannery. He was affixing a metal ring to a strap of leather, lacing the looped leather with thin leather strips. Beyond him two other men labored, and for a moment she hesitated. His gaze was clearly curious when he looked up. Seeking him out was hardly something he would expect of her. To her relief, however, he kept his expression carefully blank as he rose to his feet.

"Milady?" he questioned, giving her a short bow. "How may I help you?"

"I . . . ahh . . . I've need for something to be moved in the kitchens. If you would be so kind."

" 'Twould be my pleasure," one of the other fellows stated, jumping at the possibility to set foot inside the women's arena of work. "Here, Aric, finish this."

"Oh, well . . ." Rosalynde struggled for an effective excuse to reject the man's enthusiastic offer. "You see, Sir Roger most clearly suggested that I might use Aric." She gave the man an apologetic smile, then turned her gaze quite deliberately back to Aric. "Can you help me?"

"Aye, milady." He put the harness down without sparing a glance for the other two men. "Whatever you require."

For propriety's sake Rosalynde led him toward the kitchens. But instead of ducking through that open door, she hurried on toward the stillroom. No one would disturb them there, she was certain. And no one would overhear them either.

Before she could properly fasten the door bolt, he pulled her into his embrace.

"How now, my sweet wife? Has last evening's encounter whetted your appetite for more?" His lips moved against her hair and pressed heatedly against her temple. "I know it has whetted my own."

For a moment Rosalynde went weak. His strong, manly form pressed against her back felt incredibly good, and every fiber of her being demanded that she succumb to him. Then he turned her to face him, and the delicious feel of their full-length embrace was nearly her undoing.

"Give me your lips," he whispered as he held her breathless against him. "Open to me. . . ."

But that was the very last thing she must do, she reminded herself desperately. "Wait," she pleaded, turning her head from his searching kiss. "We must talk. Wait!" she demanded with a impotent shove at his chest.

"I seem ever to be waiting on you," he murmured in her ear. "If it is your plan to provoke me beyond my endurance, know now, sweet Rose, that you have succeeded."

His hand moved languorously down her back to the swell of her buttocks. At once her senses leapt in response. Fire rushed through her veins and sang in her ears. Yet

Rosalynde knew she must not succumb to the dangerous lick of desire. Now more than ever, she must remain firm, for his very life depended on it.

"Would you just listen to me!" She wrenched herself from his arms then stepped back a pace, eyeing him across the dim space of the little stillroom. For a minute they just stared at one another. Then the amorous look in his warm gray eyes was replaced by frustration. He folded his arms across his chest and leaned his hips back against the sturdy workbench.

"All right then, I'm listening. But, Rose," he added in a sterner tone. "Do not think to put me off any longer. I *will* have my talk with your father."

Rosalynde refused to agree with him on that point. When she firmly spurned his attentions, he would not care any longer to speak to her father. And if that didn't work, she would reveal that Sir Gilbert was here. If he had *any* sense of self-preservation he would flee Stanwood at the first opportunity.

"I have thought long on what passed between us last night," she began nervously. "I-I cannot deny that there is an attraction between us—"

"An attraction?" he mocked as he watched her face turn scarlet.

"Yes, an attraction!" she snapped. "You have a certain . . . a certain appeal. And . . . and you clearly know how best to woo an untried maiden. I was beholden to you—"

He came away from the bench, his posture gone from relaxed and waiting to tensed and menacing. "You will not put me off with this tack, Rosalynde. So do not even try. Justify your yielding to me in any fashion you wish. But I know the truth of it. And so do you."

At this blatant statement Rosalynde's control nearly deserted her. Only the dreadful fear she felt for his well-being kept her tears in check and her voice relatively steady.

"Believe what you wish. But you cannot honestly think that a maiden of noble lineage would consent to marry so far beneath her." She raised her chin a notch, trying hard not to dissolve under his dark, piercing stare. Then she remembered Cleve's words to her and her tone grew more challenging. " 'Tis not unheard of for a noblewoman to take a lesser man to her bed. But you delude yourself if you think that signifies anything." Then she held her breath, fearful of how he would respond.

There was an unnerving silence between them. In the close quarters of the small room, the air was fraught with tension. When he moved slowly toward her, Rosalynde tensed. Inside she was dying. The words had hurt him, she knew, and in so doing, they had pierced her to her very heart.

A part of her cried that it was too cruel to reject him so, when the truth was, she loved him desperately. Yet her logical self knew it was the only way. Her love for him would be his undoing; it would very likely cost him his life. His only chance was for her to deny her feelings for him. Send him away, she heard Cleve's words once more. Reject him and send him away.

When he was only a foot from her he stopped. His hard gaze pinned her before him; one of his fingers traced the line of her jaw. "Am I to take it that you've found some other man—some lesser man—to take my place? Is it this fellow you wish to have lie with you and bring your body to such shuddering pleasure?"

"No!" Rosalynde jumped at the staggering effect his light touch had on her.

"Then, if not another like myself, who?" he asked coldly. .

Rosalynde searched her mind for the right words, for the right spot to hurt him enough so that he would go. When the idea came in an angry flash, she did not hesitate nor think of the immediate consequences. "Mayhap you noticed our visitors today. One of them comes as my suitor. Since my father has allowed me my choice among those he has solicited, it remains only for me to make up my mind."

She knew at once that she had captured his attention, for his jaw clenched and his eyes grew as dark as midnight. But his voice was calm when he spoke, the menacing tone hardly discernible at all. "And have you made up your mind, my thorny little Rose?"

She took a harsh breath. "Yes," she said, daring him to say she lied. "Yes, I have decided. Under the circumstances I thought you should know. I-I will get you a horse . . . and gold, of course. You will not wish to stay here."

His smile was chilling. The icy winds of winter from across the northern seas could never be so cold. In sudden fear of him Rosalynde tried to slip past, but his rigid forearm easily blocked her way. On the other side of her also, his arm came out, trapping her quite effectively before him.

"You cannot truly think this changes anything. No matter your wishes, you are still my wife. The vow was for a year and a day."

"I will not stand by that vow!" she cried in unreasoning anger. "I will not! And if you try to force me, my father will be rid of you on the instant!"

"What?" he mocked. "You still threaten me with your father when no doubt your suitor is a more likely match should your honor require defending? Have you no faith in his constancy, then? Or is it you doubt he could carry the day against me?" he added caustically.

"He bested you once! He could do it again!"

At that unexpected revelation he went very still. "He bested me?" His dark eyes bore into hers with a fiery insistence. "Pray tell, who is this paragon among men?"

Rosalynde hesitated. What had appeared such a good idea before now seemed exceedingly dangerous. Aric looked more likely to avenge himself against the man than to be cowed by his presence at Stanwood. Had she only complicated things further with her reckless words? In vain she sought some other tact, but it was much too late.

Aric's hand shot to her chin, forcing her to face his blazing eyes. "Who is he?"

With no other recourse open to her, Rosalynde blurted out his name. "Sir Gilbert of Duxton!" Then she waited for the storm to strike.

But it was not thunder and lightning that she received from Aric. Far from it. To her complete confusion, the narrowed look he gave her was more perplexed than vengeful. And somewhat disbelieving.

"Sir Gilbert of Duxton?" he repeated. "He boasts that he bested me?"

Rosalynde was several seconds in gathering her scattered wits. As it was, she was still mightily bewildered by his reaction. "He . . . he didn't say you by name. And I did not reveal your presence here. But he *is* the one who had you captured and thrown in the gaol at Dunmow. If he knows you yet live . . ." She let the rest trail away, undone by the grim possibilities of Sir Gilbert's reaction. She could not be sure her father would come to Aric's defense, even though he clearly had begun to value the man as a soldier. Sir Edward would not wish to anger Sir Gilbert.

But while Rosalynde's thoughts tumbled in confused apprehension, Aric's were hardly so disjointed. In the space of a few seconds everything became suddenly clear to him: his unexplainable capture at Dunmow; his conviction as an outlaw. It had been Sir Gilbert of Duxton! Here was his answer, come to him when it was the last thing on his mind. Sir Gilbert of Duxton had crossed lances with him at that last tourney in London. Although Aric did not know him personally, he knew his reputation. He was well known for his skill with both lance and sword. And equally well known for his debauched habits. Money, wine, and the favors of many noblewomen, not to say even more wenches of lower birth—these were the total of Sir Gilbert's way of life. But when the man had been unseated by the newcomer, Sir Aric of Wycliffe, he had become enraged. He'd not even been honorable enough to come forward with his loser's portion, but instead had sent a lackey to deliver the coins. But now it was clear his rage had run far deeper than that mere slight. Aric had suspected that the very outlaws who had for so long been the scourge of the countryside had set him up to be hanged: He was the sacrifice they needed for their own safety. He'd thought it just his poor luck to have been on that particular road when he was surprised and overset by the villains. Now he saw that it had been no accident at all. And it had not been the outlaws either. Gilbert of Duxton must have waited for his chance at revenge, and now he no doubt considered himself well rid of the man who had humiliated him in the lists.

At that moment Aric's lust for revenge outweighed his lust for the Lady Rosalynde. He stared down at her pale, frightened face, and his anger at Gilbert focused on her. Like Gilbert, she was shallow and vain, weighing her honor and her word of far less moment than her own sense of self-importance. Were it not that he intended to slay Gilbert himself, he would say she was welcome to him, and well deserved also. But he *did* intend to kill Gilbert, and to his way of thinking, justice would be even sweeter, knowing he also would possess both the maiden and the demesne the man coveted. Oh, yes, he would have the fair Lady Rosalynde. Nothing had changed on that score whatsoever.

Slowly he pressed nearer her, flattening her body against the wall, effectively trapping her in an embrace that was at once both erotic and demeaning to her.

"Your Sir Gilbert means less than nothing to me. And I warn you, my thorny bride, you and he shall both suffer greatly should he lay a claim to what is already mine."

At her gasp of surprise and her helpless struggle to escape, he let loose a dark laugh. Then he shoved himself away from her. When she hied away in panic-driven flight, he did not try to follow. It didn't matter. Whether she revealed her tale of woe to her father or her suitor, it didn't matter. What was to come would come. It was inevitable.

20

 She had to escape.

That solitary thought pounded in Rosalynde's mind as she fled the stillroom and her disastrous confrontation with Aric. She must get away from him before she was ripped asunder by the conflicting emotions that tore at her. It should not matter that he courted disaster with her father; it should matter even less that he might now be discovered by Sir Gilbert. Yet no amount of logic would banish that fact that it *did* matter. If he was hurt she did not think she could bear it. And if he was killed . . .

She came to an abrupt halt at the stables and placed a hand to the painful stitch in her side. If he was killed, something inside her would die as well. It didn't matter how he provoked her or how angry she became. In the final analysis, she could not bear to see him hurt. But she was perversely unable to prevent it either. He seemed almost to seek a confrontation with that man, Sir Gilbert. She'd thought to frighten him away with the man's very name. Instead, it had worked more as a challenge to him, a gauntlet tossed before him that he took up with a vengeance.

Rosalynde slumped against the stable wall and closed her eyes hopelessly. It didn't make sense. None of it did. Not Blacksword's role as a common outlaw. Not his insistence that she honor the handfasting. And certainly not his unexpected reaction to Sir Gilbert's presence here.

With every move she made, everything became even more confusing until now it was beyond all hope of putting right. Before she'd only had Blacksword and her father to juggle against one another. Now with Sir Gilbert's threat, as well as Cleve's, she knew she was losing control. It was only a matter of time before it all came apart around her.

At that precise moment, Cleve rounded the corner, coming face to face with her, and Rosalynde felt as if her very thoughts had come to life. He stopped short at the sight of her pale face and defeated posture. Then his expression grew anxious and he moved nearer.

"Milady? Is aught amiss?"

She gave him an ironic smile, faint as it was. "Everything is amiss. Surely you cannot wonder at that." But as his young face reflected his warring emotions—both guilt for his part in her misery and satisfaction that she had taken his threat seriously—she felt a pang of regret for her angry remark. None of this was truly of his doing, she admitted to herself. He'd reacted only as should be expected. She knew he had always been concerned with her safety.

"Forgive me, Cleve." She sighed then turned her eyes away from him. "That was most unkind of me. It's only that . . ." She faltered, then turned a haunted face back to him. "He will not go. Indeed, it seems he is more determined than ever to stay."

"Then he shall suffer the results of his foolishness," the boy retorted in quick anger. But as swiftly as his anger flared, it faded, for he was not proof against the desperation on her face. With a muttered imprecation he looked away before sending her an impatient scowl. "No doubt he cannot believe you. Not after all that has passed between you. But he will believe me."

"You! You can't mean to threaten him, Cleve, for he will not credit it at all."

The boy's brown eyes grew bright with the light of righteous anger. His vow echoed with the timbre of a man's when he spoke. "He'll not doubt my animosity. Nor my threat."

Aric did not believe in omens. Yet the mist and the lingering drizzle worked to his advantage, and now the boy, Cleve, ventured out alone, almost as if he sought him. Mayhap he did, Aric decided as he watched the boy's cautious approach. The pup had come up in the world, it appeared, with a fine wool tunic, new hose, and a long dagger in his girdle. Remembering the boy's pluck, Aric grinned to himself. Even when he'd not had a chance, the boy had conquered his fear and attacked him anyway. Sir Edward was wise to give him a chance to become a knight. Indeed, Sir Edward seemed to have an eye for selecting good soldiers. After all, he'd picked him for a man-at-arms, with nothing to commend him beyond brute strength. But then, it was said that one good man of war could always recognize another. And Sir Edward was clearly a most adept man of war.

Aric's eyes narrowed as the boy put his hand on the hilt of his dagger. Although he was certain the lad could not see him in the dark shadows, he nonetheless had hoped not to use a weapon on him. The element of surprise should be sufficient.

Cleve paused beside a stone wall and wiped the rain from his eyes. That was the instant when Aric made his move. Like an arrow loosed from a longbow, he sprang from the shadows, pinning the boy's dagger hand to his side with one long arm and gagging his mouth with the other.

There was a split second of shock on the boy's part, when his muscles did not react to the sudden danger, but almost before Aric could tighten his grasp, the wiry little fellow began to struggle. Like a wild man he twisted and kicked, all the while trying frantically to reach his razor-edged dagger.

" 'Tis not my intent to harm you unless you force me to it," Aric muttered harshly as he tightened his grasp even more. "Hear me out fairly and no harm shall come to you at all."

There was a tense moment when the boy went very still, as if trying to decide the truth of those words. Then his head bobbed his assent and Aric immediately released him. "Smart boy." But no sooner had Cleve's feet touched the ground than he whirled around, his dagger in his hand as he crouched down, ready to attack.

"What's this?" Aric's eyes narrowed in anger. "Have you not yet learned that to be a knight you must always honor your word?"

"A fat lot you know of such things! A knight's first honor is due his liege lord. He does whatever he must to serve his lord well. And to my mind, it would serve my Lord Edward very well if I were to skewer you on my blade."

"But it would not serve my Lady Rosalynde well at all."

At those words, softly said but taunting nonetheless, Cleve lost control. With a foul curse he sprang forward, fully intending to drive his blade clean through Aric's heart. But before his blade could land, the broad target he'd struck at had moved. Before the boy could adjust his attack, Aric caught at his loose tunic with one hand and spun him off balance. Then with a sharp blow to Cleve's wrist, he knocked the dagger free. In less than a second he had Cleve by the throat and shoved him hard against the wall.

"There is no one to save you this time," Aric growled ferociously. "If you wish to live long enough to become a knight, pup, you'd best lend an ear to my words. 'Tis not my desire to harm you. But it would not cause me any great hardship either." Then with a last menacing glare he released Cleve and took a step back.

For a long minute they stared at one another, the boy visibly shaken by the bigger man's easy dominance. The dagger lay in the dirt between them, yet neither made a move toward it, for it was clear that the knife was no deterrent. It was Cleve who spoke first.

"If 'tis not your desire to harm me, why am I waylaid thus?"

Though he was defeated and his voice low, the boy's eyes still flashed with fury, and it drew a small smile of respect from Aric.

"I would form a pact with you."

"A pact?" Cleve gave him an incredulous look. "I'd as soon form a pact with the devil." But he made a nervous sign of the cross as soon as the blasphemous words escaped his lips.

"If you are sincere in your goodwill toward Lady Rosalynde, you will hear me out."

"The Lady Rosalynde!" the boy sputtered. "You take undue liberty to even mention her name!"

"So it might seem. But time will prove otherwise."

At that enigmatic statement Cleve eyed him more warily. "What do you mean?"

But Aric was not about to reveal too much to this boy who so heartily disliked him. There was too much at stake —both his revenge against Sir Gilbert and the reward he sought through marriage to Rosalynde. Cleve could too easily foul his as yet incomplete plot. It was the boy's silence he needed—no more. And as there seemed only one thing Cleve wanted, Aric reasoned that to be his best bargaining tool.

"You've made it clear you mislike my presence here—"

"I misliked your presence the first time I laid eyes on you!"

"Nonetheless, you were unable to travel and hardly able to be of service to your mistress." At the boy's answering silence, Aric relaxed a little. "Whether you wish to believe it or not, I too have Lady Rosalynde's best interest at heart."

"Lady Rosalynde does not know her own mind any longer. You have blinded her until she—" He broke off, clenching his teeth tightly. But Aric knew what he implied. He also knew that the boy would never speak ill of his mistress.

"That may be," Aric conceded as his face grew more serious. "You think my intentions dishonorable—"

"How can they be anything but! You can never hope to win the likes of a lady such as she."

"You have risen from page to squire, if I am not misinformed. And with the chance to someday become a knight?" Aric's brows arched questioningly. "Perhaps I aim as high."

Once again Cleve was temporarily silenced, but in the passing seconds Aric became aware of a new curiosity in the lad's expression.

"What is it you want of me?" the boy asked suspiciously.

Aric gave him a considering look. It was a gamble to deal with this fiercely loyal pup of hers. The boy could run just as quickly as ever to her father and thereby alert Sir

Gilbert of his own presence here. But for the promise of his departure, the boy might keep his silence.

"I agree to depart Stanwood, alone, and without the reward promised me by the Lady Rosalynde if you will agree to keep your silence." He paused as he considered his choice of words. "If you will not inform her father of what has passed between her and me."

Cleve leaned forward in ill-disguised shock. "You would leave?" Then he became suspicious once more. "When would you go?"

"After the tourney."

"'Tis a fortnight away! No. I'll not have her subjected to your odious presence!"

"Think hard before you say nay," Aric warned. "You think Sir Gilbert a good husband for her, yet I am well apprised of his vicious nature. You think to save her from two weeks of me, but you could well be subjecting her to a lifetime of hell at his hands."

It was the right thing to say—he saw that at once in the uncertainty that swept over the boy's face. "I will leave after the tourney if her father will not accept my suit for her hand. In the days 'tween now and then, I'll not seek her out. On this and the name of God I swear."

Cleve's agreement was most reluctant. But when the boy finally departed through the gloom of the heavy mist, Aric felt a surge of relief. This was a small victory, he knew. And there was much that remained yet subject to chance. It was a mortal error to underestimate your enemy. Besides Sir Gilbert, he had also to deal with the dubious certainty of both Rosalynde's and her father's feelings toward him. Where once he'd been more sure of the maiden, now he felt easier on the father's response. That one, at least, respected skill and integrity, and would give him honor when his true identity was made clear. But Rosalynde . . .

His satisfaction dimmed when he thought of their last confrontation. She wished him gone, she'd said, for he was beneath her. Though by rights he should not expect more of a noblewoman, somehow he did expect better from her. He'd hoped, foolishly it now seemed, that she could cleave to him for the man he was, without title or fortune to commend him. To win her love had seemed a real possibility until she had spurned him so coldly.

Aric thrust one hand through his damp hair, raking it back from his brow. He should be twice damned for the fool he was! She was a noblewoman, and, like most of her ilk, to be valued only for the property that came with her hand in marriage. Her comeliness was simply a thing of good fortune—no more, no less.

And yet that fair face—coupled with her desperate bravery in saving him from the gallows—had set her apart in his mind. In all honesty, he knew that his decision to honor their handfast vow had been based only on logic, and perhaps a little greed. A well-propertied wife was more than a bastard knight-errant such as himself could have hoped for. But he'd quickly come to value her for more than just the demesne attached to her. Now, however, it was clear he'd been swayed by the sharp flare of desire that crackled between them.

He pulled his hood over his head and peered out through the dreary fall of rain. As his wife, her delectable young body would be his for the taking. His passion would be well slaked upon her and he would have the castle as well. But it was the opportunity for vengeance against his newly identified foe that he must focus on now, he told himself. That was what would afford him his greatest pleasure. His challenge to Sir Gilbert would be played out before Sir Edward, and in that one moment of revenge he would obtain all he wanted.

He hunched his shoulders and moved out into the damp. At long last Sir Gilbert would be his. Stanwood too would be his. And, whether she liked it or not, the Lady Rosalynde would also be his.

Rosalynde drew her hand back from Sir Gilbert's too-firm kiss and sent him a nervous smile. First Aric. Then Cleve. Now she must deal with Sir Gilbert's unwelcome suit, meanwhile maintaining every appearance of graciousness under her father's expectant gaze. Saints preserve her, but she wished this day were done! Yet she concealed her shattered nerves behind a facade of polite welcome, hoping her jumpiness would only be attributed to a normal, maidenly shyness.

"Sit, sit." Sir Edward gestured for Sir Gilbert to take the seat of honor at his right hand. Before he could turn to her, Rosalynde quickly slid into the chair at his left, keeping her father squarely between her and the smooth Sir Gilbert.

" 'Tis very long since I partook of Stanwood's hospitality," Sir Gilbert said most agreeably as he lifted a cup, brimful of red wine, to his lips.

"I had not thought to play the host in the years after my wife died," Sir Edward admitted. "However, my daughter's presence here now demands it. I would not have her locked away from youthful companionship and the courting due her."

"Ah, and such courting there shall be." Sir Gilbert supplied the right response without hesitation. His pale eyes flicked over her, appreciation apparent in their blue depths. "I am hopeful, however, that she will find my suit the most welcome."

Rosalynde replied with a weak smile, then hastily lowered her eyes. His suit was not welcome at all. Very likely,
no man's would be if she perversely continued to compare
every one of them to Aric. However, she must give every
appearance of welcoming his pursuit if Aric was to be
discouraged. Yet even that tack seemed hopeless now,
given Blacksword's strange reaction to the knowledge that
Sir Gilbert was here.

She nodded at Cedric, signaling for the food to be
brought in, though all the while her mind struggled to find
a solution to this newest dilemma. Oh, where was Cleve?
she wondered desperately. What had come of his confrontation with Blacksword?

The first round of serving had very nearly reached the
squires' table before she had the answer to her first question. As trays and platters of roasted pork and lamprey in
raisin sauce were passed around, Cleve slipped past the
tall oak doors and made his way to his place among the
other squires. There was some good-natured shoving—
and some not so good-natured—as he slid onto the bench.
Rosalynde suspected that he might be a while earning the
acceptance of the other lads for whom becoming a knight
had always been a given. Cleve's questionable birth and
late arrival in their midst had spawned some ugliness, but
by and large she thought he had fit in. Now, however, it
was not his well-being that concerned her. He obviously
was all right. But where was Aric?

At that moment Cleve's head raised and his gaze swept
the high table. Their eyes met and held, and across the sea
of faces, Rosalynde sought desperately for an answer in his
expression. To her complete bewilderment, however, all
she received was an odd little smile and a courteous nod.
But other than that, nothing.

Confused beyond belief, and troubled anew, Rosalynde

sat back in her hide-upholstered chair. What had transpired between those two that Cleve could look so noncommittal? A frown marred her brow as she tried to reason it out. Then another figure entered the teeming great hall, and her attentions were drawn away from Cleve.

Aric's hair was damp, she noted as he pushed his hood back. He paused at the door, a tall, imposing figure as he surveyed the scene before him. Then his gaze stopped and she frowned again when she recognized the focus of his stare. Cleve stared right back at him, not smiling, but for once not frowning his dislike either. Something passed between the two, some private understanding, before the look shifted. When Aric's eyes found her she glanced quickly away. But just as quickly her gaze returned to him, drawn by the same powerful attraction that tortured her endlessly. Aric's gaze, however, was hardly as civil as Cleve's. She sensed the fury that burned behind that cool, restrained gaze. And the contempt. Then his eyes flicked casually to Sir Gilbert, and Rosalynde felt a sudden, stinging shame.

To her dismay, her ploy had not worked. She'd rejected him as beneath her, then flaunted Sir Gilbert's presence at Stanwood in the hope that Aric would save himself and flee the castle. It was clear now that her rejection had hit the mark, but instead of fleeing, he appeared, perversely, quite prepared to do battle for her. Like the boy-king of legend and his circle of gallant knights, Aric seemed plagued with a sense of honor—and of right—that was unaffected by practicality. Sir Gilbert was a powerful knight, quite able to have Aric imprisoned and hanged for his original crimes. Yet Aric seemed almost to dismiss his threat as inconsequential. It was that accursed handfast vow that he clung to, and she was convinced now that nothing would swerve him from his goal.

When Aric's eyes left Sir Gilbert and met her gaze, she felt his scorn as clearly as if he accused her with words. His curt nod to her was an insulting dismissal. Then he found a vacant spot, served himself, and began to eat with good appetite.

The subsequent courses came. Food was served and eagerly consumed. Ale and wine flowed often and well. Sir Gilbert sought in vain to draw her into conversation while her father sent her several telling stares. But Rosalynde was too worried about Cleve and Aric to do much more than reply vaguely to their conversation and poke at her food. She could not fully participate in the meal. Something was afoot, she fretted, sending furtive glances toward the two sitting so far below. Something was going on. But until she could corner Cleve and Aric, she would just have to suffer her fears in silence.

21

It was morning before Rosalynde was able to pull Cleve aside. He was in the midst of preparing to ride out with the hunt, a singular honor as evidenced by his eager manner and excited expression. He flashed her a broad grin as he led two horses from the stable out into the watery sunlight of early morn. But a restless night's sleep and her gnawing fear would not allow Rosalynde to return the smile, and under her serious stare his grin faded.

"What has happened?" she began without preamble. Then, when he only shot her an aggrieved look and continued on with the horses, she fell in beside him. "I know you've done something, now tell me what it is."

"I took care of things," he snapped. "You couldn't—or wouldn't—so I did. He'll not bother you again."

Rosalynde's heart began to pound, and without thinking, she grabbed the lead rein of the horse nearest her, forcing Cleve to a halt. "And how did you do that? Did you tell my father? Or Sir Gilbert?"

Cleve drew himself up angrily, and she vaguely noted that he had finally surpassed her in height. Then he spoke and she recognized too the new manly ring to his voice. "There was no need to threaten him with your father's wrath. As for Sir Gilbert, I've no concern with him at all.

'Tis only your safety—and good name—that I have a care for. Even though you clearly do not."

"But . . . but what did you do? Why will he not—"

"He and I have agreed," the boy interrupted her. With a yank he snatched the reins from her hands and started forward angrily. "He will stay through the tourney—I allowed him that much. But after that he will leave here, never to return again."

Rosalynde heard his words as he strode away. She understood what he said and yet it made no sense at all. How had Cleve convinced Aric to leave? And then, given that, why had the boy agreed to let him linger another fortnight at Stanwood? There was no logic in it whatsoever, and yet as she watched his stiff departure across the muddy bailey, she knew she would get no clearer answers from him.

Baffled, she made her way slowly back to the kitchens. She must see a cart stocked with provisions for the hunt, for her father would entertain Sir Gilbert in the forests today. Yet as she instructed that a butt of wine be loaded into the conveyance along with linen-wrapped breads and cheeses and a basket of dried fruits, her mind would not let go of this latest turn of events.

Aric was not a man to back down from any threat. And yet Cleve, a green boy, had somehow managed it. There was no sense in it whatsoever. With a frown marring her brow she ordered pewter mugs and wooden cups added to the cart as well as several woven rugs. Then, when the clarion call came for the hunters to assemble, she wiped her hands on the linen cloth she'd tucked into her girdle and laid the rag aside. She smoothed her hair back, tucking one damp and curling tendril behind her ear. Then, as most of the other castlefolk were doing, she made her way toward the assembly of men and horses near the gatehouse.

Rosalynde had dressed with especial care this day. Her father had been displeased with her behavior last night, although he'd not said as much in words. Still, her reticence with Sir Gilbert had been all too obvious, and it was her wish to appease her father now. She did not want to anger him. After all, he had said she would be allowed some voice in the selection among the men he would present to her. During the long, worrisome hours of the night she had recognized the foolishness of her earlier behavior. Now she vowed to be pleasant and accommodating. She would be polite and gracious to all whom her father recommended to her. She would do whatever she must to keep her father content, but she would reserve the choice of a husband for herself. The summer, the fall, the winter, and most of another spring must pass before the handfast vow she'd taken could be set aside. Only then could her choice be made.

But even then she would not be able to choose the one man she would truly want as husband.

With a sigh and a silent vow to put that thought from her mind, she held her skirts carefully above the muddy yard. Her new gown was a lovely piece of work, indeed, and she would not see it ruined. She had remade it from another of her mother's older gowns, fitting it well to her body, then letting the skirts flare wide about her ankles. The fine Raynes linen was light, woven of the finest threads and cut on the bias so that it moved in the most graceful manner when she walked. The color had been one unknown to her, somewhere between the rich purple of royal garments and the brilliant blue of the sky, only softer—somewhat like ripened plums, wet from the rain. She felt quite lovely in it despite the fact that it was simply adorned. The neckline lay just beneath her collarbones, showing only the faintest hint of her kirtle beneath it. A plain silver woven braid decorated the neckline as well as the snugly laced wrists. Besides that, only her long silver-worked girdle broke the simplicity of the gown.

To make up for the unornamented style, she had labored long over her hair. The dark waves lay loose and shining about her back and shoulders. A length of silver chain lay across her brow, then caught the hair from her crown and wove down her back in a loose braid, a style seen often among unmarried maidens.

She felt a certain guilt to wear her hair in such a virginal style, although she knew no one else would note it, save for Aric. And Cleve. But even that guilty thought was banished by her recollection of Aric's hand stroking down her back, along the freed length of her hair. "You have beautiful hair," he'd whispered. "Beautiful hair." Against all logic she wondered if he would think so today.

"By the blood of the saints!" she muttered under her breath. Why must *he* always creep into her thoughts? She did not care if he liked her hair or not.

Or at least, she *should* not care.

But the sad fact was, she did care. She cared about what he thought, where he was, and what he did to an inordinate degree. It was shameful, and terribly unwise, but it was nonetheless true.

With a sigh she stepped up onto a square stone block that had once served as a mounting block for her when she'd been but a child. Now it served nicely as a dry spot from whence to watch the men's departure for the hunt. Her father was easily recognizable in his tunic of green and gold. He was without a hood, and his graying head showed well among the younger men. His chestnut gelding was a tall steed, and Rosalynde felt a glimmer of fond pride to see him so handsomely mounted. Then her eyes focused on Sir Gilbert and her smile faded. He too rode a fine horse and was outfitted most handsomely, as was appropriate to his station. She had no doubt that under differing circumstances, she would have been quite flattered by his suit for her hand and perhaps, after but a brief hesitation, would have accepted his proposal and thought herself the most fortunate of maidens. He was young, handsome, and courtly. What more was there to ask?

Yet when compared to another taller form, one strongly muscled and forged as if of steel, Sir Gilbert of Duxton came off a distant second. As she shaded her eyes against the strengthening sun, she sternly reminded herself that at least Sir Gilbert was suitable. He was a nobleman, and he did not shirk his responsibilities if his determined pursuit of the outlaws was any indication. Perhaps when her year was done she might find him acceptable.

But Rosalynde knew deep in her heart that she could never find Sir Gilbert acceptable. There was something about him that made her skin crawl. And above all else, she knew he would not hesitate to have Aric slain if he were to identify him. That made him her foe too.

Upon spying her, Sir Gilbert cantered over, then leaned down with one elbow on his knee to address her.

" 'Twould be a pleasure, indeed, if you were to accompany us to the hunt, my Lady Rosalynde."

"My thanks, Sir Gilbert. But I've much to oversee this day. No doubt the hunt will bring us much game to be prepared. I must be certain the fires and the pits are made ready."

His watchful eyes swept over her, then briefly down to her breasts before raising once more to her eyes. He gave her a smooth smile. "Perhaps it is all to the good, for your fair face and form already dazzle these eyes of mine. I'd be sorely distracted from the hunt should you accompany us."

They were pretty words, a compliment that should have

brought a blush to her cheeks and a stammer to her words. But Rosalynde was unaffected by his remark save perhaps for a delicate shiver of distaste. However, she hid that unwarranted emotion behind a determinedly pleasant smile. To her relief, she was saved the necessity of response by her father's approach.

"Your captain begs a word with you, Gilbert," he said. Then as Gilbert cantered away, he turned with a smile to his daughter. His eyes sparkled with good humor, and his face was animated. "So, Rosalynde, you still decline to join us. I had hoped you might become better acquainted with Sir Gilbert—under my watchful eye, of course."

As much as she knew that such an "acquaintance" was impossible, Rosalynde nevertheless could not help but smile at the thought of her father playing the part of chaperon. A mother, yes. A trusted maid, of course. But having neither of those, Sir Edward became the only logical choice, no matter how poorly suited to the part he was.

"I've enough and more to keep me busy here. Besides, the hunt is not a favored activity of mine. I'll be more content to attend my daily routine."

"You won't forget your other task? The one I charged you with?"

"Other task? Oh." Her smile faded as her father's meaning became clear. He'd asked her to learn something of Aric's past, something that would help him to rest easier at the thought of the man fighting at his back.

"He was . . . that is . . . he won't—" She took a nervous breath and started again. "I've learned very little, only what you already know. He's from a place called Wycliffe. Oh, and he is the youngest son, although he has said little of his parents," she added, remembering Aric's words once before.

"A youngest son, eh?" Her father shifted in his saddle, a

puzzled expression on his face. " 'Tis curious, indeed. How did a lad of such meager beginnings come by his skills, then? 'Twould seem a man would keep such a strong worker at home."

"Perhaps there were too many mouths to feed," Rosalynde speculated, wondering herself about the mystifying man she'd bound herself to. Like her father, she felt there was more to Aric than was immediately apparent. And as her father did, she wished to know the truth of it. But not now. Especially with Sir Gilbert in temporary residence at Stanwood.

"He was no doubt not a sterling son," Sir Edward mused. Then he straightened on his horse. "I can forgive the mistakes of his youth so long as I have reason to trust him as a man."

"Do you trust him?" Rosalynde was unable to resist asking.

Her father was slow to respond. "Aye, I do. At least I trust him to do his part in a fight. But that does not mean you should abandon your efforts, Rosalynde. Today would be a good day to approach him, while the castle is quiet. There will be few enough quiet days in the next weeks. Perhaps you could send for him, say . . . oh, I don't care why. Because you would have him fitted for a new tunic," he suggested with a vague gesture of his hand. "Use whatever excuse you like. Just give it another try." Then, with an encouraging smile, he turned his horse and joined the waiting group of hunters.

In a matter of minutes they were through the gatehouse and on their way to the thick forests that stretched as far as the eye could see around the Castle Stanwood. Rosalynde was left standing on her block, contemplating her father's final words and debating whether she should approach Aric again. It wasn't her father's request that prodded her to it, however. Rather, it was Cleve's vague allusions that troubled her. His conversation with Aric made no sense to her, yet her entire future—and Aric's—seemed to hang upon it. She could not rest until she knew how he had managed to sway the heretofore implacable Aric and actually convince him to leave.

She found him at the horse pen beyond the stables, staring intently at the horses fenced there. Come upon from behind, with his wide shoulders hunched thoughtfully while one foot was propped upon the second fence rail, he struck her once again as being possessed of the most extraordinary air of nobility. There was an aura of power about him, as if he naturally expected others to bend to his wishes. As her pace slowed to an unconscious halt, she felt an intense pang of regret. Nothing ever came out as it should, she thought morosely. No one she loved ever stayed. Not her mother. Not her brother. And now not Blacksword either.

He turned his head sharply. Then when he recognized who so silently watched him, he altered his stance at the fence. "Is there something you want of me?" he asked curtly. His gaze was hard as he raked her with it, yet the anger she saw there was not cold and icy. Rather, it burned her with its ferocity and seared her with its thoroughness.

"My father sends me on a mission," she answered honestly. "He would have me learn more of your dark past. He likes you," she added with a bitter smile. "He would keep you among his men-at-arms."

His expression lifted marginally at her truthful revelation. He leaned back against the fence, studying her well before he replied. "What would you know?"

At this unexpected response, Rosalynde became even more confused. Cleve had revealed that Aric would leave after the tourney. Why, then, was the man now becoming so agreeable? Still, she was too curious about him to forgo this opportunity to learn more of his vague past. "In the years since you left your father's house—"

"I robbed and pillaged, and took whatever I wanted from whomever I wished." He straightened up and started toward her. "I honed my skills on villein and noblemen alike, and I devoured young maidens like yourself. Is that what you wish to hear?" he finished sarcastically as he stopped mere inches from her.

"That . . . that's not true," she whispered hoarsely, as much dismayed by his cruel words and taunting tone as she was by his sudden nearness. As if the heat of his strong body reached out for her, she felt an answering warmth rise quickly in her, lifting all her senses to a new and sharper awareness of him.

"I devoured you, didn't I? You sacrificed your virginal feast to my insatiable hunger, didn't you?" He mocked her unmercifully. "Isn't that how you would describe it?" His eyes bore down into hers with a fury she guessed born of her rejection and Cleve's as-yet-unnamed threats. Panicked by her chaotic emotions, she stumbled back a pace. "No . . . no, it wasn't that way."

"No? Then pray tell, describe it to me."

Rosalynde shook her head in confusion and stared at him with wide, haunted eyes. "Why are you doing this?" she whispered. "Why?"

But he did not answer. As if he struggled with his own emotions, he only stared at her, his eyes dark and opaque with his own private tortures. Then he lifted one hand and touched her chin briefly. The smile that lit his masculine face seemed to mock him even more than it did her.

"Why not buy my answers, Rose? As you did before. For a kiss you might learn something to appease your father. For an embrace, a fact he would value. Perhaps you would pay the ultimate price." His eyes burned her with their piercing strength. "Throw yourself on the altar of pure physical pleasure and finally know the truth about the man you wed." He took her suddenly by both arms and pulled her hard against the rigid length of him. "Know the truth, my sweet thorny Rose, unless you fear it." Then before one of the few watchmen could turn and notice his too-bold handling of her, he thrust her away from him.

For Rosalynde, however, the damage was done. It was impossible for her to remain aloof from him, to treat him as if he were just another of her father's men. Too keenly did she feel the imprint of him against her. Too painfully did the sweet ache of longing fill her. She wanted him, yet she would see him gone. She trusted him with her father's life, yet she knew that already he had tampered irreversibly with her own. Was ever a maiden so accursed?

"I do fear it," she confessed in a voice that shook with repressed emotions. "I fear you."

" 'Tis right that you do, fair lady. Do not press me or you shall feel the full weight of my anger."

He turned from her and stared once more at the horses, clearly dismissing her from his presence. Yet she could not go. She watched in helpless confusion as one mighty warhorse broke away from the rest and ambled toward the taciturn man. As Rosalynde remained where she was, too shaken to move, the tall black horse nudged the man's arm, demanding a caress, seeking a treat. When Aric rewarded him with a dried apple and then a scratch between the ears, she struggled with her feelings. She had hurt him with her rejection, and that knowledge sat heavily upon her. But whatever had passed between him and Cleve had aggravated the situation even further. Unaware of the soft plea in her voice, she spoke again.

"Why do you not leave here now?"

She thought he would not answer, for his attentions remained focused on the huge, amiable animal. Then he shifted slightly. "You are more than anxious to be rid of me. You make that clear enough. But 'tis my intention to stay at Stanwood."

"To stay!" Happiness leapt foolishly in her heart, to be swiftly followed by renewed fear for him. "But . . . but Cleve said . . ."

His head twisted sharply toward her and his flint-hard eyes pinned her once more. "Your rabid pup made a bargain with me. He thinks, of course, that he shall win and that I shall leave. But I have no intentions of losing, Rose. You may mark my words well. I will not lose and I will not go."

"What of Sir Gilbert?" she whispered. "He is bound to identify you eventually."

"He will not see me, because he does not expect to see me." Then his mouth curved in a mirthless grin. "Of course, you can end the suspense, if you like. Simply tell him of me."

Rosalynde was stung by his easy disregard of her honest concern for him. She was angry, but primarily she was hurt. However, she would sooner die than let him know how his cruel words cut her. Her voice was brittle and her eyes bright with fettered tears when she responded to him.

"You like the suspense, the intrigue, and the danger. Well, perhaps I do as well. If you wish to court disaster, so be it. I'll not intercede again on your behalf." She started to turn away, unable to maintain this charade of nonchalance any longer. But Aric stopped her with an angry jerk, then hauled her rudely around to face him. Beyond them the big war steed whickered softly, and Aric's furious gaze flicked briefly away from her to scan the empty bailey.

"I would speak to you privately," he said quietly, although his eyes glittered with emotions.

"N-no," Rosalynde answered shakily, as her heart's pace trebled from both fear and anticipation.

"Why this sudden hesitation?" he taunted, his face just inches above her own. "You said you sought information for your father. I'll give it to you now, only come into the stables. Unless, of course, that was not your true purpose in seeking me out." He released his harsh grasp on her then stepped back a pace and gave her a brief mocking bow. "Your servant, milady." Then he strode into the barn, as arrogant and unrepentant as ever.

Rosalynde stood against the fence, bracing her weight against it as she struggled to calm herself. How easily he played her emotions against her. How deftly he ferreted out her vulnerabilities and used them to his own ends. Yet knowing all that, she still could not resist the challenge he had given her. She *did* want whatever information he might reveal, she told herself, if not for her father, then for herself so that she could more easily shield him from the threat of Sir Gilbert's discovery. Yet as she finally forced herself toward the stable, she knew with a sinking sense of doom that those practical reasons had nothing whatsoever to do with her real reason for following him.

In the dim light of the stable she saw him in the shadows near a crude ladder. Up the ladder he went, seemingly unaware of her presence until he cast a bold glance at her as he disappeared into the loft. Rosalynde refused to hear the voices of warning clamoring in her head. Her pulse beat high in her throat as she reached for the ladder and looked warily up into the dark hole that was the loft. Then, holding her skirt in one hand, she mounted the steps, one by one, until she was half the way into the storage loft. Suddenly, before her eyes could accustom themselves to the absence of light, she was plucked from the ladder by two sure hands, stood firmly on the floor, then easily spun around to face him. Her breath caught in her chest as she stared up at his harshly drawn face, lit only faintly by cracks in the slanted roof above them. But instead of the kiss she expected—the kiss she wanted above all else—what she received was an ungentle shake and the hoarse threat of his voice.

"Ask your question," he ordered.

"What?"

"Ask your question. 'Tis why you came, is it not?"

"Oh . . . I . . ." Rosalynde faltered and unreasoning tears stung her eyes. "My . . . my father would know for certain if he . . . if he may count on your loyalty in battle," she finally managed to say.

"It seems I answered that once before." He drew her against his chest and his voice lowered to a husky rumble. "Kiss me, Rose."

She went into his fierce embrace without hesitation. Molded to his body, pressed within his steely clasp, she surrendered completely to his demand. On tiptoes she reached up to meet his lips, fired with a recklessness completely foreign to her. She felt his hesitation and his anger. His lips were hard and punishing, meeting hers, then forcing her back as if he must let her know that he—only he—was in control. But her pliant acceptance of him became her triumph, for as her mouth opened to him, accepting the heated plundering of his tongue, she sensed a change in him. The rigidity of his body relaxed, and as he bent over her, he fitted her to him more naturally.

When he lifted his head they were both gasping for breath. In the dark, low-ceilinged space she could hardly

see him. But beneath her hands and against her body she
could read him well, and she was much encouraged.

"He can rely on me," he whispered against her ear, then
searched out the sensitive curve of her lobe, sending trem-
ors of delight through her. "What else would you know?"

Rosalynde closed her eyes tightly, trying to focus on his
words as he pressed languid kisses down her neck, circling
his tongue in the exposed hollow of her throat. "I . . .
He . . ." She took a sharp breath and concentrated.
"Why did you leave your father's house?"

His mouth abandoned its sultry task and she felt his
gaze on her face. Reluctantly she raised her lashes, fearing
to see unpleasant reality intrude on this most turbulent of
interludes.

"That answer will cost you dearly," he murmured. She
felt one of his hands move down her back to sweep across
her derriere. Then his palm pressed her intimately to him
and a wave of shameful heat rose in her belly. His hand
slid back and forth. It was a mere matter of inches, and
both her skirt and kirtle rested between his hand and her
skin. Yet in that slow, seductive rhythm he raised her emotions to a new and fiery level.

His lips slanted across hers, and his tongue slid into the
warm depths of her mouth. In and out he stroked the
sensitive skin of her inner lips. Back and forth his palm
stroked. Then his thigh pressed between her legs, opening
her to his further sensual assault. Rosalynde was gasping
for breath, drowning in a splendid storm of pent-up emotions and physical desire. When he finally pulled his
mouth from hers, she let out a helpless moan of disappointment, then let her head fall weakly against his warm
chest.

"I left to fight with the Empress Matilda and then
Prince Henry, first in Normandy and later in England."

Rosalynde hardly heard his husky answer to her question. His words hardly registered in her mind. Yet as he held her there against him, his heart thudding a mirrored rhythm to her own, she realized that he was waiting for her next question. She did not reason out what it would be. The words came without thought, more from her heart than her head. Nor did she fear the price he would demand.

"Why have you stayed? Why do you continue to stay?"

His answer was swift in coming, and it stole her breath away.

"For this," he whispered as his teeth tenderly caught the fullness of her lower lip. "For this," he murmured as his hand curved around her breast and his thumb stroked with intense accuracy across her already-hardened nipple. "For this," he groaned as his other hand pressed her possessively against the thick swelling at his groin.

Everything that was feminine in Rosalynde gloried to the answer he gave. He stayed for her. He risked her father's anger and Sir Gilbert's swift punishment for her. He did all this for her. Could she risk any less for him? At that moment, none of the practical reasons that made such a liaison between them impossible mattered in the least. She refused to remember that he had once professed to want her for Stanwood only. He was a man who wanted her to the point of grave risk to himself. And she wanted him beyond all caring. That was all she need know.

As she rose to meet his masculine domination, she knew it was inevitable. She had no answers for the future, but she pushed that dampening thought from her mind. He wanted her, and though that was not quite the same thing as love, at that moment it nonetheless felt very much like it. God knew that she had begun to love him with an intensity strong enough to sustain them both.

He lay her back upon a stack of empty sacks. Her girdle fell aside; her gown was unlaced and tugged swiftly over her head, and yet she did not recall him relenting in the devouring kiss he pressed upon her. His tunic and chainse were torn from him, as much by her own eager hands as his own. Then he lay down over her, pressing her slender form into the cushion of rough-woven burlap.

"Be mine," he murmured as his lips teased hers apart with gentle nips from his strong teeth and silken strokes of his tongue. His hands caught both of hers, bringing them above her head. The full length of him weighed down on her, imprinting her, it seemed, with his possessive mark. One of his thighs parted her own, resting intimately against the damp warmth of her most private place. Her breasts rose with every labored breath to rub his shirtless chest, and even through her kirtle she felt the coarse caress of the curling hairs sprinkled lightly there.

She squirmed against him, restless from the building heat inside her. She wanted to touch him. She wanted to run her fingers through his long, golden hair and slide her palms against his damp, overheated skin. But he would not release his hold on her hands, only grasping both her wrists in one of his hands and leveraging himself up on his other elbow.

"Do you burn for me?" he whispered huskily against her throat as he marked a trail of sensuous bites and kisses down to her collarbone and across one shoulder. He slid his hard male torso against her, torturing her with the heavy weight of his arousal against her linen-clad belly. Then his mouth moved down her chest, kissing the soft upper swells of her breasts through the thin garment. When he found her nipple, he teased it at first, flicking back and forth across its puckered peak, wetting the kirtle and sending her senses reeling. Then his lips fastened on the dusky nub, and he drew it deeply into his mouth.

At once Rosalynde's entire body lifted against his much heavier weight. As he alternately circled her sensitive nipple, then lightly bit and sucked on it, she strained up to him, wanting to get away, wanting to get more—wanting everything. From one nipple to the other he moved, offering it the same torturous caress. But now his other hand drew one of her knees up, so that his insistent arousal pressed directly against the center of her desire. In dire need of the completion he teased her with, Rosalynde thrashed her head back and forth and struggled to free her hands.

"Please," she begged, her eyes closed in passionate thrall. "Please," she panted in unashamed longing.

"How sweetly you beg me, my fiery wife. How good your words sound to my starving body." Once more his lips closed on one of her nipples, biting until the passion approached pain, then soothing with hot, wet circles of his tongue. " 'Twould be my pleasure to keep you ever thus, tied helpless beneath me while I explore your tempting body and teach you all the lessons of passion." His loins ground against her as he slid up and down against her belly. "Would you like that, my hot honey Rose? Do you long for such torture at my hands?"

Rosalynde was too overcome with desire to respond to his sensory threat aloud. Yes, she told him with the raising of her other leg. Yes, she answered as she wantonly pressed her hips up to the rigid proof of his manhood. Yes, yes, yes . . .

But even as he pushed her almost to the brink of madness, he perversely pulled away, pushing off her to sit back on his heels, kneeling above her as his breath came in harsh gasps. His eyes were flaming brands scorching her

with their hot regard. She lay beneath him, writhing inside with the intensity of her longing for him, her legs still
parted, her arms still above her head. Though the kirtle
still covered her, she knew it was less than nothing, for the
naked emotion in her wide eyes revealed far more to him
than could her bared body. As if he knew that too, he
reached out one hand and let it slide slowly down her ribs
to her stomach, smoothing a wrinkle in the thin kirtle.

"Show me what you want," he murmured quietly. His
hand moved lower until his knuckles just brushed the upper curls of her triangle of hair. "I'll give you whatever
you want, but you must ask for it."

Rosalynde's mind was so dazed by her tumultuous feelings for him that she did not at first comprehend what he
was saying to her. Then a shiver that was part longing and
part fear shook her. "Please," she whispered, reaching a
hand up to him. "Please come to me."

She saw him swallow and vaguely realized that he
fought mightily for control. "Tell me what you want," he
repeated, but in a voice choked now with strain.

The words were hard to come. They seemed torn from
her and yet she could not hold them back. "I want you,"
she admitted so softly it might have passed for a rustle of
the fabric beneath her. He closed his eyes briefly and an
expression almost like pain moved across his face.

"That I know, my sweet innocent. Now tell me what
you would have me do."

Her face grew hot as she realized what he was forcing
on her. This time she would make the decision. This time
there would be no blaming another for the sinful desires
that drove her. This time she could not pretend to be a
passive receptacle for his lust. If their joining had not already been dangerous, this new slant made it much more

so, at least emotionally. Yet Rosalynde was unable to go back now.

"I would . . . I would see all of you." She caught her breath at such an admission. "Please, remove your . . . your . . . the rest."

It was done in a moment. Chausses and braies fell to the floor, and he stood above her in all his naked splendor. She lay beneath his widespread feet, feeling for all the world like a pagan offering to some mighty god, willing to make the ultimate sacrifice if he deemed it necessary.

He did not have to command her to remove her kirtle. Like one mesmerized, she reached down for the hem, then with a quick arch of her buttocks and back, slid it over her head and cast it aside. A fit of trembling took her as he continued to tower over her. Every detail of his body was boldly revealed to her in the splintered sunlight that fell through the roof joints. From his powerfully muscled legs, past the lean hips and ridged belly to the broad planes of his chest and shoulders, every muscle and sinew appeared tensed and poised. A light sheen of sweat showed on his thick arms, and even the tendons in his neck stood out. But it was the muscle that lifted so proudly from his groin that drew her eyes at last. He was an awesome figure of a man, a battle-tested soldier and a hardened criminal. But he was also a masterful lover, and she knew he prepared now to prove that once again.

"Come to me," she breathed, unconsciously writhing in artless appeal. "Please."

He moved over her almost before the words were finished. Like the pagan god she fancifully imagined him to be, he approached the offering she made of herself, lowering himself to cover her, stretching his full length and weight upon her. His skin met hers, hard heated flesh that melted her into him. Rosalynde felt his arousal hard against her belly. Her eyes closed as she slid her arms around his shoulders and ran her fingers wonderingly across the damp contours of his back.

"Tell me what you want," he whispered into the tangle of her hair against her neck. "Tell me why you sought me out today."

Rosalynde swallowed convulsively as the words sprang to her lips. More than anything, she wished to say that she loved him, that she needed to be with him, that she could not give him up. But some remnant of logic made her repress those words, and instead she pressed a line of desperate kisses to his shoulder. "Do what you did before," she pleaded as joy and fear threatened to overwhelm her. "What you did before. . . ."

In an instant she felt his hand move in a slow, torrid caress down her side to pause at her hip. Then he shifted his weight slightly and his palm slid over her belly until his fingers reached that very part of her that longed so violently for him. His mouth captured hers in a fiery kiss as his fingers parted the curls there. Then, as his tongue seduced hers into a wildly erotic dance, his fingers slipped along the wet folds of her most private place.

Rosalynde felt as if she were melting beneath that knowing touch. When one of his fingers slid deep within her then pulled out, she arched up in near agony. Then when he rubbed that same slick finger over the tensed nub where every nerve in her body seemed poised to explode, she cried out against his mouth in mindless abandon. "My love . . . my love . . ."

Blind with her need for him, she raised up against his hand. But his need too was beyond denial. With a groan of desire he moved over her, then buried himself completely within her. There was no startled pause, no hesitation or surprise in their joining. Like one born for this moment, she accepted the full length and strength of him into her. She rose in willing surrender and became strong in his domination. He plunged into her dark warmth and surrendered to her feminine demands. Like sword to sheath they fitted together, like key to lock and hand to glove. There was no learning needed as they joined their bodies in that ancient ritual. One in heart, one in mind, they strove toward that momentary perfection. His mouth devoured hers, dragging her up into a kiss that tore every emotion from her. He cleaved himself to her in a runaway rhythm that pushed her further and further. She held to him as a last reality in a world filled only with sensation. Then the explosion began and as she tightened her arms and legs—indeed, her entire body—about him, he drove into her with unrelenting insistence.

"Aric!" Her cry seemed to fill the world, though it was less than a whisper, lost in the enveloping warmth of his kiss. Her entire being shuddered in total surrender, even as he tensed and, in a final outpouring of energy, spent himself within her.

She was shaking uncontrollably as he came to a heaving halt. They were both slick with sweat and drained of emotions. She was certain he had given his all to her, just as she had given all of herself to him. It was an oddly sweet sentiment, and Rosalynde smiled as she clasped him tighter to her. He gave her the best of himself when he made love to her. She felt it as surely as she felt his heavy body pressing her down upon the rough burlap. But did he know what she gave him in return? Did he know that it was still more emotional than physical, despite the intense physical pleasure they both had found? It seemed impossible that he could not know, and she smiled in perfect happiness.

He moved and one of his fingers touched her lips

lightly. When she opened her eyes he was regarding her with a fiercely tender expression. "Save such smiles only for me." He bent and placed a sweet kiss on her lips, one not filled with the passion they had just shared but with another less clear emotion. "Only for me."

At her silent nod he let out a weary groan and let his head fall to the curve of her neck. Then he rolled to his side, bringing her with him so that she rested half sprawled upon him. One of his hands ran possessively up her arm, then down her side, just skirting the side of her breast. It was so tender and felt so right that, given her newly vulnerable state, it seemed an even more intimate gesture than all that had gone before.

She smiled once more against his shoulder, refusing to think beyond this moment in time. Lying in his arms in the aftermath of such glorious lovemaking, for a little while at least she could pretend that everything was right with the world.

22

Aric sat on a crude bench as the other men-at-arms left for supper. To the several calls to join them he gave only a silent shake of his head. Food was the last thing on his mind.

"Perhaps he's meetin' with Molly." One large fellow guffawed. "I seen her flittin' about after 'im. Now's the time when the dairy's still. What man wouldn't prefer Molly's offerin's over a trencher of mutton an' gravy!"

"Who's to be fillin' whose belly full, I wonder," another man good-naturedly threw in.

Aric looked up, forcing an appropriate grin to his face. Although it was the immodest dairymaid they jested so coarsely about, his recent meeting with Rosalynde was too fresh in his mind for him not to inwardly cringe.

"I've no doubt she's too tired to tend to my needs," he replied, but lamely. "There's a well-worn path to her door already."

"Molly's never too tired."

"She don't do nothin' but lay there and spread 'er legs. What's to get tired of?"

By the time the others trooped off to the great hall, Aric was gritting his teeth in anger. But the anger was directed as much at himself as it was at the lot of braggarts he watched depart. Molly was no concern of his; she did not interest him in the least, nor did he care that her reputation as a slut was well deserved. But he was just hours from lying with Rosalynde; her scent and the feel of her shapely body beneath his was still fresh in his mind. To hear the act they'd participated in so eagerly denigrated to the level of coupling animals disgusted him. What was worse, however, was the unpleasant fact that there were a string of Mollys in his past—the camp followers at battle; the duly impressed maidens who always gathered at the tourneys he frequented. Many a pale white body had lain beneath him in some darkened place. He'd sought temporary ease in many a warm belly and pair of parted thighs.

But Rosalynde was different.

Frustrated by the position he found himself in, he drew out his knife and picked up a sturdy length of oak. Without thinking about what he did, he began to work on the staff, whittling smooth the place where a branch had been, thinning the thick end so that the staff would be ideally balanced. Splinters were banished and the proportions of the sturdy weapon were perfected. In his deft hands the staff took shape. But all the while he worked, his mind relived his hours with Rosalynde.

She had been so sweet, an unbelievable melding of innocent reticence and passionate abandon. The very thought of her willing young body and eager response caused his blood to heat and his loins to rise in renewed desire. What had become of the anger he'd nursed toward her? The disappointment that a title mattered more to her than the man inside? He'd known it to be a foolish hope on his part. Illogical even. Yet something in him—perhaps the unrecognized bastard he'd always been—had wanted to believe it possible, and when she had spurned him for his perceived lack of position, he had been angry beyond reason. Then when the lad, Cleve, had struck his reluctant bargain, he'd promised not to seek her out. At the time, consumed as he was with his plan for revenge on Sir Gilbert, it had been an easy enough concession. No matter what did or did not transpire between Rosalynde and himself in the two weeks before the tournament, it would not affect what was to come. When he met Gilbert in the melee—and defeated him—he would reveal all to Sir Edward and, in so doing, claim Rosalynde as his wife. He had no doubt her willingness would resurface when she learned he was a knight, and although the inconstancy of her nature infuriated him, he had no intention of letting such a prize escape him. He would have both her and Stanwood, or else die at Sir Gilbert's hand.

But this day's surprising encounter with her put another slant on things.

He paused in his whittling and ran his hand slowly along the staff. He had not sought her out; she had come to him. Yet he could not help but feel a twinge of guilt. He had not broken his word to Cleve, but he had also not sent her away. Indeed, he had taunted her and mocked her, sending her a challenge he knew she would not be able to ignore. Then, when she had joined him in the low-ceilinged loft above the stables, he'd forgotten everything else but her. Cleve's forced promise, Sir Gilbert's ominous presence—none of that had mattered when he'd been faced with her intoxicating nearness. She had stood there, small and afraid, yet bold enough to follow him when she surely knew what he was about. And then she had given herself so sweetly to him.

He leaned back against the wall, the work in his hands forgotten as he relived each delicious moment. Surely the scent of the stables—horses and straw and burlap—would ever remind him of her, overlaid, at least in his mind, with

the light fragrance that was uniquely hers. His Rose. His
woman.

But was she truly his?

It was that uncertainty which kept him from the great
hall tonight. He knew it a coward's way to avoid the truth.
Yet he could not bear to see her sitting so far above him,
fawned over by that snake, Gilbert, as she gave him the
smile that should be reserved for no man but himself.
More than that, however, he feared to see her look down
upon him, to see in her eyes that she had only one use for
him, and that a purely physical one.

"Christ, damn me for a fool!" he muttered furiously.

He stood up abruptly and paced the work space restlessly, consumed with anger, overwhelmed with fear. How
had one slight maiden brought him to such a pass? he
wondered as he squinted into the now-darkened yard.
He'd always jeered at those poor fools whose brains
seemed to rest within their braies. A woman was meant to
serve her man. She was flesh of his flesh, formed of the rib
of Adam. Yet now he was consumed by his need to possess
this one troublesome woman, almost to the point of forgetting his original need for vengeance.

A sudden outburst of laughter interrupted his black
thoughts, and he cocked his head toward the sound. In the
bailey he heard several thuds, followed by a grunt and
then a cry of pain. Another round of laughter, then he
heard a voice that he recognized as one of the several
squires'.

"Bastard ye are. And a runt as well." Another thud and a
groan of pain. "I suggest you remember your place, Squire
Cleve."

Once more several voices rang out in laughter. Then a
small group of lads hurried from the darkness behind the
barn and made their way toward the great hall.

Aric stood stockstill at the stable window. So Rosalynde's pup was held in contempt by his peers, he mused. How fitting. Yet that insult—bastard—echoed most uncomfortably in his ears.

What matter if the boy was a bastard? he told himself. He would either grow strong and rise above his place, or else wither under the taunts and become a craven fool. How the boy bore his cross was not his own concern.

Yet as another smaller shape stumbled into the shadowed yard, Aric's brow creased in a frown. He had once been in much the same predicament—an outsider, the bastard son of a knight of no particular note. Had he not been taller and stronger than the other squires, he would have suffered even more at their hands than he did. But he *had* been strong enough and eventually they'd abandoned their tormenting of him. Cleve, however, did not have that advantage. As the bent-over figure limped past the stable, Aric once again cursed the perverse streak in his own nature.

"Come in here." He barked the curt command from the dark doorway. Cleve whirled into a crouch, clearly startled by the sudden order and expecting another attack.

"You!" He gasped, then pressed one hand to his side. Slowly he straightened to his normal height. "So 'tis you who are behind this." He snarled like a cornered pup.

"If I wished you harm, boy, I would not send those fools to do it."

There was a brief silence. "What do you want then?" the boy asked belligerently.

Aric let out a self-deprecating snort. He was not himself sure of the answer to that question. "If you are to survive your years as a squire, you'd best learn to handle yourself in a brawl."

"I was but one!" Cleve defended himself heatedly. "They were four or more!"

"More reason than ever." Aric shrugged. "Learn to fight, or you will be forced to crawl."

"No one will ever see me crawl."

"Brave words—now."

"I can take care of myself," Cleve charged, sending a baleful glare at the imposing man. " 'Tis none of your affair."

"I could teach you a few tricks."

In the silence that followed, Aric could almost hear the thoughts milling through Cleve's surprised mind. "I've no need of *tricks*," he snapped. But when Aric did not respond, only waited, the tone of the boy's voice changed. "Why do you make this offer to me?"

Aric smiled in the dark. "Let's just say that I'm partial to a fair fight, and I can help you even the odds."

"But why?"

In a rare moment of weakness Aric answered more honestly than he intended. "We are not so different, Cleve, despite appearances to the contrary. And I've no stomach for cowards who prey on the weak."

"As if you've not done the same. Outlaws always prey on those weaker than themselves." Yet even those biting words could not disguise Cleve's curiosity.

"There are ways to overcome a stronger opponent," Aric said, as if he had not heard the boy's accusation. "Ways of using his own strength against him. Whether you battle with a sword, dagger, or by hand, 'tis all the same. But if you're not interested . . ." He shrugged once more and turned away from the open door.

"Wait—"

He twisted his head and watched as Cleve drew nearer.

"What payment shall you exact?" the limping boy asked, still suspicious of his enemy's motives.

"None," Aric replied quietly. "I do not do this for payment."

"Hah! No one like you does *anything* without some selfish motive."

Once more Aric smiled, hearing in the boy's belligerent words a reflection of his own suspicious nature. "I had not thought of it as payment, but mayhap you are right. In exchange for teaching you how to win any fight, I would have you forgo your rabid animosity toward me in favor of, let us say, a more thoughtful observance."

"Thoughtful observance!" Cleve blurted out. But then he stopped and took a deep and obviously painful breath. "All right, then, I agree. But this changes nothing of our earlier agreement. You will not seek out milady Rosalynde. And after the tourney, you go."

"Our first agreement still stands."

"Then let's to it," the boy replied, moving purposefully into the stable.

"Are you up to it?" Aric eyed the battered boy when they stood in the light. But he knew the answer to that. Hurt, he was an even easier mark than before. Those who preyed on the helpless never gave them time to recoup their strength. As Aric squared off with Cleve, he determinedly ignored the boy's bloodied nose and swelling eye.

"All right. When I come at you, defend yourself." Then, without warning, he lunged at the lad. In a second Aric had thrust him back, undeterred either by Cleve's blows or by his efforts to escape. When Aric released Cleve, his eyes narrowed.

"First, always—always!—be aware of your foe. Where he is and what his weapons are. In my case, I have height and weight over you, as well as experience. You cannot hold me off. This is of paramount importance, so you'd best heed it well: Never push when you can pull. But never pull directly back. Instead, twist aside. Look." In a slower version of his initial lunge, he advanced on Cleve. "Step back with your right foot, pivoting on your left. As you do that, grab at my tunic or my sleeve, and pull me past you. I'm already charging, but I'm expecting you to try to stand fast. But a well-placed tug here." He demonstrated, placing Cleve's right hand on the fullness of his own tunic. "That one pull will use my own weight against me and throw me off balance. Here, try it again."

They went through the motions slowly. Then as Cleve began to understand, they tried it faster. Aric came at him alternately from either side, and then from behind as well. Each time he showed the now-eager boy how to judge his opponent's direction and to then use his own positioning to best advantage. Cleve's pains were forgotten as they practiced again and again. It was only when voices were heard from the bailey that they both drew back, winded.

"Enough for one night, I vow. Come tomorrow and we'll continue."

Cleve nodded his head as he drew several hard breaths. "Aye, I'll be here." He stepped back, but he did not at once turn away. "You have my thanks," he finally admitted grudgingly. "That changes nothing, of course," he hastened to add.

"No, of course not," Aric agreed. But he was smiling after the boy left the stables.

Rosalynde was as nervous as a cat surrounded by baying hounds. By all standards the evening meal was a most civilized affair, complete with musical entertainments and Edith's remarkable almond-raisin tarts. Yet she could not enjoy the results of her labor so long as Aric and Cleve were mysteriously absent. Perversely, she knew that Aric's presence in the hall would have unnerved her even more than his absence did.

All day she had been a bundle of nerves, jumping at shadows, starting whenever someone addressed her. She'd been quite the fool in the kitchen, giving Maud and Edith such contradictory instructions that Maud had finally given in to an uncontrollable giggle.

". . . and the plate—" She had broken off, giving the cooks a vague glance. "What is it, Maud? You seem much distracted."

"Is it the bread we must stew well while we have the meat baked till the crust turns golden? Or perhaps t'other way around?" Her eyes crinkled with good humor. "And then there's the pewter plate you said we were t'soak to remove the salt while we rubbed the dried herring until it shone!" At that, both women began to laugh out loud while Rosalynde turned pink with embarrassment.

"I . . . well . . . my thoughts are somewhat distracted."

"Aye, so t'would seem. It wouldn't have anything to do with a certain strapping fellow, would it?"

The color fled Rosalynde's face in a rush. In sudden terror she faced the two women. Was she so transparent that everyone knew? Had she and Aric been seen? "I—I don't know what you . . . what you mean."

"Ah, so it ain't that handsome Sir Gilbert who has ye so flutter-witted," Edith mocked her good-naturedly. She elbowed Maud. "An' here we thought she was just fallin' prey to a case of the maidenly jitters. Could be the gossip is wrong about 'im wantin' to marry 'er."

Rosalynde's relief was immediate. It was Gilbert they attributed her absentmindedness to—not Aric! With an enormous sigh she released the breath she'd unconsciously been holding. "I have been acting strangely, I suppose." She gave them each a rueful grin.

"No, not strange, given the circumstances." Edith laughed. "What maiden wouldn't become scatterbrained to have such a fine gentleman pursuin' her?"

One maiden wouldn't, Rosalynde was still thinking later as she sat at the high table between her father and the very man Edith and Maud linked her to. She could not be less interested in Sir Gilbert Poole, but she was enormously relieved that no one else suspected that. As long as they thought her struck foolish by his presence, they would not question her odd behavior or link it to the foot soldier Aric.

Aric. The very thought of him pushed everything else from her mind. Not the meal, nor Sir Gilbert's unavoidable presence, nor the conversation going on between him and her father could prevent memories of Aric from sweeping over her.

How had she let things go so far between them? Even now when her skin still tingled from his rough caress and her body ached from their urgent coupling, she could hardly believe it real. She'd sought him out of her own free will. It did no good to pretend she'd only done so at her father's bidding. The truth was, she'd have searched for him regardless. And though she'd had more than enough opportunity to get away from him, like the most wanton of women she had followed him up that ladder to the dark privacy of the storage loft.

Her thick lashes lowered over eyes that had darkened in remembered passion. She had followed him up that ladder. At the time she would undoubtedly have followed him anywhere. But what about now?

Rosalynde's eyes opened as noisy laughter burst from her father and Sir Gilbert. She smiled appropriately, although she'd not heard a word of their discourse. Then she bent her attention to her meal and her thoughts went back to the afternoon.

She did not know what she should do about Aric now, nor how to react when she next saw him. In the aftermath of their violent lovemaking, neither of them had spoken much. For a long while they had lain together on the burlap sacks, catching their breath, not kissing or caressing, but nonetheless getting to know more of one another. It had been a silent communion of souls, she thought with a wistful sigh. In the dim confines of the crude space she had felt safer and more cherished than a queen might, though she be ensconced in the finest castle and recline on the finest of silks. In his arms she'd felt so right, though every logic deemed it wrong beyond comprehension. She might have lain there forever, trying to force reality away, had he not moved first.

" 'Tis time you returned to your duties," he had murmured as he sat up. Rosalynde had not responded, only watched as he donned his braies and chausses, and then his chainse and tunic. He was a formidable man in the dress of a soldier. And formidable in the lesser garb of a lover, she'd thought quite fancifully. But unlike her, he'd seemed well aware of their surroundings and the threat of discovery, and his enigmatic gaze had prodded her to rise.

"Let me," he'd murmured when she had tried to tie the laces on either side of her gown. Rosalynde had swallowed hard as his big hand had nimbly tied the side slits of her gown closed, and she'd become painfully unable to speak. What was one to say after such an earth-shattering experience? How was she to act when the same man who'd brought her to such shuddering pleasure now resumed his daily role as servant and man-at-arms? How was a woman supposed to treat her lover?

It was Aric who decided the matter for her.

"It would be best if you left now," he'd said, stepping back from her. His head had nearly touched the low rafters, she remembered.

"Y-yes," she'd agreed weakly.

It would be best, she'd told herself as she'd carefully slipped down the ladder then quickly exited the stables. It was best that she left before anyone remarked on her absence, yet for the remainder of the afternoon she'd felt an aching hollowness within her at such an unresolved parting. Now as wines and ale flowed, and the din of the evening meal grew ever louder, she wondered if he'd been as disappointed to see her go as she had been to leave.

At that moment her unsettled thoughts were interrupted. "I said, Sir Gilbert has asked about the ale," her father repeated the request she'd not responded to the first time. "He wishes to compliment the alewife."

Rosalynde turned a chagrined face to her guest, glancing only briefly at her mildly exasperated father. "Oh. Why, thank you, Sir Gilbert. Thank you. I shall surely convey your remarks to her—"

"If you would be so good as to escort me to her, I would as lief tell her myself."

With her father silently urging her to it, Rosalynde could hardly refuse. But her smile was strained as she rose from the table and accepted Gilbert's proffered arm. She heard the whispers that followed in their wake as they left the room together, and she tried to reassure herself that she should be pleased. After all, no one would link her to Blacksword if they connected her to Sir Gilbert.

"Your father and I have spoken of you," Sir Gilbert began, once they were out in the bailey.

"Spoken of me?" she echoed. Although she had no

doubt of his meaning, she was surprised that he would bring it up so boldly.

"I pray you will not toy with my heart, my Lady Rosalynde. Surely you know I have spoken to him regarding you. Surely you know I seek a union between you and me, and between the castles of Stanwood and Duxton." Grasping her hand, which rested on his arm, he halted their walk and turned to face her. In the moonlight he appeared earnest and appealing. The cruel slant of his mouth disappeared in a sincere smile; the shadows made his eyes impossible to read. Yet the warm grasp of his hands made it clear what message he wished to convey.

Rosalynde tried very hard not to frown. Her heart raced, but not due to any emotional response to him. If anything, she was angry that he had lured her away from the great hall on the pretext of complimenting the alewife.

"My father has not discussed this matter with me," she replied, trying to extricate her hands from his too firm clasp.

"But he *has* told you that he seeks a husband for you."

"Yes," Rosalynde admitted reluctantly. "He has."

"And though it is an odd quirk on his part, he has promised you a say in the choice of a groom."

That reminder renewed Rosalynde's confidence. "He did. But you must understand, Sir Gilbert, that I have not yet met the other men he has approved. I am, of course, much flattered by your interest in me, and I consider it the deepest compliment. But I would do my father a disservice to rush into a decision when he has so generously granted me this choice."

Even in the dark Rosalynde could tell that he did not like her answer. But he was also not ready to concede defeat, for in a determinedly smooth tone he pressed his suit.

"Fair Rosalynde, I only pray that you will look with favor upon my offer." He raised her hands to his lips and kissed her knuckles. "Just tell me, I beg you, whether some other has caught your eye."

Rosalynde hesitated for an instant before answering him. Someone had done far more than caught her eye. Someone had caught her heart and she would be many years in freeing herself from the devastating effects, if indeed she ever could. But that was something Sir Gilbert must never know of. No one could. Besides, Gilbert's query was for those other noblemen who might try to win her and, thereby, Stanwood.

"I've met no one, Sir Gilbert. Only you. However, my father has invited a goodly number of men to a tourney. No doubt I shall be introduced to any number of acceptable nobles at that time."

"Then I am the first," he stated with a smile. He moved a step nearer, to her sudden alarm, and she hastily stepped back as well.

"Shall we seek out the alewife?" she reminded him nervously.

"In a moment."

Then before she could react, he pressed a damp kiss fully on her mouth.

Rosalynde gasped in shock and then was further affronted by the surge of his tongue between her parted lips. She stumbled back repulsed, jerking her hands angrily from his.

"How dare you—" she choked out.

"Forgive me, Rosalynde. I beg you to forgive my impetuous nature. If you did but know how your nearness affects me."

She started to reply that perhaps she should keep her distance from him, then abruptly thought better of it. If she reacted too coldly toward him, her father would no doubt wonder why and question her on it. He had already expressed his exasperation toward her constant rejection of any reference to her eventual marriage. He would see any coldness on her part as just another aspect of her resistance, and he might not be so willing to grant her the freedom of a choice. Swallowing her distaste as best she could, she faced the expectant Sir Gilbert.

"I think it would be best if we return to the great hall."

"But what of the alehouse?" he pressed. "I promise to be on my best behavior," he added with what he clearly meant to be a beguiling smile.

Rosalynde averted her eyes. It seemed pointless now to turn down his request. But as she nodded, then led the way—although pointedly avoiding his proffered arm—her emotions knotted in confusion. Sir Gilbert's wet kiss had revolted her. The thought of opening her mouth to his intimate caress quite literally turned her stomach. Yet with Aric that same act had stirred her very soul. She'd opened much more than her mouth to Aric's bold caress, and reveled in glorious abandon as he'd commandeered all her emotions. Two men, both young and handsome. How was it that the one left her cold, while the other caused her to burn with desire?

As they made their way toward the alehouse, she did not see the rigid figure in the shadows of the tannery. Aric stood as still as stone, watching the two retreating figures, and although his eyes burned with violent emotion, he felt colder than a winter storm.

His wife and his enemy! It was more than a man could be expected to endure! And yet the logical, calculating side of him knew he must let it go. Everything was falling into place; it was not yet time to act. He knew who his enemy was—who had conspired to see him hang as a common thief. Now the man was within reach, but it must be done right. Their conflict had begun on the field of honor. It would end there as well. At the melee he would confront Gilbert. He would reveal his identity at that time and challenge the man to a battle of honor—a battle to the death.

Aric watched Rosalynde and Gilbert enter the alehouse, then forced himself to turn away. His appetite was suddenly gone, and the late meal he'd anticipated in the great hall lost its appeal. He'd seen that vermin, Gilbert, kiss her, and it sickened him. And yet, when he could have easily stepped from the shadows and stopped them from going on into the alehouse, he had not. Had his need for revenge against his foe completely suppressed his adherence to his knightly code of honor? Would he go so far as to forsake the woman he loved—

The woman he loved!

He halted at that unexpected admission. *The woman he loved.* Had he truly succumbed so completely to her? Yet even as he sought some logic to deny that it could be so, he knew it was true. He'd neither sought nor avoided love in his many dalliances with women. The fact was, he'd never considered the emotion at all. But now this most difficult of all women had stolen unawares into his heart.

Unbidden the memory of her, naked and slick with sweat beneath him, came to mind. How sweetly she'd responded to him. How passionately she had risen to his possession of her. It had been a perfect communion of two spirits, something special that only they shared. Certainly no other woman had ever pushed him so far.

Then he was reminded of their circumstances and his wonder turned to fury. The woman he loved walked now with his vilest enemy. Was he mad to wait until the melee to confront Gilbert?

A shudder ripped through him and he had to fight back a blind need to seek out Gilbert of Duxton then and there, and beat the life out of him.

Your time for revenge will come, he told himself over and over. *Your time will come.*

23

A strange tension seemed to grip the castle, although Rosalynde could not quite understand it. Perhaps it was only her overwrought nerves, for she was certainly pushed to distraction by her father's unrelenting good humor and Sir Gilbert's constant presence. Yet there was something more. She was sure of it.

Cleve, who during recent weeks had quite abandoned her in favor of his duties as a squire, now appeared more and more often at her side. Just that morning he'd joined her in the pleasaunce, digging holes for the chamomile and gromwell plants she meant to transplant from the forests. Although they'd nearly recovered the easy camaraderie they'd shared at Millwort, she still detected a strange air of watchfulness about him.

Then there was Aric of Wycliffe. She had not been alone with him since their tryst in the stable loft. A part of her was relieved he had not pursued her since then, for she knew full well that she would never have the strength of will to deny him. Yet she could not pretend that her disappointment did not far outweigh the relief she felt. He was clearly avoiding her, but she had no idea why. She knew it was linked to Cleve, and yet that still seemed completely illogical. Aric was hardly likely to bend to young Cleve's will. But she could not shake the feeling that the two were somehow connected. If she had not been so busy with the preparations for the coming entertainments, she would have surely gone mad with wondering. Instead, she focused her nervous energy on the tasks at hand, trying as best she could to ignore her troublesome imaginings.

Only at night when she finally fell exhausted into her own bed did she allow herself the luxury of dwelling on the enigmatic Aric. There, as the night enveloped her in its dark protection, she relived every moment they'd ever spent together. She did not bother to pretend anymore. She was in love with him, although nothing good could ever come of it. And though she compounded her sins by her shameless remembering, she consoled herself that in God's eyes, at least, they were wed. But even that was small comfort, for eventually the year would pass, and she would no longer be able to delay the inevitable. She would have to marry someone else.

Yet as the tournament guests began to arrive—some from as far away as the border with Scotland—Rosalynde knew that though she might have to select one of them as a husband someday, she would never find love again.

"Sir Edolf is a fine man," Sir Edward remarked to Rosalynde as he watched a solid-looking knight who practiced his skills in the lists. "He is the second son of my friend Robert Blackburn, Lord of Wigan. And a good fighter," he added admiringly.

"I've no doubt that he is a noble knight," Rosalynde murmured agreeably, although she silently deplored the man's gluttony and his overfondness for ale, which she'd witnessed the previous evening.

"He shall be a demon to contend with in the melee," her father went on, unaware of his daughter's lack of interest. Still distracted, he walked off, looking for Sir Roger while Cleve moved nearer Rosalynde's side.

"Sir Edolf *is* a fine man," he echoed her father's words. "And he was much pleased upon meeting you."

"Oh? Well, his sister Margaret was much pleased upon meeting *you*," Rosalynde replied tartly, giving him an arch look.

"She's only a child!" he protested hotly as a scowl replaced his teasing expression.

"She's eleven. Certainly of an age to be betrothed. And she's certainly comely. Why else would Sir Edolf bring her here if not to seek a titled husband for her?"

Cleve did not reply, but only gave her a probing look. " 'Tis not my future nor hers but your own that you should concern yourself with during these festivities. You cannot pretend otherwise, milady."

"So everyone seems most anxious to remind me," she threw back at him. Then she sighed and her irritation fled, to be replaced instead by reluctant acceptance. "Forgive me," she said when she spied his serious face. "I've no reason to be angry with you. It's just that . . ." Once more she sighed, unable to explain why she was so unhappy.

" 'Twould almost seem that you do not wish to marry at all," Cleve said in a quiet tone. He moved nearer, keeping his brown eyes steady upon her. "But you know you must marry. 'Tis the only choice for a woman. Unless—" He faltered, as if he did not wish to say the words, or even think them. Then his jaw clenched and his eyes bored into her now-pale face. "Could it be you truly *have* given your heart to someone else—someone you can never have?"

Before she could prevent it, tears welled in her huge eyes, threatening to spill over. She averted her face, but Cleve's hand on her arm kept her from fleeing.

"Does he yet trifle with you?" he muttered harshly.

When Rosalynde turned her face up to him, she was unable to hide the naked emotions displayed there. "No," she whispered in a stricken voice. "He avoids me completely." She swallowed the lump in her throat and managed a thin smile. "I don't know how you managed it, but I know he stays away because of you. I suppose I should thank you—"

She abruptly turned and hurried away from him. But Cleve remained where he was a long time, staring after her, but thinking about the man Aric.

"Holy Mother, but where are we to put 'em all?" the stable marshal muttered as yet another string of mounts and packhorses were led into the stableyard. "An' where in the name o' God are we to keep all this armor? Here, lad." He signaled to Cleve, who as a squire had been assigned the care of the private belongings of the contingent of knights from Holyfield. "Before you unpack these loads, move that pile of things in the shed farther to the left. But have a care," he added, raising one bushy brow. "These are Sir Gilbert's belongin's, an' he's more than particular. Lord hope that *he* don't end up marrying our sweet lass," he added under his breath.

Cleve did not reply to the stable marshal's unsolicited opinion. Nor was he truly surprised by it. It had not taken him long to determine that Sir Gilbert of Duxton would be difficult to deal with at any level. Cleve was quite convinced that Lady Rosalynde was too perceptive to pick a man like that to wed. But then she seemed unwilling to consider anyone at all, he thought, recalling their earlier conversation.

His brow creased in a frown as he tied the horses to a fence then approached Sir Gilbert's belongings. Rosalynde would just have to make the choice, he decided as he carefully began to move several bulky packages well wrapped in fustian. She was unhappy now, but once she was married and had a child—

At that thought he abruptly straightened up, unmindful of the long package that immediately toppled over. A child. Could there be a child of her liaison with Aric? He'd not considered that before yet . . . wouldn't she be more anxious than ever to marry if that were the case?

Not having experience with women, Cleve was not sure *how* noblewomen dealt with such possibilities. Even though Rosalynde was enamored of the brute, she surely could not consider him an appropriate husband or father for her children. Deep in thought, he absentmindedly reached for the heavy bundle on the floor, then let out a sharp oath as the cloth bindings came loose and several weapons tumbled out. With a guilty glance around him, he quickly began to gather everything back together. These were Sir Gilbert's war tools, he realized, and that one would raise holy hell should he learn what had happened.

But when he reached for a sword and scabbard that had fallen, he suddenly paused. The sword had slid a little out of its protective sheath, revealing the base of the blade, and it was that blade which grabbed his notice. Slowly he drew the broadsword from its plain leather-and-steel scabbard. Then a low whistle of admiration escaped him. The sword was magnificent, like nothing he'd ever seen before. But it was not a fancy hilt encrusted with gold and jewels that set it apart. This sword was actually quite plain and of a simple design that appealed to him at once. What made it so remarkable was the long razor-edged blade itself, for it was as black as pitch and as wicked-looking as midnight!

Cleve stared at the weapon in his hand, all the while struggling to make some sense of his accidental discovery.

Could it be just an accident that such a black sword had appeared in the wake of the man Blacksword's arrival at Stanwood? Logically he knew there could be more than one black sword in existence. Yet he could not ignore the ominous foreboding building in him. Aric was the criminal known as Blacksword, and yet why did Sir Gilbert have this weapon?

In frustration he thrust the heavy sword back into its scabbard and swiftly bundled it with the others. The rest of his work he completed in a trifling, moving Sir Gilbert's goods and unpacking the horses from Holyfield with a heretofore unknown alacrity. Then he turned the horses loose in the stableyard before hurrying off in search of the one man who could shed light on this disturbing turn of events.

Aric was on the ramparts, taking the watch near the postern gate when Cleve found him. Beneath them the castle yard was busy with servants and guests alike. Beyond the castle itself, a field was being cut for the coming tournament. A row of serfs moved across the meadow, scythes in hand, looking from this distance like ants at work. Yet for all the people around them, Cleve and Aric were quite alone.

As the boy came to a halt before him, Aric gave him a curious look. "If you're seeking another lesson, it must wait until after the evening meal." But when Cleve did not immediately respond, Aric peered at him more sharply.

"How came you by the name Blacksword?" the boy asked bluntly.

Aric drew back warily. "I should think that easy enough to surmise. Why do you ask?"

Cleve's dark brows drew together as he studied the man before him. "Where is your black sword, then?"

At that Aric stiffened and his expression grew grim.

"Have you found it? Perhaps among the possessions of one of Stanwood's guests?" But Cleve did not have to answer, for Aric already knew. His eyes turned as cold as ice as he stared at the boy. "Have you questioned the knight who bears this sword?"

"No, I thought it better if—" He stopped, as if he wasn't sure what he thought, and his face reflected his confusion.

The revelation that his sword was at Stanwood sent a jolt of exhilaration through Aric, bolstering his conviction that the coming tourney would provide him the opportunity to confront Gilbert once and for all. But Cleve's hesitant manner made him pause.

"You came to me first. Why?"

Cleve met his hard gray stare unflinchingly. "I thought —only for a moment, of course—that perhaps it was Sir Gil—this knight—who was the true outlaw, since he had possession of that blade. But I see now, 'tis far more likely that he took the sword from you."

The tone of his words were scornful, but on the boy's face was an expression nearer disappointment.

"Aye," Aric admitted softly. "Sir Gilbert took the blade from me, in a manner of speaking." Then he stared out toward the field where he meant to avenge himself on the nefarious Gilbert. " 'Tis best you forget that sword, Cleve, and distance yourself from such matters."

"Such matters? What does that mean?"

Aric shook off his dark musings and turned back to the boy. "It does not concern you."

"If it concerns my Lord Edward—or Milady Rosalynde —then it *must* concern me."

Aric almost smiled as the boy eyed him belligerently. Cleve would make a fine man, and a good knight, he thought indulgently. He had courage and a strong sense of loyalty. All he lacked was brawn and experience, and time would eventually provide him with those. Aric's expression became almost approving as he responded to the boy.

"Sir Edward has my loyalty. Lady Rosalynde—" He halted, unable to put into words what he felt for Rosalynde and unwilling, anyway, to reveal it to Cleve. "Lady Rosalynde's well-being is uppermost in my mind. I mean no harm to anyone of Stanwood."

But Cleve would not let it go. "How did you lose your sword? I cannot see you surrendering so fine a weapon easily." Then his face creased as another thought occurred to him. "Does he know you are here?"

The last vestiges of Aric's indulgence fled. "Sir Gilbert will be informed soon enough, but by me and no other. Is that clear to you, Cleve?" The icy menace in his voice lingered in the air between them as Cleve pondered those last words.

"It would be easier for me to keep my silence if I knew more of you and your ties to Sir Gilbert," the boy answered slowly.

"Your mistrust of me has been clear from our first meeting. Do you expect me to trust *you* with things better kept to myself?"

"As I see it, you've little enough choice," the boy shot back. "I've only to point you out to Sir Gilbert—"

" 'Tis not a hard thing to silence a man. Or a boy," Aric stated quietly. He was satisfied that Cleve paled at the threat, and also impressed that the boy still did not back down.

"I cannot allow you to attack one of Lord Edward's guests."

"I've no intention of catching him unaware. A blade through the back is not my way, so you may rest easy on that score. No, he and I will meet, for justice demands it. But 'twill be on the field of honor."

At this curious remark Cleve gave Aric an odd look. "The field of honor? But you are not—" He stopped then continued on more slowly. " 'Twas your sword. And now you would meet him on the field of *honor* . . ." His voice trailed off as if a sudden thought had become more insistent. "You're a knight, aren't you? Or at least you were once."

It was in Aric's mind to deny it, to cling still to the anonymity he had forced on himself ever since Rosalynde's rejection of him as a realistic choice for marriage. He wanted her to want him no matter his station in life, and so had suffered this lowly place in her household. At times he thought his plan only a foolish exercise in pride. But other times he was certain she would soon be his. Hadn't their tryst in the stable been the proof of that? Yet he was still loath to reveal too much of the truth, not until she relented and admitted her true feelings.

"My past is of no consequence. You need only concern yourself with the future and with the knowledge that I plan no dishonor to Sir Edward or to the Lady Rosalynde."

"But you plot against Sir Gilbert, do you not?"

"That one is less than worthy of the title of knight," Aric bit out.

Cleve looked away, clearly unsettled by his new knowledge. In the castle yard all was in motion. Then his gaze sharpened as he spied Rosalynde. She was crossing the bailey, only to be intercepted by none other than Sir Gilbert himself. Aric too saw the pair below, and his expression grew as cold as a winter storm.

"Christ, but I long to face that vermin in battle!" he swore, ending with a particularly foul oath.

"Lady Rosalynde is unlikely to be fooled by such a man as he," Cleve remarked, turning back to Aric. A puzzled frown creased his brow at the sight of the other man's furious countenance. Then understanding came and a faint smile suddenly lightened his face.

"She should not encourage him," Aric growled, never sparing the boy a glance. "She should keep to her household duties and stay away from the castle yard."

"How else is she to catch the eye of any of the other knights summoned here by her father? After all, she must be wed. Perhaps she only plays one against the other—'tis not unheard of."

Aric continued staring at Rosalynde, and his eyes went nearly black as Sir Gilbert caught her hand and pressed a kiss to it. Although she swiftly freed herself from his grasp, Aric continued to scowl as he watched her out of sight, all the while unaware of Cleve's steady perusal of him.

The boy was no less concerned about his mistress's well-being. But the revelations of the past minutes had done much to alter the focus of his concerns. Lady Rosalynde must marry. He accepted that obvious fact. And she must not marry beneath her. He also knew that she was no longer a maiden.

But she still wanted this man she thought a common criminal, and he quite clearly wanted her. Cleve shook his head softly, bemused by the sudden elevation of Aric in his estimation. This cast a new light on everything.

"Do I have your silence, boy?"

Cleve nodded mutely, his serious gaze holding with the bigger man's darkened eyes. "Aye, I'll keep my peace so long as no one of Stanwood shall suffer."

24

Rosalynde could not help herself. She had watched Aric surreptitiously all through the evening meal, and there was no doubt in her mind that he was deliberately avoiding her gaze. He had come in late, eaten his fill, then departed before any of the evening's entertainments could begin. Now, even though she knew it was foolish beyond all reason, she planned to slip away from the company and seek him out. But as she made a slow circuit through the filled hall, aiming to withdraw through the servants' entrance, she felt a sudden tug at her sleeve.

"Why, Margaret," Rosalynde said as she saw the hesitant expression of Sir Edolf's young sister's face. "Is there something you need?"

The fair-haired child gave her a serious look, then heaved a desolate sigh. "Please don't think me ungrateful," she said in a voice far older than her years. "But I think I would like to go home."

Rosalynde's heart immediately melted toward the little girl who was being pushed at so young an age into the perilous world of marriage and politics. If it was hard enough for a grown woman to stomach, how much worse must it be for a mere child? Yet child or adult, a daughter was ever to be viewed as an implement of negotiation by the men who controlled her fate. Even though she herself had been given the luxury of the final selection of her husband, the men had still been carefully decided upon by her father. She was, more than anything else, simply the funnel by which Stanwood Castle's future would be secured. Margaret's fate was even worse, however, for she was a youngest child with only a moderate dowry to commend her. As a result, her rare childish beauty was being flaunted in the hopes that her very innocence might rouse some well-placed nobleman's lust.

Rosalynde caught the child's slender hand in her own. "I wish I could go home with you too," she confessed with an understanding smile.

"But you *are* home," Margaret replied. Then her sweet face grimaced in understanding. "Oh, you don't wish to marry either."

"Well, it's not precisely that I do not wish to marry. Only . . ." Rosalynde paused and a bitter smile curved her mouth. "Only, like you, I would wish for more freedom in the choice."

"If you could choose whomever you wished, who would it be?" the girl asked. Her expression was an odd mixture of childish hope and adult curiosity.

"Oh, that is hard to say," Rosalynde demurred. "No one here," she finally said, gesturing toward the noisy hall.

"I know who *I* would choose."

"You do? Who?"

Margaret hesitated, then bent nearer. "You will not tell him, will you?"

"Of course not."

"Well then, 'tis Cleve. The squire with the dark hair." Then, as if that description did not quite sum him up, she added most seriously, "The one with the sparkling eyes."

Rosalynde had never noticed that Cleve's eyes sparkled. Yet as she looked down into the girl's eager face, she real-

ized that for Margaret at least, his eyes did sparkle. How
sweet and lovely was this childish affection that the girl
felt for Cleve. Yet it would only be cruel to encourage such
hopeless dreams, for Margaret would be betrothed and
probably even wed long before Cleve would become a
knight and eligible for such an honor.

"His eyes sparkle because he has rather a temper," she
said, although she hated to see the light fade in Margaret's
face. "Besides, your brother no doubt seeks a far grander
lord for you. Cleve is but a squire."

Margaret sighed. "I shouldn't care if he were only a
stableboy."

Margaret's last words continued to echo in Rosalynde's
head long after she had seen the child to the chamber she
shared with her maid. It didn't matter to that innocent,
knowing girl that the one she pined for was not suitable as
a husband. Likewise, she herself did not care about such
things either, Rosalynde admitted. She closed her eyes
against the powerful longing she felt for Aric. If not for the
terrible repercussions it would bring down on him, she
would not hesitate to bind herself to him permanently.

An image of him as he'd first appeared on the gallows
came to her mind, and she stumbled on an uneven paving
stone. He'd been so intimidating, even bound as he was.
She'd been frightened, overawed, and drawn to him, all at
the same time. Yet never would she have predicted that
those emotions could turn to love. Never could she have
foreseen the unbelievable joy and unbearable agony that
loving him would bring her.

From a thoughtful, sensitive girl she'd become a reckless wanton, with no control over her careening emotions.
Even now, when he plainly was avoiding her, she could
not restrain herself from seeking him out. Just a word or

two was all she wanted, she told herself. Only a moment to reassure herself that he'd do nothing to risk his life.

Yet as she hurried through the dark toward the stables where she hoped to find him, she knew that words would not be sufficient reassurance. She wanted to touch him and hold him, and be held by him—to feel the strong steady beat of his heart against her own. She knew it was a madness that consumed her, but she was beyond fighting it any longer.

She found him in the stable, brushing a magnificent war-horse with sure, rhythmic strokes. Both man and beast turned warily toward her at her entrance. The horse flattened his ears, stamped one of his feet, and tossed his head up and down. Aric only patted the animal's powerful neck reassuringly and bent back to his work.

" 'Tis a fine steed," she began hesitantly, unsure precisely what she wanted to say to him.

"His lineage is the best," Blacksword replied quietly, though his eyes remained fixed on his work.

She came a step nearer, distressed by his clear disregard of her. "His lineage?" she repeated, at a loss for words. "How can you know his lineage when he belongs to Gil—to someone else?" she amended hastily.

He frowned and finally turned to look at her. "You need only look at such a horse to know he comes from a long line of fine destriers."

Rosalynde nodded silently, cursing herself for almost bringing up Sir Gilbert's name. Then the horse shoved his nose playfully under Aric's arm, and she focused more closely on the animal. "He certainly seems to appreciate your ministrations."

Aric shrugged and continued with his work, but Rosalynde was determined to drag him into conversation, and the horse seemed the only available topic. "Is this the horse you were feeding the apples to in the corral that day—"

That day!

That day they had made love in the loft that was directly above them now! Her face heated to scarlet but her eyes could not turn away from his gaze. It was clear he was remembering that day as well, for his eyes became dark and smoky. When he spoke, his voice was a low rumbling caress.

" 'Tis no great feat to tempt a wild creature. Patience and a sweet bribe will win them everytime." Then his face lifted in an unwilling and rueful smile. He leaned his weight against the horse's broad side and faced her squarely. "But who is being tempted by whom can sometimes become confused."

How true that was, Rosalynde thought as a delicious quiver of longing coursed up her spine. He had tempted her to be sure. He had tempted her to bribe him with kisses—and more. But in so doing, had he too become ensnared in the tangle that enveloped them both? His self-mockery seemed to proclaim it true, yet he still remained remote from her.

"Aric," she began, determined to steer the conversation towards her primary concern. "You have been successful so far in avoiding discovery. But the tournament begins on the morrow, and I fear you cannot long escape Sir Gilbert's eyes."

"Good."

" 'Tis not good! If you mean to prod him into a fight and thereby avenge yourself against him, you must know that my father could never forgive you for attacking a guest of his. Your punishment would be swift and severe!"

"Do not trouble yourself on that account, Rosalynde. I

am well able to fend for myself. Or is it, perhaps, Gilbert whose safety you fret for?"

Rosalynde crossed the short space between them. Without thinking she grabbed hold of his tunic, knotting it in her small fist as her fear for him took shape in anger. "Do not mock me this way! Sir Gilbert may be hanged for all I care!"

"But I may not?"

One of his hands came around hers, holding it fast against his chest. She felt the warmth of him and the steady beat of his heart, and she was reminded of another time when she'd gripped his tunic in a similar anger and fear. On the gallows of Dunmow she'd been awed by the crackle of energy that had flashed between them, frightened by emotions she'd not even been able to name. But much had passed between them since then, and now she knew where such fiery intensity could lead.

"You are ever determined to save me from the hangman," he murmured, staring down into her upturned face. "I wonder why that is."

Because I love you, her wide startled eyes made the silent declaration. *Because I need you and cannot bear to risk losing you.*

As if he heard, his hand tightened around hers. Then with a helpless groan he gathered her into his arms, burying his face in the soft fullness of her hair. He did not speak as he held her almost desperately to him, yet there was much revealed in their violent embrace. Rosalynde felt the hard imprint of his body against her softer form. She recognized the masculine strength that could easily dominate her, and the potent virility that was always her undoing. But this time when he held her it was different from before. The passion was still there, simmering beneath the surface, waiting to erupt, but there was something else. She pressed her cheek against the rough wool that covered his chest, wetting it with her unexpected tears, and felt his kiss in her hair. Her arms slipped around his waist and in the quiet stall they clung to one another, each taking comfort merely from the presence of the other.

The realization that she could find such a thing as comfort with him—a thing so rare, which she'd never completely found with anyone else—started Rosalynde's tears in earnest. She needed him so much! And she was certain beyond any doubt that he found that same ease—that same comfort—with her. It was as near to perfection as anyone could ever hope to find!

She breathed deeply. With her eyes closed she let her senses fill with him. *Oh, let this be forever,* she prayed as his arms continued to hold her. *Let this be forever.* Yet when she felt his shuddering sigh she knew it could not be.

"Rose," he began in a low murmur against her ear.

"Shh." She turned her face up to his, unmindful of the tears that wet her cheeks. "My one wish is for you to live. To be safe. I'll ask nothing else of you but that."

He cupped her face between his two hands and stared a long time into her wide, damp eyes. Then he bent to kiss her—a long, sweet kiss filled with longing, but curiously, not passion.

"I will live, Rosalynde. You must not fear otherwise." Then he stopped as several voices sounded in the night.

"I must go," she whispered as she recognized one of the voices. She clung to him for a moment with a fierce kiss of her own, then shoved him deeper into the stall before whirling and dashing toward the yard. As she rounded a corner of the stable she met with several men, including

Sir Gilbert, and as she came to an abrupt stop, so did they as well.

"Why, Lady Rosalynde." Sir Edolf gave her a surprised smile and a gallant bow. "What an unexpected pleasure."

"Good evening, Sir Edolf," she answered, all the while searching her mind for an excuse for her presence in the stables. Her eyes darted nervously to Sir Gilbert's thoughtful expression, then back to the other men. "And a good evening to the rest of you gentlemen. I trust the meal met with your satisfaction."

" 'Twas fine indeed, my lady."

"You set a fine table," another added, patting his stomach.

"Very fine," Gilbert also conceded. "But what brings you to the stables after dark? And alone?"

"The stables? Oh." Rosalynde gave him what she hoped would pass for an offhand smile. "One of the stable lads hurt his hand—a rope burn, it was. I took him a salve to ease his pain."

She began idly to ease away from the stable, trying hard to distract them with her conversation. "I know that like most of your gender, you gentlemen do not set a great store by the healing arts, nor by the herb gardens and stillroom—at least not until you have a personal need of them. But I take particular pride in the medicinal herbs I grow—and the ointments and salves I am able to make. If any of you would care to see the stillroom?"

"As a matter of fact, I would like that very much." Gilbert was the first to respond. He stepped forward, offering his arm to her.

For a moment Rosalynde faltered. It was hard enough to maintain this facade for all of them without being subject to Sir Gilbert alone. Yet she could not be certain that Aric had left the stables yet. All it would take was for Gilbert to find him in his own prize war-horse's stall!

"Oh, I did not mean tonight." She laughed weakly. "I've neither torch nor lantern to light the place. However, if you are still inclined, we may go on the morrow."

"But tomorrow is the tournament," Sir Edolf threw in, clearly pleased to stymie Gilbert's attempt to get Rosalynde alone.

"Let him go, then," Sir Andrew of Billingham laughed. " 'Twill make my plan much easier if Gilbert Poole should fail to appear in the lists!"

From there the conversation launched into good-natured boasting and laughing challenges. But as the group paused before the door to the great hall, Rosalynde was hard-pressed to keep any better than a pleasant expression on her face. Her eyes kept straying to Gilbert's peeved face.

"—'twould be a pleasure to see you unseated again, as you were in London," one of the men taunted Sir Gilbert.

"You were bested in London?" Sir Andrew asked. "I'd not heard."

An ugly expression darted across Gilbert's face, but when he turned to face Sir Andrew his features were composed once more. "It was a momentary lapse on my part, which the lucky fellow used to his advantage. I would like nothing better than to meet him once more. Then we would see who would emerge victorious." He smiled, but Rosalynde thought it forced. "Unfortunately, I have not seen him since. No doubt he will not risk losing to me in another match."

"He did not look the type to be intimidated by anyone," Rosalynde heard the same man mutter to Sir Andrew. But to Gilbert he only replied, "Perhaps you are right."

As Rosalynde entered the great hall once more, and the

knights dispersed, she did not see Gilbert's furious expression. One of the castle hounds tried to slink past him, only to be kicked viciously. As the hound leapt away, howling in fear and pain, Gilbert spun on his heel and, with a vile epithet, strode off to find his quarters.

Cleve dismissed the young page to his bed, determined to linger in the hall—even if it were only to serve the wine —until Sir Edward could give him a moment. All evening ale and wine had flowed freely, although Cleve was aware that Sir Edward and his men had drunk but sparingly. Come morning there would be many a pounding head, but not among Stanwood's contingency. He could not help but admire Sir Edward for his astute planning. It was just as Aric had told him—know your enemy's strengths and weaknesses. Sir Edward was hoping to weaken his adversaries while maintaining his own solid strength. Though a small enough advantage, as Aric had pointed out, even a small advantage could turn a loss into a victory.

At the thought of the man Aric, Cleve grew pensive. There was much more there than met the eye, and his sixth sense told him that the morrow could very well see everything brought out into the open.

At a signal from a grizzled lord, Cleve sprang forward, an ewer of wine in his hands, to fill the man's emptied cup.

"—to be settled. For I've men enough to see it done."

"Edward, Edward." Lord Virgil sighed, shaking his head. "You will be hard-pressed enough to best Sir Gilbert's men. Think you that you can outlast me and my own?" He chuckled, then brought the filled cup to his mouth and quaffed the wine in one long pull. Then he banged the pewter cup down, wiped his mouth on his sleeve, and stood up. "My compliments on the wine. How-

ever, I'm no mere boy to be done in that easily." He gave
Sir Edward a grin and an unsteady bow, then lurched
away, muttering about his knights and their many glorious
victories.

Sir Edward leaned back in his chair as his longtime
friend quit the hall. The torchieres were burning low and
only a few other knights yet lingered nearer the hearth at
wine and dicing. Sensing his opportunity, Cleve approached the quietly thinking Lord of Stanwood, ewer still
in hand. Sir Edward waved him away absently, but when
the boy hesitated to leave, the older man looked up questioningly.

"Well, lad, what is it?"

"If I may be so bold, milord, might I beg a word with
you?"

"The hour is late . . . but, yes, go ahead."

"Well, you see . . ." Cleve faltered, uncertain how to
proceed. " 'Tis about the Lady Rosalynde. Your daughter,"
he added as if by way of clarification.

"Yes, the Lady Rosalynde *is* my daughter," Sir Edward
replied in amusement. "Now, what of her?"

"Well, she and I are long acquainted. She has ever extended her kindness to me and I would sacrifice my very
life on her behalf."

"You have proven that true enough."

"The thing is," Cleve continued, gathering courage and
momentum from Sir Edward's amiable reception. "Even
though she is only a woman, she is quite remarkable. She
has said you allow her a choice in the selection of a husband. But I would implore you, as one who knows her
well, not to be too harsh on her should her choice seem ill-
advised."

Sir Edward eyed him curiously. "First of all, young
Cleve, I must thank you for your continued concern for

my only child. However, I must correct a misunderstanding on your part. Her choice of a husband is from among a prescribed cadre of acceptable lords."

"Yes, milord. I realize that, milord," Cleve stammered. "Only the Lady Rosa—"

"I have no doubt she would extend her choice wider," Sir Edward interrupted him. "Like her mother before her, Rosalynde would convert each one of my concessions to encompass much more, and use my own indulgence toward her against me." He gave Cleve a keen look but his eyes held a gleam of understanding. "No doubt there is many a young man would willingly have such a maid as she to wife. You can understand, I am sure, that it remains for me to limit her choice to those men I deem right for her." He pushed his heavy chair back, then stood up and smiled at Cleve. "Take heart, lad. In the years to come you shall come across many a fair face and soft voice. But you cannot have them all, so you'd best learn that lesson now." So saying, he gave Cleve a stern look before turning and walking away.

Cleve stared after Sir Edward, his mouth still opened to protest. It wasn't himself he'd referred so obliquely to, but Aric. Yet no matter the man involved, it was clear Sir Edward had no intention of granting Rosalynde more than the most minimal choice in this very important matter. With a sigh Cleve picked up Sir Edward's empty cup and turned to take it and the ewer back to the buttery. He had been a fool to approach Sir Edward in such a presumptuous fashion, and he was grateful the man had not called him to task for it. Once again he thanked his patron saint for landing him in the service of such a fair-minded lord as Sir Edward of Stanwood.

But fair-minded would only carry so far, he knew. Lady

Rosalynde had best resign herself to her fate, for no matter how the morrow resolved itself of the bad blood between Sir Gilbert and Aric, her father would have the final word in the choice of her husband.

25

The halls and yards of Stanwood Castle were alive with activity even before the sun crept over the eastern horizon. The meadows were still damp with dew beneath a dark-mauve sky when the villagers began streaming toward the pavilions set around the tournament lists and battlefield. Since the day before, whole pigs and calves had cooked in covered pits, and now an army of eager laborers dug away the dirt to get at the well-charred carcasses. Dogs were underfoot everywhere, waiting for their portion of the feast to come, and from the opened gates of the castle itself a constant flow of carts, pedestrians, and riders moved back and forth.

Rosalynde had also been up before dawn, directing the conveyance of the various foods to the designated area near the games. She was more than ever thankful for Cedric's calm nature, for he was seeing to the many butts of ales and wines. As she watched the armloads of breads, the huge wheels of cheeses, and the baskets of fruits loaded into the wagons, she knew she should feel relieved to have that job done, for she trusted Edith and Maud to take over from here and coordinate the serving from the many plank tables that waited in the fields. Yet Rosalynde could not take much pleasure from the completion of the main portion of her work. Indeed, as she faced the fact

that there was nothing left for her to do now, except to
dress herself, she heartily wished for a long list of details
to attend. At least if she were busy she would not be able
to dwell on the many terrifying possibilities that had tormented her all night. But Rosalynde knew that busy or
idle, she would not be able to avoid the realities that
awaited. Somehow, in some way, Blacksword would make
his move against Sir Gilbert, and when he did, nothing she
could say or do would save him from the certain explosion
that would follow.

All through the night she had prayed—and cried—and
prayed again, until her eyes had burned. Her fingers were
numb from her rosary of wooden beads—surely worn
from overuse. More than once she had risen from her unhappy bed, determined once and for all to seek out her
father and reveal everything to him. Yet she had hesitated
each time, as much because she feared he would retaliate
against Aric as because she knew Aric would never forgive
her interference. She would not be able to forgive herself
if any harm came to him; but he would never forgive her if
she stole his chance for vengeance from him. Even if he
failed in his quest and her father somehow spared his life,
she knew well enough that Aric would still not leave Stanwood—not without his vengeance on Sir Gilbert and not
without proclaiming her his wife.

As she made her weary way back to her private chamber, she reluctantly accepted the grim fact that this day's
doings were out of her hands. Aric and Gilbert would
clash. It was inevitable. Her role would be to patch up the
pieces afterward. But it seemed impossible that there
would be anything left of Aric to patch up: if he vanquished Sir Gilbert, he would be swiftly cut down by her
father. And if Sir Gilbert defeated him . . .

Unable to face either eventuality, Rosalynde retreated

into the protection of emotional numbness. Like a frozen doll, she let herself into her chamber, then automatically removed her work gown. She splashed water from a metal ewer into a shallow pan, then bathed quickly, standing in the pan and washing herself with a small portion of soft soap. Her hair she combed herself, leaving it long and loose. The tunic she donned over a fresh kirtle was another of her mother's, a gown made to be worn on only the most important of occasions. The fabric was a tightly woven linen, dyed the darkest of blues. In the light it alternately shimmered between a gleaming black and the color of the evening sky. It was laced with gold and silver cords, and fitted tightly to her body. Around the set-back neckline a wide band was embroidered so that she appeared to wear a magnificent necklace that reached the full width of her shoulders. With her silver-worked girdle and keys in place, she knew she looked almost a queen in her royal home.

Yet Rosalynde felt more a slave than a queen, for she knew—as all noblewomen must know, she realized—that she was but a pawn in a man's world. Whether she was dealing with her father or Aric or Gilbert—or even Cleve —her wishes would ever take second place to their own. She smoothed her hair back from her brow, then gnawed at her lower lip. Even a queen, no doubt, was but a pawn in the king's royal games.

A knock on her door interrupted her dark musings.

"The cart awaits, milady. Are you ready to depart?"

"I'm ready, Cedric," she answered with a fortifying breath. Then, with her head high and her back stiff, she stepped forward to watch her one true love meet his fate.

" 'Tis grand, is it not?" Cedric gushed as he drove her in the small cart toward the main pavilion. But he was too overawed by the noise and activity and crowds of people to note her lack of response.

"Edith and Maud have the kitchen well in hand. The pages have their instructions to maintain a watchful eye and keep order wherever they go. Father Henry and the two other itinerant clerics have a tent for the injured—I've two barrels of water and an abundance of linen wrappings on hand there," he rattled on. "The squires are all with the horses, of course, and setting the weapons out."

"Is it likely anyone will be hurt?" Rosalynde asked softly.

Cedric gave her a quick look, then shrugged. "With the jousting one can never tell. A bad fall, a poorly placed lance . . . But the melee." He paused as if he considered his words carefully. "The melee is but a game—as close to real battle as can ever be portrayed among friendly barons. But in the midst of it all, well, sometimes tempers rise— that, and the men's natural lust for battle. These men are all trained for war. Once the melee begins 'tis inevitable that blood will be let. But 'tis rare that a man is lost," he added by way of reassurance.

But Rosalynde was not reassured. When she stepped down from the cart and made her way toward the tented viewing stand, her legs were trembling and her stomach was clenched in a knot. It was not, however, the melee that was her primary worry. She had faith that both Aric and her father were skilled enough to protect themselves relatively well from the overeager opponents they would face. But the melee could very easily provide Aric with the access he wished to Gilbert. It also would provide Gilbert and his cadre of knights the opportunity for the same.

Had Rosalynde not been so consumed with worry, she might actually have enjoyed the jousting. One by one each of the men her father considered worthy of such a prize as his daughter urged his horse down the long course. Thundering hooves and the cries of the watching multitude culminated each time in a resounding crash. Oftimes a lance would shatter. Generally one of the knights was unhorsed, falling heavily to the dusty earth, unable to move —whether due to injury or simply the weight of his mail and armor—until two squires hurried to his aid. The victor rode off to await his next challenge.

Slowly, methodically, the field of riders was narrowed down until only two remained. With a headache pounding cruelly behind her eyes, Rosalynde watched as the two mighty knights prepared for their final run. They were well hidden by their chain-mail hoods and hard steel helmets, yet she knew them by the colors they flew. Sir Edolf wore blue and gold and rode a heavy bay destrier; Sir Gilbert wore gold and black and rode the tall black steed that Aric had groomed but yesterday.

She was not aware that Cleve had come up behind her. She did not hear young Margaret's prayer that her brother win the day. She only knew that if Gilbert was unhorsed— and perhaps hurt, but not too badly, of course—he might not fight in the melee. And if he did not fight there, then he and Aric might not confront one another! Her hands tightened on the arms of her chair as she leaned forward, her entire being rigid with tension.

At the sound of a horn, the two horses leapt forward, muscles bunching as they strained to reach their top speed. The two men catapulted toward one another, shields at the ready, lances lowered menacingly. They met with a crash of wood upon steel and the cries of a hundred throats. In less than a second the winner was clear to all, yet as Rosalynde watched Sir Edolf's stocky frame lurch back in the saddle, then slide upside down over the rump of his stunned horse, it seemed to take forever.

"No!" she cried, pounding her fists futilely on the chair. "No!"

"Edolf!" Margaret cried at the same time, jumping up in alarm.

"Hush, he'll be fine," Cleve told the child, catching her before she could hurry to her fallen brother.

"Let me go!" she pleaded tearfully, struggling in his firm hold.

"Would you humiliate him further by rushing to his side? Think you he wants a girl fussing over him now?"

Even as he spoke, Edolf rolled over. Then with stiff jerky movements and the help of a squire, he managed to rise to his feet.

"You see," Cleve said as he released Margaret. "He is fine." As the girl slowly sat down, surreptitiously wiping at the tears that had spilled onto her cheeks, Cleve turned his attention to Rosalynde.

"Milady?" he asked when he spied her pale face and still-staring eyes. Then a frown shadowed his face when he followed her gaze to the triumphant Gilbert. He moved nearer her. "Milady, did you so hope Sir Edolf would be champion in the lists today?"

At his words Rosalynde started, unaware until now that he was even there. "Sir Edolf?" she repeated in confusion. "No . . . that is . . ." She sighed and glanced once more to Sir Gilbert, who was accepting the hearty congratulations from a throng of men including her father. "I had only hoped that Sir Gilbert would lose," she murmured.

"Aye, you're not alone in that," Cleve muttered in obvious anger, and it was this unexpected emotion from him that finally drew her full attention. She made sure Margaret was well distracted before she addressed him.

"Is there something of Gilbert that displeases you?"

Cleve shrugged, not sure he ought to confide in he

something that should rightfully come from another source. "There is that about him which does not inspire my respect," he answered enigmatically.

"And yet he is a knight, well respected and a great fighter."

"There is more to a man than that," the boy replied. "I am not convinced of his honor."

His honor. The words brought a fragment of memory to Rosalynde's mind. She'd accused Aric once of having no honor. It had been an accusation born of fear and anger. But he had countered that she was the one lacking in honor for not living by her vow at the handfasting cere- mony. Perhaps in their accusations they had each been a little right and a little wrong. But now, although she had no firm reason, she was as certain as was Cleve that Sir Gilbert was a man possessed of no honor whatsoever.

"Regardless of that, he is the victor now. As such, he will no doubt be at the forefront of the melee," she mur- mured unhappily.

"Yes, the melee," Cleve repeated darkly, again piqueing Rosalynde's interest.

"Is there something about the melee that you know?" she asked hesitantly. "Is something planned—some dire deed?" Her voice trailed off in fear.

Cleve stared a long time at the field where the melee would occur before looking back at her. In the shade of the tent he somehow appeared older to her, more a man now than a boy. When he spoke it was with a mature inflection and a protective tone.

"What will be, will be, Lady Rosalynde. You cannot ex- pect a man to be other than he is, nor expect him to do less than what he must." Then, in a surprising move, he took her hand and bent low to kiss it. "By your leave, duty calls me." But before he strode off, he gave her a last anxious glance, and once more he was the boy she had known for so many years. "Try not to worry, milady. 'Twill do no good."

"And will prayers do no good either?"

He shrugged. " 'Tis hard to say. But they cannot hurt."

If the jousting had been met with enthusiasm by both castlefolk and villagers alike, the prospect of the melee raised their excitement to a fever pitch. Around the broad field of battle the various pennants snapped in a quickening breeze: Sir Virgil of Rising's red and white; Sir Edolf Blackburn's gold and blue; Sir Gilbert's gold and black; and her father's green and gold. Knights gathered alongside men-at-arms, for this melee would be fought entirely on foot in order that more men could participate in the sport.

Even from her position across the field, Rosalynde could easily identify Aric among her father's men. His great height and broad frame were a magnet for her eyes, and yet seeing him garbed in the leather tunic of battle only increased the terrible turmoil that gripped her. No good could come of this, she knew. Only disaster.

But all the worrying in the world could not prevent the progression of events to come. A shrill horn sounded and the several armies drew back behind their flags, ready for the battle to begin. Any lingerers at the food tables quickly stuffed their mouths then hurried to find a good spot for viewing the games. Then another deeper horn carried its note across the yard, and after a momentary silence, the field erupted with sound.

Rosalynde could not stay in her chair as the opposing groups of men surged forward, weapons drawn and voices raised in the battle cries of their respective houses. When the first crash was heard of metal upon metal, sword upon

sword, and staff upon staff, she clasped her hands together, sick with horror and fear. Yet she could not tear
her eyes away as the waves of men met in a great willing
crush of human flesh. Although innumerable serfs had
carted buckets of water to wet down the field earlier, dust
nevertheless rose in billows as the armies sought to pierce
their opponents' defenses. Rosalynde knew that the various armies sought only to capture one another's flags,
thereby sending the vanquished armies to the sidelines
until only one remained victorious. Yet she knew that between at least two of the combatants, the battle would be
no game.

At the beginning of the melee, she saw Aric off to the
right of her father, working his staff with devastating results. But as the dust rose and the battle thickened, she
lost sight of him and nearly panicked. Only the sight of
Gilbert's pennant and cluster of men on the far side of the
field, not yet clashing with Stanwood's forces, reassured
her that the inevitable battle between Gilbert and Aric had
not begun.

In the midst of the excited yet good-natured men, Aric's
mind also was on the coming fight with Gilbert. But he felt
neither fear nor terror at the prospect. Indeed, he was so
eager to confront the dishonorable cur who'd plotted his
death that it was all he could do to restrain himself from
truly hurting the men he now battled. With a drop of his
right shoulder he caught the long sword of one of Rising's
knights on his oak shaft. Then with an ease come of many
years' experience, he shifted his weight, lunged toward the
man, and jerked the staff up sharply, forcing the sword to
pop from the man's surprised grip.

As the man scrambled to reclaim the sword, Aric
tripped him with a sharp crack to the shins, then pressed
the squared-off end of his weapon to the man's chest.

"I claim you a captive of Stanwood," he said tersely to the downed knight. But Aric did not linger long enough to be sure the man left the field as was required, for he had another, more vital game to play out than this.

As he surged forward to meet his next victim, he noted with grim satisfaction that Gilbert's gold and black pennant also was making progress toward midfield. To his left Sir Edward wreaked havoc among the men he fought, and this fired Aric to even greater aggression. He knocked one man off his feet with a stiff elbow to the fellow's middle, then sidestepped another's rush and tripped him with the staff. With lightning-fast moves he pressed the mock-death blow to their chests, stepped over their prone forms, and forced his way farther, toward his nemesis.

As Sir Virgil's ranks gave beneath Aric's fierce assault, Stanwood's forces veered somewhat to the right—away from Sir Gilbert, who fought Sir Edolf's men now. In frustration Aric stared across the field, toward the one he was so determined to fight. But his murderous thoughts were intercepted by Sir Edward's barked commands.

"Right flank! Circle out and around. Cut off Rising's retreat while we go straight at the flag!"

For a moment Aric did not respond, but only stared fiercely toward the bobbing gold and black pennant of Duxton. He patted the sheathed sword at his side. Then Sir Roger shoved him roughly. "Go on, man! Do as you're told!"

It took all Aric's willpower not to turn his deadly staff on the glaring captain of arms. But Roger was not his foe, he knew. In frustration he clenched his jaw and turned toward the task at hand.

"Ho! We have them now. We have them now!" Sir Edward's cry rang out as his two lines pressed Sir Virgil's dwindling forces between them. As if in confirmation, Sir

Virgil's standard-bearer stumbled back, still surrounded by sweating, fighting men. But from behind him Aric's staff snaked forward, drawing one man's sword down then suddenly up. As the man's grip faltered, Aric pressed forward, grappling with the fellow for possession of the blade. Then he had it and with a triumphant cry he was through the line. With one mighty swipe of the sword he severed the pole, toppling the pennant to the ground.

One of Sir Edward's knights grabbed it, then went down as Sir Virgil himself tackled him for possession of the coveted flag. But as Stanwood's standard fluttered safely surrounded by men lined three deep in defense, Sir Virgil's fate was inevitable. When he finally rose without the flag, and lowered his weapon in defeat, the rest of his men slowly conceded as well.

In jubilation Sir Edward raised his sword, for this was the one man he most wished to defeat this day. He beamed at his circle of men. "Fine work, my lads!" he cried, breathless from his own efforts. "But there's not a moment to spare—"

Before his words were done there was a savage push from behind.

" 'Tis Sir Andrew of Billingham!" Sir Roger's choked cry came. Then there was no more conversation as Stanwood's forces staggered under the fierce attack, only muffled oaths and vicious curses. To a man Sir Edward's forces felt the brunt of the determined assault. But their long-awaited victory against Sir Virgil of Rising was too fresh in their minds to allow them to go down easily in defeat.

At the first wave of the rush Aric swiftly took stock of the situation. Gilbert's men were beyond Sir Andrew, gamely fighting Sir Edolf's forces. If he was to have his just revenge, Aric knew Stanwood must not go down. After only a moment's hesitation, he pulled back from the fight and edged around the perimeter. Sir Andrew's standard of blue and white was well protected to the fore, but behind only three men covered it. With a savage cry he launched himself at them, crashing into one man as he laid another low with one sweep of the staff. The third man turned, as did the standard-bearer, but by then it was too late. The staff came down hard on the knight's shoulder, numbing his arm, and with that defense gone, the standard-bearer fell back, colliding with his own people. The flag wavered a moment longer. Then Aric swung the long oak staff once more and the entire flag pole toppled backward. Innumerable hands grabbed at it—Stanwood hands —and in a moment the victory was secured.

Aric did not pause to savor his triumph, for now nothing stood in the way of his revenge. Across the short, dusty space his eyes found Sir Gilbert boldly leading his men in a relentless attack on Sir Edolf's flag. For an instant Gilbert lifted his head and stared back at him; their eyes met for a fleeting moment. Aric knew the other man intended only to judge the status of the other armies in the melee. But then Gilbert stiffened, and Aric sensed at once his recognition. He did not need to see Gilbert's scowl beneath his helmet, nor hear his muttered curse to know that the truth was out.

Without hesitation Aric threw his staff down and drew out the broadsword that hung waiting in the scabbard at his side. He lifted the long, dark blade in menacing salute then started forward to meet his foe. But Sir Roger prevented his attack with a tight grip on his forearm.

"Get back with the others!" he barked angrily.

"Not now," Aric replied grimly, shaking off the other's hold.

"Bedamned if you are not more trouble than ever you

are worth!" Roger swore. "I'll not have a man in my service who does not follow orders!"

But Aric was not there to hear the threat. With a sudden charge he met Sir Gilbert at the edge of the fighting, and all else was forgotten. His wicked black blade, retrieved from the stables, came down with deadly accuracy at Gilbert, but that one also was no novice at swordplay. With a cry of absolute fury he met the formidable attack, turning the strike back with a powerful thrust of his own. His eyes glittered with icy hatred as he glared at Aric.

"I should have stayed to watch you hang!" he said with a growl as they grappled then fell back.

"A mistake you shall not live long enough to regret," Aric answered in a cold, controlled tone.

"I'll see you skewered and roasted in hell first!" So saying, Gilbert swung his own sword, beginning an expert attack that forced Aric back. But Aric had waited too long for his revenge to allow Gilbert even the smallest sense of victory. He met the other man's hard sweeping thrusts with all the strength in his arms and wrists, checking the vicious chops on the cross-guard of his black sword, then thrusting his weight forward in an attempt to unbalance Gilbert. It was a daring move, for it brought him within easy reach of the other man's weapon. But as Gilbert faltered, Aric knew it had been a worthwhile risk. He pulled the heavy blade back, hearing the slither of steel upon steel, ready now to strike a death blow.

From the covered pavilion Rosalynde watched the sudden turn of events on the field in sinking desperation. Even knowing he planned to confront Gilbert had not adequately prepared her for the violent fear she felt for Aric. Gilbert might kill him! And even if he didn't, the other men surely would!

Across the yard, half hidden by the churning dust, the

two figures were hardly discernible as they struggled together. But she saw well the long, dark blade in Aric's
hands, and even in her fear she wondered where he'd
found it.

It was clear she was not alone in that. The other fighting
—done in sport—abruptly ceased as this battle raged in
earnest. Sir Gilbert's men surged forward in anger to defend their lord, but it was Sir Roger who reached the two
men first. With a furious cry he thrust his own sword between them before Aric's blade could strike, then, with a
barked command, he shoved himself between Gilbert and
Aric, protecting Gilbert even as he faced Aric himself.

"Damn you to hell for the surly bastard that you are!"
he cried, clearly outraged at such a breach of conduct at a
sporting event. He gestured to Stanwood's men-at-arms
who still stood uncertainly behind Aric. "By Christ! I said
to take him!"

Had she not been gripping the tent post so fiercely,
Rosalynde would surely have fainted. As it was, she could
only stare in horror, unable to make out all that was said.
She saw the men-at-arms crowd behind Aric. She heard
Sir Gilbert's angry voice raised in accusation.

"—unholy bastard we caught at Dunmow! . . . deserved to be hanged there! I demand he be hanged now!"

It was that which forced Rosalynde to move. She did
not think or plan as she dashed from the viewing tent. She
was unmindful of the murmurs of the bewildered crowd.
One thought only consumed her: to save the man she
loved! Her father was among the men who surrounded
Gilbert and Aric. Perhaps he would accede to her desperate please for leniency. Perhaps when he knew this was his
son-in-law!

But in her heart Rosalynde knew it would not help.
Then she saw the huge war-horse that Aric had groomed

—Gilbert's steed. With a swift change of direction she ran for the unattended animal, not hesitating even when it flattened its ears defensively. She untangled the long reins, but before she could urge the unwilling beast forward, a long, low whistle pierced the air.

At once the magnificent destrier tensed. His ears pricked forward as his intelligent eyes sought the source of the sound. Then with a low whicker, he bounded past her, yanking the reins from her hands, heading straight for the tense group in the middle of the field.

What Rosalynde saw as she stared after the horse in astonishment filled her with both fear and awe. Aric was held by four men, although he yet gripped the black sword belligerently. But Gilbert lurched forward, past Sir Roger and her father, clearly intent on striking a killing blow while Aric was helpless to defend himself. Had the horse not scattered the men with his unexpected charge, the conclusion would have been inevitable. As it was, Gilbert's broadsword was turned somewhat to the right. When the animal thundered past him, Aric leapt wildly for him.

Rosalynde screamed in horror, certain he must be trampled beneath the churning hooves of the heavy steed. In the field men lay sprawled everywhere from their terrified dash away from the huge horse. But then she saw Aric swing himself onto the destrier's back as he thundered toward the forest, and her heart leapt with joy.

Her prayers had been answered!

26

In the ensuing confusion—as the men on the field picked themselves up and the spectators milled about in rowdy curiosity—no one could get to their horses in time to prevent Aric's escape. As one, the dark destrier and its bent-over rider flew across the field toward the safety of the forest. Only at the edge of the dense woodlands did the animal pause as Aric looked back at the chaotic tournament grounds. Despite the distance between them, however, Rosalynde knew he did not look to ascertain whether he was pursued. Even across the wide plowed field she felt his eyes seeking her—finding her. In that brief moment when their eyes connected, she knew he wanted her to come to him. And as he turned his mount and disappeared into the forests, she knew she would somehow do it.

It took no great effort at moralizing—no weighing the right and wrong of it, or judging the logic. She'd spent a month and more waging that battle, arguing that debate to no avail. Now, as her heart filled with immeasurable joy to see him safe and free, she knew that logic had no place in her decision anymore. She must go with her heart now—always!—where Blacksword was concerned. She must go to Aric, her love.

But she also knew that she must be careful. Stifling the urge to flee at once, she willed herself to be calm.

Her father and Sir Roger still looked stunned by all that had happened in the last few seconds. Sir Gilbert's enraged screams only compounded the disorganization of the pursuit efforts.

"He is an outlaw, I tell you! One of the vermin that were to hang at Dunmow!"

"But he has been an excellent foot soldier." Sir Edward tried to placate the furious man. "We had no—"

"Fools!" Gilbert shoved off the help of two of his men. "You cannot even ferret out the runagates among you! Is it no wonder they prey upon the land at will!"

"I knew he was suspect!" Sir Roger swore. "I should have hanged him when I first found him—"

"I shall hang him yet!" Gilbert vowed in icy rage. He yanked his sword from the hands of a man who had retrieved it. He scowled at the circle of men then moved his narrowed gaze belligerently to Sir Edward. "And where did he come by a sword? If he was a foot soldier, why did he have a sword?"

"We'll know that when we capture him," Sir Edward bit out, clearly fuming at such an embarrassing turn of events. He turned away, signaling his men to retrieve their horses, but Rosalynde anticipated his move. Taking advantage of the attention focused on the crowd of men still on the field, she dashed back to the makeshift rope corral where most of the horses were being held. Holding her skirts high, she flapped them toward the skittish animals, stomping and yelling as she did. In a moment they were milling about, circling within their confined quarters, alarmed by the small but aggressive figure that flitted about them.

Rosalynde was unsuccessful in causing the horses to break free from their meager confines. But when the squires and knights tried to collect their mounts, the horses were too nervous and highstrung to be caught. As Rosalynde melted back into the shadows of the viewing pavilion, she could only hope that she'd afforded Aric enough time to ensure his safety.

But as the horses were finally caught and the first riders set off in the direction Aric had taken, she knew she had much more to do if she were somehow to find him. First on her list was to stay well out of her father's way. At once she headed for the still-laden food tables.

"Keep everyone well fed, and be generous with the ale," she ordered Maud when the woman sent her a bewildered look.

"What's to be made of this?" Edith cried as she hurried up.

"Too much temper, it appears." Rosalynde shrugged, giving the two a tight-lipped smile. "But there's no reason the day must be ruined for the rest of our people. Just see to the tables while I seek out Cedric."

She found Cedric near the wine butts, his normally complacent features set in a perplexed frown. "Lady Rosalynde," he said, clearly relieved to see her. "What are we to do now?"

" 'Twould be best to proceed as if nothing untoward has happened. The day is not yet done, and as it is to celebrate the spring planting, I'm sure my father would not see his people deprived of their pleasure. Be generous with the drink and they will not miss the conclusion of the melee. Meanwhile, I shall seek out my father."

"But he rode off with Sir Gilbert to seek out the errant foot soldier who attacked the man."

So much the better, Rosalynde thought as she clambered onto one of the field carts and urged the sturdy pony forward. If her father was gone he would not note her actions.

"Hie. Hie!" she cried with a flap of the long leather reins, urging the pony up the dusty road to the castle. She had medicines to get, and blankets and clean linens. And a basket of food, she added to her list as she made her plans. Aric might very well be hurt and would most certainly be hungry. When she found him—

Her jumbled thoughts were interrupted by an urgent cry. "Lady Rosalynde! Hold up, milady!"

When she saw Cleve running after her, she slowed the cart. Of all people, she did not wish to deal with Cleve, for she feared he too easily might guess what she was about.

"Cleve, thank goodness! See to the loose horses, will you? I must away to the castle for lanterns and candles." Then, without giving him a chance to respond, she slapped the reins once more and sent the cart rollicking up the road to the castle.

Cleve watched Rosalynde's departure with mixed emotions. Lanterns and candles? Surely she did not mean to aid in the search for the missing Aric? Yet it was equally unlikely that she would be worried about lighting the festivities after dark—not considering what had just happened.

Yet Rosalynde's peculiar words were of far less moment than Aric's daring confrontation with Sir Gilbert and subsequent escape. As Cleve dutifully hurried to help with the horses, his head spun with a myriad of disturbing facts.

Aric had obviously stolen that sword from among Sir Gilbert's belongings. Although Cleve knew he should feel guilty for having revealed its whereabouts to Aric, any guilt was overridden by the disturbing fact that Sir Gilbert had not accused Aric of stealing the weapon. The black sword had been in Gilbert's possession, yet it appeared that for some reason he did not wish that fact known. If he had taken the sword from Aric when he'd caught him near Dunmow, there would be no need to conceal it from this company. Yet although he had accused Aric of being an outlaw—and of having a weapon that a man-at-arms should not possess in the melee—Gilbert had not identified the sword as his own.

That was because the sword was undoubtedly Aric's, Cleve knew. His namesake weapon. And it followed, therefore, that Sir Gilbert had acquired it through less than honorable means. *That* was why Aric had been so set on confronting him.

Once more Cleve felt a certain conviction that Aric was a knight. Everything pointed to it—everything except his accursed silence on the subject. But something had gone wrong, and it was clearly tied to Sir Gilbert of Duxton.

Cleve flapped his arms, turning one loose horse back toward the horse pen. As he caught his breath he stared out toward the place where Aric had disappeared into the forest. This bad blood between Aric and Sir Gilbert was not done, of that he had not the slightest doubt. Sir Gilbert had thought Aric dead—hanged at Dunmow. He would surely not rest now until he saw him dead, and by his own hand. Yet Aric was just as clearly not afraid of such a battle, else he would not have challenged the man before everyone.

Now, however, it was unlikely he would receive a fair fight. If Aric was smart, Cleve decided, he would disappear for a while and just bide his time. He had a weapon and a horse—no doubt his very own horse, judging by the beast's uncanny reaction to Aric's desperate plight. Yes, the man should bide his time and wait for another day to get his revenge on his enemy.

It was not until Cleve made his way almost an hour later

to the castle that a wayward thought struck him. Sir Gilbert had said that Aric was to have been hanged at Dunmow. Yet Rosalynde had made no mention of that fact when she'd first brought him to the adulterine castle to help them. He'd wondered then how such a man could be without any means at all, lacking even his own dagger. Now he could not decide whether Lady Rosalynde had known all along, or just been an innocent pawn in Aric's escape.

He frowned and rubbed the back of his sweaty neck. There was still much to be uncovered in this confusing affair, he thought. A few riders had returned from the chase empty-handed, but Sir Gilbert and Sir Edward were still out. Until they returned, Cleve decided it was time for him to have a long talk with the fair mistress of the castle.

Rosalynde left by the postern gate. She'd wrapped everything she might need in a soft linen cloth and flung it over the withers of a mare she'd saddled in the stables. Now, as dusk descended over the land, she led the mild-tempered horse through the narrow gate, more than thankful for the distractions in the castle. Between the uproar caused by Aric and the lulling effects of the still-flowing ale, it had been easy to remain unnoticed and out of sight. She hoisted herself up into the saddle, and turned the mare silently for the forest. How she would find Aric when the others had failed she did not know. She only knew that she must try. Down the gravel path she guided the horse. Down the escarpment and up into the cleared field that backed the castle. A watchman hailed her—a drowsy, incoherent sound. Then there was only her and the amiable mare, heading straight toward the protection of the forest.

It seemed forever that Rosalynde had been restraining

her haste—waiting for dusk to come, waiting to sneak out of the stable, walking the horse quietly when everything in her screamed hurry! Yet once she melted into the dark-shadowed forest, she was assailed by sudden doubt. Which way to go? Where to begin her search? And what if she couldn't find him?

She sat the complacent horse, staring around her, trying to gather her bearings as she searched for a trail to follow. Somewhere in this vast forest was Aric; all she wanted was to be with him and know that he was safe. Yet as the night sounds of the woodlands began to fill the darkness, she despaired of succeeding.

She neither heard nor saw the large shape that swung down from the branches of an ancient chestnut tree and dangled an instant behind her. One moment she was completely alone, praying for divine guidance in her quest. The next, someone had slid down behind her onto the horse, startling the animal into an awkward run and terrifying the very wits from her.

"No!" she tried to cry, before a heavy hand clamped over her mouth. Then she was pulled against a wide chest and even before he said a word, she knew.

"Hush," he whispered against her ear as his arms held her steady. With one hand he took control of the rein, slowing the panicked mare, while with his other he held her so tight as to nearly constrict her breathing. Yet Rosalynde's sudden happiness was so overwhelming that she could easily have survived without breathing at all. Aric was here—that was all she need know. He was here and he was safe, and nothing else mattered at all.

As he brought the mare to a plunging halt, Rosalynde melted against him and tilted her head back to fall against his shoulder. At her compliant pose, Aric bent his head forward and hungrily pressed his lips to her exposed neck.

Like a statue melded together in an emotionally draining embrace they sat there, Rosalynde wrapped within Aric's unyielding grasp, each of them taking solace from the other, giving strength and receiving strength. Rosalynde pressed her cheek against his bowed head as tears streamed down her face. She could feel his vital warmth surrounding her; his heart beat a rhythm that matched her own. For a long quiet moment her happiness was complete. She had everything she truly wanted in Aric. Why couldn't the rest of the world simply go away?

"Ah, my sweet Rose." He breathed the words as he kissed the sensitive skin along her collarbone. "Your thorns can no longer protect you from me."

Rosalynde's hand came up to cup the hard line of his cheek. "I do not need thorns with you."

He lifted his head then and their eyes finally met. Despite the darkness of the night, there was an intensity in his eyes that she could not mistake. When she twisted around in his arms, he loosened his grip, then lifted her clear of the saddle and settled her across his thighs. Rosalynde's arms went immediately around his neck, and without restraint she pressed herself fully against him in a long, stirring kiss.

"I was so afraid," she whispered brokenly as she kissed his cheeks, his chin, his firm curving lips. "I thought you would be killed." She ran her tongue lightly along the seam of his lips, then deepened the kiss when he opened his mouth to her. The mare shifted slightly beneath them, but neither of them noticed as desperation turned into very passion.

Then, in less than an instant, Rosalynde was no longer the aggressor, demanding and receiving his passionate kiss, but instead became the receptacle for his mounting desires. One of his hands slid roughly along her thigh, finding the soft flesh beneath her skirts. At once his kiss deepened. Rosalynde was bent back over his arm, off balance, clinging to his neck, yet she had never felt so secure as he plundered the sweetness of her mouth. Their tongues met and retreated, then danced in erotic promise. His hand moved farther up her thigh, sliding around to cup her derriere, and his fingertips brushed near her feminine core. With a gasp she pressed down against his hand, mindlessly urging him to ease the fire that so quickly threatened to consume her. As her head fell back, he moved his searing kisses down her throat to where the pale skin was covered by her gown. Then he pressed his face against her outthrust breasts.

"Christ, but I burn for you! Wood nymph that you are, I need to have you beneath me here, in the presence of the entire forest. You are mine, woman!"

Rosalynde felt his hard arousal beneath her derriere. She felt his fingers tighten at the apex of her thighs. Where they were—how they could accomplish such a thing—was of no consequence to her. She wanted no more than to prove her love to him and have him prove his to her. With her hands and her lips, with her tongue and fingers and every other portion of her body she would show him her love. If they could just come together and reach that moment of oneness, that moment of completeness—everything else could be made right, or else forgotten. If only she could get close enough to him . . .

But if Rosalynde was not mindful of the dangers of their proximity to her father's castle, Aric, at least, was. With a groan as if of physical pain, he slid his hand out from beneath her skirts. His head lifted from her breasts and he pulled her upright, holding her in a last embrace several trembling seconds. Then he took a harsh, sobering breath.

"Only a wench can drive a man to such a consuming

madness as this," he muttered self-mockingly. "Only one wench." Then with a quick tug on the reins, he turned the mare for the deep woods.

Rosalynde took no note of their direction as Aric guided the horse through the night gloom. She could do no more than cling to him, leaning against his chest, listening to the familiar rhythm of his heart. Too much had happened in the past hours for her to long contemplate this new turn of events. The tournament and the melee seemed only a long ago dream, a nightmare that had nearly robbed her of all she truly wanted. But this steady heartbeat, this solid warmth and reassuring presence of the man she loved were reality now. All the rest was merely something she was just now waking from.

In less than a minute Aric brought the mare to a stop. In a slight clearing the mighty destrier he had absconded with was calmly cropping some thin grasses, but at their approach the animal raised his proud head.

"He's your horse, isn't he?" Rosalynde spoke quietly, for the still forest seemed to demand it.

"He is," Aric answered, sliding easily from the mare. Then he plucked her from her horse and brought her full length against him. "He is mine, and now you are mine as well."

His eyes were darker than midnight, but the fire in them burned her with its heat. "And you are mine," Rosalynde replied, gripping his tunic in her hands. She stretched up on her toes to meet his lips in a kiss that clung, fragile and trembling, between them.

He put her away from him almost at once, holding her at arm's length with one hand on each of her shoulders. But his breathing was ragged, and Rosalynde knew he put her off with only the most stringent effort. "This place is not safe. We must be away from here."

His words brought home to her the harsh reality of their plight. She was suddenly very frightened for them, and her hands went up to curve around his forearms, holding on to his strength.

"Where will we go?"

"I have a place in mind where we may be safe—and alone." A hungry expression swept over his face as he looked down on her upturned face and slender form. "I want you, Rose. You know that well. But my revenge is still not done. Even had your father wished to let me free, now that I have you, he must come after me. But Gilbert knows he must find me first."

"Gilbert." She mouthed the name reluctantly. "Why does he persecute you so?"

He did not answer at first, only swung her up on his destrier and tied the lead of her mare to his saddle. Then he mounted behind her and urged the animals forward.

"What is this bad blood between you and Gilbert?" she persisted. "Why did he have your horse?"

"There is no time now for that," he answered as he settled her comfortably before him. His arms circled her waist, and her back fit snugly against his stalwart chest. "I'll explain everything once we're safe. For now, just have faith in me."

Have faith in me. It was those simple words that renewed Rosalynde's spirits. She did have faith in him, she realized. Faith that he was a man of honor. Faith that he cared for her. Faith that he wanted her for more than simply the property attached to her name.

But as they rode through the thick darkness, beneath towering trees and silent shadows, it was her lack of faith in everyone else that worried her.

27

Dawn was but a vague promise in the east when they finally stopped. Aric had been silent as they rode, and Rosalynde had been too exhausted to do more than sit in his strong embrace. She had dozed intermittently in his arms, secure in the knowledge that at least he was safe, and heading away from Stanwood. But although the terrain appeared vaguely familiar, it was not until the tireless destrier splashed unhesitantly into a shallow river crossing that she realized where they were. In the purple gloom of early morning the hulking ruins of the adulterine stood shadowy guard in the hills above the river Stour.

Rosalynde shivered in the cool night air, not certain whether this return to the doomed castle boded good or ill for them.

"Will we rest here?" she asked as Aric slowed the horses and allowed the destrier to pick his way slowly up the overgrown trail. The shrill cry of a hunting curlew hushed at her words.

"We shall wait here," he answered, guiding the horse with only the slightest pressure of his knees. Beneath her thighs Rosalynde was well aware of his strong legs. One of his arms circled her and rested comfortably where her waist flared down to her hips. She felt his every breath in a silky puff against her hair and cheek. Despite her grogginess, she was acutely aware of his robust masculinity. Only with a determined effort was she able to concentrate on his words.

"Wait? What shall we wait for?"

She felt him stiffen. "We wait for Gilbert, of course. And your father."

"But why?" Rosalynde cried out in sudden fear. She twisted around to see him. "Why wait for them when we can get away so easily?"

Aric kept his profile to her. His expression revealed no real emotion, neither anger nor even concern. "It has never been my goal to escape Stanwood. You should know that by now."

"But things are different now. You've been discovered."

He turned the horse into what was once the castle bailey, then glanced down into her pale face. "The only difference now is that the players have all been revealed to one another. The secrets are all out. You are still my wife, however. And Gilbert is still my enemy."

"But . . . but if he finds you, he and his men will kill you! You will not have a chance!"

"Leave Gilbert to me, Rosalynde."

"But we can get away! Just keep riding—"

" 'Tis a hard life you describe. Hard enough for a man alone. Impossible for a man with a wife. No, I've grown fond of Stanwood. No one shall drive us from it."

With that final statement he halted them before the same little stone storeroom where Rosalynde had hidden the wounded Cleve—it seemed like a year ago, not just a matter of weeks. Aric slid over the horse's rump, then reached up to help her down with a hand on either side of her waist. Rosalynde's palms rested on his shoulders and once on the ground she started to back away, unwilling to abandon her argument. But Aric's hand held her before him and even pulled her nearer.

"To confront Gilbert again is foolhardy," she began.

"I do not wish to speak of Gilbert."

"But my father will not help you—"

"Nor do I wish to discuss your father."

"But they will find us—"

"Eventually. But not yet. And until they do, I've other things on my mind."

He pulled her nearer, until her breasts brushed his chest and she stood within the span of his parted legs. Rosalynde pushed once against his chest, trying futilely to make him listen to her. But he was adamant in his intentions, and lowered his face to capture her lips.

Without warning Rosalynde's logical protests died, swallowed up in the flame that leapt between them. She had known this was inevitable, for despite all else that might go wrong, this intense physical reaction between them flared ever stronger. Yet even as she melted beneath his fiery ardor, even as she welcomed the exquisite stroke of his tongue along her sensitive inner lips and met its increasingly bold thrust with her own, she was overwhelmed by emotions stronger than mere desire. She clung to him as she might cling to life itself—pressing herself close, clutching tightly—for there was no doubt in her mind that without Aric she would no longer wish to live. He must be safe if she was to survive. They must be together if life was to be worth living at all.

His hand slid down her back, splayed to caress every curve and hollow, then moved lower to press her hard against him, shaping the soft flesh of her belly to the rigid contours of his arousal. Willingly she came against him, and her blood sang dizzily in her ears. Here was the proof of life, she thought as she drowned beneath his ravenous kiss. His life and hers together had the force to create yet another life.

In that moment she knew that she wanted a child of him, and tears of happiness sprang to her eyes.

"I love you," she murmured silently into his kiss. "I love you. I love you. I love you—"

With a mighty groan Aric lifted his face from hers then buried it in the warm silk of her hair. "By damn, but I would not have you this way, in the leaves of a ruined castle!" A harsh laugh escaped him and he raised his head and took a shaky breath. "You should be wooed upon silken sheets or the softest furs."

"I don't need those—"

"And yet I would give them to you." He paused and in the slowly strengthening light his eyes were a rare clear shade, silver as the moonlight, yet as warm as the sun. "There are things I have not told you," he said quietly, his eyes never leaving her own. "Things you should know."

"Those things are nothing to me," Rosalynde answered as emotions choked her voice. "Just come and lie down with me. We'll make a bed—I have a blanket." She pulled away from him, letting her hand slide lightly down his arm until she took his hand in her own. "Come with me."

Aric's eyes searched her face, seeming almost to drink in her image. Then he bowed over her hand and brought it to his lips. One kiss he planted on her knuckles, another on the underside of her wrist. Then he opened her hand and pressed a warm kiss to the center of her palm. With his lips and tongue he caressed that tender spot, springing all her nerves to life. Then he straightened and pressed her hand to his pounding heart.

"You come to me when I had no reason to hope you would. For this, my thorny Rose—" His voice broke off and a wondrous shiver overtook her.

"My Rosalynde . . ."

Together they removed their meager possessions from the horses then set the animals free to graze. The blanket became the finest of rugs. The gathered leaves, a couch of rare design. The sky showed pale blue and striking gold above them, a painted ceiling that outshone the finest church rotunda. Crickets hummed softly as birds played a wild and wistful song. Serenaded they were, and surrounded by a beauty unmatched by all mankind's efforts.

When Aric drew her to him, Rosalynde would not have had it any other way. He let her cloak down lightly, then with both his hands, smoothed her hair back from her cheeks. Gently he worked the tangles free, sliding his fingers down to where her hair brushed her hips.

She touched his hair as well, running her fingers through locks that felt too soft and silken for such a hardened man as he was. His jaw was rough with the faint growth of his beard, yet the contrast was exquisite. Soft hair, rough chin, soft lips. Across his face she let her fingers roam, exploring this man of hers, learning all she could: how thick his lashes were; how fine the hairs at his temple were.

How sensitive his ears were to her touch.

As she ran one finger lightly around the rim of his ear, his eyes darkened and she heard the sharp intake of his breath. Before she could put that new knowledge to the test, he was down on one knee before her, his hands intent on her waist.

"This gown must go," he said in a thick voice as he fumbled with the ties at her sides. Then when his fingers worked the lacings loose, he slid his hands within the lace, sliding the thin linen of her kirtle sensuously along her heated skin.

"Aric," Rosalynde breathed, bowing her head to kiss the golden hair at his crown.

"Sweet Mary, but you fire my blood," he groaned. He gathered her in his arms even as he knelt there, crushing her thighs and belly to his chest. Rosalynde held the side of his face against her breasts, glorying in his nearness, in his desire for her, and in hers for him. Then he tilted his face up and she cupped his cheeks.

"Won't you show me how a husband comes to his wife who loves him well?"

"Who loves him . . ." His words trailed away, but his gaze was unshakably fixed with hers. Then a faint, wondering smile edged his harshly handsome features. He rose from his kneeling position, never letting go of her, so that she was held quite aloft, looking down upon him. For a long moment they stood there in the quiet of the abandoned castle, just looking at one another. Rosalynde felt as if her heart were filled to bursting, so much love did she feel for him. Then he slowly let her down, sliding her torturously along the hard length of him.

Once again they met in a kiss, bodies close, limbs entwined, lips clinging. Rosalynde's loosened gown found it way off, as did his own girdle and tunic, the garment forgotten and abandoned as they met in passionate recognition. They fell together onto their grand bed, cushione by leaves and well-worn wool, yet oblivious to all but eac other.

"Are you my wife then truly, Rosalynde? Before Go and man?"

Rosalynde stared up into the strong face above her, ar it was easy to answer. "Forever, as you are my husband

"Ah." He lowered his head until their forehea touched. "My wife. My love." Then he rolled over un she lay above him, stretched full length upon his hard and ready frame.

His love.

A rare and complete joy filled Rosalynde at his words, and she wanted to hear more of that sentiment. But Aric's sudden movement prevented her from pursuing it, for he lifted her upright above him, sliding his hands up beneath her kirtle as he forced her to straddle him. Pressed intimately against her, she felt the thrusting strength of his arousal. Although his braies separated them, a damp quiver began in her down there, and she arched in unthinking desire. Aric's breathing came faster, as did her own. His hands slid higher until her kirtle exposed her legs completely, and his palms rested on the naked flesh of her hips.

"Come, wife," he whispered huskily. "Be obedient to your lord husband's command."

A smile curved Rosalynde's lips as she stared down into the face she loved so well. She ran one hand down his wide chest, then lifted the hem of his linen chainse so that she could touch his skin. The smile widened further when he sighed in clear pleasure. When she pressed both of her palms against his stomach, then slid them in small circular patterns up along his ribs, then higher to discover his small flat nipples, his groan told her she was most definitely doing something right, as did his tightened clutch on her hips. But when her fingers strayed down to the ties at the waist of his braies, he exhaled noisily.

"It will not work this way," he said as he sat upright with her still on his lap. "These clothes . . ."

In one swift motion he whipped his chainse over his head and flung it aside. Her kirtle was next, leaving her covered only in the loosened tangles of her long, dark hair. But Rosalynde had no time for modesty. He lay her down and in an almost violent movement shed the troublesome braies. Then they were both naked, lying together in the roofless adulterine, ready to meet at last as husband and wife.

Rosalynde tried to resume the role of aggressor, but Aric would have none of it. When she ran one hand down his side, he caught it. When she kissed his mouth and let her fingers play at his sensitive ears, he stopped her there as well, catching both her hands in one of his and holding them captive above her head.

"If you touch me that way," he breathed hoarsely, then pressed a deep, sultry kiss to her parted lips. "If you continue this way, I shall surely explode—"

Before she could argue back, he moved his kiss down, along her chin and neck and throat. His free hand strayed even lower, brushing the side slopes of her breasts as his mouth slanted in the same direction. Then his palm cupped one of her breasts and she arched in shameless longing. His breath warmed the stiffened peak, tightening it in almost unbearable excitement.

"Aric, please—" she cried in aimless plea. But his answering kiss, taking her aroused nipple between his lips, tugging in a hot wet torture, drawing it in deep, raking it with his teeth—this relief was even more unbearable than was his teasing. Her strong young body arched beneath his superior weight, begging in a voice as clear and strong as the ages.

But Aric's answer was to offer her other breast the same attention, lavishing upon it the same exquisite torment Though she fought to free her hands, he held her immo bile until tears streamed down her face. Only then did he move down her body, planting hot kisses against her stom ach, in her navel, in the soft curving flesh of her belly.

Rosalynde's hands were in his hair, running along his cheeks and his shoulders as he edged her legs apart. When his lips found the pulsing source of her erotic desires, she arched once more in near-perfect agony. His tongue stroked a delicious wet rhythm as his fingers added their own secret caress. One of his hands pressed down on her belly. Another cupped her derriere. She was held in a sinful bondage, pressed beneath his hands as his lips and tongue fired her to unnameable heights. Then his thumb found the slick entrance to her, and she cried out in a glorious upheaval. Her hands tightened in his hair as he pushed her to the precipice of completion. Her whole body stiffened as white hot waves of passion lifted her. Her entire being—heart, body, soul—opened in that most personal acceptance as a rush of sensations washed over her. Then before she leapt over the edge into that dark, insensible pleasure, he moved over her and, without missing even one thrust, filled her completely.

The heated pressure of his manhood within her was sweet beyond imagining. He filled her and drew away, at once pleasing her and tormenting her in the same enthralling movement. Slick and hot, they moved together, the friction raising them both to monumental heights. Rosalynde's arms circled Aric; her face pressed against his thick, muscled neck as he moved faster and faster over her. He drove into her relentlessly, and with every wild plunge, she cried out her pleasure until they were moving as one, frantic for the ease they found only together.

"I love you." She heard his hoarse words as he drove on like a man possessed. "God, but I love you."

If perfection could be reached on earth, Rosalynde found it in that moment. Her heart swelled with love, even as her body erupted in violent fulfillment. It was an absolute harmony of her physical and emotional love for him. Swift hard shudders welled up from deep inside her and radiated out to encompass her entire body. Yet she was still aware of Aric's answering response as he tensed over her. With a muffled cry against her hair, his body quaked in uncontrolled passion as he poured his life and love into her.

His breath came in great gasps as he spent himself within her. And yet this too they seemed intimately to share. As they both fought for breath, they lay there together, Aric half upon her still, their arms and legs twined together in the perfect lovers' embrace.

"I love you," Rosalynde murmured through her hazy contentment. "Love you . . ."

Aric stirred at her words and lifted his head to look at her. His face was little more than a shadow in the thin light of early morn, yet Rosalynde could see him clearly. His dark-golden hair fell about his face; his eyes were dark and solemn, although she knew he was well pleased with her.

"Is it truly love you feel?"

Rosalynde nodded, her eyes direct upon him. "I love you," she repeated without hesitation.

"Why?"

A small frown creased her brow as she pondered his question. Did he doubt the depth of her feelings? She reached her left hand to cup his hard prickly cheek. "I love you because I must. I must breathe to live. And eat. And I must love you."

She felt the faint relaxation of his jaw beneath her fingers, and then her eyes closed and a sleepy smile spread over her face. "I love you," she said once more as a yawn overtook her.

When he curled her against him, cradling her head on his arm, she surrendered completely to sleep, lulled by her exhaustion and the soothing sound of his whispered "I love you" in her ear.

28

Cleve sat in a nook near the great hearth, waiting for Sir Gilbert to depart.

"By damn I will hunt him down!" Gilbert ranted, glaring at Lord Edward as if he had plotted this entire episode. For his part, Edward appeared amazingly calm, considering the disastrous conclusion of the melee and the hours he and his men had since spent searching for Aric.

"We will all continue the search in the morning," Edward put in mildly.

"I caught him once; I'll not need any help in doing so again," Gilbert retorted. "And this time I will hang him on the spot!" Then, not waiting for a response, he strode furiously from the hall.

It was only then that Edward's expression grew dark. When he spied Cleve inching into the thickening light, he signaled him to approach.

"Go bid my daughter to attend me, Cleve. I fear greatly that she may be the one with the answers to this coil," he added, more to himself than to the boy.

"Milord, the Lady Rosalynde—" Cleve halted, then grimaced to himself. There was nothing for it but to tell the man. "Lady Rosalynde is not to be found. I've searched the castle for her, but she is nowhere within. And a mare and saddle are gone from the—"

"Gone!" Sir Edward started out of his seat, his mild aggravation replaced by angry disbelief. "She is gone without my permission? With whom? And to where?"

"I-I fear she travels alone . . . to seek Aric."

Cleve watched as first fury, then fear, and finally confusion washed over Lord Edward's face. When the man slumped back into his seat, still staring in dismay at Cleve, the boy moved nearer.

"Milord," he began quietly, after casting an eye about to ensure they were alone. "I have reason to believe that Lady Rosalynde has a soft spot in her heart for Aric. 'Twould not surprise me if she has gone to help him."

"Help him? The fellow is no doubt many leagues away by now. He leaves Stanwood with a horse, weapons, and a decent tunic—far more than he came here with. He'd be a fool to linger after today's foul doings."

Cleve bit his lip, not sure how correct was his own conjecture. "Methinks he will not leave here—not without Lady Rosalynde. Nor without meeting Sir Gilbert again."

At this Lord Edward straightened up. His eyes narrowed as he stared hard at Cleve. "Tell me what you know, boy."

By dawn searchers were out again, and though Lord Edward tried to downplay his daughter's obvious absence, so many tongues already spoke of it. From maid to manservant, the tale was passed until he could not deny the truth of it to the knights who yet lingered at Stanwood. Those who might have departed, unconcerned by one rogue's escape, stayed now, outraged that a noblewoman should be stolen away from her home. For despite Lord Edward's reluctant belief that Rosalynde had fled of her own will, he refused to allow any others to suspect it. As the riders thundered down the dusty road that led from

the castle, there was a universal conviction that the runagate from the melee had somehow absconded with the
innocent Lady Rosalynde. And each man vowed to have
the villain's head for it.

Cleve's face creased in concern as he watched the activity in the bailey below. He too planned to search for
Rosalynde and Aric, for he was certain they were not long
away. But with so many searchers about, he feared greatly
for Aric's discovery. A wry grin lifted his lips at that sentiment, for there had been a time—not very long past—
when he would have relished just such an end for the
scoundrel Blacksword. Hanging would have been too good
for him. But there was more involved now. Rosalynde
clearly loved the man—and it appeared he wasn't quite
the rogue he had at first seemed.

Cleve's eyes narrowed as he saw Sir Gilbert mount his
own destrier. With an angry jerk at the reins, the man
turned the animal, then drove him forward, scattering
chickens and the pack of castle hounds as he charged
across the bailey with his men, resuming the search they'd
had to abandon the night before.

Now *there* was a man to beware of, the boy decided.
And one who must not find the missing lovers before he
himself did.

When Cleve rode out from Stanwood Castle, he was on
a sturdy pony and without any escort or fanfare. The only
eyes that noted his departure were Lord Edward's, and
that one frowned thoughtfully at his passing. While the
forest was scoured from east to west, from glen to highest
hill, the boy urged his steed on, following a hunch that had
plagued him all night. Although he spied other riders, he
avoided them, for he wished no one to mind him overlong.
As the sun moved higher into the sky and he drew several
leagues away from Stanwood, he began to relax a bit, and

even to doze in the saddle, for he'd had little enough sleep the previous night.

He did not notice the four riders who trailed him at a distance, careful to remain hidden. Even had he seen them, he would not have recognized the men in their nondescript hoods and tunics. But Sir Gilbert of Duxton recognized young Cleve very well.

"What is that trifling boy about?" he had murmured to himself when he'd first seen Cleve. He'd almost dismissed the boy as just another of the searchers who hoped to gain both glory and a reward by saving Lord Edward's daughter. But then Gilbert had reconsidered. The young squire traveled alone and did not appear to be looking for anyone. He seemed instead to have a definite destination in mind as he hurried his horse along. On a hunch, Gilbert sent his other men off with the strict orders to kill the rogue knight Aric as soon as they set eyes on him. Then he and three of his men followed Cleve.

The sun was curving toward the western horizon when Cleve approached the Stour River. Golden shafts of sunlight glanced off the tumbled granite boulders of the adulterine as he urged his weary mount across the river ford. There was no sign of life in the abandoned castle, and a shiver swept up his spine as he thought of the ghosts said to haunt the place. Yet they'd been safe there once before, he reminded himself sternly. No unhappy spirits had beset them then. None would now. It was the living they must fear more than the dead.

The pony's head was hanging low as he ambled up the littered path. Birds called back and forth through the forest canopy, and small creatures scurried through the wild blueberries and holly that almost overgrew the path. But no sound of human life could be heard. Cleve let out a short mutter of despair, but then he suddenly pulled up. A hoofprint showed clearly in a muddy spot on the trail. And another! With renewed enthusiasm he nudged his mount on. At the first wall he jumped down and tied the exhausted animal to a protruding beam. Then he hurried past the broken wall, clambered over the ruins, and jumped down into the deserted bailey.

Cleve remembered very little of the time he'd spent within this eerily silent castle—only dark flickering shadows and a place with no roof. Now as he looked around him it appeared no more than vaguely familiar. He picked his way slowly—past a wildly overgrown garden and a broken stone bench. A chimney stood lonely sentinel where a kitchen had once been. Then he heard distant voices and he froze.

Was it Rosalynde? Was she safe? On stealthy feet he made his way around an open shed and peered cautiously beyond. What he saw caused his mouth to drop open in shock.

A woman—Lady Rosalynde, quite obviously—sat upon a stone-walled well, but she had not a stitch of clothing on! She was draped only in her long, glorious hair! Standing beside her, clad in braies and nothing else, the runagate, Blacksword—Aric, he was—lifted a bucket of water and doused her thoroughly. Though she shrieked and tried to escape, it was clear she enjoyed herself immensely, for she suddenly clasped the man to her, wetting him thoroughly with her own dripping embrace.

"If I'm to bathe, so shall you," she vowed as she dropped the bucket back into the well.

A low chuckle came from Aric. "How I longed to do this to you when first we lingered here."

"Did you? I thought you disliked me then." One of her brows arched in mock disdain.

"You were more than filthy," he replied. Then when she

pounded his chest in outrage at his words, he laughed and caught her small fists. "My sweet Rose," he murmured before he lowered his head to kiss her.

In the silence Cleve was completely taken aback. How happy they appeared together! He shifted uncomfortably from one foot to the other, wondering what to do. At once Aric wheeled, sensing the presence of someone else. He grabbed up his sword, which leaned against the nearby stonework wall, and stepped protectively in front of Rosalynde.

"Show yourself!" he challenged in a ferocious snarl.

Cleve edged nervously into view, staring wide-eyed at the man and Lady Rosalynde, who tried to hide her nakedness behind him.

"Cleve!" she cried out in relief when she recognized him.

"Mi-milady," he stammered, still caught up in his embarrassment.

"Are you alone?" Aric demanded, not lowering the sword at all.

"Aye, I'm alone. But there are legions of men searching for you both." His eyes darted away from Rosalynde, then crept back of their own accord. Aric dropped the point of his sword at that news, but he frowned at the direction of Cleve's gaze.

"If you want to keep those eyes of yours, you'd best turn them away from her." Then his tone calmed. "Get you to a shed off to your right. We shall join you directly. I would have news of Stanwood. And of Gilbert."

Cleve scurried away at once, for he was chagrined to catch them in so intimate an act as bathing together. Rosalynde too was mortified to be found thus, but that emotion quickly fled for she knew that if Cleve had found them, so could Gilbert. A shiver went through her, despite the warm sunshine, and she leaned forward to wrap her arms around Aric's neck. Her bare breasts pressed against his warm back and she laid her forehead against his shoulder.

"Let us be away from here," she pleaded softly. The words caught in her throat and she compressed her lips tightly to fight back her tears. "Oh, please, Aric—my love, my husband—I would give up Stanwood gladly to keep you safe."

Aric turned, then pulled her from atop the well wall and held her close against him. A wet tendril of her hair caught between them and with one hand he slid it back from her cheek.

"Did ever a wife worry about her husband so?" he mocked her gently. "Have faith in me, my love. Have faith in me."

Rosalynde did not press him after that, for she knew it was useless. With great haste she donned her kirtle and gown, blushing when Aric's eyes stayed avidly upon her. Despite their shared intimacies, she doubted she would ever become accustomed to the possessiveness in Aric's eyes whenever he looked at her. A warm knot tightened in her belly as she let her eyes slip over his powerful arms and wide shoulders. When he picked up his discarded chainse and tunic she averted her gaze, biting her lip in consternation at the wanton thoughts that had crept into her mind. She busied herself tying the laces on either side of her waist, but when she heard him slide the black sword into its plain scabbard she looked up in dismay.

"Aric, please," she began.

He silenced her with a quick kiss. "It will be all right," he murmured once more. "Now let us hear what Cleve has to say."

Aric kept his arm about her shoulder as they walked

back to their shed, and Rosalynde took what comfort she could from his reassuring warmth. *Let him be safe*, she prayed. *Please, let him be safe.*

But her prayers seemed to go unheeded, for when they rounded the broken wall, the devil himself confronted them.

"My, my," Sir Gilbert drawled as he took in their cozy embrace. "Isn't this a pretty scene."

Despite her own shock, Rosalynde was well aware of the immediate tension in Aric. But when she would have drawn back, he would not remove his arm from her shoulder. As he stood there—to all appearances not in the least unsettled by Gilbert's unexpected presence—she saw Gilbert's face grow dark with anger even as he gave them an evil smile. Beyond him three knights stood, one huge brute with an arm around Cleve's neck. Not for a minute did Rosalynde think Cleve had deliberately led the men to them. But that hardly mattered, she realized. They were outnumbered and she could see no way out of their dire predicament.

"If you think to save yourself by the Lady Rosalynde's presence, think again." Gilbert's eyes flickered furiously to her, but he must have fought back his urge to lash out at her as well. "Your father believes you have been abducted, Rosalynde. But 'tis clear to me that he has been duped by the pair of you." He took a casual step forward. On his face was a mocking smile. "However, despite your unseemly behavior with this blackguard, it is not too late to save what is left of your tattered reputation." His voice became hard and his pale eyes bored into hers. "Come here, Rosalynde. Now."

In the heavy silence that followed his command, Rosalynde hesitated. She did not begin to consider cooperating with Gilbert. If he was Aric's enemy, then he was hers also. Yet she was consumed with fear for Aric's safety. He could not win against four men! But if she could appease Gilbert in some way—

Aric's fingers tightened on her shoulder as if he read her desperate thoughts.

"I love you," she murmured very softly as she turned her wide eyes up to him.

Although he did not respond or even smile, she felt the love in his clear gray eyes. Then he turned his face back to Gilbert. "Leave Rosalynde and the boy out of this. Our difference does not concern them."

"What does it concern?" Rosalynde interrupted. She hoped to forestall any fight, yet she also did not understand the venom between the two men.

"Has he not told you then?" Gilbert gave her a keen look. Then, as comprehension dawned, he began to laugh. "So, *Aric,*" he began, putting emphasis on the absence of any title. "You keep her uninformed about our dealings. I commend you for your foresight, for should she know too much . . . well, I can see you fear I might be forced to kill her too." He broke off with a malicious shrug, then let out a full-throated laugh.

Although she did not know what he meant, Rosalynde knew that Gilbert's words had struck a chord of truth, for she felt Aric go rigid in response.

"What is the truth?" she asked, leaning harder against Aric as she stared pleadingly up at him. "It will not matter to me. I swear it!"

"Although I mislike agreeing with him, Rosalynde, 'tis best that you stay innocent of our dealings. We shall speak on it later."

"Only there will be no *later,*" Gilbert said with a snarl, brandishing his sword menacingly. "This should have been ended in London—or in Dunmow. But we will end it now. *I* will end it!"

Before Gilbert could advance even half the way toward them, Aric thrust Rosalynde to the side and drew out his own wicked blade. Then the men met in a violent crash of metal against metal.

Rosalynde backed away in horror from the two as they locked in deadly combat, but she was unable to tear her eyes away. Although Aric had a slight advantage in height, he had only his sword and was barefoot, clad just in braies. Gilbert, by contrast, was fully garbed with leather boots and a thin mail hauberk and protective hood. In the angled sunlight Aric's skin glinted golden—and vulnerable—as Gilbert pressed his attack. Slowly Aric gave way as Gilbert hacked at him. The black sword raised to fend off the fierce assault. In desperation Rosalynde looked around for some means of help. It was then her eyes met Cleve's.

The man who held the boy was watching the battle avidly, his arms and shoulders twitching as he reacted to the two warriors' moves. Likewise, the other two men stared, absorbed in the action before them. They clearly were not concerned with the meager threat offered by the boy and the maiden, and for this Rosalynde was grateful. Carefully she eased around the two combatants and out of the line of vision of the three knights. Following Cleve's eye signals, she reached an oak staff that lay propped against a fallen stone. With the heavy weapon in hand, she crept behind the three, trying hard not to concentrate on Aric's desperate fight.

As the battle progressed, the man who held Cleve had become more and more lax, edging toward the fighters who moved across the bailey.

"By Gor!" the man crowed when Aric stumbled over a fallen beam.

Rosalynde had to stifle her own cry as Gilbert swung viciously at Aric's neck. But Aric rolled backward to come immediately up in a crouch.

Cleve's captor dragged the squire nearer the combat, and it was then that Rosalynde struck. With every bit of her strength she swung the staff at the nearest man's right elbow. When he screamed in pain and dropped his sword, she prayed she had broken his arm. At the same time Cleve slid down in his captor's arms, then stood up hard so that his shoulder lodged squarely in the man's loins. With an agonizing howl the fellow collapsed, doubling over in his misery.

Seeing his two comrades fall, the third man pulled his own sword and swung around to the attack. Cleve grabbed up the fallen man's sword and dragged Rosalynde behind him, but a chilling war cry from Aric brought all three of them to a halt.

After having retreated under Gilbert's determined assault, giving the man and his cohorts reason to think victory was in their grasp, Aric now went on the offensive. With Rosalynde and Cleve relatively safe, he began to use his full strength against Gilbert, turning back the man's attack, forcing him to defend himself as the tide of the battle shifted.

"Gregore!" Gilbert cried as he barely held off a trio of crashing blows. "Behind him, man! Behind him!"

While the other two men still rolled on the ground in pain, the one called Gregore leapt forward to help his hard-pressed liege lord. But Cleve would not allow it. With a fierce growl of his own, he blocked the man's path.

"Begone, boy, before you feel the weight of my blade." He slashed his broadsword through the air in threat. But Cleve held his ground and was quickly joined by Rosalynde.

"Shall I feel your blade as well?" Rosalynde taunted the man. "Shall you kill me also, and never fear for the consequences? What of your vows of knightly duty?" she finished, disdain clear in her scathing tone.

But although the man hesitated, Gilbert did not. Even as he fought back Aric's deadly onslaught, he screamed at the wavering Sir Gregore. "Kill the boy! Kill him!"

"And then what?" Aric goaded him. "Kill the Lady Rosalynde as well?"

"If that's what it takes!" Gilbert turned aside a slashing cut from Aric's deadly sword.

"You would kill her, and all because I defeated you in the lists in London?" The scorn in Aric's voice could not entirely hide his disbelief that a knight could stoop to so low an act.

"If you had died at Dunmow, this would not have been necessary!" Gilbert snarled as the two circled one another warily, both breathing hard.

"Why pick such a curious death for me, if my death was what you indeed desired? Why not simply slay me when you captured me?"

Gilbert glanced from the hesitant Gregore to where his other two men were struggling to their feet. A smug smile split his cruel face as the odds turned once more in his favor. "I killed two birds with one stone that night. I rid myself of the fool who dared to humiliate me." He lunged forward, forcing Aric back into a rock-strewn area. "And I found a scapegoat to take the blame for my other activities!"

Aric stumbled as his bare heel hit a sharp stone, and Rosalynde stifled a cry of terror. Gilbert was a madman, she realized, sputtering vague inanities that made no sense. But that only made him more dangerous.

"A scapegoat?" Aric met Gilbert's challenge with a swift

undercut, turning back the attack and glancing his blade off the other's hauberk. "A scapegoat for what?" Then his face went black with fury as he suddenly understood. " 'Twas you! You are the outlaw who plagued the countryside! I was to assume your guilt and hang in your stead! Only I didn't die."

"It doesn't matter," Gilbert growled. "Your death today will accomplish the same goal."

"Only now there are witnesses."

"Then they shall die as well!"

The two blades clashed as the men battled for dominance. Gilbert fought like one possessed. And indeed he was—by the devil himself. But Aric struggled as only one who fights for his loved ones can struggle—with his body and his heart and his soul.

For a scant second Aric's face was just inches from Gilbert's. "They will die and the guilt will be ascribed to you," the scowling knight taunted Aric.

Then a new voice rang out over the violent scene. "The guilt will be laid where it rightfully belongs!"

Every head turned to the sound but one. Rosalynde gave a glad cry as her father strode into view, flanked by Sir Roger and two other of his men. Gilbert's cohorts drew back in confusion, and even Gilbert froze in sudden panic. Only Aric remained focused on his goal. Only he remained fixed on his quarry.

"Now we shall see who shall die," he muttered in ice-cold rage. Then with a mighty shove he thrust Gilbert back onto a grassy area.

In the silence of the bailey, with shadows lengthening across the yard, Aric and his foe faced one another. The men's breathing came hard and fast as they weighed each other's strengths and weaknesses.

Rosalynde rushed to her father's side to beg him to stop

the fight, for she feared yet that Aric might be hurt or even killed. Her father welcomed her into his arms, but a stern shake of his head stilled her words before they were said. It was clear he would allow the men to settle their differences with the sword.

With an enraged cry Gilbert did just that. He attacked Aric with a flurry of blows and cuts, driving the barefoot man back. Rosalynde cringed in her father's embrace as the metallic crashes rang out in the air. But Aric was not overcome, though he gave way to Gilbert's rush. With nerves of steel he led Gilbert on until the blows slowed just a fraction. Then, with a sliding motion, he turned his blade, and when Gilbert's sword glanced away, he shifted his weight. With all the power in his two arms and wrists, he cut back and, with a sharp blow, caught Gilbert just below the ribs.

For a moment neither man moved. Gilbert stared at Aric as if he could not quite believe what had happened. A thin line of blood seeped onto the blade, and he turned his head slowly to stare at it. Then Aric withdrew the sword, and with a long exhalation, Gilbert dropped to his knees. At the removal of the blade from his side the blood quickly stained his tunic and hauberk, but Gilbert uttered no sound, not of pain or remorse. He only lifted his eyes up to Aric's impassive face, then pitched forward into the dirt.

Rosalynde was racked by powerful shudders; only her father's firm grip prevented her from collapsing in relief. Gilbert's men quickly threw down their weapons, and Cleve's exuberant whoop cut through the air. But Aric just stood there, gasping for breath as he swayed above his vanquished enemy. Then he lifted his head and sought out Rosalynde with his eyes.

He needed no words to bid her come to him. Although her knees trembled and her heart still thundered in her chest, Rosalynde disentangled herself from her father's embrace. She spared no glance for the fallen Gilbert as she stopped before Aric. For a long, silent moment their eyes held, and she read all he did not say. Then with a joyful cry she came into his arms.

"My love. My sweet, sweet love," he murmured into the thick wealth of her hair as he crushed her to him. Rosalynde felt him tremble and she knew in her heart it was as much from emotion as it was from his tremendous exertion. Her hands slid across his sweat-slicked skin as she tried to press him ever closer to her.

"I love you—I was so frightened for you—I love you—I love you—" she murmured brokenly. Then their lips met in a kiss of fiery emotion and perfect love.

"You have much explaining to do. And unhand my daughter." Sir Edward broke into their absorption with one another, his voice a study in confusion and aggravation. But Rosalynde shook off her father's hand on her arm while Aric pulled her into the protective curve of his embrace.

"She may be your daughter, but she is my wife."

At Sir Edward's astounded expression, Rosalynde hastened to explain. " 'Tis true, Father. We are wed, albeit in the old way of handfasting. But I love him."

Sir Edward did not respond; his eyes only moved from Aric to Rosalynde then back to Aric again. "You . . . you cannot be wed. Who would perform such a ceremony? You are a mere man-at-arms—" Then he stopped. "You fight as a knight would." He shook his head and frowned in confusion. "I foresee a long and torturous explanation for this farce, and I am weary from the ride. Let us at least build a fire and make ourselves comfortable before you begin your tale."

So saying he turned away, signaling his men to attend to

Gilbert's body. When Cleve started toward Rosalynde, Edward shook his head sharply. "Leave them. Gather wood for a fire, then see to the horses. And see if you can find food. I am near to famished."

Rosalynde and Aric stood together as the others dispersed to their various tasks. She could hardly believe that he was hers at last, whole and unharmed, declared her husband and with no repercussions! She raised her head from its place against his warm shoulder. "You are a knight," she accused him softly. "All this time you kept it from me."

His clear gray gaze met her gold and green eyes. Then he smiled, and it was the most beautiful sight she had ever beheld. "You declared your love for me, a man you thought a commoner—before your father, before them all."

Her smile trembled as her emotions overwhelmed her. "I love you," she answered softly.

"Then marry me in the Church. Make our handfast vow good before God."

Unexpected laughter bubbled to her lips and she rose on her toes to plant a jubilant kiss upon his mouth. "Our heavenly Father was most certainly with us on that awful gallows that day. To please you and my father and everyone else, I'll say my vows once more in the Church. But God knows—as do I—that we are already man and wife. For now and forever."

Epilogue

A pair of hounds lay asleep in the warm spring sunshine. Their sides rose and fell in peaceful slumber, and every now and again one of them would twitch, running to ground in canine dreams some fat and juicy hare.

At the shrill cry of a frolicking child, both hounds jerked to groggy attention. But, recognizing their rude awakener as the same sturdy little fellow who tied his mother's ribbands around their necks, tried to ride them, and often shared his supper with them, they flopped down once more with contented groans and drifted back into their dreams.

The sunshine fell as well upon another contented sou who viewed the scene in the pleasaunce with overbrim ming joy. Sir Aric, Lord of Stanwood Castle, strolled across the bailey, trailing steward and chamberlain but no really listening to their chatter.

". . . correspondence stating that the scutage fee come due at the solstice—"

"Yes, yes, Cedric. Just reckon the amounts due and I' review it with you later." Aric waved the men away, neve removing his eyes from the woman who moved gracefull along the rose hedge that enclosed the well-tended law and garden. As ever, his loins tightened at the sight of he for he'd been absent from Stanwood these four long day

But more than that, his heart swelled to see her. It filled with a nearly unbearable joy, unspeakable in its intensity.

He paused there, savoring the moment, letting his senses fill with the sights and sounds and smells of this place that had become his home in the five years past. The fragrance of roses drifted to him—a perfume that would always be linked to Rosalynde in his mind. She was clipping roses for a bouquet as he watched, unaware of his presence. Little Wyatt was carrying the overflowing basket for her. Beyond them, stretched out on a rug in the sunshine, Sir Edward dozed alongside the infant Laurel.

Aric stared at the idyllic scene and blinked at the powerful emotions that washed over him.

"Why do you hesitate?" A strong young voice broke into Aric's musing. "If you do not hurry to greet her, then I shall. And after the unholy pace you set to return home from London, I should think that would quite spoil your plans."

Aric shot Cleve a mock frown that quickly became a smile. "Dub him a knight and he becomes arrogant and presumptuous. Just give me a minute and then I shall present you to her, *Sir* Cleve."

As Aric strode across the bailey, Wyatt was the first to spy him. "Papa! Papa!" In an instant the basket of roses was forgotten. With a laugh of pure childish delight, he dashed across the lawn, hurtling as fast as his sturdy four-year-old legs could carry him.

"There's my boy!" Aric crowed as he lifted Wyatt high over his head and jiggled him to the little boy's infinite glee. He was rewarded with a tight hug around his neck and the sweet mingled smell of dirt and roses and little boy. Then Wyatt cupped his father's cheeks between his two chubby hands.

"Why were you gone so long?" the child accused. His

fair brows lowered in such an approximation of his father's expression that Cleve began to laugh.

"I came as quickly as I could," Aric answered, laughing as well. "But tell me, my son, have you tended to things at home while Cleve and I were in London? How is your little sister, and your mother?"

"Oh, they are fine. Mama showed me how to read the time on the new sundial. But Laurel didn't do anything but eat and sleep and lie there."

Aric laughed once more and then had to restrain himself from squeezing his little son too tightly. Was ever a man so blessed as he? Without warning he lifted Wyatt up and settled him on his shoulders, much to the child's giggling delight. Then he strode across the yard.

Rosalynde had stopped at the edge of the pleasaunce, trying quickly to gather the scattered roses back into their basket as father and son greeted one another. But when she saw her husband coming toward her, the oak split basket was forgotten once more. Decorum cast to the winds, she lifted her skirts and dashed forward to welcome him home.

"Papa! Mama!" Wyatt demanded plaintively, patting both their heads as he was nearly smothered in their breathless embrace. "Don't forget about me!"

Aric lifted his hand to reassuringly rumple his son' head while all the while he stared down into his wife' beautiful face. The love he saw shining in her magnificen golden-green eyes brought a lump to his throat, and hi embrace tightened around her.

It was Rosalynde who found her voice first. "Would yo like to see little Laurel?" she asked as she spied her fathe sitting up and waving to them.

"I want to see both my children," Aric murmured, sti nuzzling her neck. "But after that—" He kissed her the pulled her close enough to feel the arousal that he could not force down. "After that perhaps we can put our minds toward providing them with another little brother or sister."

Rosalynde smiled to herself as they made their way across the bailey, Wyatt shrieking with glee to be carried so high on his father's shoulders. There was no need to "put their minds toward" creating another child for their family. She had every reason to believe one already grew beneath her heart.

But she would wait to tell Aric *afterward.*